LAWLESS ROSES

Jennifer Wells

ISBN: 979-8330257072

INDEX

Part 1 - City of Sin 1

Chapter 1 - Welcome Ceremony 2

Chapter 2 - Business 9

Chapter 3 - Operation Meeting 17

Chapter 4 - The Ripper 24

Chapter 5 - Descent 30

Chapter 6 - Auction House 38

Chapter 7 - Coffee Time 48

Chapter 8 - The Warden 55

Chapter 9 - The Octagon cage 63

Chapter 10 - Falling 70

Chapter 11 - The Abyss 79

Chapter 12 - A Tree 88

Chapter 13 - Reborn 95

Chapter 14 - Lay Low 104

Chapter 15 - A Bad Student 110

Chapter 16 - Grandpa 117

Part 2 - Blooming Roses 125

Chapter 17 - The Return Debut 126

Chapter 18 - Jinxed 134

Chapter 19 - Countdown 142

Chapter 20 - The Wild Rose 149

Chapter 21 - Good Luck 156

Chapter 22 - The White Rose 163

Chapter 23 - Freelance Mercenary ..170

Chapter 24 - Impressive 178

Chapter 25 - Fake Identities 186

Chapter 26 - Sweet Lily 194

Chapter 27 - No Way to Escape 203

Chapter 28 - Chionji 209

Chapter 29 - A Harsh Journey 216

Chapter 30 - The War Began 222

Chapter 31 - Lethal Acts 230

Chapter 32 - On Fire 238

Chapter 33 - The Puppets 246

Chapter 34 - The Mole 255

Chapter 35 - The Decision 262

Chapter 36 - The Palace 268

Chapter 37 - Blood For Blood 274

Chapter 38 - Deceived 281

Chapter 39 - Tomorrow's Dream 291

Chapter 40 - Her People 299

Chapter 41 - Psycho Tsunami 306

Chapter 42 - Home 312

Chapter 43 - Family 317

PART 1

CITY OF SIN

CHAPTER 1

Welcome Ceremony

A high-clearance six-wheeled off-road vehicle raced through the desert.

After leaving Sycamore, the F777 followed a private transport convoy for a while. The convoy dropped them off a few hundred kilometers away from District F191.

The convoy captain, feeling guilty about taking the money without fulfilling his promise, explained sheepishly, "This is as far as I can take you. It's not that I don't want to help, but I fear there's no return if we go further. You'll have to make your own way from here."

Cora and her companions had to switch to another mode of transportation.

From District C to District F, the technology level dropped sharply, and they couldn't find any self-driving cars along the way.

Eventually, they settled for a traditional gasoline car, driven by Suchat.

The daytime desert sun was blinding.

Wearing goggles, they followed the navigation prompts steadily.

"Have any of you been to District F191 before?" Cora asked.

"No," everyone else replied.

Cora glanced at Onyx, who also shook his head.

This was a completely unfamiliar city to them.

After all, why would anyone in their right mind come to District F if they had a comfortable life elsewhere?

The navigation showed they were approaching the western border of the New Pacific Alliance and entering their destination's vicinity.

Cora pulled her goggles down over her eyes, opened the sunroof, and climbed out, letting the hot, sandy wind hit her face. All she could see was a desolate desert, with no trace of a city.

She was puzzled.

Was this it? Where was the infamous City of Sin?

They circled the desert countless times.

The navigation showed their destination was close, yet they couldn't find an entrance. There were no city gates, no checkpoints, and no signs of life.

The only remarkable features were several towering, oddly shaped pyramids, reminiscent of ancient pyramids, standing in the empty desert and reflecting a silvery sheen.

Cora and her team got out and approached the pyramids on foot. They found tightly closed doors on the front. They tried everything—pulling, pushing, prying.

Suchat used poison, Damian tried freezing, and Cora even attempted to shapeshift (but gave up because of rapid mental exhaustion). None of their efforts could open the doors.

The material of the pyramids was highly resistant to their Anopowers.

Navigating the desert in a wheelchair was tough for Onyx, so he switched to crutches and slowly circled the pyramids, observing the door's structure.

His gaze lingered for a few seconds on the overhead camera, the closed doors, and the nearby grooves.

"It seems this is the gateway to the City of Sin," he said.

"But we can't open it," Cora replied.

"Don't worry. If it's a gateway, there must be a 'key.' Let's keep looking."

Suchat drove around for nearly half an hour until they spotted a few blurry figures by the roadside.

Through the swirling dust, these people, hearing the engine's noise, ran to the middle of the road, waving at them.

"There's someone," Cora alerted.

The off-road vehicle slowed to a stop.

A girl with colorful braids and brown skin circled to the driver's side and knocked on the window.

Mia had been waiting by the roadside for nearly three hours. Aside from two zombies dried up by the sun, she hadn't seen another living soul. Just as the sun was setting, she finally spotted an off-road vehicle.

She knocked on the window, and the glass slowly slid down to reveal a narrow gap.

Two young men sat in the front seats.

Mia put on her brightest smile. "Hey, friends, our car broke down. Can you tow us a bit? Just up ahead."

She pointed to a pickup truck by the roadside.

Its hood popped open, and a man was tinkering under it.

"You're headed to District F191 too, right? We're on the same road. Please help us out. I've been waiting all afternoon, and you're the only ones who passed by."

Mia clasped her hands together, her voice earnest. "The desert nights are super scary. I really don't want to spend the night out here."

The two men exchanged glances, but before they could respond, the rear door of their vehicle was yanked violently.

"Bang—thud!" The person outside didn't expect the door to be locked from the inside and couldn't pull it open.

"Mu, stop that! It's rude!" Mia scolded loudly, then turned back to the men with an apologetic smile.

"Sorry about that. We've been waiting a long time, and my friend got anxious, thinking you might not help us."

A girl around seventeen or eighteen leaned out from the back seat, whispered something to the man in the passenger seat, who glanced at Mia, then nodded slightly.

Three people, Mia noted mentally.

"Okay," the handsome man in the passenger seat said.

"Great! Thank you so much. I'll have Mu attach the tow rope, and I'll ride with you to give directions."

The door finally opened, and Mia climbed in enthusiastically.

She noticed besides the girl, there were three more people in the back row: a middle-aged man dozing with half-closed eyes, a clean-looking child, and a striking woman wearing sunglasses.

Blinking, Mia greeted them warmly. "Are you a family of four on a trip? The dad, the older daughter, and the younger son... though the mom seems like a stepmother."

The girl in the front stifled a laugh.

Mia looked at her in confusion.

"Did I say something wrong?"

The girl shook her head, a playful glint in her eyes. "They're a family of three. I'm not with them."

"Hey!" The striking woman took off her sunglasses, glaring at the girl, her lips moving silently in annoyance.

Mia thought, this stepmom sure has a bad temper.

She turned to the child, trying to be friendly. "Hey, little brother, where are you from?"

The kid snorted arrogantly, ignoring her.

Mia felt a vein throbbing on her forehead.

This brat!

The two vehicles drove through the desert for another ten minutes, reaching a deserted makeshift camp. Aside from a few tents and temporary structures, there was nothing else.

"We're here. Do you want to take a break?" Mia offered.

"No need," the driver responded coldly.

Mia held the car door, speaking meaningfully.

"I suggest you take a break. The road ahead will be tough. As a thank you, I could give you some... gifts."

There was a moment of silence in the car.

Eventually, the driver and the girl got out, following Mia towards the camp.

Mia led the way, checking over her shoulder several times.

Their footsteps were so light, like ghosts, making her think they weren't following.

At the camp entrance, Mia sighed regretfully. "Why would you come to the City of Sin? You didn't fall for those rumors about fewer zombies here, did you?"

"Is that not okay?" the girl asked innocently.

"It's fine, of course. I should thank you for coming." Mia smiled brightly and shouted towards the tents, "Cha, it's time to slaughter the sheep!"

As soon as she finished, a sandstorm erupted in the camp! The ground crumbled, and a dozen people sprang from beneath the sand, surrounding the off-road vehicle.

Meanwhile, more people jumped out from behind the tents, pressing knives to the necks of the man and the girl.

The man called Cha, muscular and menacing, stared at them, a greedy smile playing on his lips.

These ambushers were all Aberrants.

"Are you... bandits?" the girl asked, puzzled.

Mia laughed heartily. "Wrong. Bandits want money. We want your lives. Who told you to walk right into our trap?"

Fire flickered at her fingertips as her expression turned fierce.

"You're surrounded. Surrender, and I'll give you a quick death."

With that, she lunged with a fiery blade towards their heads.

The girl moved in a flash, dodging effortlessly.

Mia missed completely, her flames barely brushing the girl's clothes.

The girl smiled, dimples appearing on her cheeks, and mimicked Mia's tone, "You're surrounded."

Mia sneered.

Was this girl stupid? They were outnumbered twenty to two!

A crescent-shaped scimitar appeared in the girl's hand. She swung it upwards, breaking the knife at her throat. Then she spun, slashing downwards, a dark light flashing through the sandstorm.

Mia's eyes widened as her braided hair fell to the ground.

Mia rolled away, but the tall man moved swiftly, taking down two of her companions.

"Kill the ones in the car first!" Mia shouted desperately. "Start with the weak ones and then focus on these two!"

Mu and Cha charged towards the vehicle, joined by others.

Within moments, twenty Aberrants were attacking the off-road car.

"All the greedy rivers dry up in the fragrant desert." Someone was singing.

The sand underfoot suddenly softened, turning into a swamp.

Trapped, the attackers panicked, unable to move.

From the sunroof, a fuzzy head popped out. The arrogant kid clung to the roof, standing on tiptoes. Ice shards flew from him, turning the trapped attackers into pincushions.

"Damn it!" Mia cursed.

These weren't tourists but butchers! They were the prey!

"Retreat!"

Mia shouted in a panic, turning to flee.

An icy force pursued her relentlessly, freezing her in place. Her last thought before collapsing was—We've been played.

It was an ambush.

Half an hour earlier.

"There's someone," Cora reminded.

The others peered ahead, spotting a few blurry figures.

Yuui frowned. "Standing in the middle of the road to block us. They're clearly not letting us through."

"Unfriendly," Suchat noted.

Onyx smirked. "It's almost dark. Showing up now means they want to exploit our vulnerability. They think we're easy prey."

"Who's preying on whom isn't certain yet," Cora muttered.

"We haven't found the entrance yet. We might as well try getting some information from them," Onyx suggested with a smile.

"Right. A lamb should act like a lamb." Cora's eyes sparkled.

Mia thought she had found lost lambs, but didn't realize she was facing a pack of cunning wolves.

Cora and Suchat took only a few minutes to clear the scene. They hadn't found a way into District F191 but had already encountered robbers.

The City of Sin lived up to its name.

"Hmm, what's this?" Cora found a badge-like object on Mia. It had several gray lines, with three of them already colored red. She fiddled with it but couldn't figure it out, so she tossed it to Onyx.

The last rays of the sun vanished below the horizon, and darkness enveloped the desert. Hidden dangers lurked everywhere.

Onyx examined the badge taken from Mia, deep in thought. "Let's go back to those pyramids. I have some new ideas."

They drove back to the pyramids.

"I keep wondering, what kind of authorization do we need to open this passage?" Onyx mused.

"Ever heard of the Seven Deadly Sins? Pride, Envy, Wrath, Sloth, Greed, Gluttony, and Lust, leading to Slaughter. District F191 might be called the City of Sin because it only accepts those who are guilty."

The overhead sensors picked up the scent of blood on Cora and Suchat, triggering a new reaction.

"Please present your introducer's information," a line of text appeared on the door.

Onyx raised his hand, placing Mia's badge into the recess.

The tightly closed door slowly opened, revealing an elevator-like space.

The six of them stepped inside, and the elevator descended rapidly.

"Ding—" a clear, pleasant chime sounded.

"Welcome to the City of Sin."

As the elevator doors reopened, Cora, Yuui, and Damian's eyes widened in disbelief.

A bizarre underground world unfolded before them.

"Tonight at 11, Ross Casino Grand Opening! Free drinks all night!"

"New bionic materials, check out the medical tech from Sycamore."

"Zombie beast auction!"

"We buy crystals of all qualities."

Just a few meters from the entrance, two pedestrians clashed, unleashing their Anopowers in the street. The loser was blown to pieces, while the victor laughed and walked away.

Chaos, violence, wanton crime, and a blatant disregard for life...

This was the real City of Sin.

CHAPTER 2

Business

Beneath the desolate desert lay a bustling underground city.

There was no sun here.

Artificial lighting simulated daylight, with massive electronic screens overhead standing in for the sky.

There were no seasonal winds, natural currents, or ecosystems.

The sounds of insects, birds, cats, and dogs were all artificial. The overall style was rough and flamboyant, like an eternal urban night.

After exiting the elevator, they found themselves on a long trading street, bustling with people.

The hawking they heard earlier came from both sides of the street.

Besides their entry point, there were many similar elevators in all directions.

"Ding—"

The elevator's arrival sound signaled the continuous flow of people entering and exiting, making Cora and her group blend into the crowd.

Passersby gave them cursory glances with little interest.

The unfamiliar city, noisy environment, and indifferent residents made Cora feel out of place.

Onyx suggested, "Let's look around, see if we can gather some information and find a place to stay temporarily."

The six of them wandered aimlessly through the streets.

A young man wearing a baseball cap ran towards them, his head down. He hurriedly bumped into Suchat's solid chest. "Sorry," he mumbled, taking a couple of steps back before sidestepping them.

The man brushed past Yuui, a smile slowly spreading across his face. But before he could fully smile, his forearm was suddenly grabbed by a slender hand and twisted back violently.

"Ah!!" The man's face contorted in pain as he screamed, his arm broken!

The girl with dark eyes stared at him expressionlessly, holding out her hand. "Give it back."

"What?" Yuui realized suddenly, reaching for her wrist.

Her terminal was gone!

Everyone's attention had been on Suchat after the collision, not realizing this man was a skilled pickpocket.

He had quietly stolen from her, taking advantage of their distraction.

Cora applied a bit more force, causing the pickpocket to howl even louder. "Stop! Stop! I'll give it back!"

He hurriedly produced the rose gold ladies' watch.

Cora took it and coldly said, "Get lost."

The pickpocket, clutching his broken arm, fled in a panic.

"Be careful. This place differs from other cities," Onyx reminded them.

After this incident, the six of them remained on high alert.

They hadn't gone far when someone called out to them from the side of the street. "Hey, you guys!"

Cora turned to see a sharp-eyed woman with half-shaved, half-purple-dyed hair looking at them with interest.

"I've been watching you for a while. Interested in doing some business?"

Cora asked, "What kind of business?"

"Any kind, as long as you have money," the woman replied.

"My name is Ura, and I'm a crystal trader on this street. I also sell various pieces of information. You guys are new here, right? It wouldn't do to wander around blind. How about buying some intel from me?"

"How do you know we're new?" Onyx asked coolly.

Ura nodded towards where they had just been. "That pickpocket is quite famous around here. You handled him easily, and your faces are unfamiliar. Easy to tell."

Cora's suspicion grew, eyeing Ura warily. "Why should we trust you?"

What if Ura was as deceitful as Mia, planning to fleece them?

Ura laughed heartily. "Cautious, aren't you? But don't worry. You can ask around the trading street. I'm known for being honest in my dealings. No tricks, just business. You pay, and I deliver."

Cora hesitated, then turned to her companions for their opinions.

Onyx, lounging in his wheelchair, said lazily, "If we're newbies, how can we judge the truth of your words? And if you want to do business, you'll need more than honesty."

Ura sized up Onyx.

His calm demeanor marked him as a shrewd negotiator.

Realizing she might lose this deal, she offered, "Alright, how about I give you a few pieces of newbie info for free? You can decide afterward."

"Go ahead."

"First, here's the quickest way to blend into the City of Sin. If you want to make quick money, head to the casino or the underground fighting pits. For drinking and gossip, go to the Mystery Summer Club —it's the safest bar chain in town. Avoid hotels with the 'Red Willow' sign—they're black shops that scam outsiders. And..." she pointed at Damian, Yuui, and Cora, "kids and girls should never go out alone. There are plenty of traffickers around."

Ura had nailed their immediate needs.

These tips were indeed useful.

"How do we pay?" Cora asked. "How much?"

"No money," Ura shook her head, tapping her signboard. "Money devalues fast. Only one hard currency works here—crystals."

"With your skills, you should have some good ones, right?"

Ura's eyes glinted greedily, almost drooling.

She had targeted their crystals from the start.

F777 had accumulated quite a few crystals recently, from Damian's training missions, the zombie tide in Sakura, and the chaos in Felalakas.

They had a dozen or so.

Cora pulled out a level-1 crystal.

Ura reached for it, but Cora held it back.

"We ask questions first," Cora insisted.

"Ask away. I'll answer everything," Ura said, eyes glued to the crystal.

Onyx took out Mia's badge. "What is this?"

Ura glanced at it briefly, uninterested.

"That's a criminal record, a monitoring device for released convicts. The bars show the owner's crime index. Over five bars mean they'll be arrested again."

"But it's just a piece of metal. How does it monitor crimes?" Damian asked, tilting his head in confusion.

Ura shrugged. "It's tech from District B. No one knows the specifics, but it's never wrong."

"When we entered, the gate asked for an introducer. What was that about?" Onyx asked.

"Newcomers need an introducer to open the elevator the first time they enter the City of Sin."

Realizing that they had killed their introducer, Ura's expression changed.

"You guys are ruthless."

"Just a little black-on-black action," Onyx smiled.

Understanding the City's way, Ura nodded, extending her hand to Cora. "We've asked enough questions. Time to pay up."

Cora reluctantly placed the crystal in Ura's hand.

Ura treasured it, blowing off dust, examining it with a magnifying glass, and even biting it to check its hardness.

Cora and her group felt a shiver.

That crystal had come from a zombie's head!

"We have more questions," Cora began.

"Wait," Ura interrupted, her tone serious. "That's a second question. One crystal per question."

"Scammer!" Damian cursed.

Ura retorted, "It's called transparent pricing. I warned you."

Cora, resigned, pulled out another crystal.

"How much do you know about Death Hell?" Cora asked.

"Death Hell?" Ura smiled lazily. "Just follow this street straight for about five kilometers. You'll see an underground sea. That's Death Hell."

Cora was surprised.

Such a notorious prison's location wasn't a secret?

"And how do we get in?"

Ura burst out laughing. "You really are newbies, huh? This is the City of Sin. Who hasn't been to Death Hell?"

"Look around. Most people on this street have been there at least once!"

Indeed, as they glanced around, they saw many people wore badges with one, two, even four bars.

Ura pocketed the second crystal, savoring its inspection under the artificial light.

"It's getting late. Although it's always night here, I'd suggest finding a place to rest. Don't wander around too much."

"And remember, come to me for any business!"

After leaving the trading street, the six of them walked for another half hour.

Hotels without the 'Red Willow' sign were scarce, and the ones they found were full.

They finally found one still open, though it was shabby, with a large charred spot on the second-floor wall, crumbling and shedding dust.

"Hello, we'd like to check in."

The receptionist glanced at them. "Only three rooms left. Want them?"

"How come there are only three? The display behind you shows more available rooms," Yuui pointed out.

The receptionist sighed.

"There was a fight last night on the second floor, and the entire floor got burned. We're renovating it now, so those rooms aren't available."

"Anyway, there are only three left. Take them or leave them."

Cora decided, "We'll take them."

They had been searching for a long time and might find nothing better, so it was best to make do for the night.

"Here are your room cards." After they paid, the receptionist quickly assigned the rooms, fearing they might change their minds.

Now the question was, with three rooms and six people, how should they split up?

Cora held the three key-cards, looking a bit troubled.

Damian, the little rascal, immediately hugged her leg and whined, "I want to stay with you, sister!"

Cora looked at the others.

Charles was indifferent. As long as he had a bed or even a piece of floor, he didn't care. With his nomadic lifestyle, he could sleep anywhere, no matter who he was with.

As for the rest...

Cora handed one of the room cards to Yuui. "You stay with Suchat."

This left Onyx and Charles to share a room, which seemed fine.

Cora congratulated herself, thinking she was a wise leader.

But then, Suchat spoke up quietly, "It's not convenient."

Yuui glanced at the room card in her hand but said nothing.

Huh? Cora was stunned, looking back and forth between Yuui and Suchat.

They always seemed to act together, so she had assumed they were close.

Was she wrong?

But if Suchat wasn't staying with Yuui, how should they divide the rooms? It was a tough problem.

Cora's expression showed her struggle as she mentally tried various combinations, none of which seemed right.

Yuui spoke up, "I have a suggestion."

She pulled Damian off Cora's leg. "You stay with me. I'm also your sister."

Damian flailed and grimaced in pain.

Yuui smiled sweetly. "Mia thought I was your stepmother, remember? Don't worry, I'll take good care of you."

Damian's eyes teared up as he whimpered, "Bad woman!"

Yuui ignored him and pointed to Suchat and Charles. "You two share a room."

Finally, she turned to Cora and Onyx. "You two take the last room. Is that okay?"

Onyx opened his mouth to speak, but Cora quickly agreed, "Mm-hmm."

Onyx had nothing to add.

"Half an hour later, come to my room for a meeting," Cora instructed from the hallway.

Then she shut and locked the door.

When she turned around, Onyx was gazing at her. "Cora, we need to have a serious talk."

"About what?" Cora bounced onto the bed, stretching her limbs with a lazy yawn, completely oblivious.

Onyx's voice was low and hoarse. "I think you have a very vague sense of gender boundaries."

For example, entering his room without knocking, or sharing a room with him and sleeping soundly right in front of him.

The list was endless.

"You're still a girl, although in NPA you've counted as coming-of-age. This kind of behavior could be dangerous..."

Cora, hugging a pillow and lying on her back, looked confused. "Huh?"

Onyx sighed deeply, rolling his wheelchair to the bed and staring down at her. "Do you not see me as a man, or are you just very confident in yourself?"

Even upside down, Onyx's face was breathtakingly handsome, with cold features and tightly pressed lips, his dark eyes deep enough to pull someone in.

Cora blinked slowly, then reached out—pushing Onyx's face away.

She tried to sit up too quickly, causing them to bump foreheads hard. With a thud, both fell back—Cora into the bed, and Onyx into his wheelchair.

"Cora Thornton," Onyx gritted his teeth.

"Sorry, sorry!" Cora apologized, crawling forward, only to misstep and fall off the bed, landing on Onyx.

Silence spread.

Cora laughed awkwardly, leaning in to explain seriously, "I know you won't do anything, so it's fine sharing a room."

Onyx paused, then said in a deep voice, "Say that again."

Cora, puzzled, repeated, "I know you won't do anything..."

Onyx looked up at her. "Cora, your stutter has improved a lot recently, hasn't it?"

She hadn't noticed until Onyx pointed it out.

Since her injury and subsequent recovery on Manzoni Street, she had been speaking more fluently.

Though her pace was still slow, her stuttering had significantly decreased.

"But my stutter is congenital. It never got better," Cora noted.

"How's the wound on your heart?" Onyx asked.

"Much better," Cora replied.

Less than a week since the injury, Cora's strength had recovered about 50%, and her internal blood vessels and tissues were healing rapidly.

"It must be your second Anopower," Onyx pondered.

What exactly was Cora's second Anopower? Physical regeneration? But why was her speech improving, too?

It was a mystery.

Onyx solemnly reminded her, "Keep your second Anopower a secret. Watch those two closely."

"Mm," Cora nodded seriously.

Another awkward silence filled the room.

"So, can you let me go now?" Onyx asked expressionlessly.

CHAPTER 3

Operation Meeting

Half an hour later, it was time for the meeting.

Considering the chaos of the City of Sin, it was better to be cautious.

After everyone entered the room, Suchat carefully inspected every inch along the door, walls, windows, and ceiling, ensuring there were no listening devices before giving them a nod.

As Yuui walked in, she casually asked, "What happened to your heads?"

Cora and Onyx both had slightly red and swollen foreheads.

Cora tried to cover it up. "Nothing, just a bump."

Yuui had thought little of it, but Cora's guilty expression made her linger a few seconds on their foreheads, smiling meaningfully, "Oh, what a coincidence, you both bumped the same spot."

Cora cleared her throat. "Let's get to the meeting."

The six of them either sat or stood, finding their places.

Charles's presence there surprised Cora as well.

It wasn't unusual for Charles to join, but he usually slept through these meetings, impossible to wake even if thunder struck. Today, though, he was different, his messy hair tied back, and his eyes unusually alert.

Reflecting on it, Cora realized Charles had been sleeping less since they set out for District F191.

Though he remained silent and unobtrusive, the usual look of world-weariness on his face hadn't appeared in a while.

Onyx summarized their current information. "Clearly, the City of Sin differs greatly from what we expected. Death Hell's existence is no secret, and the locals speak of it without reservation."

They had initially thought Death Hell was a remote, heavily guarded prison for severe criminals, unknown to the average person who would avoid discussing it.

But they underestimated the madness of this place, where almost everyone had a criminal record.

"I looked around the underground sea," Suchat said, pulling up images and videos on his terminal. In half an hour, he had made a quick round trip.

The screen showed a pitch-black sea, its surface deathly still, with no guards around the edges, just the familiar pyramids standing in the water.

"It's very difficult to infiltrate," Suchat frowned.

Death Hell was beneath the underground sea, with no solid ground around it.

The sea elevator was the only way in, but like the desert, it required specific authorization to activate.

Even Suchat found it challenging to sneak in, leaving the others even more stumped.

"No need to infiltrate," Onyx said after a moment of thought. "There's a simpler way to get into Death Hell."

"How?" the others asked, looking at him.

Onyx placed Mia's badge on the table. "We get in the same way everyone else here does."

"You mean by committing a crime?" Cora realized.

"Exactly. Commit a minor crime, get one of us sent in, but nothing too serious. Just enough to get released after a while. You can't catch a tiger without entering its lair," Onyx quoted a proverb.

It sounded bizarre, but the more they thought about it, the more it made sense.

The prison authorities wouldn't expect anyone to get themselves imprisoned.

"But who should we send?" Cora asked the critical question.

They didn't know the exact situation inside Death Hell yet, so sending everyone in wasn't suitable.

The chosen one had to carry both the hope and the risk, requiring strong mobility and quick reflexes.

"I can do it," Suchat volunteered.

"I can too!" Damian eagerly raised his hand.

"I can go as well," Charles unexpectedly offered.

"I should go," Cora stood up.

Onyx stopped her. "You're still recovering. Take it easy."

He then turned to Charles, "You may be an A-rank, but your Anopower isn't suited for this."

Damian was immediately ruled out.

"Little kids need to learn some good habits."

Finally, Onyx looked at Suchat. "Among us, you're the best choice."

Suchat, from the rainforest, was skilled in stealth, infiltration, reconnaissance, and assassination.

His solo combat skills were top-notch, and he was an A-rank, toxic Aberrant.

If he went to Death Hell, at least they wouldn't need to worry about his safety too much. He was often overlooked because of his quiet presence, but Suchat was indeed a powerful Aberrant.

"The next step is figuring out how to get you sent in," Onyx said.

Yuui voiced her concern, "But we do not know what kind of crime results in what length of imprisonment."

The sand isolated from the outside district F191, with no internet access inside, making it nearly impossible to gather information.

This dark, lawless underground city had no rules or regulations to follow; everything had to be explored by themselves.

If it was a minor offense and they were only detained for a few days, it would be fine. But if it resulted in several months or even a year, their plan would be ruined.

Getting the right level of offense would be very difficult.

Cora remembered something. "The people at the gate weren't arrested."

They had witnessed a street fight upon entry, where someone was killed, but the killer wasn't apprehended.

"I have another question. How does Death Hell apprehend people?" Yuui asked.

When a criminal record reached five bars, what did Death Hell deploy to capture them? Was it similar to the Anopower police in Sycamore or the AI patrol robots in Felalakas? If the criminal was an Aberrant and resisted, could they ensure they could subdue the target?

Onyx tapped his wheelchair, pondering. "You're all right. We need a demonstration first."

As they spoke, there was a commotion upstairs. They were on the third floor, and the noise came from the fourth, sounding like a fight.

Cora made a quick decision. "Let's go check it out."

In the stairwell on the fourth floor, the receptionist looked desperate, covering her face with her hands. "Not again! How can anyone do business like this?"

A burly man stood in the corridor, his arm suddenly swelling four or five times its normal size, transforming into a massive club. He swung it down with a loud crash, splintering the door into pieces. The person inside didn't even have time to scream before they were killed.

The man's Anopower was out of control, and he smashed a hole through the hotel wall, letting in a blast of icy wind.

"Four bars," Suchat quietly noted.

Cora and the others focused their attention and indeed saw the man's armband, with four bright red bars. Just as he killed the guest and destroyed the hotel wall, a fifth bar slowly lit up.

With five bars full, the criminal record reset, and the offender would be sent back to Death Hell. What luck—just as Onyx had mentioned, they now had a demonstration right in front of them.

As Cora expected someone coming to arrest the man, something strange happened.

The man suddenly clutched his head, trembling violently, his upper body curling like a shrimp as he howled in pain. A few seconds later, it was as if someone had grabbed his throat, cutting off his voice. He straightened up, eyes vacant, unconscious, moving stiffly forward, guided by the five flashing red bars passing by Cora and her companions.

"This is... Cotard's Syndrome?" Charles suddenly spoke.

Onyx nodded slowly. "That's right, caused by the criminal record device."

Yuui was confused. "What are you talking about? What's Cotard's?"

Onyx gestured. "Let Dr. Charles explain."

Charles explained solemnly, "a malfunction in the parietal and frontal lobes of the brain causes Cotard's Syndrome, also known as Walking Corpse Syndrome, leading to delusions of negation and nihilism."

"When it strikes, a normal person briefly enters a zombie. Like the state, believing their internal organs are rotting and their body is just an empty shell. They perceive the world as nonexistent, accompanied by numbness and depersonalization."

The man walked stiffly towards Death Hell, stepping into the nearest elevator to turn himself in. There was no need to send someone to arrest him. Any criminal triggering the five-bar effect would automatically return to Death Hell like a zombie.

"But how is this possible?" Cora couldn't understand.

"The criminal record device," Onyx said, taking out Mia's badge again.

"I suspect it contains particle currents with Cotard's trigger frequencies, forcibly stimulating the brain. This technology shouldn't exist in District F. The Alliance must have put a lot of effort into creating and maintaining Death Hell."

Yuui frowned.

"Wouldn't such electrical stimulation of the brain cause dementia?"

"Long-term exposure could," Charles replied gravely.

Yuui glanced at Suchat. "What about Suchat?"

"I'm fine. I don't have a criminal record yet," Suchat answered.

To the City of Sin, they were still newcomers. Their past sins were erased, making them as clean as a "blank slate." But an additional problem arose—without a criminal record, how could Suchat voluntarily turn himself into Death Hell?

It was a headache.

"Let's set aside the criminal record issue for now and think about how to commit a crime," Onyx said.

Everyone turned to Suchat, as he was the one who had to go to prison and commit the crime.

"We'll work hard to get you imprisoned?" Cora blinked, her face earnest.

At 2 p.m., the surface temperature of the desert was close to 70 degrees Celsius. It was the hottest time of the day, with the blazing sun nearly causing dizziness, and the scorching sand could cook a raw egg.

A group of Aberrants were hunting zombies at an oasis camp.

Desert zombies differed significantly from city ones: they were lean, with dried-out, cracked skin, but they were exceptionally agile, jumping around like monkeys.

They believed that the one they were targeting was a second-level zombie that had evolved.

The group had been fighting the zombie for forty minutes, exhausted and parched, on the verge of success. Suddenly, another group burst in from the side.

"Robbery!"

The lead girl, wielding two crescent blades, crossed them menacingly, shouting.

Another figure appeared behind them, shrouded in green toxic mist, sprinting towards the dying zombie.

"Swish—"

The blades flashed, and the zombie let out a piercing wail before collapsing. From its shattered skull, a green crystal glimmered, which was quickly snatched up by the man.

"Damn! Stealing our crystal? You're dead! I'll chop you to pieces!" The Aberrants were furious, having their hard-earned prize snatched away at the last moment, wanting to crush the intruders' skulls.

"Spineless, you're so spineless~" A sweet song filled their ears, and the group felt their bones soften, their mental energy extinguished, unable to lift their arms.

The man in the toxic mist swiftly dispatched them one by one with clean, precise strikes, then retreated leisurely with the crystal.

"You forgot the slogan!" A clear child's voice called from behind a dune. The girl with the crescent blades looked at the toxic mist man, urging, "Quick, the slogan!"

The man frowned, his expression awkward, mouth twitching for a moment. Finally, he steeled himself, and with a blank expression, announced to the fallen foes, "Invincible F777, I am Suchat, remember that."

With that, he vanished in a sandstorm-like rush, leaving the Aberrants stunned, muttering, "What the heck? Who's this idiot?"

...

"Hahaha haha!" Yuui clutched her stomach, tears streaming from her eyes, laughing uncontrollably, losing all semblance of her usual sweet demeanor.

She wiped her tears, exclaiming, "Oh my god, whose idea was that slogan? It's hilarious!"

Cora pouted. "I... I thought of it."

Wasn't it good?

In just a few words, it mentioned their team name and identified the culprit as Suchat. So if anyone reported it, they could find the right person.

Cora looked proudly at her companions, only to see all of them, except Suchat, stifling their laughter.

As for Suchat... his face was almost as dark as coal.

Cora felt inexplicably guilty.

"Alright, stop laughing. Suchat, do you feel any adverse reactions?" Onyx asked, trying to suppress his own smile.

"None," Suchat replied, shaking his head.

Was it that robbery wasn't enough of a crime, or couldn't be executed in the desert? "Let's try it in the underground city," he suggested.

They took the elevator back underground but still experienced no abnormalities.

"It seems the crime level wasn't enough. Robbery isn't even worth a trial in the City of Sin."

"I have a suggestion," Suchat, usually silent, made his first request. "I can cooperate with any attempts, but can we change the slogan?"

"For that, you'll have to ask the captain," Onyx replied, eyes twinkling, passing the responsibility to Cora.

Cora looked disappointed.

CHAPTER 4

The Ripper

"Hey, have you heard?"

"Heard what?"

"There's this guy named Suchat—he's pure evil. Cheats, steals, kidnaps, kills, and even enslave kids. He's so bad that he stomps on corpses when he sees them. He has wiped Mia, Gaia, out!"

"No way. Can he really take out that many people by himself?"

"Not by himself. He's got a gang. What's their name again? I can't remember..."

"F777," a voice nearby reminded him.

"Yes, F777. They're fierce. After every crime, they shout their slogan, making sure everyone remembers them. Hey, Ura, you know about these people too?"

Ura twirled a strand of her dyed purple hair, smiling silently. She thought to herself, "Know them? I know them too well. They came to me for intel just yesterday. I even know who their next target is."

The two whisperers moved closer. "Do you have any intel on them? Tell us!"

Ura tapped her sign. "Sure. Do you have any crystals to trade?"

The questioner choked, muttering softly, "Stingy. You're obsessed with money."

Ura shrugged nonchalantly. "Your rumors are too exaggerated. Kidnapping children? They were already with them. As for looting and killing, that's just a rumor Gaia spread after losing their Level 2 crystals."

"Truth or not, the more explosive the news, the better."

"Hey, Ura, why do I feel you're siding with F777?"

Ura lovingly stroked her newly strung crystal bracelet, smiling mysteriously. "Just wait, there's more to come."

Desert Camp.

Cora sighed, her face full of worry.

Damian held his sunburnt face with both hands, sighing in unison.

Their mood infected. "Ugh...", resting her head in her hands and exhaling. The atmosphere was full of gloom.

No wonder they were so depressed. F777 had become famous in the past few days, but unfortunately, it was for all the wrong reasons. They tried everything—stealing, robbing, intimidating—but to no avail. Suchat was still with them.

"Do you think those people reported us? Why is there no reaction?" Cora mumbled.

Every time they committed a crime, they practically shouted their names through a megaphone, hoping the victims would take legal action to protect themselves.

Wait, no, there's no such thing as "law" in the City of Sin.

Cora's mind wandered aimlessly under the scorching sun.

A cold bottle of water pressed against her face. Onyx kindly offered, "Drink some water. Clear your head."

The provider of the ice water was none other than Damian F777's mobile refrigerator. In this scorching environment, an ice-powered Aberrant was a lifesaver. Damian had finally become the team's backbone; now, no one could do without him.

"It seems ordinary crimes go unpunished," Onyx concluded. "So, there's only one option left."

"What option?" Suchat leaned against the wall, adjusting his knuckle gloves.

"Murder." Onyx declared each word slowly.

"But the people at the elevator weren't arrested," Cora said, puzzled.

"The elevator incident was a duel to the death after an argument. In the City of Sin, the winner isn't held responsible for the loser's death. It doesn't count as murder," Onyx explained.

"What we need to do is to kill someone with no direct conflict."

"The key is, who to kill?" Yuui asked.

Although the place was crawling with criminals, they weren't indiscriminate killers. They couldn't just pick someone at random to slaughter.

"Louis the Ripper." Onyx named a target.

"According to the intel we bought from Ura, this guy is active around Trading Street, brutal and enjoys torturing weaklings, especially children and single women. He dissects his victims after killing them, hence the nickname."

Yuui and Damian frowned in disgust and hatred. "Such scum, even death, is too good for him."

"Louis is well known in the underworld, and he's already a four-bar rank. If we take him down, Death Hell will definitely take notice. If that doesn't get Suchat arrested, we may need to think of another approach."

"Isn't this doing a good deed?" Cora felt something was off. "Feels like we're doing something right."

Onyx shook his head. "Remember, in the City of Sin, there's no good or evil. We do whatever it takes to achieve our goal."

Cora was convinced, clenching her fists. "Then let's do it tonight."

"Get ready to give Louis a nightmare," Yuui agreed.

"Let's go!" Damian pumped his little fists.

"Yes, but Louis is cautious. We need a good plan to draw him out."

"I know just the person for the job." Onyx smiled, his eyes gleaming with cunning.

Damian: Why does that sound so familiar?

Late Night, Trading Street Alley.

A richly dressed boy, about ten years old, wandered through a deserted alley. With every step, his shoulders trembled in fear, his voice quivering with sobs. "Sis, where are you?"

A chilly wind blew from behind, making the boy turn around in fright, seeing nothing.

He held back his tears, wiping his eyes as he ran deeper into the alley. He tripped over a stone and fell, helplessly rubbing his knee, before finally breaking into loud sobs.

After about ten minutes of crying, a pair of men's shoes suddenly appeared in front of him. The boy stopped crying, looking up blankly.

Louis the Ripper, his face scarred, smiled grotesquely at him. "Little one, are you lost?" The boy's pupils shook with fear as he scrambled backward.

Louis seemed to enjoy his terrified expression, licking his lips as his excitement grew. He had been observing the boy for a long time, ensuring no one else was around before revealing himself.

Tonight's delicious treat was within his grasp.

Louis raised his right arm, revealing a high-speed spinning blade instead of a hand.

"Don't be afraid. Uncle is here to keep you company. You'll fall asleep soon." Louis raised his weapon, aiming at the boy's chest, ready to strike — Suddenly, the boy flashed a sweet smile at him.

Louis's face changed drastically as his danger radar went off. He realized his legs were frozen solid! "You brat, you're an Aberrant!"

Damian quickly got up, looking composed, entirely different from his previous state of confusion and fear.

He had been crying for almost ten minutes, but Louis remained cautious, not showing himself. Now Damian's throat was dry, and he was both cold and furious, cursing Louis in his mind.

"Bleh!" Damian stuck his tongue out at Louis. "You're dead!"

As soon as he finished speaking, a ghostly figure appeared from the darkness, striking the immobilized Louis without mercy. Louis was shocked; this person had hidden so close, yet he hadn't noticed!

A burst of lethal mental energy targeted his head. Unable to move his lower body, Louis raised his right arm to block. "Clang—" The spinning blade intercepted a sharp dagger, gradually slowing down.

Louis sighed in relief, but the next second, he noticed something was wrong. Rusty green spots spread rapidly from the blade to his arm, chest, neck... soon covering his entire face.

This is... a toxic ability!

"Ah!!" A piercing scream echoed through the alley, carrying far.

"What's that sound?"

"Sounds like Louis the Ripper?"

"Is he torturing another woman or child? What a vile man!"

"No... why do I feel like it's him screaming?"

The two onlookers exchanged glances, daring to venture into the alley.

They saw Louis lying cold on the ground, his body an eerie green, eyes wide open like a poisoned frog, lifeless. On his frozen spinning blade was a small flag.

The onlookers leaned closer to read the words. "Done by F777's Suchat."

They say not to leave your name after committing a crime, but this Suchat is quite arrogant.

Louis the Ripper was dead! Killed by F777's Suchat!! The explosive news spread quickly throughout the underground city.

Criminals whispered among themselves, feeling uneasy. Who was this Suchat? Stirring up trouble in both the desert and the underground city, now he killed Louis. Who would be next? Would it be them?

And what about this F777, always shouting strange slogans? Where did they come from? Their audacity was infuriating!

"Gia, where are you going?"

"Hmph, to settle the score."

Gia, who had his Level 2 crystals stolen by Suchat in the desert, gathered a large group of persecuted Aberrants to confront Suchat. "Dare to be so arrogant in the City of Sin? I'll make him pay!"

Still Useless.

Cora rested her chin on her wheelchair, her face full of despair. Her shoulder-length hair brushed against Onyx's shoulder, some strands tickling his collarbone.

Two days had passed since Suchat killed Louis the Ripper, yet he still hadn't been arrested. Even murder didn't work? The City of Sin truly was a paradise for evildoers.

Silently, Charles Franz suddenly spoke, "Why was the man in the hotel that night able to activate the crime log?"

Yuui exclaimed, "Yeah, why was he sent to Death Hell?"

Everyone fell silent, pondering. If mere murder wasn't enough, what else could it be? Besides killing, the only other special thing was?

Cora had an epiphany. Maybe the City of Sin didn't care about the lives of criminals, but if someone undermined the city's foundation...

"Bang—"

The door burst open, and a large group of fierce Aberrants stormed in.

Seeing the danger, diners quickly fled, leaving the restaurant empty except for Cora and her group.

Gia flipped them off, taunting madly, "Suchat, today you're dead!" Without another word, they attacked, using their powers against F777.

Chaos erupted.

Suchat kicked someone flying. One Aberrant had mechanical blades for legs like Louis, but he fell back, crashing into an elevator. The blades cut into the frame, quickly forming a small crack. Suchat's toxic mist seeped in, rapidly corroding the steel.

"Screech—" A faint noise came from the elevator shaft, and within seconds, the entire frame collapsed, taking the Aberrant down into the depths.

"Boom—" The deafening crash shook the entire City of Sin, halting everyone's actions.

As Cora and her team tried to understand what was happening, the giant overhead screen shifted direction, with bright artificial lights focusing on Suchat, blinding him.

Standing in the spotlight, Suchat became the center of attention.

The screen flickered, then went dark. Two seconds later, an icy voice echoed through the city.

"Criminal Suchat, you are under arrest. Lay down your weapons and surrender to Death Hell immediately."

"Repeating, Criminal Suchat, you are under arrest. Lay down your weapons and surrender to Death Hell immediately."

"Repeating..."

After the third announcement, the lights disappeared, and the artificial sky went dark, but the danger hadn't passed.

Hundreds of heavy weapons appeared above, particle cannons aimed at Suchat, ready to fire if he resisted.

Suchat dropped his knife, slowly raising his hands. He glanced back at Cora and her team, giving them a covert nod, then walked step by step towards the underground sea.

CHAPTER 5

Descent

The elevator to Death Hell differed vastly from the one in the city. The city elevator was sleek and spacious, with a silvery exterior and a pleasant dinging sound. In contrast, the Death Hell elevator was like a black maw of a beast, cramped and oppressive.

Suchat stepped into the elevator under the threat of hundreds of heavy weapons. The oppressive feeling finally eased as the particle cannons retracted, artificial light and the sky reappeared, and the underground city returned to tranquility.

Inside the elevator, Suchat glanced at the floor index. There were no buttons, only a single black number slowly appearing "-1." The elevator suddenly plummeted, a strong sense of weightlessness hitting him. He steadied himself quickly.

About ten seconds later, fifty meters below sea level, the elevator arrived at Death Hell. The doors slid open to reveal two sturdy gates. A man in a black uniform and a police hat stood behind the second gate.

"Are you Suchat? I'm your instructor, Khun Bu," the man said.

Suchat took a small step forward, but Khun Bu immediately stopped him, harshly reprimanding. "Did I say you could move?" Suchat stopped silent, his fists slowly clenching.

"Are you mute? You should say, 'Yes, Instructor!'" Khun Bu coldly demanded.

"Yes, Instructor," Suchat replied, his expression sullen but obedient.

Khun Bu snorted, not fully satisfied, but not pressing further. "Listen carefully, I will only say this once. After the first gate opens, turn left to get your tag, then go to the room on the right for inspection. Understood?"

Suchat nodded slightly. "Understood."

Khun Bu squinted. "Did you forget what I just taught you?"

Suchat raised his voice, "Understood! Instructor!"

"Go."

The gate slowly opened, and Suchat walked left, covertly observing his surroundings. At the end of the path was a small window with a tag on the counter.

Suchat looked down and saw the gray bars on the tag, marking his "Record of Crimes." From a loudspeaker in the corner, Khun Bu's voice commanded, "Put the tag on."

Suchat hesitated before reaching for the tag. The moment he touched it, a chill ran through him. His consciousness scattered, as if his body and soul were drifting away, leaving only a void.

The feeling passed quickly, but he knew acutely that he was being watched—not by the cameras, but by a shadowy presence deep in his mind. This force would compel him back to Death Hell if he ever committed another crime. No wonder the criminals here didn't wear shackles. From the moment they received their "Record of Crimes," they became lifelong prisoners.

Unable to deal with the power of the tag, Suchat put it on and turned right as instructed, entering the opposite room.

The room resembled an interrogation chamber. Khun Bu watched him from behind another gate, gesturing towards an empty basin on the floor. "No belongings are allowed in Death Hell. Strip completely, put your things in the basin, then go inside to shower. You have five minutes."

Suchat quickly began undressing, tossing his jacket, belt, pants, combat boots, the knife strapped to his calf, the dagger hidden in his shoe, and the secret weapon given to him by Cora into the basin. Finally, he stood in just his underwear.

Khun Bu glanced at him. The man behind the gate was tall and muscular, with no excess fat. As he turned, a fierce black snake tattoo on his neck became visible, along with many scars on his back, each telling a story of past brutality.

Rainforest... Khun Bu's eyes flickered, noting: This one's a tough nut.

Suchat stepped into the shower, cold water pouring over him, his mind working rapidly. He had little time to think.

So far, Death Hell's management seemed primitive, similar to other underground cities, except for the pervasive surveillance and its unique underwater location. The only technological anomaly was the "Record of Crimes," an outlier far beyond the overall level.

Three minutes later, Suchat finished his cold shower, went to the inner room for a machine scan, then put on his prison uniform and returned to the original room.

The second gate finally opened. Khun Bu, seated at a table, opened a newly delivered file, reading through Suchat's records. "What crime got you in here?"

"Uh, vandalism?" Suchat guessed uncertainly.

"Vandalism?" Khun Bu quickly flipped through several pages. "Two months of imprisonment, a one-month sentence, and a fine of thirteen thousand NPA credits. And Warden Sherman himself issued the arrest warrant. What did you vandalize to get such a heavy penalty?"

"The city elevator."

"No wonder... That's Warden Sherman's cash cow."

Khun Bu put down the file, his hands clasped under his chin, looking serious. "I don't care who you were outside. In here, you're under my control, so you'd better behave and not cause trouble."

"Understood," Suchat replied, quickly adding, "Instructor."

Satisfied with his compliance, Khun Bu continued, "Since you're new, I'll give you some advice. Got questions?"

"Yes," Suchat nodded. "How many levels does Death Hell have?"

"Why do you want to know that?"

"Curious."

"Excluding the activity levels between six and seven, Death Hell has eighteen levels. The lower you go, the longer the sentences." Khun Bu gave him a disdainful look. "Kid, curb your curiosity. Trust me, knowing anything below level seven is painful."

"Why am I on level two?" Suchat asked.

Thinking he was unhappy with his sentence, Khun Bu explained in unexpected detail, "Ordinarily, vandalism would only get you a few days on level one. But since Warden Sherman handled your case personally and he lost money, he won't let you off easily."

"Warden Sherman?" Suchat remembered the impersonal voice reading his arrest warrant.

Khun Bu nodded. "Death Hell is managed by three wardens. Levels one to six are Warden Sherman's responsibility. Levels seven to twelve are Warden White's. And as for levels thirteen to eighteen... They're under The Pluto."

Just as Suchat was about to speak, Khun Bu interrupted, "I advise you not to ask about The Pluto."

His gaze fell on Suchat's tag, implying, "The Pluto knows everything. The moment you learn about him, he knows you, too."

"Questions?" Khun Bu closed the file. "I'll send you to your cell. I need to process the next prisoner."

"Is there any way to shorten my sentence?" Suchat asked.

A month was too long; the longer he stayed, the more likely something would go wrong. His original plan was to spend about a week gathering information on Death Hell and then out reunite with Cora and the others.

Khun Bu chuckled. "You're experienced, huh? Yes, you can reduce your sentence through labor. The maximum is eight hours a day, and if you're diligent, you can cut it in half."

"What kind of labor?" Suchat inquired.

Khun Bu's smile became enigmatic. "Test subject for new drugs in the lab, punching bag in the black boxing gym, sand filler for the underwater tunnel, and dust cleaner in the mechanical room. See how long you can endure. Which death do you prefer?"

Khun Bu led Suchat to the second floor. As soon as the elevator doors opened, countless pairs of cold, hostile eyes turned towards him —some belonging to prisoners, others to patrolling guards.

The entire second floor resembled a massive assembly line factory. It was more spacious than the market streets, with every workstation filled with laboring prisoners.

"Every day at 6:00 AM, the labor list updates. Sign up first, then scan your tag at the designated spot," Khun Bu instructed as they walked. "You must arrive at your labor point before the countdown ends. No loitering on the way."

"Here we are. Get in." Khun Bu stopped at a cell, swiped the lock open, and shoved Suchat inside. "Behave yourself and aim to get out early."

At 5:50 the next morning, Suchat woke up promptly. He climbed down from his narrow single bed and quietly waited at the cell door.

At precisely 6:00, the labor list updated. Suchat quickly selected "boxing training partner," commonly known as a punching bag. The cell door automatically opened, and Suchat headed to the black boxing gym, silently memorizing the route.

Upon arrival, he put on boxing gloves and began his eight-hour labor. The task was simple: get hit.

Suchat kept his hands up in front of his face, his defense impenetrable, while his mind wandered elsewhere. The opponent grew increasingly frustrated as he failed to land punches, resorting to dirty tricks. Annoyed, Suchat finally struck back with a single punch.

The opponent's nose was hit, sending him flying backward and crashing to the ground, unconscious. The surrounding noise abruptly fell silent.

A guard rushed over, yelling at Suchat, "What are you doing? Trying to start a fight?"

Suchat tried to explain, "No, officer..."

"You were brought here to be a punching bag, not to hit back. Get out. Your labor time is void for today!"

Reluctantly, he removed his gloves and walked out.

As he left the gym, the dejected expression vanished instantly. His eyes grew cold as he slipped into the shadows.

The second floor's cellblocks were orderly, with clearly defined divisions of labor, revealing no immediate abnormalities. Suddenly, a dark red elevator in the corner caught his attention.

Suchat's expression shifted. Could this be the elevator to the deeper levels of Death Hell? He sneaked it.

The elevator doors were tightly shut, and his tag couldn't unlock it. As he contemplated a solution, footsteps approached. He rolled to the side, hiding in the darkness.

Two guards escorted a disheveled prisoner, one of them apparently the prisoner's instructor, scolding him, "You were so close to getting out in less than a month, and now you caused trouble again. Off to the fourth floor for five years—good luck with that!"

The guard revealed a connector on his wrist, pressed it against the elevator, and the car slowly started, disappearing with the three men.

Hidden, Suchat frowned. It seemed the internal elevators required guard authorization to open. But accumulating crimes in Death Hell could lead one to the deeper levels... This was valuable new information.

For the next two days, Suchat dutifully engaged in labor reform.

In the evenings, he used a nail clipper (taken from the boxing gym) to carve a map into the wall.

The mental map in his head became increasingly detailed. The second floor housed 12,000 cells; the first floor reportedly had over 20,000. This meant Death Hell held over 100,000 prisoners, with floors one to six for minor crimes and floors seven to twelve for major ones. There was an open layer between the sixth and seventh floors, known as the activity zone, where prisoners below the twelfth floor could apply for recreational time.

There was no information on levels below the twelfth.

Suchat meticulously recalled every detail, then used the nail clipper to smooth the wall.

Death Hell was far larger than he had expected, exponentially so. Finding someone here would be incredibly challenging. He wondered where Felix Lucas was being held. Based on his crimes described by Onyx, he was likely below the seventh floor.

Eight days later.

Suchat was released.

At the elevator, Khun Bu returned his clothes. "Live a good life outside. Don't come back."

Suchat's voice was low. "Instructor, I have one more question."

Suchat had been so well-behaved over the past few days that Khun Bu found him more agreeable than when he first arrived. He casually replied, "What is it?"

"How long have you been an instructor here?"

"Seven years."

Seven years was enough time for the outside world to undergo dramatic changes—like the apocalypse, the rise of zombies, and the collapse of cities. Yet Death Hell remained an unchanging stagnant pool, aside from the influx and outflow of prisoners.

"And can you remember all the prisoners you've encountered?"

"Who would bother to remember such things?" Khun Bu said matter-of-factly. "If I forget, I can just look up the records."

Suchat nodded. "No more questions. See you next time, Instructor." He quickly entered the elevator.

Khun Bu stood still for two seconds before suddenly reacting, "Kid, what do you mean 'see you next time'? What next time!"

The pitch-black elevator ascended slowly. Suchat reviewed the information he had gathered over the past few days. "Ding—" Reaching the surface, he stepped out.

By the sea, five people of varying heights were waiting for him. Onyx and Charles Franz were chatting and looked up at him. Yuui Hayashi and Damian Blackwood were bickering, debating who had kicked off the blanket last night.

Cora Thornton, lounging on a platform with her legs swinging, spotted him first and waved. "Hey, here to pick you up. You're out."

"Yeah." After nearly eight days of minimal interaction, Suchat cleared his throat, feeling the gloom of Death Hell receding. He wasn't surprised they had tracked his position with the ethereal artifact hidden in his clothes by Cora.

"Not hurt, are you?" Yuui Hayashi asked worriedly.

"No," Suchat shook his head, "Let's talk back at the hotel."

Back at the hotel, he cautiously checked the room to ensure there were no listening devices before speaking. "There's one thing we were all wrong about."

"The true city of sin is Death Hell beneath the underground sea."

Only those who had been in Death Hell knew that the ones who were released had relatively "light" crimes. The irredeemable demons only kept falling, deeper and deeper, endlessly.

Suchat recounted his experiences to Cora and the others, then drew the floor plans of the second floor and the activity layer from memory. A master of intelligence, he pieced together the fragments, slowly revealing the mysteries of Death Hell.

Onyx analyzed, "From these two maps, the activity layer is about a third smaller than the second floor. Death Hell is likely an inverted cone."

Yuui exclaimed, "You said Death Hell has three wardens managing different levels?"

"Do they really make you strip when you go in?" Damian asked, puzzled.

"There's no need to waste time in the underground city," Suchat suddenly said amidst the chatter. "—We should all enter Death Hell."

CHAPTER 6

Auction House

"We should all enter Death Hell." Suchat rarely spoke, and when he did, it was often shocking.

Cora's eyes widened as she inhaled sharply. "You didn't get enough of prison, and now you want to drag us all in there with you?"

The others looked at him with various expressions.

Suchat paused. "...No."

"I think it's a good idea," Onyx calmly interjected, tapping the armrest of his wheelchair. "We've been gathering intelligence in the underground city for days with no progress."

Cora thought it over and had to agree. "If we're sure he's in Death Hell, it makes sense to go in as soon as possible. We might have a better chance."

"I object," Charles unexpectedly spoke up, his weary eyes lifting slightly. "Maybe I'm being pessimistic, but if we all go in and there's no one to assist from the outside, what if things don't go as planned? How will we get out?"

"And aren't you all supposed to compete in the tournament? Can you guarantee you'll find him and get out in time? We don't want to end up with nothing."

Charles's words were harsh but realistic. Entering Death Hell now meant an uncertain duration inside, potentially missing the next round of the T. T. T. For Cora, Onyx, Damian, and Charles, competing wasn't urgent, but for Yuui... she had always wanted the chance to make a wish to Ilia.

Yuui knew they were waiting for her response. She felt torn, standing at a crossroads. She had always believed the T. T. T. was the only hope to cure her family, striving for the slimmest chance. But now, Charles, an A-class healer, presented a near-certain opportunity.

Should she continue chasing a vague promise or seize the immediate opportunity in front of her?

Though Yuui had debuted with a sweet image, her true nature was decisive and fierce. She bit her lip and confirmed, "Hey, Charles, if we help you kill your target, you promise to heal us, right?"

Charles stood up and solemnly nodded. "If you can fulfill my life's mission, I will do everything I can."

Whether it was for Onyx's legs or Yuui's long-suffering relative, it wasn't something that abilities alone could cure. The best plan was to return to Sycamore, where top medical resources and Charles's surgery could provide a cure.

Yuui bit her lip and slowly nodded. "Alright, I'll give it my all!"

"Just prison? Just eighteen levels? Our goal in the city of sin is to find him. We can't fail! Even if we have to dig through Death Hell, we will find Felix Lucas!" Yuui shouted with determination, ready to storm into Death Hell.

Cora stood there, mouth agape, staring at Yuui. No matter how many times she witnessed it, she never got used to it. Celebrity personas were indeed fake. Onyx leisurely reached out and closed her gaping mouth.

"Since we all agree, let's discuss how to get in," Onyx suggested.

Suchat pulled up the floor plan of the activity layer, pointing to a level. "I suggest going directly to the fifth or sixth floor. The same warden manages levels six and above. We've confirmed that vandalism results in arrest. The only question is the severity of the sentence."

"Sentences on the fourth floor start at five years..." While the adults examined the floor plan, Damian tugged on Cora's sleeve. She turned to find him looking glum.

"What's wrong?" Cora asked, kneeling to meet his eyes.

Damian hesitated, looking around nervously.

Onyx, still expressionless, turned and said, "You don't have to strip naked. You can keep your underwear."

Of course, a man would understand a man, even if Damian wasn't quite a man yet.

Damian's eyes sparkled, and he let out a relieved "Oh," his previous dejection disappearing.

He cheerfully said, "It's nothing, sis. You guys keep planning."

Cora was left bewildered. "Huh??"

The Trade Street was ablaze with lights and teeming with people. Ura was shouting to make a deal when a group approached from a distance, led by a girl who waved and happily called out, "Ura—! We're here…"

Ura looked around nervously like a thief, hurried over to cover the girl's mouth, and led them into a nearby alley. "Shh! Keep it down! Do you know how many people hate you? I only do business; I don't get involved in your mess."

"Mm!" Cora protested, muffled.

Ura released her, flipping her half-dyed long hair casually. "What do you want? The usual rules apply—no crystals, no talk."

Cora mysteriously pulled out a green crystal they had snatched from the Gaia desert. Ura's hair-flipping stopped, and she stared, drooling at the crystal. Her eyes followed the crystal wherever Cora moved it, not blinking once.

"Business, or not?" Cora asked.

"Yes, yes, of course! It must be a big deal, haha." Ura rubbed her hands excitedly.

"What crime gets you a minimum ten-year sentence in prison?" Cora asked seriously.

"Huh?" Ura thought she had misheard. "Did you say prison? Ten years minimum? Are you out of your mind?"

Her eyes scanned the six of them, noticing Suchat and the tag on his shoulder.

Ura immediately looked understanding, pointing at him with distress. "Weren't you just thrown in? Are you addicted to prison now? And you want to drag your friends along? What kind of person are you?"

Suchat had no way to explain.

Cora smiled lightly. "It's not his fault; we want to go in ourselves."

Ura was confused. Why would anyone willingly go to prison? But... regardless of their reasons, she would not turn down business. She lowered her voice conspiratorially. "You all want in, right? It's not impossible, but you'll have to make a big scene. You know there are three wardens in Death Hell, right?"

Cora nodded; Suchat had already informed them.

"Here's something you don't know: Warden Sherman is obsessed with money. Even though he stays in Death Hell, he uses all means to gather wealth. Warden White is strict and violent, always resorting to whips and clubs. Prisoners under him live worse than death."

Ura clicked her tongue, speaking freely about the wardens' flaws.

"... But I suggest you target Sherman. Given your criminal records, if you play it right, you could get not just ten, but twenty or thirty years in there. You'll be set for life."

Cora nodded thoughtfully, but sensed something was off. Despite having three wardens, Ura hadn't mentioned "The Pluto" at all and ended the topic deliberately.

She exchanged a glance with Onyx, who slowly shook his head. Cora got the hint and didn't pursue it further.

Ura craned her neck to check the alleyway, ensuring no one was eavesdropping, and grinned slyly. "I know where Sherman's lifeblood is."

Cora and the group were led to a lavish building that wasn't open for business yet. Next to the ornate sign was a line of small, flowery script. "Rose Auction House," Onyx read quietly.

Ura crossed her arms and sneered, "It sounds glamorous, right? But inside, it's all dirty business—trafficking people. They sell everything from mermaids and zombie beasts to alien slaves and kidnapped boys and girls... Life here is the cheapest commodity. You can buy any 'product' you want."

"This is Sherman's most important moneymaker."

After she said this, Cora and the others didn't have a special reaction. Instead, they huddled together, murmuring as if they had differing opinions. Ura tapped her arm impatiently, waiting for ten minutes, during which the group still hadn't concluded. A flicker of urgency crossed her eyes.

Just as Ura was about to lose patience, Onyx stepped forward and gave her a meaningful smile. "Miss Ura, we have other ways to get into Death Hell. But you're clearly using us. You drive a hard bargain."

"Yeah," Ura admitted straightforwardly, since she'd been found out. "I do have a selfish motive. I've hated this place for a long time. But I'm a businesswoman, and profit is my nature. I'm not tricking you. The Rose Auction House is indeed Sherman's lifeline. Destroy it, and you'll all be thrown into Death Hell for sure."

Seeing Ura reveal her true colors, Onyx exploited the situation. "Since you want us to do your dirty work, show some sincerity first. This place isn't easy to mess with."

Onyx remained calm, while Ura's expression grew conflicted. The balance of power in the negotiation had shifted. After a long standoff, Ura finally gritted her teeth and said, "Fine, I'll only charge you for the information and get you in for free."

"But if the plan fails, don't involve me. I won't acknowledge anything."

At ten o'clock in the evening, the underground city was at its most vibrant. Dressed in a sequined suit, Ura entered the Rose Auction House, arm in arm with a scholarly young man with a bun at the back of his head.

The guard at the door stopped them, asking for an invitation. Ura pulled out a black and gold card from her wallet and handed it over. The guard scrutinized it, then looked up in confusion. "Miss Li, this card only has your name on it."

Ura's fingers moved slightly, and a delicate auction paddle labeled 38 appeared.

Auction participants could bring one companion, as per the rules of the Rose Auction House. The guard, satisfied, let them in.

Once inside, Ura lowered her voice and asked, "Are your people in?"

Charles, not in a hurry, replied, "Don't worry. They won't fail."

Ura had only got two invitations—one for Onyx and the other for herself. She used hers to bring Charles along, reasoning that he was the only one among them who looked like a normal "man." After all, the rest were... one was a wheelchair-bound schemer with a perpetual smile, another was a cold and violent brute, and then there was a little kid who was just too conspicuous.

The two found their seats, and Charles began observing their surroundings. The decor was ordinary, except for the scarlet auction stage at the front and the gigantic screen occupying an entire wall. Otherwise, it looked like a regular auction house, giving no hint of the dark dealings of human trafficking that took place here. The owner was clearly cautious.

Shortly after Ura and Charles entered, two more people arrived at the entrance of the Rose Auction House. A boy around ten years old, dressed in a neat little suit with a bow tie, pushed a silver wheelchair with a lazy-looking man slumped in it. As they approached, the man handed an invitation to the guard with his long, slender fingers.

The guard glanced at it and, recognizing, "Mr. Vyacheslavsky" as an esteemed bidder, respectfully nodded and prepared to let them in without a word.

As the two passed, another guard hesitated about the boy pushing the wheelchair. "Mr. Vyacheslavsky" gave him a disdainful look, brushing his fingers over the blanket on his lap. "This boy is my servant."

The guard, well aware of the dealings inside, immediately understood the implication of "servant" and quickly echoed, "Yes, yes, Mr. Vyacheslavsky, please go in."

Once out of sight of the guards, Damian let go of the wheelchair, hopping in front of Onyx and whispering angrily, "You made me your slave!"

Onyx responded calmly, "Quiet down. Do you want everyone to know we're up to no good and ruin the plan? Your sister will never forgive you."

Damian quickly covered his mouth, glaring at him.

Onyx gestured with a finger. "Come on, push me, little slave."

At the back entrance of the Rose Auction House, in the food transport passage, the checkpoint finished its inspection, and the rolling door automatically opened. A white food cart slowly entered the venue.

Yuui and Cora, dressed in white catering uniforms, kept their heads down and walked with the group. "You two, stop," the catering captain suddenly called out.

Cora froze, her right hand quietly moving towards her uniform pocket.

"Aren't you the ones delivering the vegetarian meals? You should go the other way. Don't mess up."

"Okay." Yuui nodded submissively.

Cora let out a small sigh of relief, her right hand returning to her side. She exchanged a glance with Yuui, who winked playfully before they quickly disappeared into the passage.

At eleven o'clock at night, the auction officially began.

A slick-haired auctioneer gracefully took the stage.

"Good evening, esteemed guests. Welcome to the 278th special auction of the Rose Auction House. I am Alan, a registered auctioneer with the Alliance. Your side can find all items in the catalog. Let's not waste time and begin the bidding."

Alan clapped his hands, and the staff immediately rolled out a large iron cage.

"The first item tonight is 'Pure White Grace,' sourced from District C75. Six pure and flawless girls in their prime. I can almost smell their sweet fragrance," Alan said, inhaling the air theatrically. "They're only available as a bundle. Starting bid is 50,000 NPA credits."

As the curtain was pulled back, the girls in the cage, suddenly exposed to the light, trembled with fear and huddled together.

"Scum," Yuui muttered angrily from behind the curtain. She looked up to see Cora successfully perched on the top beam, signaling her readiness.

Yuui scanned the seats and quickly found Charles and Ura, Onyx, and Damian, signaling to Cora that the four were in position. Now they just had to wait for Suchat.

'Pure White Grace' eventually sold for 350,000 NPA credits, but as a showcase, the sold items would remain on site until the auction concluded.

Alan, brimming with excitement, introduced the second item. "Next, we have something big for the pet lovers."

A covered container was rolled in, and Alan dramatically unveiled it to reveal a massive, gold-colored scorpion-like creature. Its two-meter-long body thrashed against the transparent walls of the container.

"This is no ordinary zombie scorpion but a one-in-a-million Anopower scorpion! Notice its golden eyes? Such a unique pet will surely make you stand out. We're also giving the buyer a powerful stun gun to keep it docile," Alan said, imitating the scorpion's movements.

The buyers laughed intermittently.

"Clang—" The scorpion slammed against the wall again, but Alan ignored it, continuing to shout, "Starting bid is 300,000 NPA credits, with a minimum increase of 10,000 per bid!"

"310,000." "I bid 330,000." "350,000, it's mine!"

The Anopower scorpion was eventually sold for a whopping 560,000, just like the girls, and was moved to the showcase area.

"Next up is a rare gem that's sure to delight," Alan said, his tone filled with anticipation. "Let's skip the words and see it firsthand before I explain."

Another iron cage covered in black cloth was pushed in, and a slender boy appeared in the center of the stage.

He was extraordinarily beautiful, with wet black hair clinging to his ears, honey-colored amber eyes, and an upper body so pale it seemed to glow. But below the waist, there was a dark green snake tail coiled beneath him!

Alan's voice grew even more excited. "The third item is a human-snake hybrid from U-Lab!"

From her perch, Cora's eyes widened. Onyx, in the buyers' seats, also frowned deeply.

U-Lab had branches across the Alliance, not just near Sycamore. While the Sycamore branch focused on biological genetic research, this snake boy clearly came from one specializing in human experimentation.

The snake boy gripped the bars with both hands, his clear eyes looking out curiously. He tilted his head innocently, puzzled by his situation. His naïve actions caused a stir in the crowd.

Alan had to shout over the noise, "Starting bid is 1,000,000 NPA credits, with a minimum increase of 30,000 per bid!" The bids came fast and furious, and Alan was busy confirming them, temporarily ignoring the items.

The snake boy looked around curiously, his eyes suddenly locking with Cora's on the beam, his pupils narrowing.

Cora froze. What bad luck! She quickly made a "shh" gesture, hoping he understood. Luckily, the snake boy didn't cry out. He flicked his tail lightly and nodded, unsure.

Cora exhaled in relief, silently praying: Suchat, you'd better come through. We're counting on you.

Five minutes later, a faint green mist drifted through the ventilation system of the auction hall and quickly dispersed into the air. Cora, perched on the beam, keenly sensed a fleeting mental signal. It was Suchat—he was in position!

Cora signaled to Yuui behind the curtain, who nodded in acknowledgment.

"Three million! Any higher bids? Three million once, three million twice, three million...." Alan's face was flushed as he was about to bring the gavel down.

Suddenly, the auction hall was plunged into darkness as the power was cut off!

Great! Cora silently cheered. According to their plan, Suchat had cut the primary power supply.

The buyers looked around in confusion, whispering among themselves, thinking this was some surprise event organized by the auction house. A haunting melody echoed through the hall. "Why do you~ always leave me alone in the night~ I can't control my longing~ searching for you?"

The crowd, bewitched by the song, gradually fell into a trance, meandering. Unseen frost covered their feet, slowing their movements to prevent anyone from trying to escape.

"Crash!!" A loud noise came from above. A girl wielding a massive silver axe was smashing the ceiling. She swung again, "Crash!!" The ground seemed to tremble, and the entire auction house shook precariously.

In the chaos, someone shouted, "Run! The items are being released!"

"Nonsense! That's impossible!" Alan immediately retorted.

But it was true. In the darkness, a ghostly figure appeared in the display area and opened the cages. The six girls, terrified, ran out, and Yuui directed them towards the exit. They thanked her hastily and helped each other rush towards the door.

The Anopower scorpion also broke free and began wreaking

havoc, its bright yellow flames lighting up the hall. The snake boy slithered around, enjoying himself, wrapping his long tail around someone and tossing them aside.

"Ahh!!" Alan screamed as the massive tail flung him into a broken steel beam, impaling him.

"Ha ha." The snake boy laughed joyfully.

Cora and Suchat used the chaos to their advantage, causing as much destruction as possible. Their goal wasn't to kill, but to wreck the place thoroughly. The faster and more violently they tore the auction house apart, the sooner Death Hell would take notice and come to arrest them.

Sure enough, within just two minutes, over a hundred particle cannons were aimed at the wrecked Rose Auction House. From the screen, Warden Sherman's icy voice came through, tinged with a hint of exasperation.

"Arrest everyone in the auction hall! Lay down your weapons and surrender to Death Hell immediately! I repeat..."

It worked! Cora felt immensely satisfied.

Death Hell was about to get very busy.

CHAPTER 7

Coffee Time

"Name?"

"Hey, I'm talking to you! What's your name?" The stern-faced female guard slapped the table, startling the girl in the prison uniform.

"Cora Thornton."

"Age?"

"19."

The interrogation room was dimly lit by a single overhead lamp. The guard, separated by a barrier, typed Cora's name into the computer connected to the records room but found no information on "Cora Thornton."

"ID number? Report it."

"I don't have one... Does an Aberrant Certificate count?"

The guard looked up from the computer, sneering. "We don't care about that here. It doesn't matter if you're an Aberrant or not; once you're in Death Hell, you're all the same."

Once someone entered Death Hell and was marked with the Record of Crimes, it was like wearing an invisible shackle, never to gain true freedom again. Aberrant or not, anyone who dared to act out in Death Hell would be reduced to a mindless husk.

"Without an ID, are you undocumented? From the F district?"

Cora admitted honestly, "District F199."

The guard stopped searching and opened a new file to input

information.

"How long will my sentence be?" Cora asked cautiously, watching her type.

The guard glanced at her, showing a hint of sympathy. "You are charged with intentionally destroying property, an egregious offense with serious implications. Under Warden Sherman's orders, you'll be incarcerated on the fifth floor for nineteen years and seven months and must pay a fine of 100 million NPA credits."

Cora gasped. Nineteen years and seven months? That was longer than she'd been alive! Things were really getting serious.

And 100 million NPA credits—was that number even real? Even if she served her full sentence, she could never come up with that kind of money. It seemed she had truly angered Sherman, and he had no intention of ever letting her go.

"What about the others with me?"

"You're worried about others? You should focus on yourself. Reflect on your actions and try to survive longer." The guard finished typing up her file, hit submit, and stood up from behind the desk. "Follow me to your cell."

"Get in."

On the fifth floor of Death Hell, Cora was shoved into a narrow cell. She looked around, noticing the surveillance camera that followed her every move. Apart from the single bed bolted to the floor, a basic washbasin, and a toilet, the cell was completely bare. Cora curiously inspected her surroundings before walking to the door to submit her activity request for the next day on the light screen.

Then she lay back on the bed, mimicking Charles' laid-back attitude, closed her eyes, stretched out her legs, and fell asleep.

When Suchat regained consciousness, he found himself in the familiar interrogation room, with Khun Bu sitting across from him, glaring with exasperation. "Awake? You punk, tell me, are you doing this on purpose?"

"You were out for just a few days, and now you're back. No wonder you said 'see you next time'—do you think this place is a hotel where you can come and go as you please?"

His head felt like it had been hammered, a cold, numbing pain spreading through it. Khun Bu's voice seemed distant and muffled, almost inaudible. After a long while, Suchat's vision gradually focused, and the chaotic confusion finally left him.

The Record of Crimes... So this is the impact of the Cotal Band? Terrifying.

During the raid on the Rose Auction House, the entire F777 team was captured. The others, being "newcomers," were forced to surrender, but among the buyers were some who had served their sentences, including Suchat. Regardless of how many bars were lit on their Records of Crimes, they all lost consciousness at that moment and shuffled back to Death Hell like zombies.

Suchat's memory only extended to where Warden Sherman's voice rang out; he remembered nothing beyond that.

Seeing Suchat's silence, Khun Bu assumed he was remorseful, but it was too late. He exhaled. "Adding sin upon sin, you're now assigned to the sixth floor. Your sentence... forty years, mandatory labor, and no chance for a reduced sentence. You'll suffer."

The sixth floor cells were even more cramped, akin to solitary confinement. There wasn't even a bed. Suchat, given his height, could only crouch, making even turning around difficult. By activating the light screen by the door, he saw that the labor option was greyed out and unavailable. Fortunately, he could still apply for activities, though now limited to once a month.

Suchat submitted his activity request for the next day.

The next day, during activity time, Cora lined up in the corridor. Guards escorted all the prisoners who had submitted to the activity area. She felt excited, taking quick steps and accidentally stepping on the heel of the prisoner in front of her.

The tall woman turned around slowly, her expression fierce, fists cracking. "Be. Careful."

Avoid trouble, avoid trouble, Cora reminded herself of her nineteen years and seven months' sentence. She stepped back, bowing her head. "After you, ma'am."

With the guard nearby, the woman gave Cora a once-over, snorted, and continued walking with an air of disdain.

Cora sighed in relief.

In the quiet reading room, Cora walked briskly, slipping a kunai into the collar of a man reading a newspaper in a wheelchair as she passed. She continued to the cafe, where a woman with long, flowing hair was in line for coffee. Cora stood behind her, their fingers briefly touching as another kunai was passed.

Cora found a table and sat down. Across from her, a skinny man was focused on building a model. Cora looked away, discreetly placing a kunai on the table's edge, which the man picked up naturally while gathering his blocks.

With no direct communication, soon the man in the wheelchair, the woman with long hair, and a boy bouncing in holding a guard's hand all ended up at the same table.

The activity period was only an hour, and one person was still missing.

Ten minutes later, a young man with a buzz cut entered silently and sat at the adjacent table. They were all here.

The six members of F777 had reunited in Death Hell.

This was their plan before entering—use the hour of activity time to exchange information and plan their next move. Cora sipped her coffee, lightly asking, "I'm on the fifth floor. What about you?"

"I'm on the first," Damian whispered.

"Third," Yuui said, sipping her coffee.

Neither of them had acted directly. Damian had been discreet with his frost abilities, and both he and Ura were deemed suspects involved in the incident, receiving lighter sentences. Yuui was mainly punished for impersonating the catering staff, landing her on the third floor.

Charles built a model with blocks, showing a four. Onyx folded his newspaper, revealing the same number.

They had falsified their identities and infiltrated the auction house with ulterior motives, deliberately disrupting the scene, resulting in slightly harsher sentences. As Cora listened, she discreetly passed a kunai to Damian.

Their terminals had been confiscated, and they had no communication devices. These kunai were created by Cora from materials found in Death Hell, painstakingly crafted without being detected by surveillance. Her ethereal artifact could track their mental signals, serving as a locator to keep them from getting lost.

"Sixth floor," Suchat finally said. He had the harshest sentence among them.

The others gave him sympathetic looks.

Cora flicked her fingers, sending a kunai spinning towards Suchat, who easily caught it and tucked it away.

"I've roughly estimated that the sixth floor has around 3,000 cells," Suchat said, maintaining a neutral expression. "And the bad news is that activities are limited to once a month."

Onyx's gaze dropped to the newspaper. "Since we're on different floors, we can spread out and gather information. There are seven days left in this month. Let's well use them."

With Suchat's previous exploration of the second floor, they had people on almost every level controlled by Warden Sherman.

Considering Suchat's difficulty in getting out and the risk of frequent meetings drawing guard attention, Onyx set the next meeting for the beginning of the next month. Seven days should be enough to gather substantial information.

"Agreed," everyone nodded.

As they talked, a commotion erupted behind them. Two prisoners had collided, spilling hot coffee all over the floor.

"You spilled my coffee," the victim said quickly, staring at the coffee on the ground.

The other prisoner sneered. "So what? If you really want it, go ahead, lick it up while it's still hot!"

The victim raised his head sharply, repeating, "You spilled my coffee!!"

He shouted so loudly that everyone in the cafe heard him.

"Who pissed off Jorick?" a prisoner whispered behind Cora. "Who's that?"

"Crazy Jorick. Too much electric shock therapy scrambled his brains," the whisperer said, tapping his head. "He only gets out once a month and insists on coming here for a cup of coffee."

Though the activity layer was meant for leisure and relaxation, it had strict regulations; it wasn't a place for prisoners to enjoy life. For instance, each prisoner could only receive one small cup of coffee per visit. Miss it this time, and you'd have to wait until the next activity day.

From their conversation, Jorick was also confined to the sixth floor. Missing his coffee today meant he'd have to wait another month. Jorick, who looked young and well-kept with pale skin, stared at the blister on his hand from the hot coffee, mumbling softly, "You spilled my coffee…"

As soon as he said that, Jorick suddenly exploded with rage! He pounced on the person who bumped into him, raising his fists high as his veins bulged and his mental power surged.

In front of everyone, Jorick's smooth arms became covered with thick hair, and sharp fangs grew from his mouth. He transformed into a half-werewolf and began pounding the person's face, blood splattering everywhere. Teeth and bone fragments flew as the arrogant prisoner, overwhelmed and unable to fight back, was beaten to death within minutes.

Jorick continued punching, muttering "coffee" repeatedly as he smashed the person's skull in.

"Shape-shifting ability," Onyx murmured.

A sharp whistle blared from the loudspeaker, and five bars lit up on Jorick's Record of Crimes. He writhed in pain, clutching his head, while the other prisoners in the cafe felt dizzy and experienced palpitations because of the Cotal Band's influence.

Cora frowned slightly, suppressing the agitation of her mental power, and looked at her companions.

Onyx, an S-class mental ability user, was the least affected, with hardly any visible reaction. Yuui, Charles, and Damian felt some discomfort, but controlled it. Only Suchat reacted intensely, gripping the table with trembling hands.

"The power of the Record of Crimes has been amplified," Onyx said coldly.

In the underground city, the Record of Crimes had a limitation level of 1. In Death Hell, it was almost exponentially strengthened to 10. After a while, the invisible sound of waves faded, and Suchat's breathing steadied. He signaled to them he was okay.

Jorick lay on the floor, his gaze vacant, looking even more dazed.

Suddenly, a loud voice came from the cafe entrance. "The wardens are here!" Sitting together was too conspicuous, so Cora and the others immediately stood and dispersed, pretending not to know each other.

Two men in black overcoats, exuding an air completely different from ordinary guards, slowly walked in.

Cora focused on them. The one on the left was slightly shorter, with snake-like cold eyes under his cap. His name tag read "Sherman." The one on the right had a ruddy complexion, freckled face, and messy red hair exuding a nasty temper. His name was "William White."

White stepped forward, looking at Jorick on the ground and the faceless corpse. His ruddy nose twitched, and a violent gleam appeared in his eyes. "You bastard!"

He raised his blood-stained whip high, ready to strike Jorick.

A short staff blocked his move. Sherman spoke calmly, "White, he's a sixth-floor prisoner. You have no right to punish him."

White's eyes filled with an impending storm of destruction. "This is the third time, Sherman. The third time, this bastard has attacked my men. Since you can't control your dog, why not send him to the seventh floor? I'll discipline him for you."

Sherman sneered, "No need."

Cora took a small steps back, sidling up to the prisoner who had spoken earlier. They whispered, "Jorick causes trouble every time he's out. Why not just hand him over to White?"

"Sherman wouldn't let him go. Jorick's family is loaded, and they bribe Sherman every time they visit. He's like a golden goose that lays eggs. No matter how much trouble he causes, Sherman will keep him on the sixth floor."

An unexpected discovery. The wardens could not interfere with prisoners on each other's floors. Cora pondered this new information.

Sherman glanced around at the prisoners watching the scene. Wherever his gaze landed, silence followed. The prisoners, fearing him, avoided his eyes.

Sherman raised his voice. "Today's activity time is over. Everyone, return to your floors immediately!"

Cora followed the crowd out but suddenly felt a chill down her spine. She turned back to see Sherman's icy gaze lingering on her and Suchat for an extra second.

CHAPTER 8

The Warden

Death Hell.

In a lavish, opulent office, Warden Sherman flipped through some files, casually asking, "The prisoners we brought back for destroying the Rose Auction House—have they paid their fines?"

"The buyers on the first floor have mostly paid and been released, but the two with the heaviest sentences haven't paid a cent," the guard replied.

"How much do they still owe?"

"Uh... Warden, they have paid nothing at all."

Sherman paused, a shadow crossing his face. "Understood. You may leave." After a long silence, he drawled.

After the guard left, Sherman pulled up two files.

Cora Thornton: an undocumented resident of District F199, dirt poor.

Suchat: from District E117, formerly a bodyguard in District C83. After paying off his last fine, he's now deeply in debt.

"Paupers." Sherman tore up their files with a stony expression.

Meanwhile, on the fourth floor, Charles quickly found work as an assistant to the prison doctor, thanks to his skills. He didn't have to perform any surgeries himself, just hand over tools and trays. The elderly prison doctor had a rough-and-ready approach, using sharp instruments to draw blood from prisoners feigning strokes, epilepsy, or paralysis, forcing them to stop pretending and flee in pain.

The doctor prescribed medicine in doses far from normal for humans. Charles glanced at them but said nothing. This doctor seemed like a former vet.

The old doctor, pleased with himself, hummed a tune and chatted with Charles. "Young man, do you know what's most important about being a doctor here?"

"...What?"

"Remember, it's not about curing people but ensuring they don't die. I've got plenty of experience dealing with these little bastards. Back in the day, I even treated the Pluto for gout!"

Charles was taken aback. This old prison doctor spoke openly about the Pluto. Sensing an opportunity, he asked tentatively, "How long have you worked here?"

"Hmm, let me think. About twenty years." The doctor leaned back, closing his eyes in nostalgic reminiscence.

"You've seen him then...?"

"Of course. Anyone who's been here over ten years has seen the Pluto at least once."

"Aren't you afraid to mention him... I noticed others don't dare."

"Hmph," the old doctor snorted. "That's because they have guilty consciences, afraid the Pluto knows their secrets."

"The Pluto is omniscient, the most experienced of all wardens. Death Hell is what it is today because of him. It's only in recent years, with his declining health, that those two monkeys have been causing trouble," he said disdainfully.

Charles pondered this new information.

Seven days later, outside the cafe in the activity layer, six prisoners gathered discreetly.

"Everyone, share your findings," Onyx said, flipping through a magazine, speaking quickly, but quietly.

"Nothing on the first floor. Too many people coming and going; I couldn't keep up," Damian said, rubbing his eyes, looking exhausted. He had slept little, searching for people had given him dark circles.

. Searching with Felix's distinctive ice-blue eyes, he should have been easy to spot. The first floor housed minor offenders, making it unlikely he was there.

"Nothing on the third floor, either. I tried all the labor tasks, but unless he's staying in his cell all the time, he's not there," Yuui said seriously.

"I found something else that might be useful," Charles shared his information about the Pluto.

Onyx flipped a page in the magazine, analyzing in a low voice, "It seems there's a hierarchy among the wardens. The highest authority in Death Hell should be the Pluto, who hasn't been seen in a while."

There was too little information about the Pluto, and he was too mysterious to be their primary target, so they set that aside for now.

Cora quietly raised her hand, getting the others' attention. "I didn't find him either, but I noticed there are very few Aberrants here." And the deeper the floor, the fewer there were.

Suchat nodded in agreement.

Onyx explained, "Death Hell has existed for over twenty years, but the apocalypse only started last year. Most Aberrants awakened in the past six months. The buildings here block cosmic rays, and the underwater depth reduces radiation to negligible levels, so it's normal there are few Aberrants."

"So, what's our next move?" Cora asked.

"Down to the seventh floor," Onyx decided firmly, closing the magazine.

He turned to the others. "Not all of you need to go. Stay above and keep searching."

Damian, though a powerful attacker, was still young and impulsive. Charles and Yuui were support types, not suited for unexpected combat. They knew going along could be a liability, so they nodded in agreement.

"The problem is, how do we get down there?" Suchat asked gravely.

"Kill someone? Cause destruction?" Cora suggested boldly.

Onyx rejected the idea. "No direct crimes. It would activate the Record of Crimes."

He pointed to his tag. Activating the Record of Crimes in Death Hell required a significant toll, and repeated activation could cause irreversible brain damage.

"Sherman is a control freak. He won't easily let us go down."

"Unless he realizes we can't pay the fines and are only

troublemakers, keeping us here would be a mistake."

"How do we do that?" Cora wondered.

"I have an idea," Onyx said, gesturing towards the cafe.

Jorick had just gotten his cup of coffee. Finally undisturbed, he found a table, took a deep breath, and sipped his coffee with an expression of pure bliss.

He looked white and clean, calm and well-behaved, a stark contrast to the rage-fueled killer from before.

Onyx watched Jorick, a slow smile spreading across his face. Cora felt a familiar sense of foreboding. Someone was about to be very unlucky.

Of all the labor tasks in Death Hell, the job of filling sand in the underwater tunnel was by far the hardest. It required using a heavy pump, larger than a human, to suck up silt and sand from along the way and then spray it to the outer edge to fill and prevent tunnel blockages. Most of those assigned to this grueling task were prisoners forced into labor.

Suchat, wearing a safety helmet, quietly moved closer to Jorick. Thinking about what he had to do next and the lines Onyx made him memorize, he couldn't help but feel a headache coming on.

Like a spy making contact, Suchat lowered his voice and quickly asked, "Have you ever had Mandheling coffee?"

Jorick, diligently pumping silt, paused and slowly looked up. "What's that?"

"It's a specialty from District C43, Mandheling. It has a high body, low acidity, and a rich, complex flavor with a slight herbal aroma. The taste is layered: it starts with a light bitterness, then a pleasant acidity, and finally a sweet aftertaste." Suchat recited mechanically.

Jorick swallowed, his interest piqued.

"But compared to Mandheling, I prefer Geisha coffee from Emerald City. It's the aristocrat of coffees, with a blend of natural floral and fruity aromas, and a hint of citrus acidity. It melts in your mouth, leaving a lingering fragrance."

Suchat's expression remained blank as he recited his lines, cursing his excellent memory for recalling every word perfectly.

Jorick was already captivated, his pump discarded and scattering sand everywhere. "On activity days, I have to get some."

"You can't," Suchat said flatly. "Why not?" Jorick asked, incredulous.

"The coffees I mentioned are rare regional specialties, and Death Hell doesn't have them."

"You've been here a long time, right? So you've never had good coffee. The coffee on the activity layer is average. Once you've had the good stuff, you won't want anything else."

"I've been here 11 years... or is it 13? I don't remember," Jorick mumbled.

Jorick had been in Death Hell since he was young. Frequent activation of his Record of Crimes had made his brain increasingly foggy, causing him to lose track of time. "I can't get good coffee... I can't get good coffee..." he repeated, his expression growing more frenzied.

A flash of clarity seemed to return to his memory, followed by deep confusion: Why was he in Death Hell? Why was he still here after so many years? Jorick remembered everything suddenly—his father had died, leaving him a fortune. His uncles had found him, told him there was trouble at home, and had him hide in prison for a while, promising to get him out soon. Why hadn't anyone come to get him?

Jorick clutched his head, squatting in pain.

"I heard today that while clearing the sand, the upper layer passages will be open. How do you get there again?" Suchat asked.

"Oh, follow this path to the end. Turn left, go to the end, turn left again. Repeat five times and you'll reach the surface."

"When I get out, I must have a cup of Geisha coffee." Suchat, dragging the heavy pump, muttered to himself as he walked away.

Jorick stared blankly at the end of the underwater tunnel.

"Warning! Warning! Prison break!"

A shrill siren suddenly blared through Death Hell.

Jorick, ignoring everything, sprinted forward. End of the path, left turn, end of the path... Four more turns and he could get out to drink coffee!

Just as he opened the passage to the fifth floor, his Record of Crimes lit up red, and intense electric waves shot out. Jorick screamed, clutching his head, rolling on the ground. When he stood up, his expression was vacant, forgetting what he was doing.

"Clear the sand... clear the sand." Jorick turned around, walking back slowly.

"Jorick! Geisha coffee. Don't you want to drink it?" Cora arrived just in time, using her kunai to discreetly wedge open the passage door, shouting at Jorick's retreating.

"Clear the sand... clear the sand... Geisha?!"

Jorick suddenly howled to the sky, his upper body transforming into a werewolf. Thick fur covered his face and arms, and he stood on powerful limbs, smashing a transparent wall with a single punch. The force created a crack, and cold seawater flooded in.

Jorick leaped over Cora, charging towards the fourth floor in a frenzy.

"Go, Jorick! I believe in you!" Cora silently cheered, clenching her fist in support.

In the luxurious fourth-floor office of Death Hell, a guard hastily pulled on his clothes and rushed out, shouting into his communicator. "Jorick is trying to escape and has damaged the underwater tunnel. Contact the warden immediately! I'm heading there now!"

He ran so fast that he didn't notice the floor, slippery with cleaning liquid. He slipped and fell hard, his communicator skidding several meters away. Grimacing, he looked up to see an inmate in a wheelchair leisurely mopping the corridor. The guard yelled angrily, "Get over here!"

The sound stopped abruptly as something cold and sharp seemed to pierce the guard's brain. He stood there, eyes blank, and then collapsed unconscious. Onyx slowly wheeled over to him. "Officer, do you need to return to the office? I'll take you in."

The Record of Crimes flashed briefly, detected nothing unusual, and dimmed again.

Onyx dragged the guard with one hand, using his access to reopen the office door, then turned back and closed it. He placed his mop on the ceiling, conveniently blocking the camera's view.

He went to the computer, accessed the records room, and quickly began searching through all the prisoner files.

Elsewhere, Sherman stormed through the corridors, his black coat flaring out menacingly. "Where's Jorick?" he demanded.

"He was apprehended on the second floor. He's completely lost his mind; even the Record of Crimes couldn't control him. We had to use particle cannons..." the guard stammered.

"Is he dead?" Sherman's glare was murderous.

"No, no! He's not dead, but he will need to recover for a year or maybe three to five years..."

"What about the damage to the underwater tunnel?" Sherman asked, shifting to another concern.

"There are five leaks, thirty-seven cracks, and Jorick also destroyed three... internal elevators."

"Estimated losses exceed ten billion..." The guard dared not dare meet Sherman's eyes.

"Why did Jorick suddenly go berserk?" Sherman asked after a pause, his voice rough.

"We don't know. When we captured him, he kept shouting something about 'emerald'."

"Emerald? What emerald?" Sherman looked around at the other guards, who all seemed confused. One hesitantly suggested, "Could it be some old-world jade?"

But Jorick had been in Death Hell for over a decade. It was absurd for him to suddenly develop an interest in jade.

Emerald Estate was a new, upscale coffee brand within the Alliance in recent years, carefully chosen by Onyx as an obscure name. The isolated and outdated information within Death Hell meant these guards were unaware it was a type of coffee.

Sherman's face turned icy. "Check the surveillance footage, frame by frame!"

"Yes, sir!"

"Stop," Sherman commanded, and the screen froze on a frame showing Suchat and Cora near Jorick. "What did they say to Jorick?"

The two were passing by Jorick, their lips moving rapidly. "We can't hear, but the Record of Crimes didn't activate, so it must not have been important... right?"

The Record of Crimes could only monitor direct criminal actions, not covert machinations.

Sherman closed his eyes, his fury rising. His intuition screamed that Jorick's escape attempt was linked to these two. These paupers were not only unprofitable but had caused him a loss exceeding ten billion.

Ten billion... Sherman's heart ached.

Jorick's severe injury meant his relatives would not let it go. If Jorick died, those who had sent him to prison, including Sherman, would never receive another cent!

Furious, Sherman yelled, "Execute them immediately..."

"Warden Sherman," an older guard interrupted, "if the Record of Crimes didn't judge their actions, are you not afraid of repercussions from the higher-ups? Death Hell isn't your personal fiefdom."

Sherman glared icily at the speaker. "Are you threatening me?"

"I wouldn't dare, just a reminder," the older guard replied with calm defiance.

"Warden, there's another prisoner who came in with them. He's also causing problems," another subordinate hurriedly reported.

"Who else?"

The guard pulled up another surveillance feed, showing a guard suddenly collapsing while a man in a wheelchair "helped" him into an office. Then the camera feed went dark.

Sherman crushed the cup in his hand. "Rebellion, they're all rebelling!"

He glanced at the older guard, gritting his teeth. "Throw them all to the seventh floor and let White handle them!"

CHAPTER 9

The Octagon cage

In the rapidly descending elevator, three prisoners in uniforms looked at each other, silently exchanging glances.

"Pfft~" After a while, Cora couldn't hold back her laughter, "You really are wicked."

"Jorick, coffee at the Emerald Estate. Do you want some?" Cora dragged out her words, mimicking Onyx's tone, repeating it slowly and leisurely.

Onyx raised his eyebrows, letting her tease him, since it was his idea to incite Jorick to escape.

"And then, get Suchat to trick people." Cora's cheeks dimpled with a smile, looking happy.

Suchat, suddenly reminded of his dark past, stiffened and silently stared at the elevator wall.

There was a hint of amusement in Onyx's eyes as well. "No choice, only he was on the same level as Jorick."

He straightened his expression and changed the subject. "I checked the files of all the prisoners from levels 1 to 6. Felix Lucas isn't among them."

Cora sighed, "No wonder we couldn't find him."

"Yeah, we can put Sherman aside for now. The focus next is on levels 7 to 12, under White's jurisdiction."

William White, the second warden of Death Hell, from the confrontation at the cafe. It was clear he was brutal and cruel, completely different from the cold and greedy Sherman. Who knows what the levels under his control are like?

The elevator ride from level 6 to 7 took longer than expected.

After descending for a full ten minutes, with a "ding," they reached their destination, and the elevator doors slowly slid open.

Just as the three were about to step out, they froze in their tracks.

White had come in person!

A dozen burly guards lined up, with White standing arrogantly in the center, a cigar in his mouth. It is choking smoke curling upward as he stared at the three with a mocking smile.

"Welcome, poor guys!" White slowly clapped, the sound grating at the moment.

Cora looked at him warily. Just three demoted prisoners. Was it worth the warden's personal reception?

"I heard you made Sherman lose ten billion?" White laughed wildly, cigar ash falling in flakes.

He took a deep puff, exhaling thick smoke, and pointed his blood whip at the three. "Good, very good. I appreciate your arrogance. As a reward, I'll allow you to have a good sleep tonight."

Cora frowned slightly. What did White mean by that? What did he mean by "a good sleep tonight"?

White's smile was filled with deep malice. "My territory is not like Sherman's gentle playhouse. Are you ready?"

"Take them to the cells."

The guards forcibly separated and took the three in different directions.

On level 7, the number of cells significantly decreased, with conservative estimates showing less than a thousand, and the environment was even gloomier.

The depth here had already reached the standard of the Alliance's "ultra-abyss zone" (below 6000 meters). As Cora passed by, she glanced out the transparent porthole, seeing slow-moving, dark water, with almost no life except for some sediment.

The cell was as cramped as ever, without even a bed. The walls bore many scratches of varying depths. Cora curled up on the ground, hugging her knees as she fell into a deep sleep.

A few hours later, around four in the morning, the guards banged on the cell doors with their batons. "Get out! Don't dawdle, everyone out!!"

Rustling sounds came from the neighboring cells as the prisoners were all awakened by the piercing noise. Rubbing her eyes, Cora sat up and regained her senses before leaving the cell, following the silently moving crowd in the dark. Along the way, she met Onyx, being driven out as well, and casually pushed his wheelchair.

None of the surrounding prisoners spoke; at first glance, they looked like walking corpses, their eyes filled with deep despair.

"They..." Cora hesitated.

"Are awake." Onyx knew what she wanted to ask and explained in a low voice.

They followed the major group to an open area.

Bright floodlights shone down, revealing a massive octagonal fighting cage in the center! The pitch-black netting was stained with blood, and the base exuded a dark red that couldn't be washed away, with a metallic smell that could be sensed from afar.

In the center of the cage, two shirtless prisoners were fighting. One of them seized an opening and delivered a heavy punch, sending the other flying, head and all. "Crunch—" The neck of the prisoner who received the fatal blow snapped, broken teeth mixed with blood spraying out, resembling a swarm of flying insects in the harsh light.

The bloody scene made Cora physically uncomfortable.

"Roar!!!"

The prisoners gathered outside the octagonal cage were excited, fingers clawing at the netting, reaching in desperately, cheering, taunting, shoving, all kinds of noises blending together as if they couldn't wait to rush in themselves. But such people were a minority; most, like Cora and the others, stood silently, avoiding the sight.

The scene was starkly divided into two extremes: on one side was a brutal revelry, celebrating the disappearance of a living being; on the other was a numb waiting, waiting for death to descend upon them at any moment.

Suchat noticed Cora and the others, silently approaching and standing beside them. "White is there." He discreetly pointed in a direction.

Cora looked up and saw White on a platform directly opposite the cage. He wore a black leather coat with the collar open, sitting arrogantly holding a goblet of blood-red liquor.

"Poor little Jack, look at you. When you first came to level 7, you were such a vibrant little colt. Didn't expect you wouldn't last a week. Normally, I should send you to level 8, but oh, poor thing, your head is shattered. I'll let you off."

The prisoner named "Jack" lay on the ground, white brain matter mixed with blood flowing out, lifeless. White's red nose twitched as he took a pleased sip of his drink, his gaze sweeping across, spotting Cora and the others in the crowd.

"Oh! Our newcomers have arrived!"

He put down his glass and stood up, raising his voice sharply. "To take part in your 'welcome ceremony,' I specially invited all the prisoners of level 7. How is it? Are you excited?"

Level 7

Cora scanned the area. A sea of heads, nearly a thousand people, filled the space. At least they wouldn't have to search each cell for their target.

But what was this "welcome ceremony" White had mentioned? Were they going to be thrown into the ring to fight?

"Look at those bewildered expressions. Seems like you don't know the rules here, huh?" White chuckled.

"This is where we do our 'morning exercise' every day. All inmates must take part; no excuses. The winners get to stay on Level 7 and skip a day's labor. As for the losers... well, I toss them down below."

"After all, there are plenty of hungry lunatics down there. I need to keep them fed, right?" White grinned sinisterly. "Now that you know the rules, let's get started. Who's first?"

The eager prisoners, who eyed her and her companions with predatory glares, pushed towards the edge of the octagonal cage, Cora.

These prisoners were just ordinary people. Why was White so confident? As Cora touched the iron mesh, a glow of blue energy gathered in her palm, ready to transform into her ethereal artifact. But the glow flickered and vanished.

She was stunned. She tried to release her energy again, but it dissipated instantly. Cora quickly looked at Suchat, whose grave expression showed he had also discovered their powers were being suppressed.

You couldn't use Anopower on Level 7!

"I checked your prison files. Aberrants, huh? How elite," White mocked, waving the files in the air before crumpling them and tossing them into a glass. "But I'm afraid you'll be disappointed. Levels 7 through 12 are 'zero radiation' zones. You can't use your Anopowers here."

Without radiation, there was no energy to harness, no resonance for their mental strength to sustain.

For ordinary Aberrants, losing their powers suddenly would throw them into chaos, leaving them paralyzed with fear.

But White had underestimated Cora and Suchat. Even without their powers, either of them could cruise a fight.

Suchat, trained in the deadly arts of the Rainy Forest, was a superb solo combatant. Cora, with her years of martial arts training at Mount Yue Martial Arts Hall, had never lost a match, even before the apocalypse.

She could fight just fine without Anopower.

White's rules stated winners could skip a day's labor, while losers were sent down. This was contrary to their mission; they were here to find someone. Staying on Level 7 was pointless.

Cora, unsure of what to do, gently poked Onyx's lower back. He subtly avoided her touch, then reached back and grabbed her hand.

"Warden, we can join in this 'welcome ceremony,' but can we change the reward?" Onyx called out to White.

"What do you propose?" White gazed at him.

"If we win, let us go to the next level."

The surrounding prisoners were silent for a moment before bursting into laughter. "Did I hear that right? Is he tired of living?" "Kid, you'll regret it. If you get down there, you'll find Level 7 is paradise!"

White looked at Onyx like he was a fool. "Alright, I'll grant your wish."

Suchat leaped into the fighting ring.

His opponent was Olson, a giant over eight feet tall with muscles like mountains. Olson had won ten consecutive matches before today.

Suchat's attacks were swift and fierce. He delivered a whirlwind kick to Olson's abdomen, but Olson stood firm. Suchat switched to a series of hooks aimed at his face. Olson sneered, grabbed Suchat's arm, and threw him against the iron mesh, causing the cage to tremble violently.

Olson roared like a wild beast, spitting at the fallen Suchat. The prisoners around the cage rattled the mesh with excitement.

Suchat got up calmly. The initial attack was just a probe. The more Olson underestimated him, the harder he would fall.

Like a shadowy serpent, Suchat moved unpredictably, constantly seeking openings from unexpected angles. Olson's massive body couldn't keep up.

Suddenly, Suchat stopped behind Olson's head, coiling around him like a predator. He locked his legs around Olson's waist, one hand choking his throat, the other twisting his head. With a swift, violent motion, Olson's eyes bulged as his head twisted off, his body collapsing to the ground.

Outside the cage, the loudest prisoners fell silent, staring in shock at the sudden reversal. White's face darkened as he descended from the top platform, drawing his whip.

"Crack—"

The barbed whip lashed out, striking the cheering prisoners, who screamed in agony.

"Crack—crack—"

The whip fell repeatedly, splattering fresh blood across White's face, who didn't blink as he mercilessly whipped the prisoners to death.

Cora's heart chilled. That whip, once white, was now dyed red with blood.

After venting his anger, White turned to the trio, his voice cold. "Next."

Cora protested, "Why? We've already won."

"What do you mean, why? I said every single newbie has to take part, including him! No loopholes!" The whip lashed towards the wheelchair-bound Onyx.

Cora clenched her fists. Onyx, a mental Aberrant, wasn't suited for physical combat. With his powers suppressed and his limbs disabled, fighting was a death sentence.

White had no intention of letting them go!

Cora stepped forward, shielding Onyx. "I'll take his place."

"What did you say?" White dug at his ear, thinking he misheard.

"I said I'll fight in his place," Cora repeated firmly.

White returned to his platform, scrutinizing the pair. The man in the wheelchair remained expressionless, while the slender girl, who looked like she could be blown over by a breeze, stood resolute.

What a pair of tragic lovebirds, performing a drama in front of him. Even their deaths had to follow a sequence.

"You want to fight for him? Fine." He grinned slowly.

The cage door opened, and two fierce-looking prisoners jumped in. White's smile was cold and cruel. "You want to play hero? Let's see if you have what it takes."

CHAPTER 10

Falling

The iron gate of the octagonal cage clanged shut, turning the fight into a true battle of trapped beasts.

Cora Thornton faced two prisoners, who, despite not being as physically imposing as Olson, clearly had well-honed skills. The surrounding prisoners no longer cheered carelessly; the entire area fell silent.

White lifted his goblet, sipping with a look of delight. "These are former Alliance champions. Mayweather, with a reach of 6 feet, was a genius offensive boxer. And Paris, a master of defensive counterattacks. Let's see how long you last."

The fight began. Mayweather moved with high-frequency footwork, continually closing in, squeezing Cora's space. Paris was like a slippery eel hiding in its shell, easily deflecting every attack aimed at him.

Cora launched a mid-air kick at Mayweather, who blocked with his arms. The powerful recoil pushed him back two steps while Cora landed gracefully, like a swift sparrow. She calmly assessed the situation. To deal with an aggressive opponent, she had to amplify his battle spirit and then shatter his psyche, making him lose all judgment.

Suddenly, Cora lifted her head, raised her thumb, and then turned it down in a provocative gesture. The prisoners booed loudly. Enraged, Mayweather's punches flew towards her, but Cora deflected them with ease.

Cora tilted her head and smiled contemptuously.

Spending so much time with Onyx, she had even picked up his mannerisms. Her mocking smile carried his signature blend of scorn, indifference, and casual disdain.

Mayweather's battle spirit overpowered his reason, his punches growing fiercer and his stamina depleting rapidly. Cora nimbly dodged, making him chase her around the ring fruitlessly while occasionally harassing Paris.

With their rhythm disrupted, the two champions' movements became erratic. Several times, they missed Cora and collided with each other.

Mayweather and Paris adjusted their strategy to encircle Cora, exchanging a glance. Mayweather launched a right straight punch while Paris switched from defense to offense, striking out to block Cora's retreat.

Just when everyone thought she was trapped, Cora hooked her hand on the side of the cage, leveraging herself upwards. Like a gecko, she scaled the iron mesh effortlessly, quickly reaching the top of the ring.

It was a legendary wall-running maneuver, a perfect escape!

The two champions sensed danger and looked up warily.

In the blinding spotlight, a figure leaped down. Boxing? She could do that too. Cora's fists aimed slightly upward, striking Mayweather's temple—his fatally weak spot. The blow was lethal, killing him instantly. As she landed, her right leg whipped around, kicking Paris's left jaw, disrupting the vagus nerve and causing his brainstem to shut down. Paris's pupils dilated, and he collapsed, unconscious.

This stunning counterattack took less than ten seconds. One dead, one incapacitated—Cora effortlessly KO'd the two renowned champions!

The prisoners were first stunned into silence. This was probably the quietest "morning exercise" Level 7 had ever seen. Someone nervously swallowed, glancing at White, fearing he might explode again.

Yet someone dared to pour fuel on the fire.

"Warden, you'll honor the reward you promised, right?" Onyx

asked with a smile.

He needed White to acknowledge the reward publicly. With nearly a thousand prisoners and guards as witnesses, White would risk losing face and authority if he reneged on his word.

White's sinister gaze fixed on Onyx. With a forced smile, he said, "Of course, I promise as the warden to 'reward' you three by sending you to Level 8."

The brutal "morning exercise" continued, but Cora had no interest in watching. "We need to find someone."

The three spread out, searching the crowd for someone with ice-blue eyes. After some time, they regrouped, their faces reflecting the same disappointment.

"Nothing."

"Same here."

Felix Lucas wasn't on Level 7.

"Warden, are you really sending them to Level 8?" White's deputy asked worriedly. "I feel like they have another motive for being here. They caused trouble under Warden Sherman with ulterior motives..."

White sneered dismissively. "Send them tonight. That way, they can make it for Level 8's 'morning exercise' tomorrow."

Sending them down level by level, he was certain he would soon witness their deaths. White knew about that.

The Reality Is Brutal

The next day, Suchat and Cora plowed through Level 8...

On the third day, White changed the rules, requiring Cora to face three opponents at once. The result? All three opponents perished, and Level 9 was cleared...

On the fourth day, the elite prisoners of Level 10 were utterly defeated. White smashed every vase in his office and shredded his beloved whip in frustration.

As the warden, his reputation had been trampled into the dirt. Just one more level... These damned miscreants were rampaging through his territory, figuratively pissing in his head!

White's eyes burned red with fury, his chest heaving.

His shrewd deputy seized the moment. "Warden, actually, their trio isn't without weaknesses. The guy in the wheelchair is a perfect target..."

White paused, eyes narrowing as an idea formed. A wicked smile spread across his face. "Is that disgusting creature on Level 11 still around?"

"It's there," the deputy confirmed with certainty.

During the "morning exercise," Cora, Onyx, and Suchat arrived at the octagonal cage in Level 11 on time. The number of prisoners on this level had dwindled to under 200. As Cora looked around, the prisoners silently sized them up.

Cora frowned, quickly noticing something unusual. The prisoners here seemed... deformed. Some had abnormally elongated heads with disproportionately thin arms; others had asymmetrical eyes and grotesquely split mouths. There was an indescribable eeriness about them.

Onyx observed, "Level 11 is the ultra-abyssal zone. They probably haven't seen light in a long time."

Just as deep-sea creatures adapt to the extreme pressures and darkness with bizarre appearances, these long-imprisoned inmates had undergone subtle genetic mutations. They no longer appeared "normal."

A few minutes later, White and the guards arrived.

Cora stretched her shoulders. Yesterday she had fought three opponents at once. Given White's vengeful nature, today it would probably be four.

"Wait," White suddenly stopped her. "The rules have changed." He lazily pointed his bloodstained whip at Onyx. "Today, he must fight."

Cora was displeased. White kept changing the rules on a whim.

White spoke condescendingly, as if giving a favor. "How about this? If he wins, you two won't have to fight. I'll declare you the winners."

Cora shook her head. "No need. I'll fight for him. Bring on as many as you like."

"I said he must fight today. No one gets a free ride forever. What, has he gotten used to living off a woman?" White sneered.

Onyx wasn't provoked by White's taunts, but it would be better to resolve this quickly. The wheelchair he was using now was a basic model assigned after entering Death Hell, but Cora had secretly changed it during their days of "activities," turning it into a weaponized ethereal artifact.

Onyx reassured Cora. "It's better not to confront him directly now. It'll just waste time. Remember our goal. We need to get to Level 12, the ultimate level under White's control. There's no one we're looking for among these 200 prisoners."

Cora was reluctantly persuaded. "Alright. But if you can't handle it, call for me."

Onyx smiled slightly. "I will, I promise."

With Cora and Suchat watching, Onyx entered the octagonal cage. The iron gate slowly locked behind him. Cora hesitated. Why close the gate? The opponents hadn't even entered yet!

She twisted to see White wearing a cryptic smile.

A black hole suddenly opened beneath the cage. The sound of machinery filled the air, accompanied by heavy, labored breathing growing closer. When the thing emerged, everyone except White was stunned.

A mutated zombie. No, it was an abnormally evolved zombie, adapted to the abyssal environment!

It resembled a deep-sea fish known as an "anglerfish." Its large forehead had a fleshy protrusion that glowed like a tumor. Its jaw grotesquely protruded, with large gill slits on its face. Its long, slender limbs were covered in fine scales and sharp fins.

The deformed zombie turned its head sluggishly. Seeing Onyx closest, it roared and lunged at him.

"You cheated!" Cora shouted in fury.

Regardless of why there was an evolved zombie on Level 11, White had forced Onyx to fight, wanting him dead!

"Hahaha, when did I ever say your opponent had to be human?" White laughed, feeling triumphant.

Cora gripped the iron mesh tightly.

"Don't worry," Suchat said softly. "Let's see if he can handle it."

Onyx maneuvered his wheelchair deftly, dodging side to side. Over the past six months, he had completely adapted to moving mechanically. The wheelchair moved as if it were part of his body. A blade designed for deboning popped out from the footrest—a changed ethereal artifact by Cora. Onyx aimed precisely, striking the zombie's knee.

The zombie howled and lost balance, falling down. It swiped its fin towards Onyx's face, but Onyx tapped a panel, raising an irregular shield that blocked the attack.

High intelligence was an advantage anywhere. Onyx used the wheelchair to counterattack with nimbleness while calmly observing. He gradually discovered the zombie's weakness—it seemed to lack vision, or its vision had deteriorated. The tiny pupils were almost invisible, relying on the glowing tumor on its forehead to navigate.

Onyx reached behind, pulling out a mini rapid-fire crossbow from the brake lever just as the zombie lunged again. "Pew-pew-pew!" The fine needles shot out, bursting into the glowing tumor on the zombie's forehead!

Yellowish pus splattered everywhere. The zombie seemed to feel the pain of blindness, clutching its head and wailing.

Onyx seized the moment, accelerating the wheelchair forward. He stepped on the footrest, and the deboning blade shot out again, piercing the zombie's skull!

He won! Cora jumped up excitedly, happier than if she had won herself. Onyx, breathing lightly, controlled the blade to carve out a green crystal from the zombie's brain.

He turned back and smiled at Cora outside the cage, his scholarly demeanor intact.

"We can go to Level 12 now," Cora shouted joyfully.

Onyx opened his mouth to respond.

"No, you can't. He lost," a crisp voice interrupted from behind them.

White's malicious grin spread. "Cage fights do not allow weapons. He violated the rules, so you lose."

Onyx narrowed his eyes. White had never mentioned this "overlooked" rule before any of the fights from Level 7 to Level 11. It was intentional.

"Winners get rewards, losers face punishment." White, his face flushed with excitement, pulled a small connector from his leather jacket and pressed it without hesitation.

"Boom—"

The entire cage floor shattered, and Onyx, wheelchair and all, plummeted into the bottomless abyss!

Everything happened too quickly. By the time Cora realized it, Onyx had already vanished.

"Where did you take him?" she demanded, her voice carrying the weight of an impending storm.

To descend from Level 11 to Level 12, one had to use the internal elevator; it was impossible to fall directly from the ring. White sat back in his chair, leisurely taking a puff of his cigar. The glowing tip stung Cora's eyes.

They had fought tooth and nail on the brink of life and death just to earn a chance to reach Level 12, but White? He had made the rules himself, only to break them with ease. He had never treated them as equals.

To White, what were they? Pawns for his amusement? Trash for him to vent on?

"Where did you take him?" Cora's voice rang out clear and strong, echoing throughout the arena.

White looked at her leisurely, blowing out a smoke ring with disdain. "Are you blind? He went down. Maybe to Level 13, or 14? Who knows? Below isn't my territory, anyway."

He had thrown Onyx, wheelchair-bound Onyx, powerless Onyx, into the deepest depths of Death Hell—a place of unknown horrors.

"You deserve to die," Cora said, enunciating each word.

White chuckled dismissively, extinguishing his cigar as he stood, his blood-stained whip creaking ominously.

"Look closely. I am the king of Death Hell. What are you? What right do you have to challenge me? Aberrants are impressive? Here, you're just as worthless."

Even if Cora could fight, even if she could take on three, four, or even ten opponents, what about a hundred? Two hundred? A thousand? At his command, all the prisoners would swarm and easily overpower her.

Something inside Cora burned fiercely. Was it fire? No, it was uncontrollable rage.

Her body's magnetic field pulsed with psychic energy, cells differentiating and activating, forming new combinations. Her powerful Anopower broke through the barriers, erupting from her body. Cora closed her eyes and reopened them, a blue glow flashing in her pupils. In her palm, from nothingness, a Square Halberd materialized, much to everyone's shock.

"Impossible! Anopower... you can't use Anopower here!" White was shocked. Six thousand meters below sea level, in the legendary Anopower-devoid zone, the S-class Aberrant, Cora, had ignited her brilliant Anopower.

White instinctively lashed out with his whip. Long whips were strong against short weapons, but when faced with long weapons, they were at a disadvantage.

Although White's whip had strong piercing power, it required distance. Cora swung her formidable Square Halberd, effortlessly deflecting the whip and striking White in the abdomen with a straight thrust. White staggered back, and Cora quickly closed the gap, her icy blade inches from his throat.

"Guards, stop her!" White panicked.

"Suchat, hold them off," Cora commanded. Suchat stepped in to block the approaching guards and prisoners.

Cora was like an unsheathed sword, advancing step by step. White retreated in disarray, frantically dodging, but it was futile. The Square Halberd thrust forward, piercing his throat! White's eyes bulged, blood streaming from his nose and mouth. His shattered windpipe made a ghastly rasping sound, preventing him from uttering a single word.

Cora coldly withdrew her weapon, and without an object to block the wound, blood gushed out. White's bulky body twitched a few times, then ceased its final breaths.

Those who took pleasure in others' deaths would one day witness their own. The entire Death Hell erupted in a piercing alarm. "Level One Alert! Level One Alert! The Warden is dead!"

Levels 7 through 12 shook violently. Prisoners lost their balance, falling over. The internal elevator buzzed as its doors slid open. "Get out! The levels are going into lockdown!" a senior guard shouted, waking from a daze. A Level One Alert hadn't occurred in decades, only happening when the warden's identity changed. All affected floors would lock down until the next warden took over.

Suchat darted to Cora's side. "What now?"

Cora was about to speak when the badge on her chest emitted a blinding red light, activating her crime record!

Her mind felt like it was being pierced by a thousand needles, as if it would explode. Cora crouched in pain, using all her willpower to resist. In the elusive Cotal Band, a secret call echoed, coaxing her to enter the pit in the ring.

Come down... come down...

"You... go, meet up with them," Cora pushed Suchat away. He hesitated.

"Go!" she shouted.

Suchat clenched his fists. "Alright."

Cora was clearly unwilling to abandon Onyx. Staying here was useless; it was better to regroup with the others and come up with another plan. Suchat joined the escaping crowd, rushing towards the elevator.

Come down... hurry down...

That faint voice still lingered in her mind. It was so noisy, too noisy.

Using the Square Halberd to support herself, Cora stood up, her consciousness gradually fading. In a last moment of clarity, she leaped into the pit in the center of the ring. Down she went—who was afraid of whom?

"I will find you."

CHAPTER 11

The Abyss

After falling from the Level 11 ring, the basic wheelchair was shattered beyond use. Onyx pulled a long rod from the base, using it as a makeshift crutch to limp forward. Several joints in his body had been bruised, and there were abrasions on the back of his hand. Fortunately, none were severe, except for the excruciating pain from the nerve being pinched in his injured knee.

The surrounding light was dim, revealing only vague outlines. The cells on this level were empty, with no signs of life.

After about ten minutes, Onyx stopped in front of an open cell. Inside, a skeletal prisoner with hair like knotted straw was curled up on the ground. If it weren't for the slight rise and fall of his chest, he would have seemed like a long-dead corpse.

"Forty-five years," a stern voice suddenly spoke from behind.

Onyx turned quickly to see a guard, about fifty or sixty years old, dressed in a crisp, old-fashioned uniform, calmly watching him. When had this person approached? Onyx hadn't noticed at all. His hand tightened on the crutch.

"His name is Moritick. He was one of the top three assassins in the Alliance. Imprisoned here in Year 2 of the New Era, it has been exactly forty-five years."

Moritick. Onyx recalled the name, quickly pulling up relevant information from his mental database. Like Suchat, Moritick hailed from the Rainy Forest and had been an active figure decades ago. His most famous feat was successfully assassinating a neighboring nation's leader on the eve of an international conference, leading to the Alliance annexing that nation. But... now, he was almost forgotten.

"You're not one of our prisoners," the guard stated.

"William White threw me down here," Onyx replied.

The guard paused, showing no special reaction to the warden's name. Instead, he continued, "From now on, you are. Remember, here you can enter but never leave. The eternal enemy is the stillness of time. You must get used to perpetual solitude."

Solitude? Onyx smiled silently and continued to limp forward.

Ahead was another distinct cell. In the corner was a shimmering nutrient pod. Inside, a prisoner lay submerged in a non-decaying nutrient solution, eyes closed and body naked. A small, black box connected to an energy source was embedded in the pod's exterior.

"Smyrna," Onyx whispered the name.

"You know him," the guard's impassive voice gave away no emotions.

"Smyrna is a textbook figure. Who doesn't know him?" Onyx's eyes reflected the glow of the nutrient pod. "Few know that this famous visionary from District A5 was also the creator of the 'Elder Nation' concept."

The guard was silent for a moment before objectively saying, "You come from a distinguished background and are very knowledgeable."

Onyx didn't respond to the evaluation, instead pondering silently. Even a piece of advanced technology like a nutrient pod could be found in District F, suggesting that Death Hell's creation was deeply tied to the hidden powers within the Alliance's upper echelons.

"Is he dead?"

"Biologically, no. His sentence is a hundred years. To prevent premature death, we separated his mind from his body, ensuring his consciousness survives the full term of his imprisonment."

The guard's unexpectedly calm attitude and willingness to answer questions stood out. Onyx wandered leisurely, without being scolded for returning to his cell.

Using the faint light from the nutrient pod, Onyx examined the guard's neatly pressed hat, graying hair, and clear, weary eyes.

"Officer, are you this patient with all prisoners?" the guard answered a different question. "No one has come down here in a long time."

"Is that so? How many prisoners are left?"

"Forty-two," the guard added, "alive."

Onyx tapped the floor lightly with his crutch. "Officer, look at me. I can't leave, anyway. Can I move around freely?"

"You can," the guard nodded.

Satisfied with the answer, Onyx slowly moved forward, with the guard silently following.

What did he mean by free movement if the guard was going to follow him everywhere?

Cora fell into a void.

After jumping through the gap in the arena, she found herself on a long, seemingly endless slope. There were various exits along the way, but she was unconscious, unable to struggle, and slid directly to the bottom, hitting the ground with a thud.

Cora woke up slowly, unsure how much time had passed. It was utterly dark, the darkness where you couldn't see your hand in front of your face.

Lying on the ground, she moved her fingers, attempting to release her Anopower, but failed. The mystical feeling of the earlier power surge was gone, her mental energy as dry as a desert, unable to stir even the slightest ripple. Even the wound on her chest, which hadn't fully healed, throbbed painfully.

Cora stood up and explored the winding tunnels, hitting several dead ends before finally finding an open space. She heard a faint breathing sound coming from somewhere above her.

Cora suddenly looked up, despite not being able to see. "Who's there?"

"Me."

"...Who are you?"

"I am myself. I've always been here."

I have always been here... Cora realized it must be a prisoner. Maybe she could get some information from him. She slowly felt her way to a corner, exhausted, and sat down.

"Where is this?"

"Death Hell."

"I mean, which level is this?"

There was no response.

Cora changed her question. "Besides me, has anyone else fallen down here?"

"No."

Cora lowered her head in frustration. Levels 13-18 weren't what she had imagined. How was she supposed to find Onyx? In the stillness, the young-sounding voice spoke again. "Your body is perfect."

Cora's hair stood on end, a chill running down her spine.

The indifferent tone was one she had heard from someone else before.

In front of Felalakas' public cemetery, the super AI Ilia had also said something similar about liking her body.

"What do you mean?" Cora asked, pretending to be calm.

"It's a compliment. Your limbs and joints have a vibrant life force, very healthy." The man's voice carried a hint of wistfulness.

Cora clenched her hands and asked nervously, "Are you not healthy?"

He fell silent again.

His silence made Cora relax a bit. Maybe he was missing an arm or a leg, and that's why he said what he did out of envy.

"I have a friend. His leg is broken, but he loves life, stays positive," Cora lied in the dark.

The man sounded puzzled. "Are you trying to comfort me?"

Cora. "...uh, yeah."

"Thank you, but I don't need it."

So hard to communicate, Cora thought, feeling a headache coming on.

"I'm going to look around. Do you want to, uh, come with me?"

"I can't move."

"I am a tree. Trees have roots in the soil, and so do I."

Cora was full of question marks. He seemed to be serious, but she just couldn't understand.

"Trees don't talk," Cora argued.

"How do you know? You're not a tree."

"I...," Cora stammered, "I'm not a tree, and neither are you."

"How do you know I'm not a tree and can't talk?"

Damn, he got her.

Unable to outargue him, Cora fumed silently. After a while, the man spoke to her again.

"So you've seen one now."

"What?"

"A talking tree. Me."

"Let's make a deal. After you die, can I use your body?"

"No!"

"You're very stingy."

Cora was furious. Is Stingy? Thanks, but no thanks.

His thinking was really strange—rigid, stiff, and oddly programmed. He was clearly trying to communicate, but his lack of social skills made every sentence infuriating.

"I need to go, find someone," Cora said and started walking, only to trip over something in the dark and fall.

"You stepped on me."

"Sorry!"

Cora choked up. His voice was at least ten feet away. How could she have stepped on him?

"Accepted."

A soft rustling sound, and leafy branches quickly retracted from under her feet. Cora was stunned, a ridiculous thought occurring to her. Could it be? Was she really talking to a tree?

Cora wandered around in the dark for a while. The place was vast, but she found nothing and returned to her original spot, frustrated.

"Who are you looking for? I'm sure it's just me here."

"Why didn't you say so earlier?" Cora was annoyed.

"Is that something that needs to be said? I thought you knew." The man's tone was filled with pure confusion.

Cora stretched out her limbs, lying on the ground, feeling exhausted. She needed five minutes to just collapse. At least levels 13-18 were safer than she thought. Onyx, hold on longer.

From levels 13 to 18, Onyx inspected each floor. Apart from Moritick and Smyrna, he found the remaining forty prisoners, all of whom were once prominent figures in the Alliance. However, here, they were nothing more than the walking dead.

It might have taken two or three days—without a reference point, he couldn't be sure. Onyx's palms and arms had blistered from excessive walking, and his only good leg now throbbed with pain.

"Officer, what do you think is the purpose of Death Hell?" Onyx looked at the man who had silently followed him all this time.

"Death Hell is a necessary product of the Alliance's development at a certain stage, arising alongside the emergence of classes and divisions."

"A necessary product? What about the criminal records? Are they necessary too?" Onyx chuckled softly.

The guard was silent for a second, seemingly unfamiliar with the term and unable to respond immediately.

Onyx understood instantly.

Besides the prisoners, there was only this guard on the entire level. His identity was becoming increasingly clear.

"The person I'm looking for isn't here," Onyx said.

"All prisoners from levels 13 to 18 are present and accounted for," the guard replied.

"Is that so? Then I guess Death Hell has over eighteen levels."

Onyx raised his eyes slightly. "Isn't that right, Lord Pluto?"

The guard remained silent.

"Sorry, I should be more precise—formerly known as Lord Pluto," Onyx said slowly.

From the moment this guard appeared, he had been out of place. Onyx gradually realized that the man didn't breathe, his chest didn't rise and fall, and his emotions were unnaturally stable. He remembered the prisoner Moritick, who had been imprisoned forty-five years ago, with perfect clarity, yet he didn't recognize the criminal records that every prisoner now possessed, nor did he know the notoriously violent Warden William White.

Putting all the oddities together, there was only one possibility left. But behind that possibility lay another secret.

"You keep emphasizing the living because you know you're not alive anymore. So what are you? A puppet? A doll? You don't have to answer. Whatever you are, take me to see the real Lord Pluto."

"Are you dead?"

"No." Cora lifted her leg slightly, showing she was still alive, though the other person probably couldn't see her.

"Oh," the man's voice sounded a bit disappointed, "then when will you die?"

Cora stubbornly replied, "You die first, then I'll die."

"But trees have long lifespans."

"My lifespan is long too," Cora said, holding a grudge, "longer than yours."

The man was about to engage in a logical debate on whose lifespan was longer when he suddenly paused. "Someone is coming."

Cora sprang up. "Who's coming? Are they alive? How many? Men or women? Where?"

Finally, someone was coming. She was ecstatic.

The man pondered silently for a moment, then muttered to himself, "To meet people, there needs to be light."

"Light? Why didn't you turn it on earlier?" Cora shouted in disbelief. She had been fumbling in the dark for so many days!

As soon as he spoke, faint light emerged from afar, gradually brightening. Cora instinctively closed her eyes. When her pupils adjusted to the light, she cautiously opened them and was stunned by what she saw.

A towering, lush tree made entirely of data stood in the center of the space, emitting a verdant glow. A flowing code surrounded the man who had been speaking to. His legs were missing from the thighs down, replaced by an endless stream of data forming the shape of virtual legs, which were also two flexible branches extending throughout the space. It was clear the man was part of the tree.

Silver hair! Ice-blue eyes!

Cora had never seen true ice-blue eyes before. Thyrion Lucas's eye color wasn't pure, tinged with a bit of icy blue. But now, she was certain—the man before her had the purest ice-blue eyes. It was hard to describe the color: like the first snow of winter, the frozen Mirror Lake, or clear crystal, but not rigid. Each blink revealed the flow of stars within.

Felix Lucas—this tree... no, this man was Felix Lucas! They had finally found the person they'd been searching for so long!

Two more people emerged from the darkness. One of them, a man with a cane, recognized the scene and smiled faintly. "So, it's you."

"It's been years. Why are you in such a sorry state? The Lucas family sure hit you hard, breaking both your legs?"

Felix Lucas blinked in confusion, silver hair falling over his shoulders. "I have legs."

The data shifted, the branches adorned with green 101010 leaves rustling.

"The one without legs is you," he retorted.

"Enjoying your time as Lord Pluto, I see?" Onyx said, removing the criminal record from his shoulder and tossing it in front of Felix. "You made this piece of junk too, didn't you?"

Felix glanced at the criminal record on the ground and then looked up at Onyx. His brow furrowed, and the surrounding data flowed faster, showing his displeasure.

Onyx smirked and raised an eyebrow. "What's wrong? Lost your legs and your memory too?"

The data stopped abruptly. Felix studied Onyx's expression for a long time before saying softly, "Ah, it's you."

"Onyx!" Cora rushed over to support him.

Onyx sighed in relief. He was indeed close to his limit and leaned against Cora.

"I was looking for you, but I couldn't find you. It's so dark here, I couldn't get out," Cora said, feeling wronged.

Onyx gently pinched her chubby cheeks, pulling them left and right. Cora's head moved with his actions.

"Alright, stop pouting. I'm fine."

Pouting? Cora's face turned expressionless, and she punched him in the face, knocking his head sideways.

"Ouch, so fierce," Onyx murmured.

"Onyx!" Felix suddenly called out his name, repeating it in a strange tone.

His pure ice-blue eyes fixed on Onyx, and Onyx stared back at him.

Separated by ten meters, neither spoke, but their postures were strikingly similar, even the slight lift of their chins as they looked at each other.

Spanning vast distances and time, many years ago, two equally intelligent and proud boys constantly competed, always at odds, yet ultimately forced to reconcile.

Cora belatedly recalled Onyx mentioning that Felix Lucas could barely be considered his "friend." He was friends with such an oddball?

Felix awkwardly pulled at the corners of his mouth, trying to make a "smile." "Long time no see, Onyx."

CHAPTER 12

A Tree

Felix Lucas lifted his hand, and a small cluster of glowing data branches rose with his movement, the leaves rustling softly.

Onyx discarded his temporary crutch, and with Cora's support, leaned against the wall to sit down.

He looked incredibly disheveled, his prison uniform tattered, his palms covered in blood blisters, and several scratches marred his face. These were just the visible injuries; who knew how many hidden wounds he had, considering his wheelchair was broken? It was impossible for him to be unharmed.

Sitting down, Onyx had to look up to speak to Felix. He clicked his tongue lightly. "Come down here."

Felix murmured, "I am a tree. Trees only grow taller...."

"Cut the crap and come down," Onyx interrupted.

"Why?"

"It's a strain to keep looking up."

"You're still so particular."

Flowing data formed a trunk shape, gently lowering Felix to the ground until Onyx could finally look him in the eye. Onyx tilted his chin slightly, showing another direction. "Since you are Lord Pluto, then who is he?"

Cora belatedly realized there was a fourth person present. From the beginning, this person had stood still, not moving or even breathing. She had focused all her attention on Onyx, ignoring his presence.

Now, in the light, the guard's appearance was even more incongruous. Though his eyes were clear and rational, his facial features and limbs were rigid, like a puppet covered in a human skin, no matter how lifelike, it couldn't hide the strangeness.

Cora's intuition told her he probably wasn't human.

"He's the warden here," Felix said in his usual tone. "When I arrived, he was close to death. He didn't want to die or let others know he was dying, so he found me. He wanted to separate his consciousness from his body and inject it into a new one, like that dreamer. He asked if I could help."

"I extracted all his memories, intending to transfer them into his changed new body, but there was a parameter error mid-way, and I couldn't repair it with my powers. The experiment failed, leaving only part of his consciousness. Now, he's no longer a complete person, only mechanically repeating residual commands."

"That's all." Felix moved his fingers, projecting fragmented memories of the former Lord Pluto onto the blank wall.

He had been a passionate young man who, upon coming of age, resolutely entered the prison industry, climbing from a low-ranking officer to the influential position of warden. He had both skill and cunning, continuously centralizing power, reforming, and issuing new policies, bringing Death Hell to its peak, becoming both revered and feared.

However, the law of extremes states that when something reaches its peak, it moves in the opposite direction.

After reaching the top, he declined rapidly.

Plagued by illness and age, he found himself increasingly powerless, reluctantly ceding authority and retreating to the lowest level of Death Hell. The wardens above him kept changing, while he became more and more mysterious, not because he didn't want to leave, but because his deteriorating body and depleting energy couldn't support his ambitions.

Onyx looked at the silent guard. Watching his own dramatic life story unfold, the guard seemed oblivious, like a stranger. He had built Death Hell's glory and had been defeated by his own obsession. Felix was right; he was no longer human but a puppet.

"What's his name?"

"I don't know," Felix replied indifferently, never caring to ask.

Besides the title of "Lord Pluto," his life was unknown. Now, he wasn't even Lord Pluto anymore. Just a sigh remained.

Memory extraction, conversion, and reinjection into a new body... Felix's casual words were shocking. If the former Lord Pluto's experiment had succeeded, he would have achieved immortality in a unique form, shaking the entire Alliance.

Felix looked regretful. "In the end, the body he chose was too fragile to hold a complete soul."

Felix wasn't a research fanatic passionate about such experiments. He didn't like or even find them interesting. His only attempt was because of the former Lord Pluto's request, but the failure bothered him. A genius couldn't stand imperfection.

Cora listened intently, her fingers unconsciously grasping something nearby.

Felix's ice-blue eyes suddenly turned to hers. "You're touching me."

"Huh?"

Looking down in confusion, Cora realized she was holding a branch that had extended towards her and quickly let go. The branch followed, wrapping around her wrist, its tip brushing against her arm affectionately.

"I can let you touch me because I called you down here."

Felix's gaze returned to Cora, his eyes and the branch both glimmering. "I like your body very much. How about letting me transform you? I promise it'll work this time."

"No," Cora said expressionlessly, shaking her hand, but the branch stayed.

Felix persisted. "Or let my consciousness enter you. We can share a body. Have you heard of synesthesia? It's where you and I become one, you can feel me, and I can...."

"Don't even think about it," Onyx grabbed the branch's tip and pulled it away, coldly saying, "Get lost."

Rejected repeatedly, Felix retracted the branch and pursed his lips in displeasure. He lost the will to socialize actively and leaned back against the tree roots lazily.

"Why did you come to Death Hell? Is this the result of your new research project?"

"I came specifically to find you."

"To find me?" Felix was puzzled.

"Right, before we have our proper discussion, take care of this first." Onyx removed Cora's criminal record, tossing it to the ground alongside his own.

Felix Lucas's branches picked up the two records and brought them to him. He paused for a moment, his gaze lingering on Cora, who suddenly felt nervous, fearing he might say something shocking again.

"Don't worry, she won't," Onyx said suddenly, his voice calm and assured.

Cora looked at him, confused. Won't what? His words seemed so out of context.

Felix murmured in acknowledgment, his fingers moving slightly before he crushed the tags.

Cora's consciousness shook, and she distinctly felt the persistent sense of being watched vanish. Was it really that simple?

"Did you create the criminal records?" Cora asked, surprised. She recalled the information she had got from Ura—these records were a technology passed down from District B. Could Felix have been tinkering out of boredom?

"Not entirely. It was initially a monitoring device without punitive functions. I hacked its firewall and thought it was a waste, so I added some features and improved it," Felix replied casually.

Even without his powers, Felix was a genius hacker. This was certainly something he could do.

"So, what do you want from me?" he asked.

"We need your help to hack the registry system and forge some new identities. We need to go to District C33."

Felix laughed softly. "Did you replace your brain, too? This new one doesn't seem very good."

Onyx's expression remained unchanged. "I'm serious."

"You're a genetically enhanced individual who awakened hacking abilities over a decade ago. This should be easy for you."

"I'm in an Anopower-restricted area," Felix reminded, implying he couldn't use his hacking abilities.

"I know. You misunderstood me. I want you to come out with us."

"The biggest difficulty we faced was finding you. At least that part is done. As for getting out, we can figure it out," Onyx explained.

"I'm not leaving," Felix rejected without hesitation. "Once a tree takes root, it doesn't move easily. I'm fine here."

Onyx scoffed. "Sure, you're the Lord Pluto here, the heart of Death Hell. The lives of all prisoners are at your mercy. But you're trapped here, unaware of the changes in the outside world."

"I don't care..."

"The Lucas supercomputer isn't dead. It will soon be reactivated."

"Impossible!" Felix's head snapped up. "Even if she's not dead, she can never be restored to normal."

"Why not? The Lucas family has found a replacement energy source for her."

"Who?" Felix's voice turned cold.

"A super AI with a complete personality and powerful abilities. Before we came to the City of Sin, they had already started the capture process. By now, it's probably in place."

Cora let out a sound of surprise. Onyx was talking about Ilia? But Ilia hadn't been captured; she had taken down Thyrion Lucas. As she opened her mouth, Onyx squeezed her finger joints, making her pause. Only then did she realize what was happening.

Oh... Onyx was lying again. This time even more outrageously, deceiving his own friend.

Felix's branches drooped, looking dispirited.

Onyx continued, "Back in New Era 8, the Lucas Starship was created, but for over twenty years, it remained unknown, buried among other flying terminals. It wasn't until New Era 32, when a new model emerged after a technological revolution, that it became famous overnight, known as the 'Never-Falling Bluebird.' No one knew that the one who wrote that core code was a thirteen-year-old boy—Felix Lucas."

"You perfectly integrated the key energy source, Sora Wings, into the computational core, enabling high-speed flight at great altitudes under absolute safety. You were the one who brought the Lucas family to its peak."

Cora was stunned.

The Lucas Starship, Sora Wings, Felix Lucas... Felix was the true creator of the starship!

"The Lucas family accumulated immense wealth through the starship, becoming the sole ruler of District B4. But do you know? The starship has now completely collapsed."

Felix frowned. "The code I wrote could run for another hundred years without errors."

Onyx slowly shook his head. "The code didn't fail. The Lucas family reclaimed the Sora Wings."

No matter how perfect the program, without an energy source, the starship couldn't operate. Felix's branches tightened gradually.

"Even knowing all this, do you still plan to stay here and be the Lord Pluto?"

Felix was silent for a moment, then suddenly spoke. "You're deliberately provoking me. You haven't changed a bit, pretending to be sincere but actually full of bad intentions. Once you find a weakness, you relentlessly exploit it."

Onyx smirked. "I am provoking you. I know you have Asperger's Syndrome. This place might suit you better than pretending to be normal in social situations."

Felix scoffed. "You, a psychopath, have no right to talk about me."

Cora looked from one to the other, puzzled by their conversation. What were they talking about? What A... what P...? Both of them wore stiff smiles, staring at each other without backing down.

"Are you coming or not, trash?"

"Shut up, loser."

Cora intervened, "Hey, didn't you two just make up? Why are you fighting now?"

They both looked at her.

Cora's voice grew smaller. "Can't you discuss things calmly without arguing?"

After a moment, Felix shook his branches. "I can't leave."

Onyx's expression turned stony, and Felix gave him a sidelong glance, speaking before Onyx could. "Shut up."

"If I leave the tree, I'll die."

Felix moved forward a bit and slowly turned around. Cora saw clearly that his back was full of various tubes and conduits. Data lines even connected to the nerves at the stumps of his legs. Pulling them out abruptly would likely result in instant death from blood loss.

Felix's eyelashes lowered, his expression unexpectedly calm.

Cora felt a sharp pain in her heart. It was too cruel. She didn't know what kind of grudge existed between Felix and the Lucas family, but wasn't cutting off his legs, throwing him into the deepest part of Death Hell, and nailing him to a pile of data enough? Did they have to connect his senses to countless sins, forcing him to endure endless torment for eternity?

"Do you still want to take me away?" Felix asked quietly. After a moment of silence, Cora was the first to speak. "Yes, we will definitely take you out."

Onyx suddenly asked, "How far is the boundary that restricts Anopower usage from us?"

Felix said, "As long as you leave the Ultra Abyss Zone, the straight-line distance is... twelve thousand meters."

Onyx's fingers tapped lightly on the ground, his usual thinking gesture. "I have an idea... First, let's bring down Charles Franz."

"Forget it, bring them all down," he added.

CHAPTER 13

Reborn

These past few days, Death Hell has been far from peaceful.

Warden White died suddenly, reportedly in a horrific manner, his throat pierced through. The cells on levels 7-12 were locked down, and many prisoners escaped in the chaos. Lupin Sherman was busy cleaning up the mess, leaving the management of the original levels somewhat lax. This allowed Yuui Hayashi and the others to meet on the activity floor.

Suchat had already told them about what happened below.

"Both of them went down?" Yuui anxiously gripped the edge of the table.

"Yes," Suchat said gravely.

Without Cora, Damian wasn't pretending to be cute and obedient. He sat upright, his small brows furrowed tightly.

Yuui felt a headache coming on. Normally, she wasn't the one who was deciding, but given the current situation, if they didn't act quickly, Cora and Onyx's situation would become increasingly dangerous.

"Let me state my position first. I want to go down and find them," Yuui sighed.

"I agree." Surprisingly, Charles Franz was the first to speak. Their purpose for coming to Death Hell was because of him, and now that Cora and Onyx were in danger, he couldn't stand idly by.

"I agree too." Damian bravely raised his small hand; he definitely wanted to save his sister.

Suchat nodded at Yuui.

As long as they didn't split up, Yuui felt more confident. "Alright, let's think of a way to get down there..."

As the four were discussing, their criminal records suddenly glowed red. Yuui looked at her tag in shock. How could this be? They had committed no crimes recently. Could the criminal record monitor their thoughts now?

A secret broadcast suddenly entered their minds.

Yuui listened quietly, then raised her head with a strange expression, noticing the others looked the same. "Did we all hear the same thing? The good news is that Cora and Onyx are safe, and they've found Felix."

Charles, Suchat, and Damian nodded in confirmation.

Yuui paused, then couldn't help but smile. "Did you get the rest of the message, too? Cora, you really... always bring surprises, no, more like shocks."

Lupin hurriedly walked through the office area, busy arranging various tasks. A subordinate jogged over to report. "Warden, there's a request from level 18 to transfer four prisoners down."

"Level 18? There are still people alive there? Who issued the transfer order?" Lupin was surprised.

The subordinate trembled. "It was a direct order from that person."

Lupin stopped abruptly, letting out a cold snort. "The old man really knows how to cause trouble. Reject it outright."

Lupin had never seen Lord Pluto, but since his first day as warden, this figure had overshadowed him. People constantly compared him unfavorably to Lord Pluto, insisting he couldn't change the rules set by Lord Pluto. He was fed up.

"But Warden... you don't have the authority to refuse," the subordinate stated directly.

Lupin glared at him, crumpling the papers in his hands. "Really? I don't have the authority?"

Though furious, Lupin kept his head clear. With White deceased, the priority was to reclaim the escaped prisoners quickly. Before the Alliance issued a formal order, he needed to seize control of levels 7-12.

Once he held the power, no one could challenge him. Regarding that old Lord Pluto, he would eventually be replaced. In the future, Death Hell would have only one warden: Lupin Sherman.

Calming down, Lupin asked, "Which four prisoners are to be transferred?"

The subordinate quickly handed over their files. Lupin skimmed through them. "Show me the prisoners' surveillance footage."

In the live feed, Yuui, Charles, and Damian were seen working obediently. Damian should have been released already, but because he hadn't paid the fine, he remained in his cell, leisurely drawing. The last one was a tall man temporarily placed in a cell, awaiting reassignment.

Lupin had no impression of Yuui and the other two, but when Suchat appeared, his brow furrowed. He immediately recognized him.

How is this man still around? Thrown down once and back again. Seeing him brought bad luck, reminding Lupin of the ten billion he lost. His good mood vanished, and he impatiently said, "Since Lord Pluto wants them, send them down."

Half an hour later, the guard set the destination to the designated floor, pushing the prisoners into the elevator. "Get in and behave."

As the elevator doors closed, Yuui smiled sweetly, quickly slipping a kunai into the wall.

The same small actions occurred on level 1 with Damian, level 4 with Charles, and level 6 with Suchat. The four kunai Cora had left hid in the moving elevator.

Onyx pried a usable screen from Smyrna's cell and connected it to Felix's data port, beginning to study the structure of Death Hell. "Did you send the one-way signal? You should be able to handle that without using your powers."

"Stop nagging, it's already done," Felix's branches flowed, his pale fingers tapping nimbly on the leaves, monitoring the elevator's movements in real-time. "Your people are on their way down."

"Give me the equilibrium vector data of the particles."

"Why don't you calculate it yourself?"

"I'm calculating the gravitational parameters. You should thank me; this should have been your job."

As they communicated and progressed, they occasionally

bickered, reminiscent of their younger days working on projects together. Felix rolled his eyes and quickly completed the calculations, glimpsing a figure out of the corner of his eye.

In the shadow not far away, a person stood quietly, upright and rigid.

"Wait, a moment." Felix "stood" on his data legs and "walked" a few steps towards the person, stopping in front of him.

"I'm leaving."

"Congratulations."

Felix spoke calmly. "When I leave, it might cause quite a commotion. Death Hell could be destroyed and cease to exist." The guard was silent for a moment, not understanding Felix's meaning, unable to respond effectively.

Felix's words seemed to trigger a keyword. The guard slowly and stiffly replied, "Death Hell... Death Hell is a necessary product of the Alliance's development at a certain stage, arising with the creation of classes and divisions."

His missing consciousness prevented him from processing more complex language environments, only repeating meaningless phrases. Felix waited for him to finish before speaking again. "You are one of my few failures."

"I don't understand your pursuit of immortality."

"But if you're willing, when I leave, I can use my powers to write a calculation program for you, to complete the missing part of your consciousness. But let's be clear, you won't return to your former state. At most, you'll be like an AI with factory settings."

The guard was silent for a long time, then slowly raised his arm, giving Felix a standard salute, his voice low but firm. "Staying in Death Hell is my life's mission."

"Thank you."

Felix responded nonchalantly, turning to leave, only to meet Cora's bright eyes. She wasn't eavesdropping; she had been standing there openly listening.

Cora blinked, her thoughts swirling. How could she describe Felix? His thinking seemed erratic, making communication difficult, but he had his own set of principles. How did that say go? Oh, protective.

Cora looked at him, smiling mischievously, dimples appearing on her cheeks. Felix's ice-blue eyes narrowed slightly, his branches sneaking onto her shoulder as he whispered, "Want to try synesthesia with me while he's not looking?"

Cora bristled. "No!"

Ahead, Onyx's fingers paused on the screen, his voice icy. "Felix Lucas, get back here and get to work!"

When Yuui and her group stepped out of the elevator, someone was already waiting for them. A uniformed guard with graying hair said in a deep voice, "Follow me."

The group silently followed him, continuing down from level 18 through a dark corridor until they reached an open space. Seeing the glowing data tree and Felix Lucas for the first time, the four were stunned, their eyes wide with disbelief.

Damian ran over and hugged Cora's leg. After a brief exchange of information, Charles Franz was called away by Onyx.

"Can you handle these tubes?" Onyx asked.

Charles carefully knelt down to examine the data ports connected to Felix. They already knew that below level 7 was an Anopower-restricted zone. "I can pull them out quickly, but stopping the bleeding and stitching would require Anopower, which isn't workable here."

"Don't worry about stitching. How fast can you remove all the tubes?" Onyx asked.

Charles quickly calculated, "About..."

"Don't give me estimates. I need it down to the second," Onyx interrupted.

"7 minutes and 30 seconds."

"That's too long. You only have 4 minutes and 30 seconds," Onyx said.

Charles disagreed, "4 minutes and 30 seconds accounts only for removing the tubes. Without stopping the bleeding, he won't survive."

"Then pull out the tubes from other areas first, leave the stumps for last. I'll give you an additional 30 seconds of Anopower for blood stoppage. Can you do it?"

"I can."

The seven of them sat together, and Onyx opened a projection displaying a simple structure of Death Hell. "Let's review the plan one more time and get ready to leave this hellhole."

At 5 PM, the labor period ended. All the internal elevators of Death Hell suddenly moved frantically, with no human control.

"Ding," "Dong," continuous crashing sounds echoed. The massive elevators seemed to have agreed to rush toward the same floor in the same direction.

"Death Hell is an inverted cone. The fastest way to escape is to flip it over."

"Our task is to use enough weight to forcibly change the gravitational field." Onyx switched to a 3D model, rotating it 180 degrees, making their current level 19 the top layer.

"Do you know what's the heaviest thing in Death Hell?" "The elevators!" Damian quickly answered.

"Exactly. Each internal elevator is constructed with high-density metal, making them incredibly heavy. By gathering them all, we can flip Death Hell."

An unknown virus simultaneously attacked hundreds of elevator systems, all accumulating at the oil sump on level 1. The ground tilted, heavy objects slid uncontrollably, prisoners lost their footing and fell, their vision spinning, and steel structures in the factory broke, showering sparks everywhere. Death Hell began sinking towards the ocean floor.

"But what if they use the elevators to catch us?" Cora asked.

"To prevent that, we need to cut off any chance of being pursued," Onyx confirmed.

The level where F777 was located sliced through the waves, rapidly rising. 12,000 meters... 10,000 meters... 8,000 meters... 6,000 meters! The moment they left the Abyss Zone, their mental energy flow was restored, and they could use their Anopower again!

On the 6th level of Death Hell, Lupin Sherman clung to the wall, shouting, "What's going on?!"

A guard trembled as he reported, "It seems there's a breakout from level 18. The noise..."

Level 18 again, another breakout! Lupin instantly thought of Suchat, the bastard who caused him to lose ten billion. If he had known this would happen, he would never have sent him down. Even Lord Pluto was useless, unable to control his prisoners.

"Special police team, arm yourselves and follow me down," Lupin growled, staggering towards the elevator. If it came to this, he would handle it personally. To hell with Lord Pluto and the rules; he would kill them all and end this once and for all!

Inside the crowded elevator, the four kunai suddenly glowed, charged with powerful mental energy.

"Boom!"

All the elevators exploded into ruins. Lupin, stepping into the flames, was blown out, his face scorched and unconscious.

On level 19, the cone's tip was only a few hundred meters from the sea surface. "Cora!" Onyx shouted.

Yuui sang, directing all her energy to Cora.

Cora was enveloped in a blue glow, transforming it into a giant axe five meters long. Using all her core strength, she swung the axe at the tip of level 19.

"Bang! Bang! Bang!" The sturdy outer wall shattered, and black seawater poured in. Cora was drenched, choking on seawater.

"Damian!" Damian nodded seriously, releasing his Anopower, freezing the incoming seawater into a solid escape tunnel.

"Charles."

Charles focused intensely, sweat dripping from his forehead. Only a few more tubes remained on Felix's leg stumps. He swiftly removed them with his left hand while stopping the bleeding with his Anopower with his right, moving so quickly it was almost invisible.

Felix trembled violently, his face white as snow. The excruciating pain ravaged his nerves, but he made no sound.

"The particles are deviating," Suchat warned.

Sure enough, Death Hell was falling back. Forcing a gravitational field change could only last a short time. With Felix losing control of the elevators, they had little time left.

Everyone's eyes were fixed on Charles.

Ten tubes... seven... three... the last one!

Charles pulled out the final tube just in time, quickly treating the wound. Felix was free!

"Go!!"

Several kilometers away, the citizens of the underground city looked up in disbelief towards Death Hell.

The once calm underground sea surged with terrifying waves, soon triggering a massive tsunami that swept through the trading street, drenching everyone. People were stunned.

Could it be that something happened to Death Hell?

"The criminal records are gone!" someone in the swimming crowd shouted in delight. Others quickly checked, finding the tags on their criminal records had disappeared, turning them into useless pieces of metal.

Ura, busy saving the crystals in his shop, suddenly remembered something. He retrieved the terminal left by the previous group and ran towards the underground sea.

"Hey." Felix called out to the guard just as they were about to escape.

Pale fingertips flowed with data, touching the guard's forehead. Felix's cold and powerful Anopower surged in, completing the missing fragments of the guard's soul with a new code.

"I, Felix Lucas, never leave things incomplete."

After saying this with pride, Cora promptly grabbed Felix by the collar and dragged away.

The thawing seawater gradually returned. Level 19, just steps away from freedom, fell back into the sea. The guard's vision narrowed, and he barely saw a woman with strange hair assisting Felix and the others at the shore.

Onyx pulled out two wheelchairs from the space, sitting in a high-end one while tossing a basic one to Felix.

Felix fumed, "I want yours!"

Onyx sneered, "There are only two left. Take it or leave it."

"Stop arguing and move!"

The shoulder-length-haired girl pushed both their heads aside, lifted them up, and ran off.

"Boom!"

Death Hell crashed back into the abyss, flipping back over.

The silent guard sealed off level 19, slowly walked back to level 18, and sat in the dark alone for an unknown amount of time until a commotion broke the silence.

"Level 18, the breakout... Lord Pluto!" Several middle-aged guards saw his face and cried out in shock.

The former Lord Pluto stood up slowly and spoke in a deep voice, "Ryo, Ryu, long time no see." He didn't actually remember their names, but the implanted memories told him so.

"Sir, are you returning to manage Death Hell?"

The two guards asked excitedly. With the upper two wardens dead or severely injured, Death Hell was in chaos. Lord Pluto's return would be a strong stabilizing force.

"Yes, I am back," the former Lord Pluto nodded solemnly, but his mind drifted. He could remember everyone's name, but what was his own? It didn't matter. He would create a new one.

"From now on, don't call me Lord Pluto. Death Hell has no Lord Pluto anymore."

"My name is Hugh Young."

CHAPTER 14

Lay Low

"How is he?" Cora asked, her eyes filled with worry as she looked at Felix, lying pale on the bed, his silver hair spread across the pillow. Even in his sleep, his brow was tightly furrowed.

Since escaping from Death Hell, Felix had only made it to the safe house before passing out.

"He's not in immediate danger, but he needs time to recover," Charles Franz said, his hands glowing with healing energy as he continuously transferred it into Felix's body. The surgery to stitch up his hundreds of wounds had gone smoothly.

"Why is he unconscious?" Cora asked.

Charles's expression was grave. "All those tubes were connected to his nerves. While he could control Death Hell's data, his own life force was being drained. So, when the connection was cut, he became even weaker than an ordinary person."

No wonder Felix had said he was like a "tree."

Trees absorb nutrients from the soil and then transport those nutrients to their branches and leaves. If Felix weren't a powerful mental Anopower user, he would have long been drained to death by the constant torture.

The pain Felix endured when the tubes were removed must have been unimaginable.

Yuui sighed deeply beside them. "Is there any hope for his legs to recover?"

Felix's legs were completely gone under the blanket.

Charles slowly shook his head. "We can only consider using prosthetic materials or mechanical replacements."

There was a long silence, broken only by a faint sigh.

Onyx spoke coldly, "Felix is a hacker-type Anopower user. Even without legs, it doesn't diminish his abilities."

"But I still suggest you put away your sympathy and pity. He doesn't need it. He's always been an oddity. Your excess emotions will only trouble yourselves, not affect him."

Yuui mused, "You're right. My sigh wasn't out of sympathy, but out of awe. Knowing that the criminal records, which could zap our consciousness into nothingness, were his creation, makes me shiver."

"You've never been zapped," Suchat cut in unexpectedly.

Of all of them, Suchat had suffered the most from the criminal records. The cold, invasive Cotal Band drilling into his mind was something he'd never forget. If Felix hadn't disabled the records, a few more zaps might have turned him into a mindless shell like Jorick.

"It's a metaphor, emphasizing how powerful he is. Don't you understand?" Yuui shot him a glare, her beautiful eyes full of intensity. Today, she had put on a full face of makeup, and her glare carried the imposing aura of a star, dazzling and unapproachable.

Suchat paused, then nonchalantly turned his head away.

Talking about the criminal records reminded Cora of Anopower. She tugged on Onyx's sleeve. "What level is he?"

"Felix awakened before Doomsday. His mental power potential was tested to be 97%, just a step away from S-class," Onyx explained. "Even after a few years in Death Hell, he should have no problem breaking through to S-class."

"S-class mystic hacker Anopower," Cora exclaimed in awe, stars in her eyes.

Damian pouted, seriously counting on his fingers how long it would take him to break through his 90% potential.

"So, who's stronger, him or Ilia?" Cora asked, directly excluding Thyrion Lucas. Just by looking at Felix's pure ice-blue eyes, he seemed more formidable. Among those she knew, the most skilled in data manipulation was Ilia, the lord of Felalakas.

"They've never fought, so it's hard to say," Onyx said, his pause full of meaning. "But AI inherently fears his abilities. Don't forget, Felix created an AI just before he escaped."

Felix used his Anopower to "enlighten" the former Lord Pluto, giving him a complete soul. Just saying it was shocking enough. If Felix could create AI, he could certainly destroy it. An S-class hacker-type Anopower user was the number one enemy of all AI.

Cora couldn't help but imagine. If Felix had gone to Felalakas instead, how would Ilia have dealt with him? Would she have easily subdued him and taken his body like she did with Thyrion Lucas?

No, Ilia wanted an "unrestricted body." Felix's legs were broken, making him unsuitable. Besides, he and the Lucas family were arch-enemies, so he wouldn't have worked for them either....

Thinking it over, having S-class Anopower user Felix join F777 would significantly boost their overall strength. As the captain, she felt responsible for protecting this golden asset.

Cora turned to Onyx, her smile ingratiating. "Why don't you give him your wheelchair?"

Onyx's eyes narrowed, his voice cooling. "Cora, are you that biased? Fickle?"

"No, no, it's not like that," Cora stammered, shaking her head.

"Or are you dissatisfied with me?"

"I, I'm not. Don't say that!" Cora hurriedly waved her hands, feeling wronged. She prided herself on being the fairest captain!

"Knock, knock."

Ura's timely entrance saved Cora from her awkward situation.

Thanks to Ura's timely help, they had escaped quickly. She provided this safe house, although Cora had to part with quite a few crystals—after all, a merchant never takes a loss.

Cora turned to greet her, while Yuui asked, "Boss, I want to go out and buy some supplies. Any suggestions?"

Ura immediately stopped her. "No, don't go out!"

Cora was taken aback. "Why? What's happening outside?"

Ura laughed. "You guys are famous now!"

"The entire street is talking about F777—mighty and domineering, taking down Lupin Sherman's ten billion, killing Warden White, rescuing a mysterious Death Hell prisoner, and flipping Death Hell upside down. Now, everyone in the City of Sin knows your fearsome reputation!"

Cora asked nervously, "Will we be hunted?"

Ura shook her head, still laughing. "Quite the opposite. Thanks to you, the criminal records are useless. Sherman and White have fallen, and the new warden has taken over. Death Hell is thriving, and people are praising you like crazy. If you go out, you'll be swarmed by fans."

"But there's one thing I'm really curious about..." Ura said, stroking her chin and eyeing them. "You've caused such a huge mess, turned Death Hell upside down, yet there's been no arrest warrant. Why?"

"Who is this new warden?" Onyx suddenly asked.

"He just showed up recently, named Hugh Young. With White dead and Sherman severely injured, the... senior figure remained reclusive, leaving no one to manage Death Hell. Hugh Young stepped in and quickly took control. The guards inexplicably follow his orders, and he's swiftly restored order. He's already ordered a review of prisoner records—releasing those who should be freed and capturing those who need to be. The City of Sin is in for a major shake-up."

Cora and Onyx exchanged a knowing glance, both thinking of the same person.

The silent guard—indeed a formidable character—even without his previous personality memories, he fulfilled his mission in a new form.

"Thanks for letting me watch a great show for free. As a reward, I'll handle the procurement of supplies," Ura said, standing up, her purple-dyed half-length hair flipping as she smiled with a shrewd glint. "As for the service fee, I'll give you a discount."

Cora clutched her money bag tightly in Ura's smile.

The next morning, Cora went to see Felix Lucas.

To her surprise, he was already awake, sitting in a wheelchair, the sound of various electronic adjustments filling the air.

Curious, Cora peeked over.

Felix had made his mechanical legs—gleaming silver and integrated with the basic wheelchair. When seated, he used the wheelchair for movement, but when he wanted to "stand," the mechanical legs would extend, supporting him as he stood, towering over two and a half meters tall, exuding a formidable aura.

Cora stared up in awe as Felix proudly displayed his new legs. "What do you think? With the current materials, this is the best possible state."

"Amazing!" Cora clapped her hands, genuinely impressed. She hadn't expected Felix to be not only a top hacker, but also incredibly talented in mechanics.

"My GPA in 'Practical Theory and Structural Mechanics Design' was 5.0," Felix said, lifting his chin, seemingly nonchalant but clearly taking a jab at someone. That "someone" was obviously Onyx.

Cora thought of something. Felix had just mentioned "current materials." "Where did you get the materials?"

He had been unconscious yesterday and hadn't left the safe house. Where did he get the parts to change the wheelchair?

"Oh," Felix said, his expression unchanged, his tone casual, "I dismantled Onyx's wheelchair."

Cora choked on her saliva, coughing violently.

Felix continued righteously, "He has two legs, albeit crippled, so why should he use a better wheelchair than me? Does he deserve it?"

Cora felt an impending crisis. If the petty Onyx found out, there would be trouble. She needed to check on him quickly.

"You should rest..."

"Wait," Felix called out, "Can I borrow your terminal?"

He had been isolated in Death Hell for over five years, desperate to catch up on the world. As for F191 not being connected to the network? Ridiculous. As a hacker-type Anopower user, as long as there was data, there was nothing he couldn't access.

Cora rummaged through her backpack, hastily pulling out the terminal and an old screen, and handed them to Felix.

Then she rushed to Onyx's room, pressing her ear to the door. There was no sound; he probably wasn't awake yet. She needed to get a new wheelchair quickly.

Cora fully geared up, wearing a hat and mask, and hurried out. The overall atmosphere in the City of Sin was indeed different, with more law enforcement officers on the streets.

"Jane!"

A thin man ran past Cora, embracing a woman in front of him.

"Jack, how did you get out?" The woman was both surprised and delighted. "I was released. I'm innocent!"

A special police officer in a Death Hell uniform passed the two, entering the Red Willow Hotel next door.

"Judd, you are suspected of intentional murder. You are under arrest."

The trading street was as bustling as ever, but the mood varied—some were happy, others worried.

Cora passed by the restaurant where Suchat was captured. It was business as usual, bustling with activity.

"Have you seen F777?" someone asked excitedly.

"Not only have I seen them, but they also robbed my crystals!" Gaia, a burly man, put a foot on the table, spitting as he bragged, "It was a scorching afternoon, and my brothers and I were hunting evolved zombies in the desert..."

"Who are the members of F777?" a listener asked eagerly. "I only know Suchat, who seems to be the most famous, and there's a woman who wields a curved blade. I don't remember the others."

Cora pulled her hat brim lower and walked by inconspicuously.

CHAPTER 15

A Bad Student

Cora found a medical equipment store at the end of the trading street.

In a maze of alleys, the shop remained tucked away, with dim lighting that prevented artificial light sources from reaching. She stepped into several puddles along the way and felt the icy sea breeze from the nearby underground sea, less than a kilometer away, chilling her to the bone and waking her up fully.

Because of the shop's remote location, business seemed slow, with the storefront looking rather deserted.

Cora walked into the store, where a middle-aged man behind the counter was busy with a calculator, greeting her indifferently, "look around if you need anything."

The store was spacious, and Cora headed straight for the wheelchair section. There were various models, colors, and functions, but after examining them for a long time, she couldn't make sense of it all. She originally planned to buy several, but after feeling her money bag, she realized it was beyond her means.

Thinking of Onyx's picky eyes, Cora painfully chose the most expensive one. The function description was detailed, presented in a small booklet. While paying, the shopkeeper glanced at her. "Buying it as a gift?"

"Yes." Cora nodded.

"New or replacing an old one?"

"Replacing an old one, the previous one broke."

The shopkeeper said plainly, "This wheelchair isn't very cost-effective. Many of its functions are useless. If you're looking for practicality, check out those in the display case, made by Green Pine Bio. They're much cheaper."

Surprised by the shopkeeper's straightforwardness despite his initial indifference, Cora went to the display case and found a familiar silver-white wheelchair similar to Onyx's old one. Satisfied, she carried it to the counter to pay. "I'll take this one."

The shopkeeper's forehead twitched. "That's a sample! Let me get you a new one from the warehouse."

The shopkeeper went through a small door, leaving Cora waiting. Suddenly, the main door swung open, and two figures burst in, laughing and playing.

First was a six or seven-year-old boy with a dirty face covered in sand, followed by a beautiful teenager with a green snake tail. This time, the boy wasn't naked; he wore an old cartoon T-shirt with rolled-up sleeves, and his tail wagged happily, banging against the counter.

Startled by Cora's presence, both froze, trembling. The boy quickly regained his composure and pushed the snake-tailed boy. "Go, you need to go!"

The shopkeeper emerged from the warehouse, seeing the scene, and scolded sternly, "Yanosh, I told you not to bring him here!"

The boy clung to the snake-tailed boy, yelling.

"Papa, don't give Gabriel to the bad people. Don't give him away!"

The snake-tailed boy's amber eyes stared at Cora for a long time, his tail rings rustling, before he suddenly smiled happily.

Cora awkwardly waved. "Um, I think we know each other."

Yanosh's crying stopped abruptly, and his snot bubble burst with a pop.

Cora explained the incident at the Rose Auction House, and the shopkeeper sighed. "Yanosh found Gabriel at the seaside. I told him not to do that. Alien pets are kept by rich people and will be taken back, eventually."

"But Yanosh didn't listen and kept playing with him, so I made a rule that Gabriel couldn't be brought into the store."

"He... I mean Gabriel, probably doesn't have an owner yet," Cora kindly informed the shopkeeper. After all, the auction was disrupted before it could be completed, and the snake-tailed boy likely escaped on his own.

Yanosh asked hopefully, "Papa, can we adopt Gabriel?"

The shopkeeper yelled, "Go wash your face clean!"

Yanosh shrank back, leading Gabriel outside to play by the sea and wash his face.

The shopkeeper finished Cora's transaction and hesitated. "You said the auction house is destroyed, and no one will come after him?"

"Yes," Cora nodded. With the downfall of Lupin Sherman, who owned the Rose Auction House, and Hugh Young taking over, it was unlikely these shady dealings would resurface. "You shouldn't have any trouble adopting him."

The shopkeeper looked thoughtfully at Yanosh and Gabriel playing in the water outside the window.

As soon as Cora stepped out, Yanosh ran up with Gabriel in tow. Gabriel circled around Cora a few times, affectionately brushing his tail against her leg.

"Gabriel likes you. He wants you to pet him," Yanosh translated eagerly.

Unable to refuse, Cora cautiously reached out and touched Gabriel's green tail. The scales were smooth, with a rough, sandy texture mixed with seawater.

Gabriel enjoyed her touch, closing his eyes in pleasure as his belly scales flared out, revealing a faint waistline.

Cora noticed a small line of characters at the junction of his human body and snake tail. They weren't tattooed or carved; it looked like they naturally grew there. She bent down to read the text: RYK1275.

It was a U-Lab experimental subject number.

Gabriel broke free from Cora's hand and circled behind her, staring intently at her waist.

Cora felt uneasy.

"What is he looking at?"

Gabriel made a few "ah-ah" sounds, tilting his head in confusion. Yanosh seriously translated, "Gabriel is asking where your tail went."

Gabriel seemed to find it incomprehensible that she didn't have a tail, surveying her arms, neck, and face. Then he suddenly straightened up, bringing his pretty face close to hers, staring into her eyes with a gradually puzzled look.

"Gabriel, no! You can like me the most, but you can only like her second!" Yanosh said angrily, pulling Gabriel away, jealous of his affection for Cora.

Gabriel laughed, his tail flicking up the sand, covering both Cora and Yanosh in the dirt.

Cora spat out sand, thinking expressionlessly: Gabriel's affection is too much for her to handle.

Returning to the safe house, Cora tiptoed to Onyx's room and quietly placed the new wheelchair at his door.

After a moment's thought, she decided she should tell him in person and try to convince him not to be angry with Felix. Just as she was about to push the door open, she remembered Onyx's strict insistence on "maintaining a proper distance" between genders, and opted for a more polite approach, knocking on the door instead.

"Knock, knock," she tapped lightly.

No response.

"Knock, knock," she tried with a bit more force. Still no response.

"Bang, bang!" This time, she hit the door too hard, and it swung open. Cora peeked her head in, scanning the empty room.

Not good, Felix might be in trouble!

Onyx, hobbling with a crutch, barged into Felix's room unceremoniously.

Felix was busy adjusting his new "legs," and although he noticed the unwelcome guest, he only paused for a second before continuing his work, seemingly unfazed.

Onyx leisurely walked in, leaning against the wall, observing the familiar-looking mechanical legs without a word.

Felix, adding fuel to the fire, boasted, "I replicated them according to the 'Practical Theory and Structural Mechanics Design.' What do you think? Oh, I forgot, your GPA was only 4.2. You probably don't understand."

Onyx immediately retorted, "At least I had a 4.2, unlike someone who failed the elective 'Language, Social Skills, and Arts.'"

Felix rose to his full height of two and a half meters.

"Objection, I failed because I misremembered the exam time."

Onyx ignored his protest. "I've told you before, I don't enjoy talking with my neck craned up."

Felix scoffed and slowly lowered himself back into the wheelchair.

"How did you hurt your leg?"

"Accident."

"I thought you had 'accidentally' died long ago."

"Sorry to disappoint you."

"So, you couldn't make it on your own, and now you've found yourself a protector?" Felix asked curiously.

"What, are you jealous?" Onyx shot back.

"What's your relationship with Cora? Are you using her?" Felix's ice-blue eyes glinted, his attempts at social interaction always laced with aggression.

"No," Onyx replied without hesitation, then paused, his expression turning serious. "She is my protector, but I won't use her."

Felix was silent for a moment before pressing, "Why did you skip my first question?"

Onyx coldly countered, "Why haven't you learned to read people's expressions?"

Felix scoffed again.

Onyx tapped the floor with his crutch, his eyes full of warning. "Don't mess with her. She grew up in District F, doesn't have your crooked thoughts, and might take you seriously."

"District F?" Felix repeated, his expression turning slightly odd.

"What, is there a problem?" Onyx's keen senses picked up on Felix's unusual reaction.

Felix pulled out the old screen Cora had given him before she left. "This screen is ancient, but it's a special commemorative model from twenty years ago, only sold in District B. Your family ordered a large batch, which prevented me from getting the first release, so I remember it well."

"So what? The screen could be second hand."

"The screen could be resold, but what about the data inside?"

Felix opened a book titled "Particle Physics Advanced Microbiology," flipping through a few pages. "These textbooks aren't within District F's access."

Onyx frowned. He had used Cora's screen before but had noticed nothing special. However, he had always accessed it from his understanding level. If it were Cora... could she understand it?

Felix continued, "There's something else interesting. I found a hidden database. It took me 45 seconds to crack it."

Onyx took the screen, and inside the folder Felix had found were innovative research papers and materials on genetics.

"This screen..." he began.

"Bang!" The door burst open, and Cora rushed in, flustered.

"Don't, don't fight!"

To her surprise, instead of the bloody scene she had imagined, the atmosphere in the room was harmonious. Onyx and Felix both turned to look at her.

Cora froze, her words stuck in her throat, wishing she could disappear on the spot.

"Cora, come here," Onyx called.

"What for..." Cora hesitated, but approached slowly.

"Where did you get this screen?" Onyx asked.

"Huh?" Cora blinked, confused. "It was my grandfather's."

Onyx and Felix exchanged a glance, silently agreeing to drop the previous topic. Cora had mentioned she was an orphan, picked up and raised by her only grandfather. Until they figured out the screen's original owner, it was best not to worry her with unnecessary details.

"I remember you saying your grandfather specifically left this screen for you," Onyx emphasized the word "specific."

"Yeah, he wanted me to study every day," Cora nodded.

"He wanted you to study this? Particle physics?" Onyx pointed to the complex textbook.

"Hold on," Felix interrupted with a light cough.

"In my humble opinion, your grandfather likely wanted you to study the contents of this database."

Felix quickly switched to another system, and the cracked screen displayed a set of children's textbooks, along with some oddly named e-books.

"Learn Local Dialects, Travel the Alliance Without Fear."

"100 Tips for Independent Living," "Everyday Legal Knowledge Applications."

And more...

Cora was stunned.

No way she had been studying the wrong books all along? No wonder she worked so hard every day and learned nothing!

CHAPTER 16

Grandpa

"Cora, you're thirteen now, and you need to learn to cook for yourself. Even when Grandpa's not around, you need to eat well to grow tall and strong. There's a cookbook I wrote myself on the screen; follow the videos and remember not to eat your failed dishes!"

"Cora, you're fourteen this year, right? Try not to fight at school, but if you do, don't break anyone's head. We can't afford to pay for that. Find places where you won't get caught... cough, cough, keep going to school and become knowledgeable and cultured. Study the materials I left for you."

"Oh, one more thing I forgot to tell you: don't be stingy with money. Our family isn't as poor as you think. I left three backup funds for you. One is with Old Cheung, another in an anonymous account I opened, the password is xxxx, withdraw it before it expires. The last one is hidden three inches behind the headboard of your bed. Dig into the wall; there's a small box with a piece of rhenium in it. If you really run out of money, sell it. I heard it's precious."

Along with the children's textbooks, there were also voice messages from Cora's grandfather, Old Thornton, left for her since the year he passed away. There were two to three messages a year, nearly twenty covering every aspect of her life, filled with his love and care.

"Cora, Grandpa can't see you anymore, but I hope you've grown up well. This world is more beautiful than you think. Stay happy, safe, and healthy. Do what you want to do, and most importantly, live well."

Cora finished reading the last message, her nose tingling, staring blankly at the screen until it automatically turned off.

She missed her grandfather so much.

A gentle hand rubbed her head, saying nothing but providing a comforting touch. Cora nuzzled into Onyx's palm, smearing his hand with tears.

Onyx paused, then slid his hand down her head, teasing her like a cat, pinching the back of her neck and... returning the tears.

Cora's melancholy disappeared, and she turned to glare at him, her cold eyes now lively and back to normal.

Onyx's lips curled into a faint smile.

Unfortunately, the third person present, Felix, was oblivious to the atmosphere, his mechanical voice breaking the moment. "This screen is designed for researchers, with the primary feature being its dual independent systems and deep firewall. Its practicality is average."

Cora pouted. "I don't really know how to use it."

She wasn't familiar with high-tech products and must have accidentally switched systems without knowing how to switch back. Not only did she couldn't learn anything, but she also missed her grandfather's messages.

Cora sighed silently, feeling stupid for the first time.

Felix, oblivious to her distress, continued in his matter-of-fact tone. "I'd recommend revisiting 'Kali+Linux Penetration Testing Techniques.' With a bit of effort, you can crack the hidden database. Given your current knowledge, starting with web security and DOS commands might be more appropriate..."

Cora looked bewildered, "Huh?"

Felix paused. "Perhaps starting with 'Basic Screen Usage Tutorial' is better, and the 7-14-year-old version would be more suitable for you."

Onyx's icy gaze swept over. "Shut up."

Felix shrugged.

Cora hugged the screen, blinking at Felix, and sincerely said, "Thank you!"

Despite everything, if it weren't for Felix, she might never have heard her grandfather's messages.

Half an hour later, Yuui, Dr Franz, and the others gathered in Felix's room for a meeting.

"Now that we've found Felix, our next step is to go to Deep Woods," Onyx said.

Cora nodded solemnly. This mission to the City of Sin had been fraught with difficulties from the start, and unexpected challenges arose along the way. But thanks to everyone's combined efforts, they ultimately succeeded.

"Before we leave here, I suggest we all reintroduce ourselves and get to know each other better, as we'll be traveling together for a while," Onyx said, leaning casually in his new wheelchair. "Let's start with our captain."

Being called upon, Cora straightened up, a faint blue light forming a blade in her palm.

"Cora, S-class offensive gold-type Anopower. I can materialize spiritual weapons and am very skilled in combat."

Damian clapped enthusiastically from the side. "Big sis is the best!"

Onyx chuckled. "Our captain's strength is undeniable, as everyone here has seen firsthand."

The others nodded in agreement.

"Next is me, Onyx, from the Qilian Research Institute, S-class mental Anopower."

"Felix Lucas, from District B4, Grass Pit, S-class hacker-type Anopower," Felix followed.

One couldn't simply categorize these two abilities as offensive or support. As S-class Anopower users, their strength was formidable.

"Charles Franz, from District C40, Sycamore, A-class support healer Anopower. I used to be a surgeon."

Though not a combatant, Charles's role in the team was indispensable. Without him, Cora wouldn't have received timely treatment for her severe injuries, and Felix wouldn't have escaped Death Hell so easily with all those tubes.

"Yuui Hayashi, from District C83, Felalakas, A-class support sound Anopower. I'm not good at fighting, but I can buff you guys."

"Suchat, from District E117, Rainforest, A-class offensive poison-type Anopower."

Onyx smiled. "These two are temporary members."

Yuui glanced at him, her long eyelashes lowering without a word.

Her reasons for joining F777 were indeed mixed: half because of Cora's pressure and half for her own personal gain.

Everyone had introduced themselves except Damian.

He looked left and right before suddenly bursting into tears, choking out, "My name is Damian...sniff, B-class offensive ice-type Anopower, from District F199...sniff."

Everyone else was S-class or A-class, leaving him as the only B-class. Damian's self-esteem was cut, and at this moment, he understood why Onyx kept pushing him to improve his skills—he didn't want to be useless!

Cora hurried over to comfort him. "Little Diamond, you're very strong. You're a crowd control specialist."

Damian sniffled. "Really?"

"Yes!" Cora nodded firmly. "You still have 90% potential, and there's hope for you to level up."

Damian wiped his tears, glancing sneakily at Felix, who had successfully leveled up, and made a silent vow.

"So, where are we headed next? To District C33?" Felix asked.

Yuui checked her terminal and reminded everyone, "T.T.T. is about to start."

The third round of the T.T.T. tournament, which had been suspended for three months, was scheduled in three days, with the 16 runner-up teams announced.

Suchat said in a deep voice, "If we head back now, we might not make it in time."

They had spent too much time in Death Hell, and District F's transportation system was underdeveloped. Three days weren't enough to return to Felalakas. Were they just going to give up? Yuui bit her lip in frustration.

"Why won't we make it?" Felix suddenly asked.

Yuui explained, "When we came, it took a week. First, we followed a transport convoy to the outskirts, then switched to an off-road vehicle to get into the desert."

Felix asked, "Why didn't you use a more efficient mode of

transport?"

Not that they didn't want to; they simply didn't have the means. Speaking of the most advanced flight terminals in the Alliance...

Cora looked helplessly at Felix. "Did you forget? The starship is broken."

Felix tried to smile, though it came out awkwardly, looking strange. "It's only lost its power source. You can't say it's 'broken.'"

"What do you mean? Do you have a way?" Yuui's eyes lit up.

Felix ignored the question and instead asked, "This tournament you mentioned sounds interesting. Can I take part?"

"Huh? Do you have a wish you want to fulfill, too?" Cora asked. She had already promised Yuui that if they won the championship, she would give the wish to her. But if Felix wanted it too...

"No, I just like being number one," Felix replied matter-of-factly.

Everyone fell silent.

The genius's thought process was indeed incomprehensible to ordinary people.

"Fine, then you can participate in the next match. Captain, any objections?" Onyx asked for Cora's opinion.

Cora was worried. Felix had just recovered and looked frail. Could he do it?

Felix's new "legs" suddenly stood up, his two-and-a-half-meter height towering over everyone. His ice-blue eyes gleamed, his silver hair fluttered, and his mental energy poured out, filling the room with a silver-white code.

Cora said, "No objections."

Felix wasn't just capable; he was more than capable.

Felix sat back in his wheelchair, satisfied. "Then let's go find a starship."

Before leaving, F777 went to bid farewell to old friends.

Ura's business was booming, keeping her busy around the clock. Just as she saw off one customer, she saw the familiar seven approaching.

Only Onyx was in a wheelchair; Felix Lucas was "walking" on his own. At two and a half meters tall, he stood out among the crowd. Thankfully, the City of Sin was filled with many oddities. While mechanical bodies were rare, they weren't entirely unheard of in the black market. Thus, the group mainly garnered curious looks.

As they approached, Ura's gaze lingered on Suchat for two seconds before she couldn't help but laugh. He wore a hat pulled low, a mask, and a thick coat, completely concealing his identity.

Suchat's face was now known all over the City of Sin. Without a disguise, he would be mobbed by fans the moment he stepped outside.

"Boss Ura, we're leaving," Onyx greeted her. "We'd like to do one last piece of business with you before we go."

Ura stroked her cropped hair, taking a deep breath. "Where are you planning to hit next?"

Onyx laughed. "You misunderstand, Boss Ura. We just want information about the starship port. How much for that?"

Ura thought for a moment, then surprised them. "I'll give you the information. No charge."

She pointed toward Death Hell, her expression calm, conveying everything without words.

"I don't know who you really are, but thanks to you, the City of Sin has changed—for the better."

"The Rose Auction House has changed hands. Now, human trafficking is classified as a serious crime. Anyone thinking of reviving it better think twice."

Since Hugh Young took over, he hadn't rushed to assert his authority, nor had he shown himself or given a public speech. He remained in the darkness of Death Hell, slowly correcting "mistakes."

The removal of the criminal records didn't mean freedom for the prisoners outside. New regulations were issued in the underground city. Although it was still chaotic and filled with villains, it was gradually moving toward order.

Ura laughed heartily. "Consider the information about the starship port my gift to you." Even the most profit-driven merchant has a heart.

Suchat drove the off-road vehicle across the desert. According to Ura, the starship port in the City of Sin had been almost abandoned since before Doomsday, with only a few flight terminals left. She wasn't sure if they were still there or had been sold for scrap.

As they approached their destination, an interesting thing happened.

A gang of armed bandits jumped out. "This is a robbery! Hand over all your valuables!"

"Uh…" Cora and her teammates exchanged glances, finding the situation both amusing and absurd.

When they first arrived, a treacherous Mia ambushed them. Now, as they were about to leave, they were being robbed again. Even with recent changes emerging, the City of Sin still lived up to its name.

Suchat, having been in a foul mood throughout the journey, angrily removed his hat and mask, and said coldly, "You have three seconds to leave." The lead bandit stared at him for a full four seconds before responding arrogantly, "Who do you think you are? You think you can just tell me to leave? That's humiliating!"

"Boss, maybe we should back off. These people don't look easy to mess with," one of his men suggested.

"Back off? Don't you know you have to make trouble to survive in the City of Sin? We finally escaped here; we can't give up now!" Ah, they were newcomers. No wonder they didn't recognize the infamous F777.

Damian stepped forward, hands on his hips, and shouted with authority, "I said leave! Didn't you hear?" A massive blizzard blew in, freezing the bandits into ice sculptures. The leader's mouth froze crooked mid-shout.

"Little lion, let us go. We'll leave right away!"

Damian snorted and loosened his hold, letting the bandits flee in a panic.

They quickly put the minor incident behind them and entered the starship port, finding it indeed dilapidated. Several terminals were buried in the sand.

Felix picked a relatively intact one and climbed into the cockpit, with Cora curiously following. He easily brought up the control panel, his ice-blue eyes reflecting the data, rapidly rearranging and reconfiguring the parameters.

"With no Sora wing, we can use other energy sources: wind, water, sunlight… anything you can see can power the starship." Felix Lucas was the true cornerstone of the "Never Falling Bluebird."

The old starship slowly lifted off, its jets stirring up sand.

The others, seeing this, quickly boarded and found seats. Felix closed the hatch. Though he didn't smile, everyone could see his happiness. "We're ready to go."

"Boom—"

The engine roared to life, and the starship took off like a meteor.

Inside the cockpit, Cora and the strong acceleration threw the others back, gripping the handrails tightly.

Yuui, who frequently flew on starships because of her work, shouted, "Wait, aren't you flying off the star track?"

Straying from the star track meant they couldn't use autopilot or navigate the route, increasing the danger significantly.

Soon, Yuui noticed another fatal issue and screamed, "Hey, aren't you speeding?"

The meteor sped up again, flashing a few times in the endless desert before disappearing above District F191.

"Felix, you madman!!!"

Part 2

Blooming Roses

CHAPTER 17

The Return Debut

Long absent for three months, Felalakas was still as neon-lit as ever.

"This is the city ruled by artificial intelligence?" Felix Lucas lowered the starship and leaned out to look. A passing cruise ship floated by, with a floating ad screen featuring a sweet starlet with princess-pink hair smiling gently at him.

Felix stared for two seconds, then turned back, accurately finding someone in the back seat.

Yuui Hayashi awkwardly covered his face. "Yes, it's me. I'm used to dying of embarrassment by now."

"A virtual city with fake personalities," Felix criticized sharply.

"Ugh—" Across from Yuui, Cora and Damian lay on their seats, their faces pale. The intense dizziness from the high-speed ride made them, unaccustomed to starships, dry-heave uncontrollably.

Charles Franz also looked unwell. He had always followed safe driving rules and had never ridden in Felix's "black market" vehicle. Fortunately, being an Aberrant with healing powers, he wrapped himself in his mental energy and overcame the discomfort after a few breaths.

Felix navigated the starship, blending in with the cruise ship fleet, and found an empty spot to land.

Cora stumbled out, dizzy, and sniffed a burnt smell. She looked around and quickly noticed the problem. "The engine's on fire!"

At high speed, the four engines of the starship sizzled and smoked "pfft" twice, and were completely scrapped.

Felix turned off the control panel, slightly regretful. "Unable to break the speed threshold—this is the main reason solar energy was eliminated. Next time we get a starship, I'll consider other energy sources."

Cora repeated in shock, "Next time we get a starship?"

It's true, you don't know the cost of running a household unless you're the head of it. Thanks to Ura not charging them this time, who knows where the next starship will come from? At Felix's rate of destroying one per ride, they'd soon be bankrupt!

The poor captain silently clutched her purse.

The group returned to the hotel they were familiar with and booked the largest suite. Without another word, they collapsed on the sofas and beds, sleeping deeply. After spending so long in the dark and cramped cells of Death Hell, their legs felt stiff. The soft mattress of Felalakas was incredibly comfortable. It was midnight when the seven of them woke up one after another, yawning as they headed to the media room for a meeting.

The screen played the previous competition's footage on a loop, and Onyx projected the new rules.

The top 16 advancement round was a team challenge mode. The top names from the previous A-G group matches would be the champions, while the remaining teams would be challengers. Each round, they could choose a champion to challenge. If they won, they would replace the champion.

The advancement rules were simple: a champion could directly advance if they won three rounds by default or undefeated in single rounds. However, each team member could only take part once per round, meaning if they started as challengers, they only had five chances to challenge. Choosing the right champion was crucial.

If the champion was strong, the challengers might avoid them, sending a weaker member to exhaust them and wait for another opportunity. Conversely, everyone knew "you squeeze the softest persimmon first." If a champion seemed weak, they might face multiple challenges in a single round.

As the top name of Group G, F777 naturally became the champion. They just needed to win three rounds to advance. Before that, Yuui and Suchat also canceled their temporary names and joined the team, increasing their combatant number to seven.

In choosing the champions, Onyx first excluded the two support members, Yuui and Charles, as they had no advantage in this type of competition.

"For the first match, Felix, you haven't appeared before, so the others have no information on you. Because of a certain underestimation, many should challenge you, but they won't be strong. You can win quickly and take the victory."

Felix nodded calmly, and the others had no objections.

"For the second match, Suchat, your solo combat ability is powerful. Win quickly."

"Okay," Suchat responded coolly.

Onyx smiled. "For the last match, our captain will take the lead."

Cora nodded confidently.

"I... I want to join, too," Damian raised his hand, speaking eagerly. He was already the weakest in F777. If he didn't hurry and improve, the gap between him and the others would only widen.

"Then, Damian, second, Suchat third, and I'll be fourth," Cora patted Damian's head. Let the kid get some practice. With her there, losing wasn't a problem.

"Since you've decided, I don't need to show up tomorrow, right?" Yuui summoned his terminal, revealing a rose-gold invitation. "Though it's a fake persona, I have to work to make a living. I've been invited to be a special guest for tomorrow's match."

Cora was puzzled. "Aren't guests usually artificial intelligence?"

Yuui answered, "I'm not entirely sure. After the Felalakas riot, Ilia seemed to relax the regulations. The top ten rising stars even recorded a short video together."

"It's not relaxation," Onyx analyzed calmly, leaning on his cane. "In the three months we've been gone, Ilia hasn't appeared publicly, but his abilities have been constantly growing. He's far beyond human now, indifferent to any commotion we cause."

Everyone fell silent. No one knew how powerful the AI ruler would become.

"Then I'll take a day off tomorrow?" Yuui asked.

"Sure," Captain Cora waved her hand in agreement.

The media room fell silent. Onyx suddenly spoke. "What are you doing?"

Cora turned and was surprised to see Felix's hand reaching for another wheelchair in the room. He answered seriously, "I need materials for a second modification."

A cane stretched out, blocking him. Onyx squinted slightly, his tone sharp. "Felix, some things I can only tolerate once."

Felix nonchalantly withdrew his hand. "Oh, then get me some materials."

"I'll handle the procurement," Charles volunteered. Everyone had a task; he couldn't stay idle.

"Here's the list." Felix's ice-blue eyes flashed as a large amount of data transferred to Charles's terminal. "Oh, and if possible, get another terminal. We're heading to District C33, and I need the equipment to hack into the C District household registry system."

Charles paused. "Okay."

Two days later, the top 16 advancement round of the T.T.T. officially began.

The host, the ever-energetic AK, introduced the competition rules. Then, with a mysterious twist, he said, "Today's guest is special. Please welcome one of the top ten rising stars, Yuui Hayashi, performing his new song 'Drizzle'."

The spotlight lit up. Unlike before, the star on stage wasn't a hologram, but emerged slowly from an elevator platform. Yuui Hayashi was dressed in a luxurious costume, his makeup flawless, with tiny glittering sequins at the corners of his eyes. His ethereal and melodious voice rang out. "I love... love... your smile, like a drizzle falling in my heart..."

In the contestants' area, Cora Thornton swayed left and right, humming along with the enthusiastic fans, "Love... smile... drizzle... falling in my heart..."

She was completely off-key, but she didn't seem to notice.

Onyx turned to glance at her, and Cora was oblivious. He couldn't help but smile slightly.

On the other side, Ellyn the Wild Rose looked at the radiant Yuui on stage and cast a glance towards the F777 team. The mysterious masked contestant was indeed not among them.

She turned back to continue watching the performance.

After the song ended, Yuui stood with AK, blurring the lines between real people and AI. From a distance, they were indistinguishable. AK enthusiastically asked, "Yuui, it's your first time at our venue. Do you have anything to say to the audience?"

Yuui flashed his signature smile. "I'm honored to be invited. I've actually been following the competition."

"Oh? Do you have a favorite team?"

"Of course, but I can't say now. I hope they win."

"Great! Let's all look forward to it."

After the opening, the seven champions took the stage one by one. The audience's murmurs grew louder. "What's with the champion from Group G? Did they get lost?"

"F777, weren't they the dark horse last time? Why have they changed players?"

Among the star players like Zephyrion Stormrider, Master Stark, and Ellyn, Felix Lucas in a wheelchair with crippled legs looked weak, like a lamb lost among wolves.

Onyx's prediction was spot on. Felix indeed became a popular target for challengers. In the first round, fifteen people saw him as an easy point to grab.

"I choose him!"

"Me too!"

The first challenger was an old acquaintance, "The Star of Felalakas," a bassist he had met at Mirror Lake. The smoky-eyed young man immediately started playing his bass, emitting a disruptive noise with his Anopower.

Felix quietly listened for a moment, whiffling his head, concluding that the opponent's musical taste was too poor to bear. His ice-blue eyes flashed, and a Cotal Band wave struck the bassist's face.

The bassist's eyes went blank, and he collapsed twitching. The audience hadn't even seen what happened, and the match was over.

The second challenger was noticeably more cautious. He had an awakened defensive Anopower that could turn his skin to steel, protecting him from external attacks. But seeing Felix without legs and limited mobility, he circled around him mockingly.

Felix followed him a few times, unable to catch him head-on. Growing impatient, he "tsk"-ed, and six giant mechanical arms sprouted from his back, like a spider. They quickly intercepted from mid-air, and the cold appendages precisely pierced the challenger's chest.

The crowd fell silent. Even the surrounding battles paused for a moment, followed by a thunderous cheer.

Zephyrion Stormrider and Master Stark, who had already won by default, watched Group G's fight, their expressions growing serious.

Zephyrion had suffered a loss for Cora before and remained wary of her. Although he was upright and wanted to defeat Cora fair and square, Master Stark, who was scheming and often eliminated rivals, hadn't targeted F777, which puzzled Zephyrion.

Zephyrion quipped, "Master Stark, letting an opponent grow isn't like you."

Master Stark snorted, unusually not retorting.

He wanted to suppress F777 and eliminate his enemies early, but he couldn't catch them!

After the Mirror Lake battle among the top 64, he sent men to gather information on F777. Just as they got a lead, the team disappeared the next day, impossible to find even after searching for all of Felalakas.

When F777 reappeared in the top 32, he ordered an immediate assassination, but before they could act, Lion's rebellion and a zombie horde plunged Felalakas into chaos. By the time he recovered, they had vanished again!

Seeing the opponent grow stronger and potentially threaten his championship, Master Stark couldn't stay still. Today's top 16 match was his last chance. If F777 made it to the finals... who knows what could happen?

F777, this time, no matter what, I won't let you leave Felalakas alive.

Group G

Felix Lucas was unstoppable, defeating all challengers. He even unfolded a data panel on one of his mechanical arms, leisurely working while fighting. His arrogant ease made people grit their teeth in frustration. Those who had underestimated him regretted their misjudgment bitterly.

In the first round, F777 secured an easy victory.

In the second round, it was Damian Blackwood's turn.

It was his first time fighting solo. Nervously, he climbed onto the stage, glancing back to see Cora Thornton swaying to the music, cheering him on. Beside her, Onyx wore a faint smile. Suchat looked expressionless, and Charles Franz appeared half-asleep.

Damian tightened his small face and nodded heavily.

One would think a child would attract many bullies, but the champions in the neighboring groups were even weaker. Everyone had studied the match footage. Compared to others, Damian, who had once single-handedly killed an Anopowered zombie, was still a standout. In the end, only three challengers chose him.

Damian, who had been the weakest in F777, suddenly became a strong opponent in others' eyes. Before he could react, the "swish" of ice spikes had already taken down his three challengers.

F777 won two consecutive rounds!

The third round was Suchat's turn. He leaped onto the stage like a graceful leopard.

Suchat, with his 6'3" height, buzz-cut, and tattoos, looked wild and untamable. But other teams were at the breaking point and had no choice but to challenge him. Five people went up against him.

Suchat, honed by the trials of Death Hell, didn't even use his Anopower to effortlessly defeat his opponents.

Cora, watching from below, was puzzled. "Why? It feels like they've gotten weaker."

Onyx shook his head. "They haven't gotten weaker; we've gotten stronger."

Their seven-member team's strength had far surpassed the other competitors in the Throne Tournament. From an evenly matched qualifier to now being far ahead, they were no longer on the same level.

Suchat knocked down the last challenger. F777 won three consecutive rounds and advanced to the finals! As AK excitedly announced the finalists, Cora and her team walked against the crowd to meet Yuui Hayashi outside.

Onyx quietly asked, "How's the entry permit for Deep Woods?"

Felix replied lightly, "Done."

With a flick of his mechanical hand, seven convincing IDs appeared before them, all showing District C33, Deep Woods, as their place of residence.

"Let's not waste time. Let's go."

"Correction, we need a new starship to leave."

"You've got some nerve. If you hadn't wrecked the last one, we wouldn't need a new one!"

Cora noticed someone lagging and turned back. "What's wrong?"

Charles wiped his face, trembling with emotion. He took a deep breath. "Nothing. Let's go."

They took some time to infiltrate Felalakas' starship port, disappearing through the gate.

Seconds after they entered, the surrounding space distorted, and a group of Aberrants emerged from the shadows.

"Is everyone here?" the lead spatial Aberrant asked coldly.

"Yes."

"Finish them quickly. This is the third time. If we fail again, Master Stark won't spare us. Understand?!"

"Yes!"

Just as they moved, the familiar sound of jet streams echoed from the starship port. It sounded like... a starship taking off. The spatial Aberrant felt a shadow over his heart. "Damn, hurry!"

Before he could finish speaking, a sleek silver starship shot into the sky, skillfully weaving through steamships and cruise ships, disappearing into the neon depths in an instant.

The pursuers could only exclaim, "WTF!"

CHAPTER 18

Jinxed

"Why are all these IDs showing mercenary as the profession?"

During the flight, Yuui, bored, flipped through the fake entry applications Felix had forged and noticed the common point.

"Mercenaries are the best choice."

Felix assumed everyone's intelligence was on par with his and didn't bother to explain further.

The rest exchanged glances.

They didn't get it, but no one wanted to seem ignorant by asking.

Cora turned to the "Alliance Know-It-All," Onyx, giving him a discreet look.

Onyx coughed twice and explained, "Deep Woods has a strict social hierarchy. People are divided into different classes. At the top is the Governor, or 'General,' who holds supreme power. He is the rule-maker, and his word is law."

"Below the General are the warlords and various military officers. They monopolize weapon production channels, enjoy many privileges, and even have private armed forces. As beneficiaries of the current system, they staunchly support the General's rule, acting as his loyal dogs."

"The third tier comprises the wealthy and merchants. These people serve as middlemen for arms trade, amassing wealth. Though they appear glamorous, their assets are illicit, and they must rely on the warlords' protection, often becoming their accomplices."

The starship glided through the sky, and the navigation system showed they were approaching the border of District C33. Surrounding Deep Woods were several D-level cities, encircling it like stars around the moon.

Onyx quickened his pace. "From the fourth tier downward are the mercenaries, workers, and peasants. Mercenaries are many and relatively free. Workers are mostly locals who have lived there for generations. Though they live mundane lives, at least they're secure. The peasants, also known as outcasts, are at the lowest level, only doing menial labor with the constant risk of expulsion."

Everyone understood. No wonder Felix chose mercenary identities. Officers and wealthy people were local big shots; disguising themselves as such would draw unnecessary attention. Workers and peasants had too many restrictions, making it hard for them to swing. Mercenaries were just right.

Felix slowed the starship. "We can't go any further. Unidentified flying devices are shot down within Deep Woods' range."

"There seems to be something up ahead?" Yuui squinted out the window, but the limited view made it hard to see clearly.

Cora donned a hood, opened the starship door, and hung onto the railing with one hand, leaning out to look ahead.

The high-altitude wind was icy and biting. Below them, countless zombies and mutant animals wandered aimlessly between the wasteland and ruined cities. The sounds of gunfire and roars echoed sporadically.

The cities they had visited before, whether Felalakas or Sycamore, had relatively cleared out the zombies. The Sin City, because of its unique location, required elevator access and was far from the calamity.

But Deep Woods laid bare the most brutal aspect of the apocalypse.

Between several D-level cities, a road enclosed by high-voltage iron fences stretched out, leading to the foot of the city wall.

"That's Deep Woods' 'Lifeline.' Only those who pass through it are qualified to enter the city," Onyx said.

Cora squinted, seeing the solid walls of Deep Woods at one end and endless zombies at the other. She smiled. "To enter the city, we must pass the test?"

"We'll fight our way through."

With no one around, there was no need to hide their strength. After lowering the starship to a low altitude, the seven of them jumped off one after another. Cora drew her twin swords. Suchat unsheathed his dagger, Felix's six mechanical arms bristled menacingly, Yuui's singing voice resonated, and Damian followed closely, shooting ice spikes. F777 worked seamlessly, unleashing their full power.

A group of gray-eyed beasts suddenly pounced, resembling dogs but smaller than wolves, snarling and drooling. These were zombie jackals, a ferocious species unique to Deep Woods.

Cora quickened her pace, charging forward and slicing a jackal in half with a spin of her twin blades!

Various Anopower lights flashed, and in less than five minutes, the small-scale battle was over, with F777 easily eliminating the threats.

Even Charles held a long Ethereal Artifact blade. Though he was a support type, he couldn't always rely on others for protection and needed to learn to defend himself, stepping in when necessary.

The Lifeline was about four or five miles long. Along the way, they encountered other teams hunting zombies, taking photos with their terminals to tally kills. When Cora and her team passed by, these people, intimidated by their aura, retreated a few steps, quickly abandoning the zombies and running away.

Judging by their mental energy, these people were clearly Aberrants too.

Cora asked curiously, "What are they doing?"

Onyx replied, "They're probably scavengers."

"What are scavengers?"

"A specialty of Deep Woods, mostly made up of mercenaries and peasants. They clear monsters outside the city to prevent hordes of zombies from gathering."

In the abandoned buildings they passed, there were signs of human activity—half-built camps, unfinished drinking water...

"Why are they living here?" Cora frowned. Surrounded by zombies, camping out wasn't a good choice.

Onyx's eyes darkened. "Without entry permits, they can only

linger on the outskirts."

Felix pulled up the new laws issued by the General after the apocalypse. "Deep Woods revoked permanent residency for peasants, switching to a quota system, offering 300 temporary slots daily for scavengers. Only after completing their clearing tasks are they allowed into the city."

"Isn't this forcing people to their deaths?" Yuui frowned.

Zombie hunting was extremely dangerous. One wrong move, and they wouldn't make it back. Though peasants were low, this level of oppression was too much. Charles, who had been silently walking, spoke coldly. "In the eyes of a tyrant, peasants are just pigs and dogs. Who cares about pigs and dogs? Bark a few times, and they'll stop."

The group sighed. This was a cruel city.

After half an hour of walking, the number of zombies dwindled, and the towering city walls gradually appeared in the distance. Along the battlements, tanks and heavy artillery were stationed at intervals, with patrol drones circling the skies. This was clearly the Alliance's armory, and these heavy weapons were a blatant deterrent to any outsiders.

At the city gates, there were long lines of scavengers waiting to turn in their tasks, stretching out of sight.

As Cora Thornton and her team walked along the lines, they overheard hushed conversations. "Did you meet the quota?"

"Barely, but I got back late. I'm afraid I won't get in."

"Who's on duty at the gate today?"

"Cơ Đan Vi."

"... That lapdog? Forget it. I'll try my luck tomorrow."

Cora's ears perked up at the unfamiliar name, Cơ Đan Vi.

As they approached the gate, the team chose the line marked "Green Channel (Mercenaries Only)," which had significantly fewer people.

The guard on duty, performing his routine checks, said, "Show your entry permits."

Cora raised her terminal and pressed it against the connector, displaying the forged identity information Felix had created.

The guard glanced at it and operated the machine, allowing them through. "Proceed to the verification booth."

"Wait, a moment." A deep voice suddenly interrupted, followed by the sound of heavy military boots.

The guard stood up, looking fearful. "Sir Cơ Đan Vi, what are your instructions?"

Cơ Đan Vi, dressed in a mercenary's uniform, with brown skin and a strong, burly frame, narrowed his eyes. "Your mercenaries? Whose mercenaries are you? I've never seen you before."

Cora's heart skipped a beat, nervous. Damn, this Cơ Đan Vi is also a mercenary and well-acquainted with Deep Woods' mercenaries?

Facing Cơ Đan Vi's questioning, Onyx remained calm and composed. "We're freelance mercenaries. We left Deep Woods for a mission before the apocalypse and have just returned. It's not surprising you haven't seen us. But ignorance is no excuse to block our way."

Cơ Đan Vi stared at him for a couple of seconds, then snorted, studying their ID information word by word. The household registration was indeed District C33, Deep Woods, with no flaws to be found, but his instincts told him this group didn't look like local mercenaries.

"You, go for verification." Cơ Đan Vi pointed at Cora.

Silently, Cora walked forward, with Cơ Đan Vi following closely behind.

Cora reached the booth and entered a scanner-like machine. Countless beams of light swept over her from head to toe, capturing her facial and body data. The screen displayed "Verifying..."

Seconds ticked by, but no result appeared.

Cơ Đan Vi's expression turned stony. He pulled out a particle gun from his waist and aimed it at Cora's head, ready to pull the trigger.

"What are you doing!" Yuui shouted, his heart pounding.

Franz and Suchat clenched their fists, and Damian's expression tightened, his lips trembling. Onyx moved subtly, shielding Damian with his body, remaining composed.

Cora was also anxious, glancing surreptitiously towards Felix, mentally urging Felix. You better have this right! Felix sat in his wheelchair, looking unconcerned, even yawning lazily as if saying, "You doubt me?"

Onyx gave her a barely perceptible nod. Somehow, it made Cora feel a bit relieved.

Five seconds later, the scanner screen flashed. "Verification passed. Welcome home, mercenary."

Cora straightened her back, trying to maintain a calm expression while internally sighing with relief.

Cơ Đan Vi moved the gun aside, signaling Cora to leave, but still did not lower his guard. "Next." The remaining six entered the scanner one by one and all passed without issue.

Only then did Cơ Đan Vi holster his particle gun, saying sarcastically, "Welcome home, freelance mercenaries."

Under Cơ Đan Vi's hawk-like gaze, they entered Deep Woods, only relaxing once the piercing scrutiny was behind them. Cora muttered, "Who is that guy?"

Felix swiped his fingers across his terminal. "Just found out. Cơ Đan Vi is a private soldier of the warlord, Mục Tân. Also, Mục Tân has an extremely notorious reputation in Deep Woods."

Deep Woods' mercenaries were categorized into two types: freelance mercenaries and those loyal to the aristocracy. Freelance mercenaries, nicknamed "free birds," had no constraints and could choose their missions, relying on their skills to find work.

In contrast, mercenaries employed by warlords were called "house dogs." Despite their comfortable living conditions, their association with warlords earned them the disdain for others.

"Felix, you're amazing." Cora sincerely praised him.

While standing in the scanner, she had a moment where she imagined "verification failed" and felt her heart in her throat. Felix accepted her compliment with ease.

Damian followed behind, sneaking a glance at Felix and moving closer to him, his big eyes blinking as if he had decided about something.

As they turned a corner, the entire city of Deep Woods came into view.

Compared to other districts, Deep Woods' technology was not impressive. The architectural style was common, similar to the D-level cities of Blossomville and Glass Port they had visited. However, the scent of gunpowder was especially strong here. Mercenaries walked the streets, weapons at their waists, and restrictions were frequent. Weapons factories were everywhere, each belonging to different families, with armed guards glaring at passersby.

In the distance, atop a mountain, stood a grand golden palace, its spires reaching into the sky, symbolizing power.

Huge holographic projections hung on either side, displaying a middle-aged man with sharp silver hair, wearing the highest commander's uniform of Deep Woods, his chest adorned with ribbons and medals. His stern face, with prominent eyebrows and a hooked nose, exuded an oppressive aura.

"Ne Kon," Charles muttered, trembling, his voice filled with hatred.

Tyrant Ne Kon, the supreme ruler of Deep Woods, the General at the pinnacle of the power pyramid, and the man Charles wanted to kill but couldn't.

"We will succeed," Cora said softly, placing a reassuring hand on his shoulder. Charles' reaction was too intense; they were on a street, and it could easily arouse suspicion.

Onyx suggested, "Let's find a place to stay first."

Compared to other districts in the C Zone, Deep Woods' technological level wasn't particularly impressive. The architectural style was common, similar to the D-level cities of Blossomville and Glass Port they had visited. However, the air here was thick with the scent of gunpowder. Mercenaries walked the streets with weapons at their waists, and restrictions were everywhere. Weapons factories were ubiquitous, each belonging to different families, with armed guards glaring at passersby.

In the distance, atop a mountain, stood a grand golden palace, its spires reaching into the sky, symbolizing power.

Huge holographic projections hung on either side, displaying a middle-aged man with sharp silver hair, wearing the highest commander's uniform of Deep Woods, his chest adorned with ribbons and medals. His stern face, with prominent eyebrows and a hooked nose, exuded an oppressive aura.

"Ne Kon," Charles Franz muttered, trembling, his voice filled with hatred.

Tyrant Ne Kon, the supreme ruler of Deep Woods, the General at the pinnacle of the power pyramid, and the man Charles wanted to kill but couldn't.

"We will succeed," Cora Thornton said softly, placing a reassuring hand on his shoulder. Charles' reaction was too intense; they were on a street, and it could easily arouse suspicion.

Onyx suggested, "Let's find a place to stay first."

Since they were planning to stay in Deep Woods for a while, they rented an apartment.

"We'll need some time to explore Deep Woods. For the next few days, we'll split up and gather information," Onyx said seriously.

"Don't worry, we have plenty of time," Cora said, cracking her knuckles in a relaxed tone.

They had successfully infiltrated their household registration as Deep Woods, and they had no entry restrictions. As long as they were careful, they wouldn't be discovered.

"Beep beep—"

Their terminals all simultaneously chimed with a notification. It was a district-wide broadcast, received by all residents in Deep Woods.

"Effective immediately, entry restriction validity periods have been changed. Please strictly adhere to the following regulations: Peasant entry is reduced to three days, worker and freelance mercenary permanent residency is revoked, changed to work seven days, freelance mercenary fifteen days. This period can be extended by completing tasks from the City Hall."

Onyx's voice suddenly turned grave. "The General has issued new laws."

This was the "tyrant" of Deep Woods, capable of altering local laws at any time.

Their IDs now had an additional line: "Your entry application is valid for: 14 days 23 hours 59 minutes 42 seconds." The countdown continued.

Everyone in the room, including Onyx, instantly turned pale.

They were freelance mercenaries, thinking they could relax once inside Deep Woods. But now, before they even settled, they had to go out and work as scavengers. Cora, who had just said they had plenty of time, silently covered her mouth.

Great, she jinxed it.

CHAPTER 19

Countdown

Countdown: 15 days.

When the date they could stay was solidified, F777 felt an inexplicable sense of urgency. If they made no progress within these 15 days, they would either have to become scavengers or face expulsion from the Deep Woods. The new law amendment meant that the admission application would cover constant mobile reviews. Their household registration was forged, and Felix tampering with it again would only increase the risk of exposure.

More intriguingly, the amendment specifically mentioned "freelancers" but made no mandatory provisions for "domesticated dogs," showing that the General had left some leeway for his supporting warlords.

"Time is limited. Let's split into groups and take action tomorrow," Onyx said solemnly.

The groups were Cora Thornton and Onyx, Yuui Hayashi and Suchat, and the remaining three—Felix Lucas, Charles Franz, and Damian Blackwood.

After a brief rest, at dawn the next day, F777 set out in different directions to gather intelligence.

Cora and Onyx arrived at the Golden Palace, the General's residence, also known as the Unity Palace.

Armed soldiers heavily guarded the main entrance of the Unity Palace, marking a restricted area where no one could approach.

Although there were no signs of heavy weaponry, the air was thick with a sense of foreboding.

Cora cautiously explored the perimeter. Boldly, she was about to climb over the wall when Onyx grabbed her hood. "Don't. There are infrared sensors."

Cora retracted her foot silently and released a wisp of mental power, confirming many hidden mechanisms inside the wall.

The infrared sensors swiveled, and the smell of gunpowder thickened. Cora's hair stood on end as she swiftly retreated. She had a hunch that if she dared cross the boundary or made any unusual moves, countless gun barrels would aim at her, ready to blast her to pieces.

Onyx surveyed the surroundings and quickly decided, "Let's go to the opposite hillside."

They changed their route and climbed to the hilltop. Although far away, the vantage point provided a panoramic view of the Unity Palace.

"Help me up, please," Onyx extended his left hand, openly seeking support.

"Aren't you using a cane?" Cora mumbled softly but instinctively supported his arm.

The mountain path was uneven, and as Onyx stood up, he accidentally stepped on a loose stone, causing him to lean toward her. Cora instinctively looked up, and their breaths intertwined unexpectedly. Onyx's deep eyes curved slightly. His magnetic voice seemed to drill into Cora's ear, "I need to draw; leaning on you is more convenient."

Cora blinked slowly and spun her head, feeling her ears heat.

"... Oh," she stammered, not knowing what to say.

Onyx manipulated a light screen, drawing as he spoke. Cora watched in amazement as he sketched a three-dimensional structure of the Golden Palace, even creating a model and dividing it into sections. She stole glances at his focused profile, then another, and another, gradually getting lost in thought. How could someone be so intelligent? Not only did he know so much, but he was also skilled at everything, even drawing.

"The General's residence is larger than we thought. Sneaking in rashly is too risky and might alert them," Onyx continued as he noticed Cora's odd expression. "What's wrong?"

Cora looked up and said seriously, "Felix Lucas is an S-level; he's shown his strength, and I know it. You are also an S-level, but I don't know how strong you are."

Except for that time on Manzoni Street, when he saved her from Bloody Hunter Punk, Onyx rarely made a move. Most of the time, he was strategizing. As an S-level mental-type Aberrant, his true strength remained a mystery.

"You should think of it this way: because there's a reliable captain, it hasn't been my turn to shine," Onyx said with a smile. Cora turned her head, puffing her cheeks slightly, "Hmph, sweet-talker."

On the other side, Felix and his group arrived at the commission center in the Deep Woods. This place was teeming with mercenaries and Aberrants, a crowded hub perfect for outsiders to gather information.

Felix found a self-service terminal and fiddled with it for a while before suddenly exclaiming, "Hmm?"

"What did you find?" Charles asked quietly.

Felix pulled up a newly released announcement. "The Mu Family issued a recruitment order for their Royal Guard two days ago."

Charles read the recruitment order carefully. "There will be a Hero Banquet held at the family residence in seven days to recruit the Royal Guard. All ambitious individuals in the district are invited, regardless of identity, but a Level 3 crystal must be submitted."

The Mu, Mieu, and Nguyen families were the three major warlords of the Deep Woods. They not only controlled the core weapons development technology but were also said to have close ties with the General. Joining their Royal Guard could grant one officer status and elevate one's social rank.

Level 3 crystals, or blue crystals, were extremely rare. They were only produced by evolved Level 3 zombies or B-level and above Aberrant zombies, making the threshold exceedingly high.

Felix returned to the main hall and found a secluded corner. His eyes locked onto the central floating screen, scanning countless data streams that flowed through his pupils. He quickly filtered through them, occasionally stopping at seemingly unrelated fragments.

"Cover me while I look for something," he said. Charles and Damian immediately moved to shield him.

After a while, Felix's hands stopped moving. "Ah, so that's it."

Before sunset, the entire F777 team safely returned to their apartment.

"We went to the munitions factory, but private soldiers heavily guarded it. Suchat couldn't sneak in. Here are the images we captured," Yuui Hayashi said, projecting the footage. The video showed Suchat blending into the surroundings, barely approaching the perimeter before the camera shook, and the sound of patrolling footsteps echoed. A tank-like behemoth could be vaguely seen being loaded onto a vehicle and transported away.

"We went to the Unity Palace," Cora Thornton added, displaying Onyx's architectural drawings and noting that both infiltration and forced entry were impossible.

Everyone looked dejected. A day had passed with no leads, and only 14 days remained.

"We made a discovery," Felix suddenly announced, catching everyone's attention.

"We found that the Mu Family is about to hold a Hero Banquet to recruit the Royal Guard."

"And how does that concern us?" Cora asked.

"Of course, it concerns us," Felix's icy blue eyes gleamed as he projected all the information about the Hero Banquet. "The timing of the Mu Family's Hero Banquet is unusually early, a full three months early. I have firm evidence to suspect that, because of the urgent situation, they are actually helping the General recruit talent."

Felix's revelation was shocking. "The General might have been ambushed, and either frightened or injured."

He pulled up news fragments extracted from the data: A month ago, several media outlets reported refugees attacked the General during a "hunt." Fortunately, the defense was timely, and he was unharmed. The Guard killed the troublemaking refugees on the spot.

"Whether the General was harmed, his Guard must have suffered significant losses and urgently needs fresh blood."

"I searched through surveillance footage of the General over the past twenty-six years. There were about 132 original faces among his guards. If we can determine how many are left now..."

"95," Onyx interjected. "There are 95 guards left in the Unity Palace."

"Are you sure?" Felix questioned.

"More certain than your 'about'," Onyx retorted calmly.

Felix was silent for two seconds before clicking his tongue.

"But what refugees could cause the General's Guard to lose nearly 40 men?" Yuui wondered. "Could it be something else?"

Aberrants selected for the Guard were at least B-level and highly skilled. How could they be overwhelmed by a disorganized group of refugees?

"Regardless of the truth, this is an opportunity for us. If we can attend the recruitment, we might infiltrate the Guard," Onyx stated. He didn't say the rest, but everyone understood: being close to the General would provide opportunities to act.

Cora rummaged through her backpack, looking dejected. "But we don't have a Level 3 crystal."

The highest quality crystal she had was a dark green Level 2 crystal from the Mirror Lake monster. She had never even seen a Level 3 crystal.

Suchat suggested, "We could go to the Lifeline. I saw Level 2 zombies when we entered the city." When we entered the city, I saw Level 2 zombies. With careful searching, they might find a Level 3 zombie.

"Sigh..." Yuui sighed. Thinking about zombies gave her a headache. "Looks like we can't avoid being scavengers for a while."

"Then it's settled. We'll head out tomorrow," Onyx declared.

Cora cautiously sought the others' opinions. "Since we're going out, can I take on a commission?"

As the team leader, she needed to be thrifty and support the entire group.

The other six members. "... Do as you please."

Da Nang, a D-class city near the Deep Woods.

Yuui searched for signs of zombies among the rubble and ruins. Because F777's most "dedicated" captain, Cora, had taken on more than a dozen commissions, they were worried about running out of time. So, they split up to complete the tasks, though they weren't too far from each other—close enough to call out if anything happened.

Yuui emerged from a collapsed office building, dusting herself off. Just as she looked up, a group of fierce-looking mercenaries approached. Seeing she was alone, they stopped with ill intentions.

In the apocalypse, amidst the ruins, a young, fragile, and beautiful woman was an easy target for many twisted thoughts. Mercenary Mulberry was such a base animal; he stared at Yuui, licking his lips with excitement.

His companion, Hu Chao, guessed what he was thinking and warned, "Mulberry, a prize like this should be offered to Lord Mieu."

Mulberry dismissed this. "Lord Mieu has seen countless beauties. He won't miss one. I'll enjoy her first."

He stepped out from the rubble, whistling lewdly at Yuui. She frowned and coldly said, "Get lost."

Mulberry advanced instead, his lecherous eyes roaming over Yuui's face and chest. Anger flared in Yuui, and she slapped him hard across the face.

For a moment, everyone froze.

Mulberry was stunned, spitting out a mouthful of blood. "Feisty, I like that."

His body suddenly turned into black sludge, moving behind Yuui and reforming, his thick wrist grabbing her arm as his foul breath neared her face.

Yuui, furious, tried to retaliate but realized she couldn't sing! Oh no! The Silent Field—an innate counter to her powers. She couldn't even call for help.

Yuui looked up in shock to see a thin man with one eye covered, his bloodshot right eye staring deeply at her. Under his gaze, Yuui's world fell silent—she couldn't hear or make any sound.

Yuui could already smell the foul breath from Mulberry's yellow teeth, feeling nauseated. Her sleeve moved slightly, and a dark blue arrow slipped into her hand, slashing her skin.

The world remained silent, but — A gust of wind rushed past Yuui, and a lithe figure darted toward the thin man. Yuui sighed in relief.

Cora Thornton's dagger flashed blue as it pierced the man's evil eye. "Ah—" His gut-wrenching scream broke the Silent Field instantly!

At almost the same moment, Mulberry, who had been restraining Yuui, was kicked hard in the chest, spewing blood as Yuui escaped. In front of Mulberry stood an enraged Suchat, his wild mental power surging like thunder.

Realizing the imminent danger, Mulberry's body quickly dissolved into black sludge, trying to escape.

A haunting song echoed in his mind, filling Mulberry with boundless fear, paralyzing him. It was Yuui's A-level power, a debuff control!

Suchat's venom enveloped the writhing black sludge, the corrosive pain forcing Mulberry back into human form. Just then, a green-tinted dagger plunged straight into his heart. Shocked, Mulberry turned to see Yuui, using Suchat's dagger, had stabbed him to death herself.

In just a few seconds, the tables turned, and the two mercenaries attacking Yuui were dead! Cora landed beside Yuui. "Are you okay?"

Suchat's towering figure looked down at her, a trace of regret in his eyes. Yuui patted his shoulder, "I'm fine."

Not far away, Onyx and the others, hearing the commotion, quickly arrived.

Having witnessed Mulberry's death, Hu Chao's face darkened. "Who are you? Do you not want to live after killing Mieu's mercenaries?"

Cora stared back fearlessly, "We are freelance mercenaries."

"Freelance mercenaries? South District or West Street, who's your leader? Which faction?"

Freelance mercenaries have factions? Cora couldn't answer.

Hu Chao grew suspicious, "Who do you really work for?!" The mercenaries behind him took combat stances, surrounding the group.

F777 prepared for battle, the tension palpable.

"Boom—"

A micro-missile struck the ground between the two groups, sending debris flying and dust rising.

"They are with me."

A familiar voice rang out.

CHAPTER 20

The Wild Rose

A figure jumped down from a sniper position on the rooftop.

Black combat boots, camo pants, a hot vest, and a mobile cannon slung over their right shoulder, with their left arm missing from above the elbow. The figure was tall and muscular, with a buzz cut and a resolute, commanding gaze that exuded a rare leadership quality.

Ellyn.

Cora silently repeated her name. The leader of "Guns N' Roses" and their rival in the Throne Tournament—why was she here?

"The infamous sly fox of West Street heard you moved to another district. Why are you back?"

"Probably because nobody wants her. What kind of woman is so rough?"

"Look at her hand. She's lost it. Now she's a stray dog, haha!"

The mercenaries recognized Ellyn and started laughing and taunting her. However, faced with the ominous cannon and her expressionless face, their laughter gradually weakened and ceased.

Hu Chao spoke slowly, "Sly fox, haven't heard from you in six months. How have you been? Do you have time to sit and catch up?.."

Ellyn interrupted coldly, "No need for your concern. Have your men withdraw."

The fake smile disappeared from Hu Chao's face as he raised his voice sharp, "Withdraw? These people killed Mulberry, Lord Mieu's private soldier. Are you standing up for them, ready to oppose the entire Mieu family?"

Ellyn remained unfazed by Hu Chao's threat, "I'll say it again. They are my people. Mulberry's death was his own doing. Hu Chao, you can report today's incident to your master and see what his reaction will be."

Hu Chao was at a loss for words. Mulberry had been killed because he coveted Yuui Hayashi's beauty and wanted her for himself. If this reached Lord Mieu, it would be seen as disrespect and betrayal, and even if Mulberry were alive, he would not fare well.

Seeing Hu Chao's silence, Ellyn added, "What's wrong? Need me to report it to you?"

Hu Chao's heart trembled. Ellyn was threatening him. Everyone knew that Lord Mieu's new favorite was from West Street. If Ellyn hinted to her, even Hu Chao, who had just stood by, might be implicated.

Hu Chao, though not as bold as Mulberry or as capable as Cơ Đan Vi, prided himself on being the most adaptable and able to survive better than others.

After much consideration, he spoke in a low voice, "Nothing happened today. Mulberry and Para were killed by zombies, regrettably."

Para was the one with the Silent Field power.

"No! Mulberry can't die in vain!" An agitated mercenary shouted, drawing a particle gun from his waist.

"Boom—boom—"

Without hesitation, Ellyn fired three micro-missiles, creating a deep crater at the feet of the shouting man.

Shards from the explosion tore through the mercenaries' clothes, and flying debris cut their faces, silencing them. The particle gun was laughably inadequate under such overwhelming firepower.

Ellyn was practically a madwoman, more unhinged after losing a hand!

"Have we understood?" Ellyn ignored the mercenaries and stared at Hu Chao.

"... Yes," Hu Chao's expression turned stony. This was not an agreement, but coercion by force. Ellyn, a B-level Aberrant with an innate talent for guns and cannons, intended to protect them today. And angering her would be unwise.

"Withdraw," Hu Chao commanded through gritted teeth.

"Hu Chao, they..."

"If you don't want to die, keep your mouth shut!"

Hu Chao led his men away, leaving Mulberry and Para's bodies behind. Only F777 and Ellyn remained at the scene.

Ellyn retracted her cannon and glanced at F777, her gaze lingering on Onyx and the others before settling on Cora.

"If you're hiding from Old Master Stark's hunt, this isn't a good place. Find somewhere else," she said.

"What hunt?" Cora asked, puzzled.

"You don't know?" Ellyn was taken aback.

Cora shook her head, genuinely unaware.

Ellyn's brow furrowed deeper.

"If it's not because of the hunt, then why are you and the celebrity here?" Ellyn ignored the men and pointed at Yuui Hayashi, who was trying to hide behind sunglasses. "Why are you in the Deep Woods?"

Yuui awkwardly smiled. "When did you recognize me?"

"I had my suspicions before. During the top 16 matches, I didn't see you among them, so I confirmed it." Ellyn paused. "I don't understand why you came here when you could have everything in Felalakas."

"We're looking for a Level 3 crystal," Cora explained seriously.

Ellyn turned to her, "Level 3 crystals are rare, but you didn't have to come to the Deep Woods to find one."

"Oh, we want to attend Mu Family's Hero Banquet."

Ellyn's grip on her cannon tightened, her expression turning cold, "What, you want to become warlord lapdogs?"

"No, no, no! We... we're..." Cora stammered, wanting to explain, but with Ellyn's uncertain stance, she couldn't outright say, "We're here to assassinate the General." Panicked, she struggled to articulate.

"Seems complicated. Aren't you going to step in?" Felix asked, as diplomacy had always been Onyx's responsibility.

"It's not appropriate for me to intervene. Let the ladies handle it," Onyx replied, smiling, with his chin propped on his hand. Ellyn clearly didn't like them, only speaking to Cora and Yuui. His intervention wouldn't help.

"I'll explain," Yuui patted Cora's back. "Ellyn, we're here for something specific. We can't tell you exactly what it is right now, but to accomplish it, attending the Hero Banquet is our best chance. But we oppose the warlords and would never become their 'domesticated dogs.'"

"Thank you for helping us just now," Yuui added sincerely.

Ellyn scrutinized Yuui's expression, assessing her sincerity. Cora vigorously nodded beside her to add credibility. After a moment, Ellyn nodded slightly. "Do as you wish."

She lifted her cannon, pausing before she left, and whispered with her back to Yuui, "A word of advice: the Deep Woods is not for you. Finish your business and leave as soon as you can."

Yuui was momentarily stunned. Ellyn's words were clearly directed at her. A few zombies emerged from the ruins, and Ellyn calmly retreated, set up her cannon, and blasted them away before pulling out a terminal to take photos and count.

"Huh? Is she doing a scavenger mission?" Cora exclaimed in surprise.

Felix Lucas's icy blue eyes flickered, "Ellyn, 27 years old, bio ID: MUD3220875, registered in the Deep Woods, occupation: freelance mercenary. According to current laws, her entry permit has expired. To re-enter the city, she must complete a scavenger mission. Her current progress is at 15%."

"How do you know so much?" Cora asked, eyes wide.

Felix replied, "When she took the photos, I hacked into her terminal."

Cora: Can't you give people some privacy!

Felix misinterpreted Cora's exasperated look, thinking she also wanted to learn this skill. "It's actually quite simple. Use your Anopower to first release mental energy..."

"No, I don't want to know," Cora said, waving her hand, feeling exhausted.

"I have an idea," Yuui suddenly spoke. "The hierarchy in the Deep Woods is complex, even among mercenaries. Our only option now is to attend the Hero Banquet. If we have local help, maybe there's another way."

"You want to ask Ellyn for help?" Onyx asked.

"Ellyn's personality makes asking for help difficult... How about negotiating a deal? I'll find out what she needs." Yuui remembered the unique merchant Ura from Sin City and brightened up. "Do you think it's workable?"

"It's worth a try," Onyx said. "From her attitude earlier, even if she's not on our side, she won't be our enemy either."

"We could help her complete her scavenger mission faster," Cora reminded them.

F777's goal was Level 3 zombies, which didn't conflict with Ellyn's mission. They could help her along the way. Charles and Damian had no objections and nodded in agreement.

"Alright, I'll go talk to her."

Yuui jogged over and caught up with Ellyn. After a few minutes of conversation, Ellyn and Yuui turned back together.

"What kind of deal do you want to make?"

"We'll help you complete your mission first."

"Fine, but I must enter the city by tomorrow at the latest."

"No problem," Cora nodded.

Ellyn temporarily joined the team, and they moved toward the center of Da Nang, clearing zombies along the way.

Cora and Suchat, along with Felix in his six-claw mode, attracted zombies, drawing them together within a few kilometers. Yuui sang to slow the zombie horde. Damian froze them, and Ellyn, positioned on a rooftop, adjusted her angle and fired a micro-missile.

"Boom—boom—"

Destructive smoke rose, and most of the zombies were blown to pieces. The trio swiftly finished the few remaining, attracting them, leaving the ground glittering with crystals.

Onyx and Charles cleaned up the battlefield. Charles moved precisely among the zombie remains, extracting whole crystals without spilling brain fluids. He wiped them clean with a cloth and put them in a bag. Most were white Level 1 crystals, with the occasional Level 2 crystal.

Ellyn jumped down from the rooftop, her combat boots hitting the ground. She took out her terminal to photograph and count the kills. With F777's help, her progress had significantly sped up, reaching

85% in half a day. Unfortunately, there was still no sign of Level 3 zombies.

As it got darker, visibility became challenging. Onyx suggested, "Let's find a place to stay for the night and continue tomorrow."

Ellyn checked her position. "Follow me."

She led Cora and the others through the ruins of Da Nang to a high-rise building. It seemed to be a camp with tight security measures, occasionally surrounded by circles of fire from Anopower. Ellyn knocked on a copper bell at the camp's entrance with the base of her cannon.

"Who goes there?!" A booming voice questioned from a distance, and lights turned on, illuminating the area. Cora sensed an unfamiliar mental power; the speaker was an Aberrant.

The next moment, mechanical whirring sounds came from above the camp, and unseen dangers aimed at them. "West Street, Ellyn." Ellyn raised her hand, signaling Cora to stay calm.

"So, it's the sly fox. Long time no see," a deep voice responded.

"Samuel, there are eight of us. We need a place to stay for the night."

The door slowly opened a crack, and the person inside didn't show himself. His loud voice echoed, "Left to the first floor, help yourselves. Sly fox, I'm letting you in out of respect. Tell your people to stay in line, or they'll face the consequences."

"Thanks."

They entered the camp. The first floor had several makeshift dormitories. Ellyn pointed to two rooms. "The conditions are basic, but make do for the night. This is a West Street mercenary base, relatively safe."

They divided into separate rooms for men and women. Cora and Onyx parted ways at the door, and Cora followed Ellyn to the left room.

Yuui picked a relatively clean bed and sat down, "I heard a person call you 'sly fox'."

"A nickname," Ellyn replied nonchalantly.

Yuui got straight to the point. "Ellyn, we want to know more about freelance mercenaries."

Ellyn put down her cannon within reach. "Freelance mercenaries in the Deep Woods mainly gather in the South District and West Street, divided into two factions. The South District is larger and has more people, but in recent years, some have secretly pledged loyalty to warlords, like Hu Chao. The members are mixed and hard to identify. The mercenaries of West Street live on the edge, all reckless madmen with no rules. Even the warlords' lackeys don't dare to provoke them lightly."

The three of them lay on their beds in silence. Cora turned over, quietly glancing at Ellyn's profile, "Ellyn, why did you take part in the Throne Tournament?"

Ellyn didn't move. "I'm not sure how you got in, but you know the entry restrictions to the Deep Woods are very strict." Cora and Yuui nodded in the darkness.

"The application for a change of residence is even stricter."

"You want to leave the Deep Woods?" Cora sat up in shock.

Ellyn was silent for a moment. "Something like that."

"But you didn't need to join the competition..." Yuui said softly. "You're a B-level Aberrant. If you apply, I'm not sure about other C-districts, but Felalakas would definitely accept you."

Ellyn lay with one hand under her head, her resolute eyes staring at the dark ceiling, her solitary severed arm resting on the bed's edge.

"You don't understand the Deep Woods."

"I can leave, but some people, even if they give their lives, are trapped here. I have to take them away."

CHAPTER 21

Good Luck

The next morning, F777 and Ellyn prepared to leave the temporary camp.

During the day, many people were out and about. Surprisingly, this camp housed not only Aberrants but even more ordinary people: the elderly, children, and women... Everyone had something to do with the smell of food and smoke rising into the air, creating a strong sense of life.

A burly mercenary leader sat on the open ground at the entrance, shirtless, with a massive tattoo of a giant serpent coiled on his back. The snake's open mouth and sharp fangs were so lifelike they could scare anyone to death. He was assembling an L39 anti-tank rifle, a weapon with immense destructive power, capable of splitting an elephant in half if fired at close range.

Several mercenaries spoke respectfully to him, "Samuel, someone from Saya wants to meet you again."

Samuel sneered, "Hmph, just a bunch of refugees, thinking too highly of themselves. I won't see them."

As they saw Cora and her group approaching, the speaking mercenary's expression turned wary, and he immediately fell silent.

Ellyn nodded slightly towards Samuel. Samuel's sharp eyes swept over Cora and the others, and he returned the nod indifferently.

After leaving Samuel's camp, Cora asked, "Is this Samuel also a freelance mercenary?"

"Yes," Ellyn replied, "The mercenaries of West Street each have their own factions and rarely interfere with each other. Samuel didn't want to submit to the entry restrictions and moved out of the city after the apocalypse. Many people join him recently. He acts tough, but he's still a decent guy."

Cora had long understood not to judge by appearances. Samuel might look fierce, but his willingness to resist the general's rule and take in the elderly and children showed he was no villain. No wonder Ellyn brought them here for the night.

They spent some time nearby, killing zombies. Ellyn's scavenger mission was 100% complete, but F777's level 3 crystal was still missing. Cora sat on top of an overturned car, exhaling.

In the distance, the sound of hurried footsteps echoed briefly. Despite the short duration, the keen senses of those present quickly detected the anomaly.

Suchat silently drew out a dagger. "I'll check it out."

He returned shortly, "It's Samuel. He's heading southeast with 17 Aberrants from the camp."

"Are they armed?" Ellyn asked.

"AK-47s, G36s, FAMAS, and small cannons. Samuel has the L39," Suchat answered.

With these weapons, they could destroy a small city.

Ellyn picked up a turret with one hand and nodded towards Cora. "If Samuel is getting involved personally, it's definitely something big. Maybe you'll find what you're looking for. Want to check it out?"

"Let's go." Cora immediately jumped off the car.

With Suchat, an expert tracker, they didn't have to worry about losing Samuel. They followed at a distance and reached the southeast corner of Da Nang. To be cautious, Cora found a distant office building and climbed to the top to observe below.

As soon as she saw the scene, Cora couldn't help but gasp. It really was no small matter. Hundreds of Aberrants were fighting a zombie in the ruins below.

This zombie had clearly evolved. It was twice the size of a normal zombie, with no signs of decay. Its muscles bulged all over its body, and its massive hands had sharp nails half a meter long. A single scratch on the ground left deep marks. Compared to its robust body, its head seemed small, hiding between its shoulders. Its pupils were jet black, darting around quickly.

Nearby mercenaries threw out Anopower chains, tightly binding it. The zombie roared in fury, breaking free, the chains snapping into pieces. It grabbed the broken ends and threw the mercenaries into the steel ruins.

Several fires of Aberrants rushed forward, attacking with flame guns. The zombie agilely dodged behind a nearby truck, disappearing from sight. The others cautiously surrounded it. Suddenly, a thick arm reached out, grabbed one by the leg, and dragged him back. The sound of a skull being crushed was horrifying.

The mercenaries quickly surrounded the truck, firing wildly, but the area was empty. The zombie had long escaped.

Two seconds later, it leaped from a broken window of another lofty building, instantly killing another mercenary. This zombie not only had intelligence but also used guerrilla tactics, openly toying with humans.

Seeing this, the newly arrived Samuel joined the battlefield, leading his men in a rapid advance, firing as they went.

On the office building's top floor, Onyx observed for a moment and concluded, "An evolved zombie, at least level 2 or higher."

"Why so many people?" Cora wondered. Was everyone aiming for the Hero's Banquet?

"It's not just about the Hero's Banquet. It's more likely for money or resources," Felix Lucas said. "I just checked. On the Deep Woods black market, the value of a level 3 crystal has surpassed ten million."

Cora gasped. Ten million? She'd never seen that much money in her life!

Below, the evolved zombie continued its slaughter, with more mercenaries dying. The ambushers revealed themselves one by one as Ellyn quickly reported their positions, "Target at 3 o'clock, moving left 10-70, close 23, enemy mortar position."

"Target at 6 o'clock, moving right 10-40, low ground, enemy grenade team formation."

Suddenly, Ellyn paused, her voice growing colder, "Coordinates X6742, Y5878, Nguyen Van Tuan's men are here."

Nguyen Van Tuan, one of the three warlords of Deep Woods. If

Mục Tân was cunning and Miao Lun was a hedonist, then Nguyen Van Tuan was a complete war fanatic. He had the most private soldiers and reveled in the thrill of smoke and destruction.

Cora turned her head blankly. 3 o'clock... 6 o'clock... low ground. Where exactly were these places?

Onyx sighed lightly, wheeling forward. He gently tilted Cora's head, left 30 degrees. "Here, 3 o'clock." Then right 70 degrees, "6 o'clock."

He then pulled her close, appearing as if embracing her, "From my position, look ahead. Nguyen Van Tuan's men are there."

"Got it?" Onyx whispered near her ear, the tone teasingly intimate.

Cora shrank her shoulders uncomfortably. "... Oh."

She saw it clearly now.

Ellyn's bitter voice unexpectedly sounded. "Nguyen Van Tuan has made his move."

Cora snapped back to attention, watching as a formidable line of tanks slowly entered the scene. Gunfire and explosions were incessant. Although the evolved zombie continued killing, it lost its best chance to escape. With the human wave tactic surrounding it, defeat was inevitable.

Cora was eager. "Shall we join the fight?"

Onyx pondered briefly. "We can try."

"How do we join?" Cora asked.

"Blend into the chaos. We only have one chance. Whether we succeed, we must retreat immediately," Onyx replied.

They were only eight people. Stealing the kill on the zombie was extremely risky. After all, being surrounded by so many Aberrants wasn't a joke, and if their faces were seen, attending the Hero's Banquet later would be troublesome.

Onyx used Cora's terminal to create a temporary group chat, and assigned tasks to everyone.

"Ellyn, switch to heat-pressure shells. You're in charge of disrupting the enemy and causing confusion. The messier, the better."

"Got it," Ellyn's microphone icon lit up, her steady voice coming through.

Heat-pressure shells were extremely lethal and released explosive dust clouds, making them highly effective in underground caves and densely built environments.

"Yuui, do you have a debuff that can temporarily blind the enemy?" Yuui Hayashi's Anopower required songs to be released. She quickly scanned her mental lyrics library. "Yes."

"Duration?"

"Maximum of 20 seconds."

"20 seconds, a single hit. Can the captain do it?"

Cora thought for a moment. "I'll try it."

"Suchat, you hide. If you get the crystal, grab it immediately."

"Okay." Suchat's figure vanished on the spot, blending into the surroundings.

Once everyone was in position, Onyx spoke softly. "Ladies, good luck. It's up to you now."

In the middle of the ruins, the evolved zombie, having taken several heavy weapon hits, sensed something was wrong and retreated. At that moment, many shells tumbled from the sky.

"Boom—Boom—"

Ellyn, positioned in her sniper spot, unleashed her Anopower, firing shell after shell. The heat-pressure shells she launched exploded on impact, sending debris and smoke flying, burning the air, and causing mercenaries to clutch their throats in pain as they desperately fled.

With the shelling, Ellyn's location was exposed, and several Aberrants quickly moved toward her position.

"Ellyn, retreat," Onyx ordered promptly.

"Roger." Ellyn swiftly packed up her turret and ran, taking winding paths until she vanished.

Amid the swirling dust, Yuui's soft and graceful song echoed, "Why can't you see, see the red and black dried up, letting sin fall asleep, at ease~,"

The mercenaries went blind, unable to see after already struggling to breathe. With this double blow, the scene descended into chaos. "Cora, one chance," Onyx turned, his deep eyes full of trust.

Cora's fingers brushed over a large stone slab, and moments later, the slab vanished, leaving a giant dark blue longbow in her hand.

She drew the bow, pulled the string, and nocked an arrow. The bow's flexible arm slowly opened, and a dark blue arrow formed, gathering energy. Cora's dynamic vision was excellent; she had locked onto the evolved zombie's position even before Ellyn started shelling. Now, with mental power aiding her, she tracked its movements, and the arrow quickly homed in.

"Roar—!!"

A deafening roar echoed as the enraged zombie went on a rampage, instantly killing two more people.

However, its roar gave away its position. Cora's eyes focused. She released the arrow!

"Whoosh—" The arrow moved at high speed, piercing through the fog and smoke, flying straight at the evolved zombie. "Pfft—" The metal-infused arrow hit its forehead accurately.

The next second, the arrowhead split, scattering hundreds of tiny needles, shredding its brain. The zombie's eyes widened in anger, its fragile head fatally penetrated, and it crashed heavily to the ground.

"Hit!" Cora shouted joyfully.

"Quick, retreat." Onyx grabbed her wrist and pulled her to run.

"Cough, cough, how did the zombie die?" The nearest mercenary shouted instinctively. The others froze, then frantically rushed towards the body.

In the crowd, a vague green mist floated over, faster than everyone, pausing at the zombie's head for two seconds before quickly drifting away. When the others eagerly reached the body and searched, the zombie's brain was smashed like a crushed watermelon —no trace of the crystal.

"Who the hell stole the crystal!!!"

Having successfully snatched the crystal, F777 ran for ten kilometers before daring to stop and catch their breath.

Everyone looked at each other and burst into laughter. Even Chief Franz's mouth curved into a slight smile. This was the legendary "hit and run," frustrating their opponents to no end.

"Suchat, check the crystal," Cora urged impatiently. Suchat opened his palm, revealing a transparent crystal, glowing with a bright blue light.

"Sis, it's a level 3!" Little Diamond, sweating profusely from the run, jumped up and down in excitement. Cora's cheeks dimpled with joy. This trip was worth it.

"Where's Ellyn?" Yuui looked around. "Why didn't she come with us?"

Ellyn's voice came through the temporary group chat. "My task is done, and you've got what you wanted. This trade is even. I'm leaving now. Contact me if you need anything." With that, she left the group.

Yuui couldn't help but hold her head. Ellyn's personality was indeed carefree.

"Let's go back to the city," Onyx said.

After a long queue at the city gates and tedious checkpoint verification, they finally returned to their apartment past midnight. They had 12 days left until their admission deadline and only 2 days until the Hero's Banquet.

Onyx's slender fingers tapped the table. "One crystal means one spot. Now let's discuss who will attend the Hero's Banquet."

CHAPTER 22

The White Rose

Who should attend the Hero's Banquet? That was a good question.

"I'll go," Cora said confidently.

"No way!" Yuui, Suchat, Franz, and Damian all objected in unison.

"Why?" Cora felt deeply hurt. Did her teammates see her as so unreliable?

Damian clasped his hands behind his back, sighing like a small adult, "If you go, Sis, you'll definitely get into a fight."

The others nodded in agreement, thinking Damian made a valid point.

Yuui added, "If you get all riled up and kill that warlord, our plan will be ruined."

Suchat coldly agreed, "Exactly."

Cora couldn't believe it. "How... how could that happen?"

She was so mature, so steady. How could she possibly get into fights... uh, probably not, right? Facing their skeptical looks, Cora felt a little uncertain.

This time, the Hero's Banquet hosted by Mục Tân had an entry requirement of a level 3 crystal. It wasn't just a gathering of hidden talents; it was a den of experts. It might even be a trap.

In F777, Onyx and Felix were physically handicapped, Yuui and Franz were more supportive roles, lacking offensive capabilities. Damian was clever but too young, likely to get nervous in big scenes.

After considering all factors, Cora and Suchat were the most suitable candidates.

Suchat's strength lay in stealth and intelligence gathering, like during the Death Hell mission. But this time, the event was open, and participants would be under scrutiny. Suchat's abilities wouldn't be helpful, making him and Cora equally suitable.

Cora also had her considerations. Given the unknown risks, F777's representative would face great danger. Compared to her companions, her strength was better suited for handling risks. "I'm the captain. We don't know what will happen, but at least I can handle it," she said.

Cora raised two fingers, promising confidently, "Alright, I'll try… not to fight. If things go south, I'll run." The others still looked hesitant.

Cora turned to Onyx, her eyes pleading for help. "Please back me up."

Onyx cleared his throat. "You can go."

Everyone was surprised, expecting Onyx to be the most opposed, but he was the first to agree?

"The situation at the Hero's Banquet is unpredictable, and their concerns are valid. We worry you might not think things through," Onyx said, "So the best solution is to bring an external brain."

"What?" Cora was confused.

Onyx turned to Felix, tapping his wheelchair with a cane. "Hey, those materials you requested, you should have some left. Our captain paid for them."

Speaking of Felix's list… when Franz brought the bill to Cora for reimbursement, she almost cried, clutching her money pouch.

Cora had gathered a group of highly talented individuals, but they were all broke. The wealthiest among them was Damian, but he inherited his money from Victor Blackwood, and Cora couldn't use it. Next were Yuui and Suchat, but Suchat's savings were spent paying a hefty fine after the Death Hell mission, leaving him penniless.

The rest were even worse off. Franz had to change his identity, resulting in no access to his previous accounts. Felix and Onyx didn't have legitimate identities and couldn't contribute a penny… It was no wonder Cora had gone from being indifferent about money to cherishing every cent. These people had molded her.

Felix's mechanical arm flexed out, blocking Onyx's cane. "What do you need? Just say it."

"Trackers, detectors, I need to know every detail of Mục Tân's residence. Also, portable communication devices that any surveillance can't detect," Onyx listed.

"Although the captain is going alone, if we can see real-time situations, we can help with strategies."

"Can you do it, 5.0?" Onyx deliberately used Felix's boasted GPA to provoke him.

Felix's icy blue eyes flickered. The pride of a genius couldn't be trampled. "Of course."

Two days later, Cora arrived alone at Mục Tân's family estate.

The buildings had a distinctive local Woodmoon style, with sprawling bamboo houses forming an extensive manor. In the center was a luxurious villa complex, surrounded by strict patrols of mercenaries with Anopowers.

Adjusting her black collar, Cora discreetly touched a small protrusion on her neck, hiding a miniature microphone. "Hello, can you hear me? Can you hear me?" she asked nervously, feeling surreal.

A faint static came through her earpiece, followed by a man's magnetic voice, "I can hear you."

Onyx's voice felt like a breeze in Cora's ear, making her face inexplicably warm.

"Sis, Sis, I can hear you too!" A boisterous child's voice suddenly broke in.

"Thud!"

"Ow! Don't hit my head!" The child jumped up, rubbing his head, and the chair clattered over, creating a mess of noise.

The momentary flirtation vanished.

Cora's face turned expressionless. "Keep it down!" Her ears were about to explode.

To enter the main house, she had to register and complete the on-site check-in.

Cora arrived at the side gate, where a middle-aged man in a private soldier uniform was verifying each registrant's identity. The floating screen beside him showed the entry count had reached 26 people, and in a flash, it updated with three more entries.

"South District freelance mercenary, Wild Wolf." "South District worker, Losang." "West Street corporal, Mandaya."

"They're checking identities," Cora stepped back, finding a corner to report to her companions. After a moment, Felix's unfluctuating voice came through. "I'll handle it, don't worry."

Cora followed the line forward and first presented the bright blue level 3 crystal.

Suvongsa, the middle-aged man in charge of verification, took the crystal with gloved hands and gently placed it in a transparent instrument. Several rows of sparkling level 3 crystals were already inside, with one particularly unique, emitting a faint red hue amidst the blue.

"Please present your identity information."

Cora pressed her terminal to the connector, and the floating screen flickered imperceptibly, showing a momentary data stream no one noticed. Suvongsa glanced at the screen. "West Street freelance mercenary, Cora Thornton."

"That's me," Cora said, standing tall and righteous. "Welcome, and good luck today," Suvongsa nodded slightly.

Cora was about to step forward.

"Suvongsa, something's happened up front!" A patrolling mercenary rushed over.

"Why are you panicking?" Suvongsa reprimanded with a stern face.

"At the main gate, Lord Miêu Luân has arrived!"

Suvongsa's expression tightened. This year's Hero's Banquet was held earlier, and Lord Mục Tân hadn't invited Miêu Luân. What was his uninvited arrival about?

"You, report to the lord," Suvongsa turned and pointed at several mercenaries, "You, come with me."

Seeing Cora still standing there, Suvongsa patiently said, "Mercenary, you need to go inside. Just follow the signs."

"Oh, no problem." Cora was eager to comply.

Once inside the side door, Cora looked around. Confirming no one was watching, she shook her sleeve, and several small mechanical spiders fell to the ground. They spun around dizzily before scurrying off, quickly hiding in the shadows.

These were miniature detectors Felix had developed,

reprogrammed to have basic artificial intelligence. They could move autonomously and capture images of the surroundings, helping Onyx and the others monitor the situation.

"I released the spiders. Can you see them?"

"Yes, keep wandering around and release all the detectors."

"Got it."

Ignoring the large directional signs above, Cora pretended to be lost, wandering around the estate. Here, she dropped a few spiders, circled the pond twice, and released a few more.

"How's it going?"

"Building the model, 45% complete."

Miles away in their apartment, the complete architectural model of Mục Tân's estate was gradually taking shape. The real-time images came through, and Onyx and the others focused intently on the projection.

Felix's fingers paused on the light screen, clicking his tongue softly.

"Here," he pointed to a corner where Cora was headed, "there's a strong high-frequency band. Risk level H (high danger). Cora's microphone signal will be detected."

In the estate's surveillance room, a mercenary monitoring the site noticed something amiss and pulled up the footage of Cora's location, projecting it onto the central screen. "What's this person doing? Sneaking around, almost at the forbidden garden."

The person next to him immediately pulled up Cora's registration information. "She's here for the guard recruitment. Maybe she's lost?"

"Even if she's lost, she shouldn't wander around. That area is near where the two lords are meeting. Get the patrol team to drive her away!"

Cora dodged the patrolling guards and was about to enter the courtyard ahead when Onyx's voice came through her earpiece. "Cora, danger ahead. Turn off your microphone and follow my instructions."

Cora touched her collar, turned off the microphone, and switched to a one-way input mode. In this mode, she could hear Onyx's commands, but her voice wouldn't be transmitted.

Danger ahead? Cora thought for a moment, then abandoned the main path, opting to climb the wall and jump onto the roof. Her movement suddenly stopped — By the pond ahead was a graceful figure. She lifted her head slightly, looking towards the closed window in the distance.

The woman wore a simple dark green long dress that highlighted her pale skin. Her black hair cascaded down her shoulders, her waist was slender. Though not young, her beauty was undeniable. Her side profile was stunning, with eyebrows like mist, exuding charm and frailty, making it hard to look away.

Cora, inexperienced, was entranced.

"Hey, get down here, catch her!" "Don't let her go inside!"

Noisy footsteps approached from behind, and several mercenaries lunged at Cora. Startled, Cora saw the woman turn towards her, revealing her full face.

Wow, she's even prettier up close…

Stunned by her beauty, Cora's mind went blank. She instinctively smiled at the woman, dimples appearing on her cheeks.

"Stop her!" the pursuing mercenaries shouted.

Cora agilely dodged the attacks, landed on the ground, and obediently raised her hands. Since the spiders were deployed and the model was built, she had no intention of running.

The mercenaries quickly surrounded her. "Who are you? Who sent you here, and why?"

Cora answered honestly, "I came to attend the Hero's Banquet."

"The Hero's Banquet isn't here. Didn't you read the signs?" the questioning mercenary snapped.

Cora gritted her teeth, deciding to throw caution to the wind, "I-I can't read. I didn't understand them."

This wasn't the old civilization era. Illiteracy was unheard of in the Alliance. Who would believe that?

"Even if you couldn't read the signs, you shouldn't have conveniently 'gotten lost' and ended up here. Tell the truth, who sent you?" The leading mercenary didn't believe her weak excuse and asked harshly.

Cora was momentarily speechless. She really didn't know what this place was. Black muzzles instantly aimed at her.

"I told her to come." In the dead silence, the woman by the pond suddenly spoke.

The wind in the hall lifted her skirt. The woman looked like a pure white rose, slowly blooming in the night.

"She's my friend. I told her to come here."

A good person! Cora was almost moved to tears.

CHAPTER 23

Freelance Mercenary

After the beautiful woman, who shared a rose-like elegance, finished speaking, everyone, including Cora, stared at her. The pursuing mercenaries seemed wary of her, exchanging uncertain glances without rushing to act. The leader stepped aside, lowering his voice to communicate with his superior via earpiece.

The remaining mercenaries occasionally glanced at the woman, their eyes showing a mix of awe and other indescribable emotions that Cora couldn't understand. She turned her head and mouthed a thank you to the woman. The woman's gaze lingered on Cora's face for a moment before coldly turning away. Although she had just helped Cora, her current demeanor clearly showed she didn't want any association with her.

The leading mercenary returned, glaring at Cora and the woman. "If you want to talk, I can arrange a meeting room for you both to have a proper chat, but it has to be outside the forbidden garden."

"No need, I don't want to talk," the woman interrupted coldly, rejecting the offer.

The mercenary sneered, "In that case, it's getting late. I will 'escort' your friend to the Hero's Banquet venue." Saying escort, but meaning to guard her closely, ensuring she didn't wander off again.

Cora felt a hard push on her back. "Move!" How infuriating. Her fists clenched in anger.

"Cora, don't start a conflict." Although unaware of her situation,

Onyx timely reminded her. "Judging by the layout of the estate, you're probably in the council hall. Mục Tân and Miêu Luân might meet inside."

Fine, she would endure it. Cora tucked her head down, looking pitiful as she was driven away. Before leaving, she couldn't help but glance back. The beautiful woman was still staring at the closed window, her solitary figure as elegant as a painting.

Once out of the forbidden garden, the mercenaries started chatting frivolously, "She's just a plaything, Banya, why did you give her face?" "That's not right. Even if she's a plaything, she's Miêu Luân's canary, thinking herself so noble." "I heard she's been favored for nearly three months now. That's quite long." "With such a pretty face, I wonder how skilled she is in bed?" They exchanged lewd looks and grinned wickedly.

Fuming with anger, Cora wanted to blow their heads off on the spot.

The mercenary leader named Banya spoke coldly, "Shut up! Don't drag me down with you if you want to die. Do you think this place is so secure that no word gets out? If Miêu Luân hears you gossiping about him, being skinned alive would be the least of your worries!"

Miêu Luân's top Aberrants included some with eavesdropping talents. If their words reached his ears... The group fell silent instantly, cold sweat dripping.

The fierce mercenaries escorted Cora to a heavily guarded large bamboo house, the primary venue for the Hero's Banquet. "Banya, who is she?" The guard at the door looked at Cora, confused. "Watch her closely. This guest likes to wander," Banya said.

The guard glared, lowering his tone. "The Hero's Banquet is about to start. Please enter promptly." Only after seeing Cora enter did Banya and his men leave.

Cora walked silently into the bamboo house like a quiet quail. "You're safe now. You can turn the microphone back on."

Cora pretended to adjust her collar, pressing the receiver switch. "Are you alright?" Onyx asked, unable to determine if she was in trouble since they couldn't hear her.

"I'm fine. Didn't get into a fight. I'm inside now," Cora whispered.

Since she was the last to arrive, countless scrutinizing gazes fell on her as soon as she entered. The room was filled with men and women of various builds, some familiar faces chatting in small groups, while loners sat quietly. It was clear they were all powerful Aberrants. Cora counted 36 people besides herself.

Knowing no one, Cora tried to minimize her presence, finding the most inconspicuous spot to sit. The banquet hall was spacious enough that people at opposite corners might not even see each other clearly.

Hiding under her large coat, a tiny ladybug crawled out of her pocket and fluttered up to the ceiling, scanning the room with its mechanical eyes.

Felix, always proud of his intellect, rarely showed interest in anything. But Onyx knew how to provoke him precisely. This time, Felix's modifications—the spider detectors, collar microphone, and ladybug camera—left Cora and the others in awe.

"Real-time feed loaded, Cora, your task is done. Adapt as needed," Onyx's voice softened with a reminder, "And be careful."

Ten minutes later, a series of exquisite bamboo curtains were rolled up by the servants, and a group of people, guided by Suvongsa, slowly entered.

Leading the group were two middle-aged men in high-ranking military uniforms, exuding extraordinary presence. One was a sturdy man with sharp facial features, a neatly trimmed mustache, and narrow but piercing eyes. He strode confidently to the chief seat, and everyone present showed great respect. Cora immediately knew this had to be Mục Tân.

What surprised Cora was the man next to Mục Tân. This was a man with kind eyes and a gentle smile, looking very approachable. In contrast to Mục Tân's robust build, his face and body were rounder, with his belt barely restraining his protruding belly.

Cora didn't let her guard down; instead, she furrowed her brows slightly. She had a hunch that this man was far more dangerous than he appeared. Behind him, Cora noticed Cơ Đan Vi, who had clashed with F777 at the city gate. Based on the current information, this smiling Buddha was likely the other warlord, Miêu Luân.

Sure enough, after Mục Tân sat down, he scanned the room with a sharp gaze and said in a deep voice, "Everyone here is a top Aberrant from Deep Woods. Thank you all for honoring me by joining the Mục Tân Family's guard. I vow that as long as you pass the selection, you will be rewarded with both wealth and status!"

"Good!" The participants cheered enthusiastically.

Mục Tân raised his left hand and pointed to the guest seats. "Today, I'm honored to have Brother Miêu Luân here with us."

Miêu Luân waved his hand amiably. "Oh, I'm just here to join the fun. No need to mind me."

Cora's earpiece crackled with her companions' discussions.

"Are Mục Tân and Miêu Luân on good terms?" Yuui Hayashi asked doubtfully.

"On the surface, the three warlords coexist peacefully, without conflict. Their genuine relationship is unknown," Onyx replied.

Mục Tân stood up from the chief seat, his powerful voice echoing through the hall, "Now I will announce the selection rules for tonight..."

"Lord Nguyen, wait, you can't go in!" "Stop him! Report to the lord quickly! Ah—"

Suddenly, the sounds of intense fighting erupted outside the banquet hall, followed by muffled grunts and screams. Three or five of Mục Tân's private soldiers tumbled in disarray as another team's footsteps gradually approached.

"Bang—"

A fierce Anopower burst out, shattering the bamboo door into pieces. Amid the debris stood a tall figure. Wearing the same high-ranking military uniform and exuding the same imposing aura, but far younger than Mục Tân and Miêu Luân. His features were more delicate, with pale skin and neatly pressed black hair under his cap. He harshly kicked aside the mercenaries, blocking his way with his half-length black boots.

"Lord!" Banya rolled a few times, spitting blood, and cried out to Mục Tân on the chief seat.

Mục Tân sprang up, his full aura unleashed, countering with his own Anopower. Judging by the intensity of their mental strengths, both were Grade A Aberrants. The people present were caught between their overpowering pressures, forcing them to release their own Anopowers to withstand it, causing a fierce dark wind to swirl in the hall.

Cora felt no suppression at all. She ate some fruit from the plate, glancing left and right, observing the situation. Suddenly, she noticed that Cơ Đan Vi, with his full Anopower unleashed, was standing firmly in front of Miêu Luân.

Cora pondered. After awakening, Aberrants generate a special mental force field. Even if outmatched by higher-grade Aberrants, they would only be immobilized at most. Only normal people would be seriously injured or even die from the pressure.

Could it be... Miêu Luân doesn't have Anopower?

"Nguyen Van Tuan, barging into my residence without warning. What do you mean by this?" Mục Tân shouted angrily from his chief seat.

"Nothing much. Two days ago, my people lost a Grade 3 crystal in Da Nang inexplicably. I was very displeased. I heard you're hosting some kind of hero banquet here, so I came to find the culprit. Not welcome?" Nguyen Van Tuan responded nonchalantly.

Da Nang, Nguyen Van Tuan, Grade 3 crystal... Could it be the one they stole? Cora choked on her fruit, silently patting her chest.

"Even if you're not welcome, today I must find the person and slice them to pieces." Nguyen Van Tuan flicked his coat and strutted in. The people along his path quickly stepped aside in fear.

"Hah, it seems these two aren't on good terms," Yuui quipped.

"Like fire and water," Felix Lucas commented sharply.

As the tension between Mục Tân and Nguyen Van Tuan reached a boiling point, Miêu Luân stood up leisurely, playing the role of a mediator. "It's just a Grade 3 crystal. Is it really worth getting so worked up over? Let's put away our Anopowers and not scare our future guards."

Under protecting Cơ Đan Vi's Anopower, Miêu Luân walked up to Nguyen Van Tuan and greeted him warmly. "Brother Nguyen, why don't you take a seat first? Everyone's here, so you can search slowly. If you can't find the person, I'll make up for the crystal myself. Is that good enough?"

Nguyen Van Tuan's delicate face twisted with a hint of malice and bloodlust. "A mere Grade 3 crystal? I don't care about that. Those who dare to challenge me will die."

Miêu Luân laughed heartily. "We just need to clear the air. You're looking for someone, right? That's easy enough." He then turned to Mục Tân, patting his own round belly. "Brother Mục Tân, look, Brother

Nguyen isn't here to cause trouble. Why not do me a favor today and let everyone sit down and talk?"

"Thanks to you, other than meeting the General, it's a rare occasion for us to sit together, hahaha," Mục Tân said, trying to mask his irritation.

Nguyen Van Tuan was clearly unwilling to let it go, but under Miêu Luân's persuasion, he reluctantly agreed. "Guests are guests. Take a seat."

Nguyen Van Tuan, who did not want to sever ties completely, left his men at the door and entered the banquet hall alone. Now, with the three warlords of Deep Woods gathered, the atmosphere in the room was incredibly tense. Some Aberrants were already sweating from the pressure.

"This smiling tiger really knows how to play both sides," Yuui said in awe. "Such a scoundrel, just like Onyx," Damian cursed, insulting both men in one go.

After a moment of silence, the earpiece crackled again. "Sis, help me!"

Cora rolled her eyes dramatically, feeling quite exasperated. This distraction caused her to miss the two young people who slipped in through a side door and sat behind Mục Tân.

Nguyen Van Tuan's interruption made the atmosphere cold and stagnant.

Mục Tân reiterated the selection rules. "If you can defeat my subordinates in a one-on-one duel, you will officially join the guard."

A duel? Just like that? Cora was surprised. She had expected multiple rounds of rigorous testing, but winning a single duel could secure a spot on the guard. It seemed strange to her. The entry requirements were so high, yet the actual test seemed too lenient — more like an open gate than a mere letting off of steam.

"I'll go first," said a mercenary from the Southern District named Wild Wolf, volunteering to step forward.

Suvongsa made a few hand gestures, and a private soldier stepped out from behind Mục Tân.

A transparent isolation chamber rose in the banquet hall, allowing the two to fight. Wild Wolf and his opponent engaged in a fierce battle.

On the guest seats to Mục Tân's left, a servant respectfully offered Miêu Luân a cigarette. Miêu Luân reclined in the large chair, unbuttoned his collar, loosened his belt, and puffed away contentedly. After a while, he whispered a few words to the person next to him.

Soon, the servant brought over an exquisite bamboo screen and escorted a beautiful woman to Miêu Luân's side with grace. Miêu Luân wrapped his arm around her without restraint, pulling her into his embrace.

The beautiful woman showed no expression, neither flattery nor resistance, and sat down obediently.

Even though Cora had heard Banya and the others' discussions earlier and was prepared, actually witnessing this scene left her with a sinking feeling, a sense of world-crumbling devastation. She couldn't eat the fruit in her hand anymore.

So, the beautiful woman was indeed Miêu Luân's new favorite. She felt a dull ache in her heart and a sense of discomfort.

Perhaps she was staring too blatantly, because Cơ Đan Vi suddenly glanced in her direction with cold eyes.

Cora quickly lowered her head, avoiding his gaze.

In the field, Wild Wolf successfully defeated his opponent, winning the match.

Mục Tân nodded in satisfaction. "Southern District mercenaries are indeed brave and skilled. Congratulations on joining the guard. You will officially be enlisted tomorrow."

Wild Wolf was overjoyed. "Thank you, sir! I will serve you diligently from now on!"

Nguyen Van Tuan toyed with his sidearm, letting out a disdainful snort.

Meanwhile, Miêu Luân gently stroked the smooth shoulder of the beautiful woman, exhaling a puff of smoke, his face becoming increasingly obscured and his smile deepening.

Several more Aberrants were called up to the duel. Overall, more won than lost, and by the eleventh match, only two had been defeated.

"Next," Suvongsa checked the list on his light screen, "Cora Thornton, freelance mercenary from the Western District."

It was finally her turn. Cora wiped her mouth and stood up from the corner.

"Go get them, sis!" Damian cheered.

"If they're weak, just beat them quickly," Felix advised.

"Keep a low profile," Onyx reminded her softly.

Keep a low profile, finish the fight quickly. Cora repeated the sage advice in her heart as she rushed to the center of the room.

Suvongsa announced, "The mercenary to face her is..."

"Click—" The sound of a bamboo chair being pushed back echoed as someone stood up behind Mục Tân.

"You little trash, what are you doing here?!" a young man with a dark brown face suddenly exclaimed.

Cora froze, inwardly panicking. Oh no, it's Eamon! She also wanted to ask, how did Eamon end up here?!

But Eamon's next words made her mind go blank.

"Freelance mercenary? Aren't you from District F?"

CHAPTER 24

Impressive

Eamon's words made Cora the center of attention.

Eamon, Mieu Luân, Nguyen Van Tuan... all the participants' scrutinizing gazes fell on her.

"Don't panic, stay calm." At this critical moment, Onyx's calm voice sounded.

In just a few seconds, Cora's emotions went through a roller coaster ride. Fortunately, she kept her composure and didn't reveal any clues.

"Heh," Nguyen Van Tuan's eyes were sinister, showing a slight interest in the spectacle. "A hero's feast, and yet a little rat sneaked in."

The shrewd Eamon didn't get angry immediately; instead, he thoughtfully stroked his beard. "Eamon, come here."

Eamon walked to the chief seat, his arrogant attitude completely restrained, his hands tightly pressed against his thighs. He respectfully called out, "Uncle."

Eamon gave him a look, and Eamon immediately corrected himself, "... Sir."

Eamon pointed at Cora, who was standing in place. "Explain what you just said clearly."

Eamon raised his head, meeting Cora's gaze. They hadn't seen each other for over half a year, but his eyes were still full of malice. Despite having trained together every day, Eamon's hostility toward her had never faded.

He had attacked her with a particle gun before, and today, he could betray her with no hesitation.

"Starting two years ago, I was training in ancient martial arts in District E104. This person is my fellow student and has been there much longer than I have. She has been a student there for at least a decade. I'm certain she's not only from District F, but also an unregistered citizen."

Eamon exposed Cora's background in a few words.

Cora couldn't just sit there and do nothing. She quickly defended herself. "No, I've already registered in the Deep Woods."

Some participants below immediately scoffed, "What a joke, someone from District F registered in the Deep Woods?"

District F, the most impoverished and backward numerical district in the Alliance, was a rundown place where even flies didn't want to stay. The Deep Woods (District C33), not only ranked in the middle of the C districts, but also had a notoriously strict admission policy.

Cora's words were entirely unbelievable. To put it simply, it was like the lowest class of society suddenly becoming a second-tier military officer. It was not only ridiculous but also impossible in the Deep Woods.

"It's true, I'm a freelance mercenary," Cora stubbornly defended herself.

"Freelance mercenary? Which faction?" Wild Wolf, also a freelance mercenary, asked suspiciously.

Again with this question, what's the obsession with asking about factions among mercenaries?

"I... I'm from West Street, under Ellyn the Wild Rose." Cora, flustered, had no choice but to use Ellyn's name as an emergency measure.

The beauty in Mieu Luân's arms suddenly raised her eyes, looking at Cora in the center of the hall.

Eamon's eyes were deep, and he didn't speak. Private soldiers in the hall had already surrounded Cora.

Cora clenched her fists but remained motionless.

Eamon tilted his head slightly. "Check when she last entered the district."

Suvongsa hurriedly confirmed, "Six days ago."

A smile tugged at the corners of Eamon's mouth, hidden beneath his beard.

A small fry like Cora, whether from District E or F, couldn't cause any significant trouble. Eamon didn't care about her true identity; he was more interested in another matter that he could exploit.

"Mieu Luân, I remember you volunteered to handle entry verification with the General, right?"

"How do you plan to explain this oversight to the General?" Eamon said meaningfully.

Mieu Luân's hand paused as he lit a cigarette, his smile fading slightly.

Cơ Đan Vi had recognized Cora as soon as Eamon shouted, and he quickly knelt down, leaning close to Mieu Luân's leg and whispered, "Sir, I checked... facial recognition... no mistake."

Mieu Luân's hand, holding the cigarette, pressed lightly on Cơ Đan Vi's shoulder, causing him to tremble uncontrollably.

"Eamon, are you questioning me now?" Mieu Luân, usually easy-going, suddenly became serious, with hidden currents in his eyes. However, he only stayed serious for a second before bursting into laughter. "Who said it must be a mistake? Since everyone is so curious, why don't we verify it on the spot? If what she says is true, it would be quite inspiring, wouldn't it?"

"If the identity information is forged," Mieu Luân's smile was chilling, "I'll take her head to the General to apologize."

Mieu Luân let go of the beauty in his arms and gestured backward. A plain-looking short man stepped forward.

"Is he... Hasa?!" The Aberrants below recognized him and couldn't help but exclaim.

Hasa, an A-level Aberrant, the strongest white-hat hacker in the Deep Woods, with the ability of data tracking. It was said that as long as there was a network, no secret could hide from his eyes. Unexpectedly, he was under Mieu Luân's command.

"Hasa, reveal all the information about this person from birth." As long as someone existed, they would inevitably leave traces. By digging into those clues, one might discover surprises.

Hasa nodded silently, took out several light screens from his ability space, and projected them onto the bamboo curtains in the banquet hall, allowing everyone to see clearly. He then set up a dozen supercomputers in a row.

Cora: Oh no, they're going to dig up everything about me. Urgent, urgent, urgent. She was so anxious.

On the ceiling, the mechanical beetle's compound eyes slowly rotated, transmitting all the activity at the scene back to a distant apartment.

"Not good. Mieu Luân is checking Cora's records!" Yuui exclaimed.

"Even if the identity information is fine, her resume could easily give her away. She hasn't even submitted an entry application," Charles said.

Worry appeared on everyone's faces.

The wheelchair moved, and Felix Lucas's flat voice sounded, "Please make way."

He watched Hasa's every move in the projection, his icy blue eyes gradually showing interest. "A white-hat hacker? Let him check."

Onyx glanced at him, instantly understanding, and whispered into the earpiece, "Cora, Felix will handle it. Don't worry."

In the banquet hall, Cora was on pins and needles. After receiving Onyx's instructions, she breathed a sigh of relief.

Felix had only one lonely terminal and an old, outdated light screen with cracks. In contrast, Hasa was fully equipped with the latest model of floating technology light screens that could connect to six supercomputers simultaneously.

Hasa operated a sophisticated device with a camera on top that extended to scan Cora from head to toe. As it retracted, a miniature mechanical beetle fell, wedged into the gap of the mechanical arm, and a hidden trojan horse program was implanted.

Hasa collected Cora's biometric information and quickly traced the data.

"Cora Thornton, originally from District F199. Activity tracks include District E104, District D56, District C83, District D139, District C40... Parents unknown, date of birth unknown, attended High School of the Blossomville in District D56, dropped out midway."

Hasa's eyes flickered as he activated his ability to track more detailed information.

Felix's silver hair fluttered on his shoulders, both hands operating simultaneously, one typing rapidly on the terminal, the other writing complex attack programs on the light screen.

In the network world, the two forces collided head-on, one charging forward bravely, the other disintegrating into countless points, merging into the vast ocean. However, the dissipated starlight didn't disappear; instead, it subtly changed the direction of the opposing data flow.

The battle between the white-hat and the black-hat hacker was invisible, yet intense. Whoever took the high ground first would utterly defeat the other. Hasa's tracking hesitated for a moment, disrupted by the chaotic stream of code rushing toward him, leading him astray. He began muttering incoherently.

"October 2, New Era Year 46, special permission granted to register in District C83 Felalakas because of close personal ties with the Governor." "November 15, New Era Year 46, awarded the Outstanding Youth title in District C40 Sycamore, received an entry green card."

"February 6, New Era Year 47, submitted a household registration change application after successfully exterminating zombies. The application was approved, and registration was granted in District C33 Deep Woods." "Current identity: freelance mercenary."

Page after page of detailed records were revealed, causing an uproar among the crowd.

It was the first time they had heard of someone from District F successfully changing their registration to the Deep Woods. The review process was excessively stringent. Could it be that, faced with Cora's "impressive" resume, the reviewers had a moment of madness and made an exception?

No way!

Cơ Đan Vi suddenly looked up. He remembered clearly the day Cora entered the city; they had a group of seven. The reason given was "residents leaving the Deep Woods on pre-apocalyptic missions." How could it now become a change of registration? There was definitely a contradiction.

Hasa, what are you doing?!

Cơ Đan Vi's eyes were red with anger, ready to shout furiously, but then he saw Mieu Luân's face. That face, shrouded in smoke, was eerily calm. No, it was the calm before the storm.

Like a bucket of cold water poured over his head, Cơ Đan Vi instantly sobered up. He couldn't speak out. Cora's identity had to be "real." Otherwise, not only would it mean he had been incompetent, but Mieu Luân would also lose face in front of Eamon, Nguyen Van Tuan, and even the General. In that case...

Cơ Đan Vi trembled all over, suddenly realizing Hasa's intention. He lowered his head humbly and submissively, remaining silent.

Cora looked at her dazzling "resume" and couldn't help but exclaim inwardly. Felix Lucas, you're amazing at making things up! She almost believed she was a hero who had saved the Alliance!

In the apartment.

While altering Hasa's data, Felix Lucas sarcastically commented, "After a few years, your skill at lying has improved remarkably."

Onyx entirely fabricated Cora's resume in a short period.

Onyx smiled slightly. "Not as much as your declining skills. If you were any slower, they'd have understood it."

Felix Lucas grumbled in dissatisfaction, "I protest. You distort the facts. What equipment does he have compared to me? A pile of scrap metal!"

Despite his words, his fingers moved deftly, quickly erasing the genuine records Hasa was about to find about Cora.

In the banquet hall.

Mieu Luân smiled at Eamon, "Eamon, this is quite a talent. If you don't want her, I'll take her in."

He turned to Cora, "Mercenary, if you want to make a name for yourself, you don't have to join the Guard. You can come to me just the same."

Eamon responded coldly, "Mieu Luân, it's too early to say that. Let's see her beat my people first."

At this moment, the most embarrassed person in the hall was none other than Eamon.

He had revealed Cora's identity on purpose, hoping to curry favor with Eamon and get noticed. Unexpectedly, this little nobody had genuinely made it into the Deep Woods and earned a freelance mercenary status. How could someone from the lowly District F achieve that?

"Sir, I request to fight," came Eamon's voice was hoarse as he volunteered to face Cora.

After the apocalypse, he had awakened his abilities. The humiliation of losing to Cora before, he would repay in full.

"Father, I also want to play with her." Another young man, with three diamond studs on his brow and roughly the same height as Eamon, stood up from the back. His expression was rebellious, with half his mouth curled up in defiance.

"Nguyen!" Eamon glared at him, paused, then lowered his voice. "You're still not used to your new abilities. How about?"

Nguyen glanced at him indifferently. "How about what? You're just a B-level, and I'm an A-level."

Eamon's back stiffened, and he pierced the skin of his palm.

Nguyen asked curiously, "Do you know her? Is she strong?"

Eamon lowered his head, his expression unclear. "Her... average, no, she's weak. Definitely not your match."

Nguyen's confidence soared. "Father, let me do it. I want to test my abilities."

A stern look from Eamon silenced Eamon when he called him uncle. However, Nguyen called his father, and Eamon's expression remained unchanged, even somewhat indulgent. "Alright, you go."

Cora and the young man named Nguyen entered the isolation chamber.

"Hey, what's your level?" Nguyen asked contemptuously.

"A-level," Cora replied, since her Aberrant Certificate showed that.

"Same as me," Nguyen smiled, and without another word, raised his arm. A row of miniature cannons appeared, and bullets fired in rapid succession.

Whoa, the legendary barrage of bullets.

Cora quickly moved, her figure almost flashing in a Z-line. Finding an opportunity to counterattack, she delivered a spinning kick! Nguyen was kicked hard, flying out and crashing to the ground, the cannons falling silent.

Huh? Cora was stunned. Wasn't he A-level? How did he go down with one kick?

Nguyen struggled to get up, wiped the blood from the corner of his mouth, and his hands gleamed as countless crystals appeared, mostly level 2 and 3. He drew energy from them using his mental power. Once the crystals dimmed, he discarded them and charged at Cora ferociously.

Cora was stunned. She had seen people use drugs, but never anyone doping with crystals during a fight! She dodged his attack and cautiously threw a punch.

"Bang—"

Nguyen didn't dodge again, and her punch landed squarely on his nose, sending him tumbling backward.

"Cora, he's a pseudo-Aberrant."

Cora was puzzled. What did pseudo-Aberrant mean? Onyx seemed to know her confusion and quickly provided a detailed explanation.

"A pseudo-Aberrant is someone who can't awaken their abilities naturally and relies on external stimuli, like crystals, to form a false magnetic field within their body." "You can think of it as... a weakling."

Nguyen, like a wobbling toy, struggled to get up again, pulling out another handful of crystals and began absorbing energy.

Cora was still confused, but seeing Nguyen coming at her again, she responded with her mental power.

A domineering and powerful mental force struck Nguyen head-on. Unprepared, he was instantly dazed, charging forward with such momentum that he crashed into the transparent glass of the isolation chamber, knocking himself out!

Eamon stood up abruptly. "Nguyen? Doctor! Where's the doctor?!"

"The match is over. Everyone take a ten-minute break," Suvongsa shouted in a panic.

Cora stood there, bewildered. What just happened?

In the chaotic scene, the screen to the right of Eamon's guest seat moved slightly, revealing half the face of a beauty, like smoke and mist, signaling Cora. Huh? Cora blinked.

The beauty seemed to have something to say to her.

CHAPTER 25

Fake Identities

In an instant, a group of people rushed into the banquet hall, carried the unconscious Aemond onto a stretcher, and quickly took him out for treatment.

With a dark expression, Mục Tân followed them out. Suvongsa hurriedly announced the suspension of the competition, busy maintaining order at the scene. Meanwhile, in the isolation room, the other protagonist, Cora Thornton, was left alone, ignored and isolated.

In the previous rounds, participants won effortlessly. Everyone understood that the so-called selection was merely a formality. Allowing Aemond to take part was a calculated move by Mục Tân, given everyone was aware of Aemond's "young master" status and assumed no one would really hurt him.

However, the result was that Cora Thornton didn't even make a move, and Aemond knocked himself out, which was absurdly comical.

Could she be blamed for this? She didn't expect this Aberrant to be so weak!

After Mục Tân left with his people, Nguyen Van Tuan leisurely stood up and looked at Miêu Luân across the hall. "May we have a word?"

Miêu Luân smiled and nodded, leading Cơ Đan Vi and a few other mercenaries out of the bamboo house and into the room across. Meanwhile, Cora noticed that the beautiful woman beside her was giving her a meaningful look.

Through the noisy earpiece, with background sounds chaotic, Damian cheered for her victory, while Onyx and Felix bickered back and forth. Cora, unable to interject and fearing she might appear suspicious, turned off all her communication devices.

Following the beautiful woman to the bamboo curtain, she asked, "Are you with the Sora Wings?"

"... Yes," Cora reluctantly answered, thinking to herself that she must apologize to Ellyn for borrowing her name later.

"You're lying." the woman's expression turned stony. "I'm from the West Street, and I've never seen you before."

"..." Busted. Cora sighed. Unlike Onyx, she wasn't good at lying.

"In truth, I'm not with anyone. Sora Wings is just a friend of mine..."

"A friend? What's her name?" the woman interrupted.

"Ellyn," Cora answered honestly. "I said it out of desperation just now."

The woman still eyed her suspiciously.

Cora raised her device, "I can contact her right now..."

A soft palm pressed against Cora's wrist. The woman's brows furrowed slightly. "No need. It's inconvenient here."

"You really know Ellyn?"

"Yes."

"Has she returned to the Deep Woods?"

"Yes, we met a few days ago."

"Will you be able to contact her once you return?"

"Yes."

"Give me your address."

"What?"

"I need your help to ask Ellyn to come to you. I want to meet her tomorrow."

"Okay." Cora quickly gave her apartment address and then realized the woman, despite wearing an expensive dress, had no accessories, not even a device.

The woman memorized Cora's address, then gazed at her face, her expression growing distant as she reached out involuntarily. Cora held her breath, standing still, not daring to move.

Just before her fingertips touched Cora's cheek, the woman

suddenly snapped out of it and withdrew her hand.

"Here's a piece of advice: no matter the reason, do not join the Guard. It's a conspiracy." Her tone was calm, but there was a discernible kindness in her words.

"What do you mean?" Cora was taken aback.

The woman glanced back; Miêu Luân and Nguyen Van Tuan were already returning. There was no time left.

"The Guard is just a cover. Their actual target... is Saya."

"Remember to set up a meeting with Ellyn for me?" They brushed past each other.

Cora was left alone under the bamboo curtain, even more confused. Not joining the Guard? But she couldn't think of another way to get close to the General.

She turned her receiver back on, and immediately, Onyx's voice came through. "What's going on over there?"

"Yeah." Cora briefly explained what had just happened.

"Wait, a moment. I'll contact Ellyn to confirm," Yuui said.

Cora returned to the banquet hall nonchalantly. Before long, Mục Tân and his group returned. His glance swept over Cora with no sign of anger.

"Congratulations on passing the selection. You will officially join us tomorrow," Mục Tân announced calmly.

Cora secretly breathed a sigh of relief. It seemed that Aemond was okay.

Miêu Luân, with a knife hidden in his smile, interjected, "Mercenary, my offer still stands. Coming to my side is also a good choice."

Cora, looking awkward, silently retreated to a corner. A gaze followed her like a lurking viper. Cora glanced sharply and saw that it was Eamon.

The following matches proceeded smoothly. When only a few contestants remained, an Aberrant named Takbear entered the arena. He took a bit of time, but eventually defeated his opponent, joyfully retreating to his seat.

Nguyen Van Tuan suddenly spoke up. "Stop. Where did you get that crystal?"

In Takbear's registration, there was a uniquely designed level-3 crystal, emitting a bright red amidst a dark blue hue. Both its color and purity made it the best of today's crystals.

Takbear hesitated, a hint of discomfort flashing across his face. "I, uh, got it from killing a mutant."

Nguyen Van Tuan sneered, "Is that so... Check the production date of this crystal."

With Mục Tân's nod, Suvongsa immediately arranged for the crystal's radiation levels to be tested.

"Master Nguyen, this crystal is new, produced within the past week."

"Within a week... within a week..." Nguyen Van Tuan muttered repeatedly, his military boots thudding as he slowly descended the guest steps. His tall, imposing figure and the sinister look under his brim made everyone shudder in fear.

He stopped in front of Takbear. "Tell me exactly when, where, and how you killed the mutant?"

"I, I..."

Takbear was only a B-level Aberrant. Under the pressure of Nguyen Van Tuan's imposing presence, his eyes darted around, and his words became increasingly mumbled, eventually barely audible.

Miêu Luân took a sip of tea and added fuel to the fire with a light but deliberate tone, "Well, well, the Hero's Banquet indeed hides many talents. This crystal's quality is top, close to level 4. The zombie that hosted it must have been formidable. If you killed it, your skills must be impressive."

Nguyen Van Tuan sneered coldly, "Did you really kill it, or did you steal it?"

"Three days ago, in Da Nang, the one who shot a level-3 zombie with an arrow —was that you?"

"No, no, no, it wasn't me!" Cold sweat broke out on Takbear's forehead.

Cora Thornton crouched lower, silently hiding under the table. Nguyen Van Tuan was clear after the crystal she had stolen.

Takbear's denial did not soften Nguyen Van Tuan's expression. Without a word, he drew his sidearm and fired several shots into Takbear's right leg. "Ah—!!" Takbear clutched his bleeding leg, screaming in agony. Nguyen Van Tuan's special ammunition exploded inside the flesh, causing excruciating pain.

Nguyen Van Tuan ground his boot into Takbear's wound, twisting it mercilessly. "You're going to die, anyway. Confess now, and I'll let you die quickly. This is your last chance. Did you steal the crystal?"

"It wasn't me!! This crystal, I... I bought it from Saya," Takbear sobbed, his voice full of despair. "I wanted to join the Hero's Banquet and become an officer, so I bought it at a high price from Chionji's men. They were the ones who killed the zombie and stole the crystal, not me!"

"Chionji."

Upon hearing this name, both Mục Tân and Miêu Luân's expressions changed noticeably.

Nguyen Van Tuan's aura of spiritual power surged, a sign of his rising anger. His eyes were terrifyingly cold. "Who did you say?"

Takbear's face turned even paler. "Chionji, the leader of Saya's refugees. I don't know his real name; they all call him Chionji."

The hall fell silent. The participants in the banquet hall didn't even dare to breathe.

The smile disappeared from Miêu Luân's face. "In less than a month, someone already has the power to kill a level-3, no... nearly level-4 zombie?" The transparent instrument held the crystal Takbear submitted, which caught everyone's attention with its vivid red hue.

"Though it's the common duty of warlords to combat refugees, perhaps Mục Tân and Nguyen Van Tuan need to act more swiftly?" Miêu Luân's meaningful glance at Mục Tân was a clear return of the suspicion thrown his way earlier.

Suppressing rebellion and banditry were primarily under these two warlords' jurisdiction, especially Nguyen Van Tuan, known as the war maniac. If he couldn't handle a small group of refugees, his position would indeed be in jeopardy.

"The General is quite concerned about this matter," Miêu Luân added pointedly.

"Colluding with refugees is a crime punishable by death," Nguyen Van Tuan coldly declared.

"Bang!" The gunshot echoed, and Takbear's head exploded.

Cora looked at Takbear's corpse, silently sighing at the scapegoat who took the fall for her.

After this episode, Nguyen Van Tuan lost interest in the competition and left the banquet hall with his men. The remaining few matches finished quickly, and the Guard recruitment concluded hastily.

Cora left the mansion, her mind heavy with thoughts, ready to exchange information with her companions. Just as she was about to leave, she noticed Eamon standing behind Mục Tân, making a shooting gesture at her head. Cora paused for two seconds, then slowly mouthed back, "Idiot."

She couldn't understand Eamon's deep-seated animosity towards her. It couldn't be because he never won against her in the fights, could it? But then again, he never won against Chi Zhang either. Shouldn't Eamon hate Chi Zhang equally if that were the case?

Grumbling internally, Cora hurried back to her apartment. She opened the door to find Onyx and the others waiting for her.

She took the water Onyx handed her and drank it down in one gulp, listening to her companions' discussion.

"There's something off about the Hero's Banquet," Charles Franz, who rarely spoke, said.

"Yeah, it was too hasty. The threshold of the level-3 crystal misled them, but now the truth is out," Onyx added.

Cora recalled Aemond's frantic use of crystals during the fight. Mục Tân must have been hoarding crystals for him.

Initially, they thought Mục Tân was using the Guard recruitment to send high-level Aberrants to the General, filling the gaps in the Guard Corps. But given today's selection, the participants' skills varied widely. Sending them as the General's close guards seemed rather far-fetched.

"So, should I still go tomorrow?" Cora asked.

Onyx pondered for a moment. "You mentioned that Miêu Luân's associate wants to meet Ellyn. What did Ellyn say?"

Yuui Hayashi brought up the terminal screen. "They know each other. Ellyn has agreed to come tomorrow."

"Then let's wait until after the meeting. She might know something. Try to get more information," Onyx decided. "Also, investigate Saya's refugees and Chionji further. I have a feeling this could be an important lead."

The next morning, Ellyn knocked on the apartment door.

Yuui Hayashi opened the door, and Ellyn's first question was, "Where is she?"

"She hasn't arrived yet. Come in and wait," Yuui said softly.

Ellyn cautiously moved to the window, setting up a small cannon to monitor the street outside for any followers.

Cora confessed the truth about borrowing Ellyn's name. Ellyn shook her head. "It's okay."

"Ellyn, is that beautiful lady really your person?" Cora asked.

"She's not entirely under my command," Ellyn said calmly. "She came to the West Street six months ago. We're more like partners."

Cora wanted to ask more, but Ellyn suddenly signaled her to be quiet. "She's here."

A few minutes later, there was another knock at the door. The beautiful woman, wrapped in a shawl, stood quietly in the hallway.

Ellyn aimed her cannon at the figures loitering outside the apartment. "You brought a tail."

"They're Miêu Luân's private soldiers. They're just monitoring me. They won't come in," the woman replied.

The four of them sat down, and Ellyn skillfully handed over paper and pen. The beautiful woman began sketching, creating lifelike portraits.

"I've found these people so far. They agreed to wait for your message. The others... I couldn't locate."

Ellyn examined the drawings. "They're from West Street. Thank you for the information."

The woman responded softly, "That's all for today..."

"Are you planning to stay with Miêu Luân?" Ellyn suddenly asked. The woman paused.

Cora and Yuui exchanged a glance, Yuui barely shaking her head, and both held their breath.

"I've thought for three months and still don't understand what you're trying to do," Ellyn continued, her gaze unwavering. "You're not the person who loves vanity. Miêu Luân is unpredictable. The longer you stay, the more dangerous it becomes. Why are you deliberately getting close to him?"

The woman remained silent.

At that moment, the guest room door opened, and Onyx and Charles walked outside by the side.

Physical therapy alone can prevent muscle atrophy. Charles's voice trailed off as he looked towards the living room, his face struck with shock.

"Rao?" He called out, his voice trembling.

CHAPTER 26

Sweet Lily

Dr. Franz's voice trembled as he called out the name.

The beautiful woman's reaction was equally intense. She accidentally knocked over the paper and pen, her calf hitting the chair with a loud scrape. Her face turned ashen as she stared at Charles in disbelief.

"How are you here? I mean, in the Deep Woods, weren't you..." Charles took two steps forward, his words jumbled, "You clearly said you wanted to leave Sycamore and start anew somewhere else. No, no..."

Charles glanced at Ellyn, then at the beautiful woman, and suddenly a terrifying guess formed in his mind. His face reflected a mix of shattered hope and immense pain. "Rao, what are you doing?"

The only reason she could be here was as Miêu Luân's mistress.

Coincidentally, Cora had turned off her receiver both times she encountered the beautiful woman, so none of the F777 members had heard her voice. In the banquet hall, the servants had set up screens, drawing everyone's attention to Cora, making it easy to overlook someone less important.

From Charles' reaction, it was clear they knew each other well.

Felix, Suchat, and Damian came out of their rooms, sensing the tension but remaining silent. Cora tilted her head slightly and saw the beautiful woman's entire body trembling, like a rose in a storm, ready to collapse.

Charles slowly reached out but didn't dare to touch her. "Rao, please stop. Let me handle the rest. Trust me one more time. I'll do it, even if it kills me."

Something in his words seemed to sting her. The beautiful woman suddenly lifted her head, eyes red, "What can you do? What can you achieve?"

Her voice grew more sorrowful. "Seven months. Do you still remember Lily? Do you remember what she looked like? You don't, but I do. Every night, I see her crying. She was my daughter, a part of my life. You can move on easily, but I can't."

Her eyes filled with tears, but none fell. "Charles, you're just a coward."

"We have nothing to do with each other anymore. You don't need to care about what I do... I need to leave, or Miêu Luân will get suspicious."

She stumbled towards the door. Cora wanted to stop her but was held back by Ellyn and Yuui, who signaled her to stay quiet. Before leaving, she said, "The Guard will make a big move soon. You'd better not get involved."

The apartment door closed slowly, and soon the trackers outside disappeared. Inside, silence reigned. Cora hesitantly spoke, "Charles..."

Charles stood still, slowly covering his face, hot tears streaming through his fingers. Neither had cried during their conversation, but now, alone, Charles broke down, sobbing uncontrollably.

Cora had never seen someone cry so heartbrokenly. Though he made no sound, each tear expressed his agony. Her heart ached, and she felt like crying too.

After a long while, Charles steadied his breathing. "I'm sorry for always troubling you with tasks without explaining why. I want to kill Ne Kon because I need revenge, deep and bloody revenge."

"You and..." Cora struggled to find the words.

"Rao, her name is Rao Cheung. She was my wife," Charles forced a smile, though it was more of a grimace of deep sorrow, "my ex-wife."

Unlike Rao Cheung, Charles Franz hadn't dreamed in a long, long time.

There was a time when he dreamed. In those distant and beautiful dreams, Charles would return from the Ninth Hospital on a sunny afternoon, unlock the door, and see a graceful figure with her back to him, wearing an apron and painting at an easel. A smile would spread across Charles's face as he silently stepped forward and hugged the woman from behind, nuzzling his chin into her neck, inhaling deeply, letting all his exhaustion melt away in her warm embrace.

Rao Cheung would turn halfway around, holding her brushes and palette awkwardly, her eyes twinkling with a gentle reprimand. "Dr. Franz, how many times have I told you to change your clothes when you come in? Paint stains are hard to clean."

Charles, stubbornly refusing to let go, would mumble, "I'll wash them. I'll wash them. I'm so tired. Let me lean on you for a bit."

Rao would push back slightly with her elbow, "What about the thing I mentioned last time?"

"Hmm," Charles would groan dramatically, "Be gentle, are you trying to kill me? Don't worry, you go to the art exhibition. I'll take care of Lily this week. I've rescheduled almost all my surgeries, just one patient left."

"Still that one from the Deep Woods?" Rao frowned slightly.

"Yeah, he's someone important. I couldn't refuse."

"Don't be ridiculous. It's because he has a rare disease and you can't resist the challenge, right?" Rao would see through him instantly. Charles, a medical genius, had little interest in common ailments but was always eager to tackle the most difficult surgeries.

"He's only thirteen. After all, he's just a child..." Charles would cough lightly, trying to change the subject. Ever since becoming a father, his once sharp edges had softened considerably. "Where's Lily? Isn't she done with class?"

"I'm here, Daddy."

A sweet voice would pipe up, and an eight- or nine-year-old girl with neat pigtails would pout unhappily, "I'm right here, but you only see Mommy and not me."

Charles would lift his daughter with one arm, affectionately nuzzling her nose, "Who says Daddy can't see you? Seeing you make Daddy's heart burst with joy." Lily would giggle, dimples appearing on her cheeks, looking especially adorable.

"Our great artist, Mommy, has to work. How about you play with Daddy during your vacation?" Charles would ask his daughter. Lily would hug his neck and plant a kiss on his cheek, "Okay, I love playing with Daddy the most."

As a chief physician, Charles had his own office and lounge. While playing dress-up with Lily's dolls, a colleague would burst in, "Dr. Franz, the patient in VIP Room 3 is in critical condition!"

VIP Room 3's patient was Ne Win, a thirteen-year-old boy, and the only son of the governor of District C33, Ne Kon. He suffered from a rare bone disease, McCune-Albright Syndrome (MAS), complicated by aberrant conditions, with his symptoms worsening with age. His body was covered with distinct brown patches, and during flare-ups, he experienced excruciating bone pain.

"Prepare for surgery. I'm coming right now," Charles would say, standing up. "Oh, and ask the head nurse to assign a colleague to look after my daughter." He would kneel to Lily, "Lily, Daddy has to save someone. Be good and wait for me, okay?"

Lily, though unhappy, would puff out her cheeks but agree reluctantly, raising two soft fingers, "Okay, but I want two strawberry ice creams."

Charles would smile indulgently and kiss her head, promising, "Daddy will buy you three. Don't tell Mommy."

Ne Win's surgery would last fifteen hours. Charles, fully focused, would race against death, pulling Ne Win back from the brink. Just out of the operating room, he would collapse to the floor in exhaustion, falling asleep almost instantly.

Lily, who had slept through the night in the lounge, wouldn't see her father return the next day. Holding her doll, she would sneak out while the nurse dozed off. VIP Room 3... Lily vaguely remembered the number, thinking Daddy didn't want to buy her ice cream and was hiding from her.

She would finally find the room, but as she approached, a menacing guard would stop her.

"Let her in," a weak voice would call from inside.

Lily, timid, would enter, not finding her father but being startled by the sight inside.

A frail boy in a hospital gown, about her height, lay on the bed, his gaze cold and hollow, with a large brown birthmark-like patch on his left cheek, making him look scary.

Clutching her doll tightly, Lily would back away, wanting to flee.

Ne Win's eyes would remain fixed on the little girl before him. He knew he was gravely ill, having faced death countless times. His body wracked with pain, yet beneath that agony, a hidden, sinister excitement would quietly spread, as if telling him that all his suffering needed an outlet.

Ne Win would force a stiff smile, coaxing softly, "Come here, I'll give you some candy."

Lily, well-taught not to talk to strangers or accept their gifts, would shake her head vigorously, "No, I want to leave."

She would turn and run towards the door.

"Stop her!" Ne Win would command.

The guards' powerful arms would pin Lily to the ground, making her cry in terror. Ne Win's voice, cold and light, would say, "I'm in so much pain. Why am I the only one in pain? Play with me."

Listening to the screams from inside, one guard would hesitantly say, "This … we're still in a hospital. Isn't this too much?"

Another, eyes downcast, would respond, "It's the same everywhere. If you don't want to die, mind your own business."

Ne Win ran rampant in the Deep Woods, where the class system was twisted. No matter how badly he behaved, there was always someone to clean up after him. He had done such things many times before; no matter how big a fuss he made, it was always covered up.

When Charles woke up, his head ached fiercely.

He held his head, getting up from the cold floor. Though he had only slept for less than an hour, he had been on his feet in the operating room for nearly a day and a night. Even a body made of iron would be exhausted. Unable to bear it any longer, he had dozed off briefly.

Rubbing his temples, Charles headed towards the lounge. Remembering something, he detoured to the hospital's downstairs store and bought three boxes of strawberry ice cream. He didn't want to be a father who broke his promises.

Returning to the lounge, he found several hospital leaders standing at the door, their faces grim.

"What's going on? Don't worry, the surgery was a success. Everything will be fine." Charles smiled and moved to open the door.

"Charles..." The hospital director placed a hand on his shoulder, stopping him.

"What is it?" Charles asked, confused, holding up the bag. "Let me in first. The ice cream is melting. Lily will be upset if it melts. Little girls are hard to please."

"Charles..." The director repeated, tears welling up in his eyes.

Charles suddenly had a bad feeling.

In the cold morgue, Charles Franz saw Lily's body. A torn doll had been stuffed into her arms, its limbs disjointedly pieced together, her exposed skin covered in bruises. Charles's world collapsed.

"I'll kill him!!!"

People nearby hurried to restrain him as Charles's eyes turned red. He struggled and thrashed, but they gripped him.

The director, with a pained expression, said, "Charles, Ne Kon has arrived from the Deep Woods with his Guard Corps. They've surrounded the entire hospital, and their troops are stationed around Sycamore. This incident has caused a diplomatic crisis, and news of Lily's murder has been temporarily suppressed."

"Even if you rush out now, it won't help. You'll only lose your life," the director continued, knowing the following words were cruel but necessary. "The governor insists that the surgery still be performed by you, and he'll be overseeing it."

"Get out, get out... I'll kill him, I will kill him with my own hands!" Charles was pinned to the ground, his head pressed against the floor, vision blurring. "I was wrong... Lily, it was Daddy's fault...."

"Daddy, why do doctors save people?"

"Because it's our job."

"What if it's a bad person? Do we save them too?"

"Yes."

"Why?"

"Because a bad person is still a person first. Doctors don't have the right to judge, but the law will punish them."

Would the law really punish the guilty? Not in the Deep Woods.

Countless times, Charles had raised a knife, wanting to kill Ne Win, but Ne Kon had him imprisoned, forcing him to perform surgeries on Ne Win. Charles refused to comply, spending countless sleepless, painful nights in the dark rest room.

Then the apocalypse came.

Charles fell into a fever. He had treated several Aberrants before and knew the secrets of awakening. A flicker of hope ignited within him. "If only I could awaken my power. Any power, I must kill them."

Reality dealt him another cruel blow.

Charles awakened his power, but it was the most useless type—a healing ability, only capable of saving lives. How laughable that when his heart was filled with hatred, fate still demanded he continue to be a life-saving doctor.

On the third day post-apocalypse, there was an upheaval in the Deep Woods. Ne Kon and Ne Win left Sycamore. Charles regained his freedom and returned home in a daze. He opened the door to find a much thinner Rao Cheung waiting for him with a calm expression.

"Rao..." Charles murmured, reaching out to hug her, his head resting on her neck as tears poured down.

"Charles Franz, you killed your own daughter."

But this time, Rao pushed him away.

Charles froze, and the equally emaciated Rao transmitted a divorce agreement to him.

"All these days, what have you done? You couldn't even avenge her. You're unfit to be a father, and you're unfit to be my husband."

"I can't face you anymore. I want to move to another city and start over."

Charles, too tired to think, reached out to grab her. "No, Rao, I..."

Rao dodged his hand and hurried to the door.

"You, you... Charles Franz," her back trembled, her words cold and harsh, "No matter how much you suffer, you must live and spend the rest of your life atoning for Lily."

Charles stood stunned for a few seconds before stumbling after her, but Rao had already disappeared.

He wandered the streets like a ghost, his last memory being of zombies lunging at him.

"Let him rest." Yuui closed the door, leaving Charles alone in the room, while the rest sat in silence in the living room.

"Ne Kon, damn him," Cora said each word with emphasis.

Should Ne Win, who killed Lily, die? Yes, but killing Ne Win wasn't difficult. The challenge lay in Ne Kon, the governor of the Deep

Woods. This "tyrant" allowed his son to commit evil acts and then used force to suppress any fallout, even forcing Charles to continue performing surgery on the murderer, treating him as less than human.

Cora finally understood why Charles and Rao often looked lost when they saw her. Her dimples reminded them of Lily, their sweet little girl. Perhaps that was why Rao had helped her multiple times.

Ellyn's solitary hand brushed over the cannon, her voice heavy. "Among the three warlords, Miêu Luân has the closest relationship with the General and meets him the most. I initially thought she was trying to get close to Miêu Luân, but now it seems..."

Ellyn sighed silently and left the apartment with the drawings. F777 reconvened.

"So, what do we do now?" Cora asked. "I believe she wasn't lying to us."

Rao Cheung had specifically warned them before leaving. Cora believed it was out of goodwill, showing the importance of the matter.

"From her words, it seems Mục Tân's recruitment of the Guard might not be for the General, but related to Saya's refugees," Onyx pondered for a moment before deciding. "Let's hold off on our original plan. We'll proceed on two fronts: keep monitoring Mục Tân's actions and investigate Saya."

"I'll follow Mục Tân," Cora volunteered.

"And I'll check out Saya," Suchat said, taking the other task. He was the best-suited for it.

Saya (District D78), Da Nang (District D94), and Emerald City (District D103) were all large D-level cities around the Deep Woods. Given Suchat's skills as an A-level Aberrant and his expertise in stealth and concealment, no one worried about him going alone.

After dividing the tasks, Cora and Suchat left one after the other.

In the evening, Cora returned on time, but they waited until midnight with no sign of Suchat.

Messages sent by Yuui to Suchat vanished without a trace, with no response from the other side, which was unlike him.

"Do you think something happened?" Yuui was anxious.

"Should I go look for him?" Cora stood up.

A loud bang echoed from the apartment door, making everyone

turn their heads in alert.

Cora's hand twitched, conjuring an ethereal dagger. She waited cautiously for a moment before yanking the door open — Suchat, covered in blood, held on until the door opened. He raised his blurry eyes slightly, gasping, "Saya... there... there..."

He couldn't finish his sentence and collapsed into a pool of blood.

"Suchat!!"

Cora quickly bent down to check. Suchat's body was battered, with a fatal wound piercing through his abdomen, seemingly a sword wound.

CHAPTER 27

No Way to Escape

Suchat's face was ashen, and his limbs were ice cold. Cora helped him lie flat and checked the pulse on his neck, finding it very weak. Yuui dropped her terminal and rushed over, kneeling on the ground, her expensive silk dress getting soaked in blood, but she didn't care. She wiped the blood off Suchat's face while calling his name. "Suchat, wake up."

Onyx patted Damian's back. "Go get Charles."

Damian, the only one available, turned and ran towards the guest room.

He tiptoed, about to knock, but Charles had already heard the commotion and emerged from inside.

His eyes were slightly red, and his mental state wasn't great, but he was fully awake and no longer overwhelmed by grief. Seeing the situation at the door, he quickly walked over to Cora.

"Let me." Charles gently took over Suchat, placing his palm over the most severe penetrating wound. A white glow of his Anopower flowed out; the immediate task was to stop the bleeding, or Suchat wouldn't survive the wait for further treatment and would go into shock and die.

"Prepare for surgery immediately. I need the following drugs and tools..." Charles's tone was calm and clear as he began listing the items.

After their experience with Cora, Yuui and the others were

already familiar with the emergency procedures and swiftly moved into action.

On the makeshift operating table, Charles made precise incisions, preparing to clean and treat Suchat's wound. To his surprise, despite the severe internal damage, there were no signs of infection, only the residual unstable Anopower.

"A physical object did not cause the wound but by an Anopower," Charles whispered. "The attacker was decisive, hitting Suchat in one strike."

Everyone felt a chill. Suchat was cautious; for someone to injure him so badly, they had to be exceptionally skilled.

The stitching was straightforward, and Charles quickly finished, removing his mask. "Don't worry, Suchat is in good health. He lost consciousness because of excessive blood loss. With a night's rest, he'll wake up tomorrow."

Relieved to hear Suchat was out of danger, everyone sighed. Cora stood up abruptly and headed outside.

Onyx quickly grabbed her wrist. "Where are you going?"

"Saya."

"The situation is still unclear..."

Cora dragged Onyx and the wheelchair forward like a stubborn calf, impossible to hold back.

Seeing she was about to break free, Onyx tightened his grip, interlocking his fingers with hers. "Saya is more dangerous than we thought, you..."

She dragged him another two meters. Wow, the girl is strong.

"I want to fight back."

Cora's eyes burned with fierce determination. The flame of anger had been ignited long ago, growing stronger with each injustice—from hearing Rao Cheung and Charles's story, Sweetie's experiences, to Suchat's injury. The anger towards Ne Kon, this wretched place, and its heinous inhabitants made Cora feel a rage she'd never known before.

She turned to face Onyx, not letting go of his hand, just staring at him with stubborn, blazing eyes.

Cora's life philosophy was simple: whoever bullied her, she would fight back. And the same went for anyone who bullied her companions.

Onyx's brows furrowed, understanding he couldn't dissuade her.

He quickly assessed F777's combat capabilities and decided. "Let's go. I'll go with you."

"Add Felix and Damian." Felix's mechanical arm nodded in agreement, for once not objecting to Onyx's plan.

"You two stay and take care of Suchat," Onyx instructed Yuui and Charles.

With three S-class Aberrants and one B-class attacker, even if Saya was a den of dragons and tigers, they could storm through. "Get ready. I need to talk to Charles."

Cora took Damian's hand and left first.

After the door closed, Onyx turned to Charles. "Give me two doses of Closure."

Closure injectors, developed by Charles using his Anopower, mixed high-intensity radiation and anesthetics to suppress pain and stimulate nerve activity, allowing Onyx to stand on his own for a short time with no external support.

But this treatment had severe side effects. Improper injection could cause irreversible damage to bones and muscles.

Charles gave him two doses but cautioned out of medical instinct. "This stuff is still unstable. It's best not to use it. If you do, remember, only one dose in ten days, or the consequences are unpredictable."

"I know, just in case." Onyx palmed the Closure doses into his space.

"Keep in touch. Any news about Suchat, update us immediately."

"Got it. Be safe," Yuui nodded.

When Rao returned, a large group of private soldiers guarded the courtyard in front of Mieu Luân's mansion.

She glanced at them and turned to leave, but was stopped by Hu Chao. "The master wants you to wait inside."

"I'm exhausted and want to rest first," Rao said coldly.

"The master said you should wait inside," Hu Chao insisted.

Rao stepped forward. From inside, she could hear women's screams, and the bamboo windows cast the shadows of several tall figures—Aberrants. Mieu Luân was just an ordinary person and was extremely fearful of his life, allowing no one to be over five meters away from him, even during intimate moments.

A wave of nausea surged from her stomach, and Rao fought the urge to vomit, standing expressionless in the courtyard.

Unlike new aristocrats like Mục Tân and Nguyen Van Tuan, who rose to power through their own strength in recent generations, Mieu Luân's family had been warlords in Deep Woods for generations, with local influence deeply rooted, existing even longer than the general's reign. Many of the general's unsavory tasks that he couldn't handle were accomplished through Mieu Luân. As a result, Mieu Luân had the closest personal relationship with the general among all the warlords.

Mieu Luân, despite being an ordinary person, had cunning and ruthless methods that secured his position as one of the three major warlords. Even though Mục Tân and Nguyen Van Tuan had gathered many private soldiers, Mieu Luân's local influence was second only to the general's.

Over half an hour passed before the noise inside gradually subsided, and the door opened. A bloodied girl was dragged out. Rao, wearing only a simple dress, shivered, her lips frozen. The girl passing by her suddenly moved, her bleeding fingernails accidentally catching on Rao's dress.

"Nung sau..." The girl mumbled incoherently, using the Deep Woods dialect for "sister," before being ruthlessly dragged away.

"Come in," Mieu Luân's voice called from inside. Rao Cheung looked away and crawled inside.

Mieu Luân, his collar open and expression relaxed, was puffing on a cigarette, with Cơ Đan Vi standing submissively behind him. "Come over here."

Rao Cheung sat at Mieu Luân's feet. His hand, holding the cigarette, pressed down on her shoulder, forcing her head onto the cold floor and her waist to bend in a submissive posture.

"Do you know why I favor you?" Rao remained silent, knowing Mieu Luân wasn't really asking.

"Because you are obedient, gentle, and smart. You know what to do and what not to do. I can give you some privileges and let you have a little temper, but crossing the line is not good."

Hot ash fell, leaving a shallow burn on Rao's shoulder. "Don't see the people from West Street anymore, okay?"

Rao's heart sank. Mieu Luân knew she had seen Ellyn. He might also know she helped Cora yesterday. Bad! The others in that apartment...

Rao Cheung panicked for a moment, but quickly calmed down. From Mieu Luân's current reaction, he was only warning her to stay away from the West Street people and didn't know their true identities. Someone as arrogant as him would never pay attention to nobodies.

"...Yes," Rao replied softly.

Mieu Luân smiled, exhaling smoke, satisfied with the submissive rose at his feet.

On West Street, Ellyn walked alone. Her terminal beeped with a video call from her teammates far away in Felalakas.

Ellyn answered, seeing several smiling faces crowded on the screen. "Ellyn, we're at the Rainbow Band concert! Look! Fireworks and flower floats, so beautiful. Felalakas is amazing. I'd stay here forever..."

These girls, all Aberrants, were ones Ellyn had smuggled out of Deep Woods over the past six months. For ordinary people, especially women, leaving Deep Woods was almost impossible.

"Ellyn, when are you coming back? We miss you..." Ellyn lowered the terminal, her eyes moist, wiping away tears with her left arm.

"I'll be back before the competition, for sure."

After a few seconds, Ellyn picked up the terminal again, smiling as she answered.

Just as she ended the call, a commotion erupted ahead. Ellyn's eyes turned cold as she quickened her pace.

"Masha, you've been requisitioned. Come with us immediately."

Several private soldiers were roughly dragging a girl from a house. Masha's parents ran out but were shoved to the ground.

"No, let me go! I won't go!!" Masha struggled desperately.

"Smack—" A slap across Masha's face disheveled her braids, and the soldier's expression was arrogant.

"You lowly people should feel honored to join Lord Mieu Luân's 'Rose Army.'"

"Enough talk. Just knock her out and take her."

Ellyn jumped onto the roof, switching her weapon to a Barrett

M82A1 sniper rifle, slowly aiming at their heads.

Masha continued to resist. "You already took my sister. I won't go with you!"

The soldiers grew impatient, ready to act.

"Thump—" The silenced gun made a faint sound. A dark flash and the bullet imbued with mental energy tore through bodies, shredding the soldiers on the spot.

Scalding blood splattered all over Masha. She stood stunned. Ellyn jumped down from the roof, walking lightly towards her.

It wasn't until Ellyn's face emerged from the shadows that Masha muttered, "Ellyn."

Most people on West Street knew the "Cunning Fox."

Masha threw herself into Ellyn's arms, crying. "My sister was taken by them. Ellyn, can you take me away too?"

Ellyn patted Masha's head. "I killed their men. They'll find out soon. It's not safe with me."

Masha looked desperate. "What should I do? I won't go with them."

Ellyn thought for a moment. "Go to Da Nang and find Samuel. Life might be tough, facing zombies every day, but at least no one will force you to do things you don't want to do. Are you willing?"

"Yes!" Masha nodded tearfully.

"Uh, excuse me..." A hesitant voice came from the street corner. Ellyn immediately aimed her gun at the intruder.

A young man in his twenties jumped out of the alley, raising his hands obediently. His face seemed somewhat familiar, likely from West Street. "Cunning Fox, right? I'm Cẩm Tú. I joined the Free Mercenaries two months ago. I've admired you for a long time..."

Ellyn's expression remained stern as she pressed the trigger of her sniper rifle.

"Wait, wait!" Cẩm Tú finally realized he was babbling too much, sweating profusely. "I mean no harm. I just got back to the city and overheard you. I wanted to warn you."

"Warn us about what?" Ellyn asked coldly.

Cẩm Tú scratched his head. "You might not make it to Samuel's place. I just came from there. He announced this morning that he's officially joined Saya..."

CHAPTER 28

Chionji

D78 District, Saya.

Before the apocalypse, Saya was a well-known heavy industrial city, along with Da Nang, which developed the marine industry, and Emerald City, which mined rare minerals. These cities served as satellite cities for District C33, Deep Woods, diverting population and providing significant resources.

Because of its overdeveloped steel, petroleum, and chemical industries, Saya's environmental pollution was severe. The overdeveloped steel, petroleum, and chemical industries in Saya caused severe environmental pollution, resulting in perpetually overcast skies, streets and buildings shrouded in a gloomy, dark haze, and very low visibility.

Cora and her group of four moved quickly, occasionally encountering zombies, which they swiftly dispatched with a single stroke.

It was nearing dawn. As they advanced from Saya's outskirts, they saw remnants of artillery and smoke, buildings destroyed by Anopower, shattered roads and bridges, and piles of zombie and human corpses forming small mountains—a horrific sight.

As they approached Saya's city center, the situation improved slightly. The destruction was less severe. Cora's keen ears caught human voices from an abandoned steel plant. She signaled her companions, and Onyx and the others immediately understood, tiptoeing.

They initially thought they had encountered refugees, but the reality was quite different.

About twenty Aberrants, mostly C and D class based on their spiritual power, were working together under command to hunt a group of zombie jackals. Various Anopower lights flashed as the coordinated effort quickly decimated the monsters. Several ordinary people then emerged from behind the group, expertly cleaning the battlefield and collecting fallen crystals.

"Organized and disciplined—they're not ordinary refugees," Onyx analyzed calmly. After cleaning up, the group of refugees headed back.

"Follow them," Onyx whispered, switching his wheelchair to a quieter mode. Felix Lucas's mechanical arms extended, lifting him up as he switched to walking mode. Cora and Damian held their breath, carefully following behind.

After tracking the refugees for about half an hour, they arrived at a camp. Calling it a camp might not be accurate; something like Samuel's, occupying several buildings, could be called a camp. But the scale of this steel forest before them reached the level of a city—it was more appropriate to call it a "base." The base's front guard station had two rows of huge, bright searchlights scanning back and forth, leaving no room for intruders to hide.

Even Suchat, with his stealth skills, got injured here. Cora was even more cautious.

She gripped her short, ethereal sword tightly and drifted a few steps forward. Suddenly, a strong sense of danger overwhelmed her, making her hair stand on end. Though nothing seemed out of place around her, it felt like she had stepped into an invisible forbidden zone. Flowing spiritual power swept over them like a tidal wave, pinpointing their location with two rows of searchlights.

Damn, it's a detection Anopower!

Almost simultaneously, a piercing alarm sounded. Over a dozen Aberrants jumped from the guard station, rushing towards them. Onyx quickly issued commands, "Damian, retreat five steps, ice at the 9 o'clock direction."

Damian's short legs moved quickly, creating ice spikes at the specified location, slowing down the first wave of attackers. Felix's six mechanical arms moved in unison, rapidly deploying a code wall of

101010, cutting off the attackers' retreat and trapping them.

Seeing they could handle the situation, Cora confidently charged into the fray.

Her short sword danced as she tangled with four or five enemies. These Aberrants were strong and ruthless, but they struggled against Cora's fierce attack. She forced one Aberrant back, releasing a domineering spiritual power that caused him to hesitate, creating an opening. Cora took him down and kicked him away.

A wind blade slashed from behind, and Cora dodged sideways, only to feel the ground tremble and crack beneath her. She had to steady herself while three other Aberrants leaped at her, throwing countless dark orbs at her face.

Cora's eyes narrowed as her ethereal short sword transformed into a three-foot-long sword, slashing out with powerful sword energy.

"Beep beep—" Damian's terminal suddenly lit up. He glanced at it, eyes widening, and quickly handed it to Onyx. Onyx looked down; Yuui's voice message was urgent.

"Where are you? Suchat woke up. He said there's an S-class Aberrant in Saya. Be very careful!"

Cora's sword energy not only shattered the dark orbs but also ended the attack of three Aberrants, who fell from the sky in panic. She seized the moment to counterattack, aiming her sword at an enemy's throat — Suddenly, thousands of golden talismans descended, surrounding Cora. A low, ethereal chanting echoed in the mist, "Heaven and Earth, profound and everlasting, cultivating billions of kalpas, manifesting my divine power."

In an instant, the talismans disappeared, transforming into countless golden swords, descending with overwhelming force. "All gods worship, commanding thunder, demons, fear, and spirits vanish."

This is... the Golden Light Incantation! These talismans were driven by an Anopower! Cora's heart trembled. The power of these Anopower talismans was immense, capable of obliterating all impurities. Getting hit was no joke!

The ground beneath her still shook, and the surrounding Aberrants watched menacingly. Cora, caught between two forces, could only dodge the omnipresent golden light. She rolled into a pile of debris, her right hand touching a discarded steel bar, instantly transforming it into a giant shield, blocking the incoming swords. The impact forced her back dozens of meters in the debris pile before she could stop.

Amid the swirling dust, a tall man in a black Daoist robe, his face hidden in a hood, walked forward.

"Chionji!" The Aberrants attacking Cora called his name. "These people trespassed in the forbidden zone and attacked first." "Nguyen Van Tuan's dogs are everywhere, coming after the scent."

Dust choked her lungs, and Cora coughed violently.

The hooded man remained silent for a moment, then suddenly raised his hands to form a seal. His middle and ring fingers interlocked, with the index, little fingers, and thumbs extended, lifting the golden light seal to his forehead. Thunder roared in the void behind him.

Another wave of talisman attacks was about to fall. No, she couldn't let him cast it!

Cora wouldn't sit idly by. Her long sword thrust out, interrupting his seal formation without hesitation.

Unexpectedly, this man's close combat skills weren't weak either. They exchanged dozens of moves. Though his techniques were slightly inferior, he remained calm, patiently waiting for a chance to counterattack.

As they fought, Cora felt an inexplicable familiarity, as if they had battled like this countless times before.

She summoned her core strength, suddenly changing her fighting style, delivering an upward strike. He failed to dodge, and the sharp sword wind sliced through half his hood, revealing his face.

Black hair, black eyes, sharp eyebrows, and starry eyes, with a chiseled jawline, clear lips tightly pressed, looking hard to approach.

Cora's mind went blank. "... brother?" He suddenly withdrew, watching her warily in silence.

Realization dawned on Cora as she hurriedly wiped her face. She was filthy from the debris pile, barely recognizable. After cleaning the mud and dust, she looked up, revealing her clean face.

"Cora?"

The man stopped his left-hand mid-air, a hand drawing

talismans, and slowly called her name.

Cora took a step forward, like a nimble swallow, and called out again in surprise, "Senior Brother!"

Chi Zhang responded, took off his hood, and looked down at her. "It's me."

"Everyone, stop."

Then he turned and gave the command, and the Aberrants immediately ceased their actions.

"It seems Cora knows this S-rank, so we don't need to fight." Felix retracted his six mechanical arms and calmly sat back in his wheelchair.

Onyx lightly tapped the wheelchair, glancing over nonchalantly. Over there, Chi Zhang said something, and Cora began frantically brushing off the dirt on herself, accidentally choking and coughing violently. Chi Zhang reached out to help dust her off.

Onyx's movements paused, his almond eyes narrowing dangerously.

Chi Zhang keenly sensed something and suddenly looked up. Ten meters away, a man in a wheelchair was staring at him from a distance.

"Your people?" Chi Zhang asked.

"Huh? Oh, yes, they're my companions." Cora glanced back and happily waved Onyx and the others over.

Chi Zhang's gaze returned to her. "What are you doing here?"

Cora recalled the matter with Suchat and was about to speak when another group jumped down from the sentry post, releasing a chaotic wave of mental power. They were all A-rank or B-rank, and the leader shouted arrogantly, "Where's that Nguyen dog? Come out and die!!"

As they charged closer, these people hastily braked, their faces shocked as they looked at Chi Zhang and Cora.

"Damn, am I dreaming? Seeing things?"

"Little Junior Sister!" Morgan jumped in front of Cora, excitedly pinching her cheeks, which she pushed away with a punch, annoyed.

These people were the elite that Chi Zhang had taken from the Yue Mountain Martial Arts Hall to take part in the Azure Force assessment. After the apocalypse, they had lost contact and never expected to meet here today.

Cora's expression turned serious as she brought up the issue, "Senior Brother, why did you injure Suchat?"

"Who is Suchat?" Chi Zhang asked.

"Suchat is my companion, good at stealth? He returned from Saya yesterday, seriously injured." Cora gestured to the wound on her abdomen.

The Aberrants, who had jumped down first, reminded, "Chionji, isn't she talking about the person who appeared with Nguyen's spy?"

"That guy was quite a fighter. We couldn't stop him, so you intercepted him."

Cora was stunned. These people were calling Chi Zhang—Chionji.

No way could Senior Brother Chi Zhang be the refugee leader, Chionji, who was a thorn in the sides of the three warlords and generals of Saya? Chi Zhang quickly recalled the Aberrant he had fought yesterday.

"Sorry, it seems like a mistake. The situation was chaotic. He almost infiltrated the base, and I thought Nguyen Van Tuan sent him."

He had struck hard, and even if the person had survived, their condition would be dire. Chi Zhang added, "There's a B-rank healer on the base, bring him over."

"No need. Suchat can't move for now." Onyx's crisp voice came from behind them.

Chi Zhang and Cora turned to look, Onyx lazily leaning in the wheelchair, his smiling almond eyes sparkling. "Chionji, right? I have a suggestion. Since we're not enemies, there's no need for so many people to crowd around and discuss things here, right?"

"Who are you?" Chi Zhang's expression remained unchanged.

"Me? Just an ordinary researcher." Onyx smiled in response.

Cora glanced at him speechlessly, wondering why he was acting again.

Chi Zhang looked at Cora, recalling her mention of "companions," and nodded slightly. "Let's talk inside the base."

The group tidied up the scene a bit and headed towards the base gate.

Morgan warmly slung his arm around Cora's shoulder, switching from pinching her cheek to rubbing her head since he couldn't pinch her face anymore. "Little Junior Sister, you chased all the way here? Are you determined to marry him?"

Cora's beaming face instantly fell. "No way!"

Morgan winked at her. "I get it, I get it. You're shy. Look at Chi Zhang, thick-skinned as ever, never denying it."

Chi Zhang gave him a light glance. He couldn't understand why these people found the same joke funny for over ten years.

Behind them, Onyx's wheelchair suddenly stopped without warning.

"What's wrong with you?" Felix asked.

"Nothing."

Felix glanced at the crowd, seeing Cora being rubbed on the head and Chi Zhang standing tall. He then turned to look at Onyx, whose usually fake smiling face was now expressionless, faintly showing some of his youthful arrogance.

Felix watched and suddenly, his emotionless brain lit up with an idea.

"Huh." He let out a merciless laugh.

CHAPTER 29

A Harsh Journey

From the outside, the Saya base looked like a crouching beast. They used reinforced concrete for the bottom, and they concentrated on the main activity areas about thirty meters above ground. The overall structure was a dual purpose for offense and defense, resembling an impregnable fortress.

Crossing a few swaying iron suspension bridges, Cora reached the beast's gaping maw. The steel doors at the entrance of the base slowly opened, revealing the full view of Saya base.

Unexpectedly, the inside was bustling and lively, filled with signs of life. Children ran noisily on the streets, young women occasionally glanced up from their sewing, and strings of red chili peppers and fragrant smoked meat hung under the eaves of the buildings. Aberrants of various ranks walked the streets, calling out to each other as they prepared to go hunting.

Seeing Chi Zhang and the others return, people greeted them warmly.

"It's Uncle Chionji! Uncle Chionji is so awesome!" The children excitedly surrounded him.

"Back already? No trouble outside?" passing Aberrants casually asked.

"Auntie has breakfast ready. Go eat before your stomachs get upset." An elderly lady advised them kindly.

Though Chi Zhang was not talkative, the people in the base

greeted him with respectful nods, radiating a sense of closeness. The atmosphere here was entirely different from Deep Woods. Senior brothers and sisters mingled freely with others, chatting and laughing, reminding Cora of her days at the martial arts hall.

It had always been like this; Chi Zhang possessed a unique charisma. Anything he said or did naturally earned people's trust. Despite his young age, his mature demeanor and steady actions made him universally recognized as the "Senior Brother."

At the top of the base were several tall lookout towers. One of them had been scorched by artillery fire, partially collapsed, and a huge crane had fallen, creating a deep pit on the ground. Following Cora's gaze, Chi Zhang explained, "We've been clashing with Nguyen Van Tuan these past few days, with damage on both sides."

Another senior brother, Ewen Van, in his thirties, spat angrily, "Just thinking about it pisses me off. Lately, Nguyen has been attacking us like a mad dog, non-stop."

Nguyen Van Tuan has been frantically attacking Saya these past few days?

Cora paused, remembering the bluish-red crystal from the Hero's Banquet, suddenly feeling guilty. She confessed the entire story to them, guessing that Nguyen was blaming Saya for the stolen Level 3 zombie.

Everyone was speechless after hearing her. "Well, Little Junior Sister, letting us take the blame for you?" "Give us back our innocent Little Junior Sister!"

Morgan clutched his chest, pretending to be heartbroken. "Little Junior Sister, you diverted trouble our way and made us lose a lookout tower. Hey, Chi Zhang, aren't you going to do something about it?"

Chi Zhang didn't get sidetracked, making a fair and just decision. "If I remember correctly, you were the one who misfired and hit the lookout tower. Since you want me to handle it, you'll be in charge of the repairs."

"Bias, how can you be so biased, Senior Brother?" Morgan jumped in frustration.

"Haha, Morgan, are you stupid? You still want Chi Zhang to get justice for you?"

Having known each other for over a decade, Cora knew her senior brothers and sisters were just talkative and harmless, so she laughed along.

The front was noisy and lively, while the back was cold and quiet.

Justin tugged at his curly hair, turning it into a bird's nest, and grumbled unhappily, "Sister got snatched away..."

The more he thought about it, the more agitated he became. Clenching his fists, he shouted at the man in the wheelchair, "Hey you, my sister ran off with someone. Aren't you the most capable? Go get her back!"

"Did you hear that? Go get her back." Felix's two mechanical arms vividly mimicked a pulling motion behind him.

Onyx said, "Everyone, shut up."

It was breakfast time. Chi Zhang led them to the dining hall. Since they were all familiar with each other, there wasn't much formality. They grabbed their breakfast and sat wherever, just like in the martial arts hall, chatting casually.

"Senior Brother, how did you become Chionji?" Cora finally found the chance to ask.

"It's a long story." Chi Zhang explained slowly.

After leaving Yue Mountain Martial Arts Hall, Chi Zhang and the others hurried to District B to attend in the Azure Force assessment. Along the way, team members fell ill with fever one after another, forcing them to stop and rest. After everyone had recovered from their fever and awakened their miraculous abilities, the existence of Aberrants was no longer a secret, and the apocalypse inevitably descended. Zombies and ferocious beasts were everywhere, city traffic paralyzed, and order collapsed. Every step forward was exceptionally difficult.

As the captain, Chi Zhang had to consider their plans: continue heading north to join the Azure Force assessment as originally planned, or turn back to slowly develop their strength at Yue Mountain?

He quickly decided not to move forward. Chi Zhang had a premonition that the world had changed. The Alliance was undergoing a dramatic transformation, and joining the Azure Force no longer made sense. Since they had awakened their abilities, they should take control of their own fate.

"After returning to Yue Mountain, we saw twenty-three tombstones. Not knowing what had happened, we had to dig them up to check."

Chi Zhang still remembered his feelings. Dark clouds loomed overhead, and everyone's expressions were grim. Seeing the martial arts hall's trainees turned into zombies was hard for anyone to bear.

"Master Zhang, and the others..."

Cora choked up, finally having the chance to tell Chi Zhang what had happened at the martial arts hall, including how she killed her fellow students. "You did nothing wrong," Chi Zhang said. "If he were here, he wouldn't blame you."

Although there had always been rumors in the hall that Chi Zhang was Master Zhang's biological son, their relationship wasn't particularly close. Chi Zhang was always a role model for all the trainees, and the Master held him to especially high standards. Whenever others made mistakes, Chi Zhang would also get punished, making him the most frequently punished person.

Chi Zhang spoke in a deep voice, "When you arrived at the hall, he... was already dead, right?"

"Yes, Master had a hole in his chest." Cora meticulously described the scene from memory.

Chi Zhang remained silent, lost in thought.

"Senior Brother, what happened next?" Cora couldn't help but ask. "After that..."

After leaving Yue Mountain again, they continued to wander, passing many refuges and camps established by Aberrants, but never stayed. Until they passed Saya, where Chi Zhang saved a group of refugees from Deep Woods. His strength and reputation grew, and more and more people sought refuge under him, growing from dozens to hundreds, thousands... to today's tens of thousands.

In the apocalypse, strength reigned supreme. Chi Zhang's awakened S-rank rune ability was renowned, unbeaten. Under his leadership, Saya base grew increasingly strong, now capable of shaking Deep Woods's foundations, drawing the attention of tyrant Nacon and the three warlords.

Chi Zhang himself also became the fearsome "Chionji."

After recounting their journey, Chi Zhang looked down at Cora.

"And you? Why are you here?"

"I..."

Cora rarely hesitated. F777 had only one mission in Deep Woods: to assassinate Governor Ne Kon. But this matter was too shocking. Her senior brothers were already struggling against Nguyen Van Tuan's pursuit while protecting Saya Base and the refugees. They were in a difficult enough situation. Should she really say it and add to their troubles?

Cora found it hard to decide. She instinctively turned to Onyx for help, asking with her eyes, Should I tell them? Onyx ignored her, completely unmoved.

Thinking he didn't understand, Cora widened her eyes and gestured with her fingers. Onyx sighed inwardly. Finally, she knows to ask his opinion. He gave a slight nod.

Receiving his answer, Cora turned back and said honestly, "Senior Brother, I want to kill Ne Kon."

Everyone was stunned. "Damn, Little Junior Sister, you're crazier than Chi Zhang!"

"Your ambition is too big! What, are you planning to become queen?"

"Seriously, don't go through with it. If the Governor of District C33 dies, it will definitely cause a tremendous problem!"

Chi Zhang didn't respond immediately. His gaze shifted from the little interaction between the two, his brow furrowing.

The senior brothers and sisters were still chattering, trying to dissuade Cora. Chi Zhang gave a discreet nod to Ewen Van. He immediately stood up. "Hey Little Junior Sister, Rita doesn't know you're here yet. She's out on patrol. Let's go, I'll take you to her."

Senior Sister Rita is in Saya too?

Cora's eyes sparkled. "Okay."

As soon as Cora followed Ewen out, the atmosphere in the dining hall changed abruptly. The senior brothers and sisters who were laughing and talking just moments ago instantly put away their smiles, each turning around, some clenching fists, some folding arms, quietly surrounding Onyx and the other two.

Chi Zhang sat in the center, adjusting the sleeves of his robe, and unexpectedly spoke, "May I know your name?"

Onyx smiled calmly, "Onyx."

"Where are you from?" Chi Zhang continued to ask.

"Nowhere in particular. I come from the Arashi Research Institute," Onyx replied steadily.

No official registration, so he's a refugee? Chi Zhang's brow furrowed even more.

"Although Cora said you are her companions, there are some things I still need to confirm. If there's any offense, please forgive me."

"What do you mean?" Onyx raised an eyebrow.

"Exactly what you think. Cora has no family now. I... we have the responsibility to take care of her and can't let her be used to do dangerous things for dubious people."

Chi Zhang made a gesture, and a calm-looking woman stepped out from behind him. "Ruby Bai, A-rank Aberrant, with the ability of psychic lie detection."

"So, you want to interrogate me?" Onyx sneered.

"It's not an interrogation, just a simple inquiry," Chi Zhang said.

Onyx remained composed, slowly leaning back in his wheelchair. "Fine, go ahead."

CHAPTER 30

The War Began

Ruby stepped forward and sat opposite Onyx. Her pupils rippled, and her mental power turned into a trickling stream, carefully sensing the fluctuations in his emotions.

"When did you meet Cora?"

"Seven months ago."

"Was it your idea to assassinate Ne Kon?"

"No."

"Did you ever use persuasion, suggestion, or provocation to influence her thoughts?"

"Never."

Ruby frowned. Ordinary Aberrants facing psychic lie detection would show some nervousness or panic, but this man was like a still, undisturbed pool of water. She couldn't detect anything.

Was he too good at lying, deceiving himself? Or had he secretly built a mental barrier, blocking her detection?

Ruby steeled herself, releasing her power to the extreme. The trickling stream merged into a rushing river, planning to break through and forcibly invade Onyx's mind to extract information. However, as soon as she had this thought, she collided with a cold mental force. It was like a giant hammer pounding her mind, making her consciousness chaotic for two seconds.

"What's your purpose in traveling with Cora?" Ruby gritted her teeth and asked.

"No particular purpose. After she saved me, we traveled together." Onyx replied calmly.

"From start to finish, have you ever lied to her?" Ruby Bai's body swayed.

Onyx curved his lips, his eyes void of any smile. "How do you define 'lying'?"

Ruby Bai's cold sweat flowed more and more. She was supposed to be the interrogator, yet the man before her remained calm and unperturbed, while she felt like she was on the edge of a precipice. Her power was completely suppressed, unable to move. His mental power was clearly stronger than hers.

Ruby was shocked, and a terrifying thought rose in her mind: Could he be...

"Ruby, stop."

Chi Zhang sketched in the air, sending a calming spell to Ruby. She snapped back to reality, gasping for breath.

"Are you S-rank?" Chi Zhang asked coldly.

"Exactly." Onyx replied with a smile.

As soon as he spoke, two powerful S-rank pressures were simultaneously released, clashing head-on. The onlookers' expressions changed, and they retreated, avoiding the center of the confrontation. Tables, chairs, and dishes clattered to the ground.

In the chaotic scene, Felix, the only one unharmed, complained, "If you want to fight, do it outside. Can't you consider others?"

Chi Zhang and Onyx paused and retracted their powers.

Chi Zhang knew he couldn't get anything out of Onyx, so he turned to the other two. He glanced at the nonchalant Felix, who continued eating, and fixed his calm gaze on Damian.

Damian wanted to cry: He knew it! Among F777, he was the weakest and always the one to be squeezed for information.

At the critical moment, Onyx cleared his throat, drawing everyone's attention. "May I say a few words?"

Chi Zhang nodded slightly. "Go ahead."

"You oppose Cora's idea out of concern. Why not seriously consider the feasibility of it?"

"What? Assassinating the Governor? How could that be workable?" Morgan shouted.

Onyx smiled. "From Cora's perspective, it seems like a fantasy, but what if... we consider it from Saya's standpoint?"

Morgan and the others were stunned, while Chi Zhang's eyes flashed.

Onyx's next words seemed almost hypnotic. "Saya Base has grown to its current scale and has long become a major threat to Ne Kon. You will inevitably clash with Deep Woods. Passive defense will only get you beaten continuously."

"Chionji, you are ambitious. Are you willing to live under Ne Kon's shadow, waiting for the day he attacks you on a whim? Since you've come this far, why not take the initiative? If you eliminate Ne Kon, all of District C33 will be yours."

Everyone had the same thought: This guy is definitely crazy! But on further thought, while his suggestion was shocking, it... it made some sense!

Chi Zhang remained silent. He didn't expect his deepest secret to be revealed by this person in one sentence.

Why didn't he stay at others' bases? Why didn't he continue the Azure Force assessment after awakening his power? Going even further back, why was his conflict with Master Zhang so deep? The root cause was their ideological conflict.

Chi Zhang couldn't understand why, with Master Zhang's capabilities, he would choose to live humbly in Mount Yue, running a small martial arts hall. Master Zhang always accused him of being overly ambitious, arrogant, and greedy, always striving to stand out.

Onyx said meaningfully, "So, from a long-term perspective, Cora is clearing the way for Saya's bright future. Instead of stopping her, join forces with her to take down Deep Woods."

Everyone thought: This guy is terrifying, too good at persuasion!

Sure, here is the revised translation with correct names:

In the Saya Base, Ewen Van led Cora along the regular patrol route looking for people. After walking for about ten minutes, a figure with a high ponytail, standing tall and sharp, appeared in front of them.

"Senior Sister!" Cora recognized the person and rushed over like a little bird. Rita turned around in surprise, and when she saw Cora, she beamed with joy. "Cora? Is it really you? How did you find this place?"

The two of them held hands and jumped around, chatting for a while to catch up. It was only then that Cora noticed a girl standing beside Rita, curiously staring at her. Feeling a bit embarrassed, she scratched her head and asked softly, "Senior Sister, who are they...?"

Rita's expression turned stony. "They escaped from the 'Rose Amy.' Hmph, I've never seen a place so filthy and vile."

Rose Amy? What is that?

Cora was stunned.

Deep Woods, an ordinary apartment.

Yuui sat by the bed, bare-faced, with her long hair tied casually, propping her chin up as she dozed off, with faint dark circles under her eyes.

Suchat leaned against the headboard, his fingers curved over his knees, silently observing her. As a popular star of Felalakas, Yuui always paid attention to her image and rarely appeared so unkempt. She had a small mind and a bad temper. If someone outshined her at an event, she would sulk for several nights.

Suchat had spent the first seventeen years of his life in the Rainy Forest and had never seen someone so contradictory. When he first started following Yuui, she often scolded him for being "clumsy" or "dull-headed." Despite being six feet three inches tall, he would often lower his head in confusion at her reprimands. However, he never thought Yuui was "bad." After all, when he was at his lowest, she was the only one willing to take him in and even paid him a generous salary. To Suchat, no matter how "bad" she was, Yuui was good.

Although Suchat excelled at stealth and reconnaissance, he had no experience in spying girls. Surprised, he locked eyes with the suddenly awake Yuui and was caught red-handed. He paused, awkwardly looking away.

Yuui's lips curved slightly. "Oh, were you sneaking a look at me? Did you get mesmerized? Do I look good?"

"No," Suchat immediately denied, "...you should wash your face."

Yuui almost choked, "You know, you really..."

At that moment, the terminal beeped. Yuui looked down and saw a voice request from Ellyn the Wild Rose. She answered, and the sound of roaring artillery came through, followed by Ellyn's hoarse voice.

"Are you still at the apartment? I need a favor." "Yes, what do you need?"

"I have a few friends who have nowhere to go temporarily. Can they hide out with you?"

Yuui quickly thought it over. Cora had already informed her about the situation at Saya. They had originally planned to head to the base once Suchat recovered a bit, and then they would vacate the apartment.

Yuui reminded Ellyn, "Sure, but remember, this place's address has been compromised."

People from Miêu Luân had followed Rao Cheung to the apartment building before. It was no longer considered completely safe.

Ellyn responded, "That's fine. We just need a place to stay for a couple of days."

Yuui waited at the apartment entrance. About an hour later, Ellyn led four or five girls across the street and into the hallway. They had injuries on their faces and bodies, with Ellyn being the most severe. Her intact left arm was bleeding profusely, and the hand holding the cannon kept trembling.

Yuui quickly fetched medicine to bandage them up. After a simple treatment, Ellyn stood up again. "Wait here; I need to find a few more sisters." There were still two people from the photos Rao Cheung had given her that hadn't been rescued.

"Ellyn, I'm not afraid. I'll go with you!" The young girl with brown skin grabbed Ellyn's arm. "Masha, you don't have any abilities. It's too dangerous to go out," Ellyn shook her head, insisting on going alone.

Yuui sighed helplessly, "You're injured. Isn't it more dangerous to go alone?"

Ellyn. "It's fine, I can still fight."

"Alright, alright, I'll go with you," Yuui said. "You?" Ellyn raised an eyebrow.

"Are you looking down on me? I'm still an A-rank. I'll assist you. The two of us working together is better than you going alone, right?" Yuui had spent enough time with Cora that she had picked up some of her boldness. If reasoning didn't work, she'd use force. She stepped onto a stool, cleared her throat, and loudly chanted, "Sisters, raise your cups together, break through the mist and rise again! Fight the heavens, fight the earth, fight until we're unstoppable. Let me turn the world upside down again!"

The apartment filled with dark mist, and countless blades flew around. This was Yuui's new combat style, transitioning from pure support to a controller with both defensive and offensive capabilities. She could attack or retreat, giving her some combat ability.

The lyrics, though... had nothing to do with elegance or romance. They were ridiculously cheesy, but as long as they worked, it was fine.

A slight noise came from behind.

Yuui turned around to see Suchat, wrapped in a jacket with bandages around his abdomen, looking at her with a complicated expression. With her current appearance, no one would associate her with the former "sweet songstress" of Felalakas, even if she were thrown into the central square of Felalakas.

"..." Yuui awkwardly lowered her leg.

"Alright, you can come with me," Ellyn agreed after witnessing her abilities.

Just as they were about to move, Masha grabbed Ellyn again, "Ellyn, actually I..."

Miêu Luân's Headquarters.

Rao carried some medical supplies to the backyard. The "pets" here were those Miêu Luân had not yet tired of. Once he lost interest, he would send the conscripted "Rose Amy" members to various private camps under the guise of "resource sharing."

Sadly, only the pets discarded by Miêu Luân had a slim chance of escaping.

Rao opened the courtyard door and roughly counted; a few more rooms were empty.

She walked to the right, where she saw a girl she had met a couple of days ago, covered in blood, awkwardly bandaging her wounds. The girl struggled to reach with one hand and stopped in frustration.

Rao stepped forward, took the gauze, and skillfully treated the wounds. "Let me do it."

The girl quietly looked down at her. The woman in front of her was beautiful, with faint lines at the corners of her eyes that did nothing to mar her beauty, instead adding a touch of vulnerable charm. Unfortunately, there were dark scars on her shoulders and wrists, marring this perfection.

Rao took her time, carefully stitching up all the wounds, snipping the threads, and checking them. Everything was tidy.

"You did a great job. Are you a doctor?" the girl asked softly.

"No," Rao paused, her gaze momentarily softening, "but my husband was. He was the best surgeon."

They both knew the "husband" she referred to was definitely not Miêu Luân.

"My name is Marie."

"Rao Cheung."

"I was captured. I didn't join the Rose Amy willingly." Marie clenched her fists, her expression filled with hatred.

"Many people here weren't," Rao sighed lightly.

Marie was silent for a moment. "But I heard others say you volunteered."

Rao stiffened. "I did."

Marie's expression showed confusion. "But the way you spoke about your husband sounded so happy. I don't believe you volunteered. Do you have a purpose?"

Rao did not answer. "If you want to escape, I can help you..."

Marie interrupted her. "No, I won't run."

Rao looked up in surprise, seeing a determined belief in Marie's eyes.

"My grandfather was a brave mercenary. He taught me you have to avenge your own grievances," Marie said, quoting a local saying from West Street. "I cannot flee in shame. I must kill Miêu Luân and avenge myself."

"Shh." Rao quickly covered her mouth, silently pointing outside the wall. The place was filled with Aberrants; they had to speak carefully.

Marie lowered her voice. "You have companions, don't you? You've been contacting people outside, helping those girls' escape."

Rao frowned slightly. "I used to, but now I'm restricted. That path is closed."

Marie blinked, assessing her credibility, then dropped a bombshell. "If you can find powerful allies, I can help you contact them. I'm an Aberrant."

Rao was stunned. "Didn't they test you when you were brought here? Only ordinary people can enter Miêu Luân's quarters."

Marie clasped her hands together, a faint thread of mental power seeping out. "My level is very low, only E-class, so the machines can't detect it. But I have a twin sister, and our power is telepathy. We can know each other's thoughts within a certain range."

Rao's brow furrowed with concern. "West Street has been chaotic lately. Are you sure your sister is still in Deep Woods?"

As they spoke, a thunderous noise erupted outside. The city-wide announcement in District C33 was triggered, and the General issued a new law.

"From this day on, an extermination order is issued against all refugees fleeing to Saya. The United Guard, Imperial Guard, and Iron Hawk Squad are to conduct a sweep. The entire Deep Woods district will be mobilized. Spare no effort, eliminate the rebels within three days."

Ne Kon finally lost his patience and officially declared war on Saya.

CHAPTER 31

Lethal Acts

On the desolate and barren lifeline, a force of over 3,000 Aberrants marched towards Saya in a grand procession. Besides Deep Woods' regular garrison, this joint force included over 800 high-level Aberrants (Class C and above). Among them, the United Guard, Ne Kon's personal bodyguard, had nearly 100 members fully deployed. The Imperial Guard, led by Mục Tân, was composed of about 200 conscripted soldiers, while the remaining 500 came from Nguyen Van Tuan's Iron Hawk Squad.

Ironically, the Aberrants recruited during the previous Heroic Banquet were also included. Mục Tân, having pocketed the expensive Class 3 crystal admission fee, wanted to preserve his strength and sent them out as cannon fodder to "ease the General's troubles."

All the residents of Saya took refuge in the bunkers beneath the base. Chi Zhang convened an emergency defense meeting.

"How many Aberrants do we have on the base?" Onyx asked.

"About 1,500, but less than 300 are high-level Aberrants," Chi Zhang replied.

Recently, the two had been at odds, but now they were calmly discussing strategies. Unfortunately, 300 against 800 seemed like an uphill battle no matter how one looked at it.

Chi Zhang and Ewen Van discussed the city's defense layout. Considering Onyx's injured leg, Chi Zhang spoke to him while deliberately lowering his head. Tall and broad-shouldered, Chi

Zhang's black robe made him appear even more slender and upright.

Onyx remained silent for a moment before pulling a cane from his space and standing up, matching Chi Zhang's height.

Felix glanced at him. "You look like a peacock showing off its feathers."

This guy never enjoyed looking up to talk to people and often asked others to lower themselves. Now, he actually stood up himself.

Onyx coldly retorted, "You seem quite idle. If you have nothing better to do, optimize the surveillance."

Merlin, the detection Aberrant behind Chi Zhang, stepped forward. "Uh, Brother Felix, I'm familiar with the surveillance. Let me show you."

Felix Lucas snorted and followed Merlin out.

Onyx lowered his gaze to the 3D projection map and fell into deep thought. Given the current situation, the outcome of this war didn't look optimistic. Chi Zhang turned his head and calmly asked, "Do you have any suggestions for defense?"

As Maya's leader, Chi Zhang was trusted because he wasn't stubborn or dictatorial. Despite being only twenty-five, Chi Zhang was steady and humble, open to suggestions and willing to adopt good advice.

Onyx pondered for a moment before slowly shaking his head. "We can't hold."

"Given Deep Woods' firepower, holding the line is impossible, but winning isn't out of the question," Onyx continued.

"Big brother, isn't that contradictory? If we can't hold, how can we win?" Morgan was puzzled.

Chi Zhang remained composed. "Explain your plan."

Onyx smiled slightly. "Have you read the ancient military tactics? 'Capture the ringleader to catch the bandits.' If we take down Ne Kon, the joint forces will fall into chaos."

Chi Zhang's deep voice hit the mark, "Your focus is always on Ne Kon, not on Saya."

"But that doesn't conflict with helping Saya win," Onyx didn't deny it, calmly analyzing, "To win, we must achieve victory through unconventional means. Our biggest advantage is that Ne Kon is unaware of Saya's true strength."

Ne Kon might be confident about suppressing the rebellion, but he miscalculated one thing: Saya currently had four Class S Aberrants.

On the eve of the battle, Cora Thornton tried to contact Yuui, but couldn't get through. She then called Suchat.

"How's your injury?"

"Charles just treated it again, it's almost healed," Suchat's voice sounded normal, "Do you need me to come help?"

"Not yet. Stay put." Saya base was on lockdown, and the roads out of town were filled with the joint forces. Moving now would be too dangerous.

"Shifu asked me to apologize to you on his behalf."

"No problem."

Chi Zhang had injured Suchat accidentally and had explained that if Suchat had any issues, he could come to the base for proper treatment.

Cora instructed the three to stay in the apartment until the chaos of Saya settled. She then asked, "Where's Yuui? I can't reach her."

Suchat was uncharacteristically silent for a moment. "She went out with Ellyn to rescue people, probably didn't see it."

Shortly after hanging up, Cora received a call from Yuui. As soon as she answered, the sound of intense artillery fire erupted from the other end. Yuui shouted roughly over the noise, "Ellyn, they're here! Retreat! Hey, Cora?"

What are they doing? Cora was surprised.

Yuui briefly explained the situation with the Rose Amy, and Cora informed her of the plan to avoid coming to Saya for now. After exchanging information, Yuui sighed, "I was going to tell you, don't cancel the apartment yet. I might be delayed a couple of days."

"Stay safe," Cora advised. "You too," Yuui replied.

Merlin led Felix Lucas through the base. As they passed a factory, Felix Lucas paused.

"What's this place?"

"Oh, it used to produce engineering vehicles and cranes, but they're all broken now."

"What's broken?"

"Seems like a programming issue, so they were all scrapped." Merlin wasn't too sure about the specifics.

Felix's wheelchair rolled into the workshop. He glanced around, and his icy blue eyes glowed with a strange light. All the control panels of the mechanical vehicles lit up, and the codes on the panels rapidly changed. A few minutes later, the engines roared to life, and the abandoned vehicles started moving in unison.

"I don't think they're broken," Felix said matter-of-factly.

Dense steel machinery surrounded the two tiny humans, but Felix Lucas remained calm and unruffled. Merlin...

Merlin was trembling, staring wide-eyed.

Cora, Onyx, and Chi Zhang waited in the observation tower. Felix joined them. "I've reinforced the defense system, but some facilities are too outdated to be effective. Also, look at this."

He motioned with his finger, projecting the screen image in front of them.

On the lifeline dozens of miles away, massive and cumbersome siege engines advanced slowly: large battering rams with metal heads, trebuchets loaded with cannons, spruced ladder trucks, long-range cannons, and howitzers...

Occasionally, zombies and fierce beasts would escape along the way, only to be instantly shattered. The joint forces marched forward as if on flat ground.

Felix zoomed in on one camera, revealing Nguyen Van Tuan and Mục Tân in full armor, leading to the front of the formation. In the middle of the ranks, a middle-aged man with a stern face sat atop an armored tank. He wore the gold-edged uniform of Deep Woods' highest ruler, his upturned eyebrows, hooked nose, and fierce, gloomy eyes glaring at them through the camera as if he was staring right at them.

Cora was shocked when she saw his face. Ne Kon was commanding the battle? Not only that, he was brazenly sitting in such a conspicuous place, as if daring someone to assassinate him. Was he that strong, or did he have some hidden support?

"Is Ne Kon an Aberrant?" Cora asked, puzzled.

Chi Zhang slowly shook his head, "Not sure. I've never faced him directly, and no information has ever leaked from the Unified Palace."

Cora's expression grew increasingly serious. No matter what schemes or backing Ne Kon had for attacking Saya, she was determined to kill him.

The four Class S Aberrants, either sitting or standing, waited side by side at the top of the base. The wind carried the news of battle from afar, and even the air seemed to have a strange, murderous aura.

In the evening, the joint forces finally reached the outskirts of Saya Base. "Boom—" A long-range missile fired, marking the start of the war.

"We can't let the siege engines get close," Chi Zhang pressed the communicator, issuing a deep command. "Morgan, move out."

Deep Woods' military might be renowned throughout the alliance, and no matter how sturdy Saya Base was, it couldn't withstand such relentless bombardment.

Morgan led a team of high-level Aberrants, taking a roundabout route to use their abilities to sabotage the siege engines. Explosions echoed continuously. Cora and Chi Zhang donned their hoods and, under the cover of the thick smog, leaped off the city walls, rushing towards Ne Kon.

Cora gripped her Serpent Spear, her entire body enveloped in Aberrant energy, cutting through the enemies like a hot knife through butter.

"Mighty God of All Directions, make me natural... The evil dissipates, and the Dao remains."

Chi Zhang supported her from behind, his powerful "Heaven Purification Mantra" painting the sky, causing dark clouds to surge and the earth to tremble. Thousands of talismans rained down, striking the Aberrants and causing them to fall, writhing in pain with burned skin.

Cora successfully broke through to the armored tank, just a short distance from Ne Kon. Ne Kon's gaze was icy, and he neither dodged nor flinched, merely raised his hand. The United Guard immediately fired their cannons at Cora.

Cora leaped high, gripping her spear with both hands, and aimed it at Ne Kon's head. "Boom!" A cannonball flew from an angle, hitting the spear and sending Cora flying.

She caught herself with one hand, her knee bent, barely stopping her momentum. She grabbed her spear again and charged at Ne Kon. At that moment, the tank beneath her shook violently, causing her to lose balance and fall.

A chill ran down her spine. Why? Every time she tried to kill Ne Kon, she always "just missed." Was her luck that bad?

Chi Zhang supported her back, his tall figure moving past her. He quickly formed a seal, and a Seven Star Sword with a "Purification Talisman" flew straight out. As it neared Ne Kon, the sword suddenly vibrated violently, grazing his scalp and leaving him unscathed.

Even Shifu missed? Cora and Chi Zhang exchanged a surprised look. This wasn't right!

They had intended to strike quickly and retreat, but their successive failures left them in place too long, and they were soon surrounded. Dozens of high-level Aberrants closed in, with a short, fierce-looking man stepping forward, glaring at them.

"The leader of the United Guard, Juramani, is an A-Class Aberrant but with strength close to S-Class. His ability is spatial distortion," Chi Zhang said quickly. "The others are easier to deal with. Take him out first."

Cora glanced at Ne Kon from a distance, shook her spear, and faced Juramani head-on.

High-angle cannons continued to hit various parts of the base, causing buildings to collapse with loud crashes. The joint forces' firepower was overwhelming, and progress on Cora's side was worrying. The survival hope for Saya was shrinking.

Nguyen Van Tuan, bloodthirsty and excited, continuously commanded the siege engines to bombard the high-voltage iron net behind Saya. Once the lifeline was broken, thousands of zombies would flood in, and the residents hiding in the underground bunkers would be slaughtered.

Onyx observed the battlefield from above. On Ne Kon's side, Cora and Chi Zhang were still engaged in a fierce battle, unlikely to end soon. Meanwhile, the zombies, drawn by Nguyen Van Tuan's indiscriminate bombardment, were gathering around the iron net, their numbers increasing, including several noticeable Class 3 zombies.

Frowning, he thought for a moment, then took out a sealed injector from his space. Felix Lucas glanced at him but refrained from making a snide remark.

Onyx's expression remained unchanged as he injected the fluid into his right leg. A slightly numbing liquid flowed into his bloodstream, followed by excruciating pain. The cells in his damaged leg, influenced by radiation, began to renew and activate, reaching a peak of activity.

"I'll handle Nguyen Van Tuan. You deal with the rest," Onyx said, pushing himself up with no external support and standing up from his wheelchair.

The high-voltage iron net was on the verge of collapsing under the relentless attacks.

Nguyen Van Tuan's expression revealed a hint of madness. Refugees were like straw, and the masses like pigs and dogs. He didn't care about their lives. As long as he could win and defeat Chionji, he would relish in razing the city.

"Whoosh—" A crossbow bolt flew from behind, lightly aiming at him.

Nguyen Van Tuan dodged, glancing in that direction. Through the smog, a figure slowly emerged, and his gaze gradually moved up. He saw a handsome man in a trench coat.

Where did this fool come from? Nguyen Van Tuan glanced disdainfully and ordered his men, "Take him out."

The Aberrants of the Iron Hawk Squad set up their high-caliber sniper cannons, ready to fire. Suddenly, a sharp pain cut through their minds like a knife, causing them to clutch their heads and wail. The cannon muzzles turned uncontrollably, firing towards Nguyen Van Tuan's position.

"What are you doing!" Teammates cursed amid the thick smoke.

A magnetic, light laugh echoed around them. "Lord Nguyen, you're still so impatient, just like in Da Nang."

Da Nang?

Nguyen Van Tuan's eyes narrowed dangerously. "How do you know about Da Nang? Are you Chionji?"

Bold indeed, daring to face him alone.

Onyx's smile stiffened, but responded nonchalantly, "Of course I know. Thanks to you, we got a fine Class 3 crystal."

"Sold it to some sucker for a million Alliance credits. Lord Nguyen, you're Saya's benefactor. Should I thank you in person?"

His words hit a sore spot, and Nguyen Van Tuan instantly flew into a rage. "Blow him to pieces!"

Amid the roaring cannons, Onyx ran swiftly around the iron net, dodging and rolling. Occasionally, he would pause at certain points. Aberrants in Nguyen Van Tuan's team lost control one after another, either collapsing unconscious or turning their cannons on their comrades.

A psychic Aberrant? Nguyen Van Tuan sensed something was amiss. No matter, he'd still die by his hand.

Nguyen Van Tuan focused his mental power, not needing any firearms. With a flick of his fingers, psychic bullets shot out. Onyx dodged awkwardly as Nguyen Van Tuan relentlessly pursued, gradually isolating him and cornering him against the iron net.

Onyx's back slammed against the net, the zombies outside eagerly reaching for him. He sighed, "Oh my, Lord Nguyen, you're still so careless after all these years."

"Facing death, and you still have the nerve to talk back," Nguyen Van Tuan snorted coldly, spraying a hail of bullets to turn Onyx into a sieve.

Onyx smiled faintly. "Carelessness can get you killed."

The high-voltage iron net finally collapsed under the strain. Dozens of three-meter-tall evolved zombies roared in, absorbing the hail of bullets. Zombies felt no physical pain. They roared in anger, their expressions utterly enraged.

Nguyen Van Tuan's pupils contracted. Class 3 zombies typically had territorial instincts. How could so many gather in one place?

However, the more terrifying fact was that the zombies ignored Onyx, rushing past him to attack Nguyen Van Tuan. Nguyen Van Tuan desperately tried to fend them off with bullets. Suddenly, his body froze as a sharp, cold psychic force pierced through his mental barrier, disabling his abilities.

Before being completely torn apart by the zombies, Nguyen Van Tuan looked at the man standing leisurely before him in disbelief. How... was this possible?

Onyx took a couple of steps forward, nonchalantly finishing Nguyen Van Tuan with his spirit crossbow. Zombies were mindless creatures, but evolved zombies were not.

CHAPTER 32

On Fire

After Nguyen Van Tuan was torn apart, Onyx raised his rapid-fire crossbow, aiming at the remaining members of the Iron Eagle Squad. Level 3 zombies possess a certain level of intelligence, which allows them to control their behavior simply through mental power, such as encircling, feigning surrender, or retreating.

With his trench coat forming a graceful arc, Onyx walked forward with unhurried steps, standing amidst the monsters, one hand in his pocket exuding a gang leader's aura, followed by a dozen Level 3 zombie henchmen.

Onyx motioned with his fingers towards the Iron Eagle Squad, and the zombies immediately pounced fiercely.

The artillery team near the iron net panicked, abandoning the catapults and fleeing in all directions. The Level bit those who ran too slowly in the neck. 3 zombies falling to the ground as their necks were crunched and shattered.

"Nguyen Van Tuan is dead, and the United Army's defeat is inevitable!" Onyx shouted. At such a moment, he had to demoralize the enemy. His clear voice, amplified by mental power, echoed across the battlefield.

The United Army's formation noticeably faltered, but unfortunately, it quickly regained order. There was more than one warlord on the battlefield. The cunning Mục Tân took over command, identifying Saya's weakness and changing tactics to focus fire on the base.

After clearing the field, Onyx looked off into the distance in another direction - where Cora and Ne Kon were.

The defenders mounted countless scaling ladders on the city walls, giant battering rams rolled down the roads, and metal hammers smashed against Saya's foundation. Stones and dirt fell from the ceilings of the bunkers where the residents hid, huddled together, silently praying.

"No time left. I'll take out the catapults first!" Morgan shouted as he ran.

"Kid, get back here!" Ewen couldn't hold Morgan back, who dodged and rushed into the heart of the United Army.

Morgan navigated through the smog, throwing precise fireballs at the siege engines. Everywhere he passed, flames erupted. Faster, faster... Morgan urged himself, moving swiftly.

Several rows of howitzers suddenly appeared in front of him. Morgan's eyes lit up, and he concentrated all his energy, forming a giant fireball larger than his body, just about to throw it — A cannonball flew from behind, landing at his feet, exploding with a thunderous roar.

As Saya Base was about to be overwhelmed by artillery fire, a high suspension bridge suddenly lowered.

"Clang—clang—"

A dense array of steel machines charged out from the base— engineering vehicles, bulldozers, cranes, new tractors... stretching as far as the eye could see. More terrifyingly, they had basic AI modules, fearlessly crashing into the scaling ladders and battering rams ahead.

"Boom—"

A crane, like a fierce beast, swung its arm and knocked down the scaling ladders on the city walls, its sturdy tracks crushing them mercilessly!

"Bang—"

Hundreds of unmanned bulldozers charged through, carrying large amounts of explosives, launching suicide attacks on the catapults and missiles. Mercenaries nearby couldn't escape in time and were blown away, while more deadly weapons continued to emerge from Saya Base.

What... are these things?! Mercenaries shouted in despair.

The major battlefield's situation reversed in an instant, with the United Army on the defensive and Saya gaining the upper hand!

In the base's watchtower, Felix stood surrounded by six mechanical arms, his eyes closed, silver hair dancing on his shoulders, his entire body enveloped in layers of binary code. He seemed like a giant ancient tree made of data, each branch executing different commands, simultaneously controlling all the steel vehicles with his powers.

Once, in the pitch-black depths of the Sea of Death, Felix was the Pluto who ruled over prisoners' lives with the Record of Crimes. Now, the mechanical barrier he built became Saya's strongest defense line.

Ne Kon looked up at the higher place, his expression serious and solemn. Unexpectedly, besides Chionji, Saya had a second S-class Aberrant!

"Mục Tân, send snipers, take him out immediately!" Ne Kon's stern command came through the earpiece. Mục Tân, commanding the siege, quickly organized a team of high-level Aberrant snipers, their red aiming lasers flickering across Felix's face.

Merlin, next to Felix, was anxious. Gritting his teeth, he rushed forward, spreading his arms to shield him.

Merlin was merely a support Aberrant, his primary role being surveillance and enemy detection. Now, with all of Saya's offensive Aberrants fighting, he could only watch nervously. Felix was crucial and couldn't afford to be harmed.

Snipers locked onto their target, about to pull the trigger.

Suddenly, a group of Level 3 zombies leaped at their positions, their landing precise. "Roar—" With the zombies' roars, the snipers' positions turned into a bloody mess, their attack completely disrupted.

In the chaotic battle, Onyx quickly passed by, saving the situation. However, he didn't stay on the major battlefield, disrupting the sniper's attack before continuing to charge forward, disappearing into the mist.

At the rear of the United Army, Ne Kon sat in the commander's seat of an armored tank, coldly controlling the situation.

Cora's snake spear fiercely struck at Juramani's throat. He caught the spearhead with his palms, forcefully pulling it down, locking it with his elbow. Then he wrapped his legs around the spear shaft, hanging upside down, immobilizing Cora's attack.

Cora's eyes sharpened. His moves... were the Ghost Fist techniques that Shifu had mentioned!

Ghost Fist, originating from Deep Woods, is an ancient martial art known for its power and agility. In combat, practitioners use their fists, legs, elbows, and knees as sharp weapons, moving like spiders. Therefore, Ghost Fist is also called "Eight-Armed Boxing."

Mastering Ghost Fist, Juramani was clearly a formidable opponent in close combat.

"Buzz —"

The air around vibrated as Chi Zhang's Five Thunder Curse flew towards Juramani. This curse had immense killing power; a hit was fatal. Suddenly, several invisible distortions appeared around Juramani, forming three or four black holes that absorbed the curse entirely.

Juramani's ability, "Space Distortion," naturally countered Chi Zhang's spells, requiring preparation time. Realizing this, Chi Zhang switched to a longsword from his waist, moving to close combat, teaming up with Cora.

As the three fought fiercely, a group of Level 3 zombies suddenly jumped from behind Ne Kon, claws aimed at his face! At such close range, the agile evolved zombies missed, their dark eyes showing confusion.

Through the pervasive smog, a pair of long legs slowly emerged.

Onyx looked up at Ne Kon, a thoughtful expression in his eyes.

Cora, surprised to see him, didn't have time to wonder when his right leg had recovered, turning back to fight Juramani.

Onyx flashed to Chi Zhang's side, blurting, "I'll handle this. You go defend the city."

Chi Zhang looked back, seeing Mục Tân adjusting formations against Felix. With his mobility limited and focus divided in controlling the machines, Felix couldn't hold on alone. Nodding, Chi Zhang swiftly retreated.

Onyx's peach blossom eyes held no humor, staring intently at Ne Kon. He sensed a faint mental power from him. Undoubtedly, Ne Kon was an Aberrant, appearing confident on the battlefield, assured that none could kill him.

Onyx raised his rapid-fire crossbow, firing a test shot. As expected, missile fragments deflected the bolt from nowhere before reaching Ne Kon.

Onyx squinted, rapidly assessing the situation. A mystic Aberrant? It seemed to be the complex causality type. Without identifying the "cause," he couldn't affect Ne Kon, the "effect."

He abandoned attacking Ne Kon, directing the Level 3 zombies to assault other Aberrants, seeking a breakthrough opportunity.

On the other side, Cora abandoned her snake spear, facing Juramani bare-handed. Fighting an opponent skilled in Ghost Fist, weapons would only become a burden and might even be twisted away by his abilities.

After exchanging hundreds of moves with Juramani, she identified his weakness.

The strength and lethality of Ghost Fist were its strengths, but also its weaknesses. Because of its emphasis on power, the speed naturally slowed down. The harsh force of each punch left little room for variation between moves.

Cora adjusted her breathing and entered a state of free fighting. She moved quickly around Juramani, no longer meeting him head-on but moving nimbly, finding opportunities to kick, punch, and throw him at his weak joints. Her mental power continuously revitalized within the magnetic field, using every inch of her muscles to the fullest. Her feet barely touched the ground, her moves were unpredictable, so fast they left afterimages, making it impossible for Juramani's "eight arms" to hit her.

Juramani fell into a disadvantage but remained unflustered, seizing the gap between Cora's two attacks. He raised his knee! Hooking her neck!

Just as planned! Deliberately exposing a flaw, Cora was delighted, mimicking his move exactly. She lifted her knee, thrusting upwards with greater force, dismantling Juramani's attack. His balance disrupted, his eyes widened in fury as he fell backward. Cora spun and leapt up, landing heavily on top of him, her knees pinning him down. She twisted her hands sharply — Juramani's head was severed, instantly killed!

"Crack—" There seemed to be an invisible fracture in the wind. The moment Juramani died, Ne Kon's expression changed dramatically, and he opened the top hatch, attempting to escape.

Onyx, who had been watching him closely, keenly sensed the loosening of the "cause" on Ne Kon. His mental power shot out! Ne Kon's body stiffened suddenly, his consciousness filled with excruciating pain, unable to escape into the tank in time. Simultaneously, Onyx shouted loudly, "Cora!"

Cora's head snapped up, locking eyes with him for 0.0001 seconds. With no verbal exchange, she understood Onyx's intention—seize the opportunity.

She sprinted with all her might, leaping towards the armored tank where Ne Kon was. Her right hand transformed back into a snake spear, which she aimed at Ne Kon's back, thrusting it down fiercely!

Time seemed to slow down. In Ne Kon's terrified expression, the spearhead pierced through his uniform, bulletproof vest, skin, and muscle... just as it was about to penetrate his bones and reach his heart, the "causality" on Ne Kon shifted again. Cora's feet suddenly slipped, stumbling back two steps, her spear's momentum lost. Ne Kon seized the chance to dive into the tank.

"What?!"

For the third time, she failed? She wanted to curse out loud!

After Ne Kon disappeared from the command position, the armored tank hastily retreated, abandoning the main United Army forces and fleeing. Onyx quickly approached Cora, who stood dejectedly with her head down, stabbing the ground repeatedly with her snake spear in frustration. Onyx looked at the top of her head, reached out, and ruffled her hair. "It's not your fault." Cora looked up at him with a hurt expression.

Onyx smiled inwardly, using his slender fingers to wipe the dirt off her face. "A good girl like you, always ending up dirty." He said, "Ne Kon has a mystic ability. Until it's broken, even you can't kill him."

"Mystic?" Cora was stunned. So, her and Chi Zhang's repeated failures weren't their fault but because of the influence of his ability?

"Yes, I have a rough understanding. Let's finish this battle first, and I'll explain when we get back," Onyx said.

Chi Zhang arrived at the major battlefield, his black Taoist robe resembling a death reaper harvesting life. His Purifying Heaven and Earth Curse erupted, changing the color of the heavens and earth, scattering the regrouped snipers once more.

With Chi Zhang and Felix controlling the field from above and below, plus the siege engines being destroyed by successive sneak attacks and suicide bombings, the United Army was defeated overwhelmingly.

Mục Tân withdrew his gaze from the rear, making a decisive call. "Retreat."

Eamon shouted incredulously, "Uncle, we're about to win. Why retreat?"

Mục Tân's face was grim. "Win? Which eye of yours sees victory? Nguyen Van Tuan is dead. The general has fled. If I don't leave now, am I supposed to take the blame for this defeat?"

Mục Tân spoke coldly and walked away from the battlefield without looking back.

Eamon glared furiously ahead. This United Army operation was something he had begged Mục Tân to join. If he couldn't seize this opportunity to make a name for himself, when would he ever rise?

A black-robed figure flashed by, killing a large group of mercenaries with a single wave of his hand. Under the hood, half of his face was visible, with sharp eyebrows and starry eyes, exuding heroic spirit.

Chi Zhang. Eamon gritted his teeth, calling out this name in his heart.

If there was anyone Eamon hated most in his life, it was Chi Zhang.

The deep-seated hatred stemmed from nothing more than jealousy. Chi Zhang, about his age, had been the senior brother at Mount Yue Martial Arts School since birth. He was stronger in martial arts, more popular. Even though Master Zhang often scolded and beat him, his gaze always lingered on Chi Zhang when no one was around.

Family, friendship, even love... Chi Zhang had everything without effort. His future was a hundred times brighter than Eamon's. Eamon would never forget the martial arts combat in his first year at Mount Yue, where Chi Zhang easily defeated him, pinning his head to the ground with one hand, giving him a humiliating lesson in front of the entire dojo.

Blinded by rage, Eamon raised his shoulder cannon, charging at Chi Zhang. Now a high-level B-class Aberrant, he intended to make Chi Zhang beg for mercy this time.

CHAPTER 33

The Puppets

Eamon's awakened ability was called "Battle Frenzy." As long as he gained the upper hand in a duel, it would trigger his battle spirit, stacking layers of power, making him fight better and better, eventually overwhelming his opponent.

He carried a rocket launcher on his shoulder—the "Viper," the latest anti-tank weapon from the Deep Woods armory. The shaped-charge rounds it fired would cause burning, penetration, and explosive effects upon contact with a body, along with blinding flashes and incendiary effects. Even high-level Aberrants would be pulverized if hit.

Eamon hid behind a slope, activated the scope, aimed at the moving Chi Zhang, and pulled the trigger without hesitation, firing four armor-piercing rounds in rapid succession!

"Boom—" Blinding flames shot up into the sky, engulfing Chi Zhang in an instant. Battle spirit layers activated successfully. Eamon smirked coldly, discarded the Viper, and switched to his sidearm, charging forward.

In the rolling smoke and dust, Chi Zhang was nowhere to be found. Eamon was shocked. Realizing the danger, he spun around. It was too late; Chi Zhang, surrounded by protective spells, flashed behind him and struck down with a fierce knife-hand.

Eamon had no time to react and was hit squarely, dropping his weapon. Chi Zhang transformed his hand into a claw, grabbing

Eamon's neck and slamming him into the ground. Half of Eamon's face landed on the still-burning flames, the smell of burning flesh filling the air. His face contorted in pain, wailing miserably, and the battle spirit he'd accumulated dissipated instantly.

"It's you," Chi Zhang recognized his voice, loosening his grip slightly. "Just as well. If you didn't come, I would have gone to find you."

"What, the great senior brother of Mount Yue, reduced to being Saya's lackey?" Eamon rasped, his eyes darting around, looking for a chance to turn the tables. He deliberately provoked, suddenly swinging his right hand back. A small cannon once used by Odin emerged from his arm, ready to unleash a barrage of bullets — Chi Zhang bent his second and third fingers of his left hand, pinched the middle joint of his thumb, and formed a seal with one hand. A soul-binding spell immobilized Eamon. Chi Zhang then pulled out a knife and stabbed it through Eamon's right arm, pinning it to the ground.

"Ah—!!" A piercing scream rang out.

"Ignorant and incompetent. Didn't you consider my identity before attacking?" Chi Zhang unleashed his mental power. The pressure of an S-class Aberrant bore down on Eamon like a heavy mountain, making it hard for him to breathe.

"You—you are Chionji?!" Eamon suddenly realized the horrifying truth, his eyes nearly popping out of his head.

Chionji, the infamous leader of Saya's refugees, was rumored to be an S-class Aberrant. This was no secret among the Deep Woods' high command. However, Chionji's origins, background, and appearance were mysteries. He rarely showed himself, and the arrogant warlords disdained to infiltrate the refugees to gather information, so no one knew who he was.

Eamon's right hand trembled, his face alternating between fear and regret. "Chi Zhang, you've humiliated, destroyed, and killed me repeatedly. Don't pretend to be honorable. You're just a hypocrite!"

"From the beginning, I opposed your entry," Chi Zhang said sternly. "Martial arts are always judged by strength. If you could have beaten me fair and square, you could have stepped on my head, but your dark nature always harbored resentment every time you lost."

Mount Yue Martial Arts School required significant funds to operate. Master Zhang, a pragmatic man, accepted Eamon because of his substantial "entrance fee." However, during their first duel, Chi Zhang noticed Eamon's twisted psychology. Winning and losing were common; even he often lost to Cora seven or eight times out of ten. But Eamon's eyes looked like he wanted to kill everyone who defeated him.

"What happened at the dojo before and after the apocalypse?" Chi Zhang demanded loudly.

They had searched every mound, including the Master's. Master Zhang hadn't turned into a zombie, and the wound on his chest was man-made.

Rita had once said she left Mount Yue two days before the apocalypse. Eamon was among those who stayed. Now, with the dojo wiped out, if anyone knew the truth, it was likely Eamon.

Eamon, pressed by Chi Zhang's questioning, was initially stunned, then burst into laughter.

"Senior brother, even as an S-class, there are things you can't do. Want to know how your father died? Beg me!"

"When he was alive, you refused to acknowledge him as your father. Now you want to play the filial son, mourning for him, hahaha!"

"Incurable scum. You don't deserve to be a student of Mount Yue." Chi Zhang said coldly.

Eamon, certain that Chi Zhang wouldn't kill him, mocked recklessly, "Senior brother acting as a righteous avenger, expelling me? Such grand authority!"

"Ruby!" Chi Zhang called out, "Even if you don't speak, I have other ways to find out."

Ruby ran over with a stony expression. She couldn't deal with an S-class like Onyx, but a B-class was no problem.

Her psychic probe forcefully invaded, her deep mental power searching through Eamon's mind, leaving no corner untouched. Cold sweat poured from Eamon, his scalp feeling as if it were being peeled off, unable to even scream.

Fragmented memories flowed like a tide. A particular scene flashed by, and Ruby seized the part she wanted.

On the first day of the apocalypse, Master Zhang locked the mutated students in the warehouse and silently guarded the door. Shortly after, a group of uniformed men broke into the dojo. After a brief conversation with Master Zhang, a fierce dispute broke out, escalating into a duel. Their strange techniques were unlike anything Master Zhang had ever seen. They joined forces to kill Master Zhang and then ransacked the place, searching for something.

Having overslept and stayed an extra day in a single dorm, Eamon woke to find the dojo deserted. He went to the monitoring room and witnessed the entire process of Master Zhang's death. He didn't dare make a sound until the men left. Then, he hastily gathered his belongings and fled from Mount Yue.

Ruby Bai, after reading his memory, shed two lines of tears and angrily cursed, "Eamon, you are a disgrace to Mount Yue."

When Cora and Onyx arrived, Chi Zhang, with an emotionless face, had already stabbed Eamon through the head.

"...Senior brother?" Cora called out softly. Chi Zhang withdrew his knife, saying only four words, "Clearing the house."

After Ne Kon and Mục Tân left, the United Army abandoned much of their damaged supplies and difficult-to-carry siege equipment, hurriedly retreating from the battlefield.

Chi Zhang, Cora, and the others were cleaning up the aftermath when Ewen Van suddenly ran over, carrying someone in his arms. His face was covered in ash, and the nearly six-foot-tall man spoke with a voice on the verge of tears, "Chi Zhang, please save Morgan!"

Morgan had gone alone to destroy the catapults and was caught in a cannon blast, half of his body mangled beyond recognition. His limbs hung limp, barely breathing, on the brink of death.

Chi Zhang quickly ordered, "Get him to Cho Lu."

Cho Lu was the only healer on the base. Before the apocalypse, she was just an ordinary student at Saya, having finally been admitted to Sycamore Medical School. She hadn't even attended her first class when the apocalypse struck. Previously, she relied half on her level and half on self-study for treatments. In life-and-death situations, her limited skills were often insufficient.

Seeing Morgan's condition, Cho Lu immediately activated her ability, but soon said in a flustered voice, "No, his mental power is depleting too fast. I can barely sustain him, let alone treat him."

Chi Zhang's body tensed, and Ewen Van's eyes filled with tears. If even a B-class healer couldn't help, was Morgan really going to die here? Cora quickly spoke up, "Senior brother, my companion is an A-class healer and a doctor. I'll call him right away."

An A-class healer.

Those few words reignited hope among the group. Healers were notoriously rare, especially A-class ones. Chi Zhang nodded immediately, "I will clear all checkpoints. Please have him come to Saya as quickly as possible."

Cora contacted Suchat, who answered almost instantly, "Suchat, bring Charles to Saya immediately. Hurry!"

Suchat paused for a moment but didn't ask questions, responding firmly, "I'm on my way."

Even with an Aberrant running at full speed, it would take four to five hours to travel from Deep Woods to Saya. Cho Lu's mental power might not hold out that long. Rita brought a box of Level 3 crystals, a dozen of them donated by Saya's Aberrants. They would provide energy if Cho Lu couldn't keep up.

Time ticked by, with everyone's hearts tightly clenched. Cho Lu grew paler and trembled uncontrollably, while Morgan's breathing became almost imperceptible.

At the critical moment, Merlin led Suchat and Charles Franz in, shouting, "They're here!!"

Charles, his hair disheveled, the ponytail at the back of his head undone, and half-shaven stubble on his face, immediately took over. He expertly cut open Morgan's clothing, cleared the dust and sand from his trachea to prevent asphyxiation during surgery, then restored his heart, lungs, and kidneys. The pearly white healing power flowed in, visibly improving Morgan's condition.

Cora glanced back at Suchat, who was in terrible shape from the extreme rush. His abdominal wound reopened, blood soaking through his jacket. Yet he stood quietly in the corner, not saying a word, not daring to disturb Charles.

"Cho Lu," Chi Zhang noticed Suchat's condition and called softly.

Cho Lu, who had been intently watching Charles work, immediately stood up. "I'll help you."

Suchat nodded, "Thank you."

Charles remained focused, undisturbed, his hands never stopping. The others didn't dare speak or even breathe loudly, their eyes fixed intently on him.

After over two hours of emergency treatment, Charles put down the scalpel and took a moment to rest. "He's saved. Fortunately, his limbs aren't damaged. Just make sure he doesn't move much for a few months and let his mental power slowly recover."

Ewen Van clenched his fists and finally couldn't hold back his tears.

An A-class healer could snatch people from death. And Charles was no ordinary A-class healer. He was a skilled surgeon, experienced and calm under pressure, able to use his powers to their fullest.

Chi Zhang bowed slightly, expressing his gratitude, "Thank you."

Seeing their leader, Chionji, bow in person, all the high-level Aberrants behind him stood at attention and bowed 90 degrees, shouting in unison, "Thank you!!"

Merlin, crying uncontrollably, wiped his tears as he shouted.

Their overwhelming gratitude startled Charles, making him step back in surprise. Cora discreetly supported him, keeping him steady.

After Morgan was out of danger, everyone breathed a sigh of relief and busied themselves with arranging the residents and cleaning up the battlefield. Gradually, most of the people left.

Cora turned to Onyx and reached out her finger, gently poking his right leg once, then again, with a curious expression. "How did your leg get better?"

"Temporarily."

This was still amazing. Remembering how he had commanded on the battlefield just now, Cora's eyes sparkled. "Can you control Level 3 zombies?"

"Yes, I am an S-class after all. I won't embarrass you."

"Amazing." Cora clapped her hands enthusiastically.

Onyx shook his head and smiled lightly. Cora's compliments were always the same. Whether praising him or Damian, there was no actual difference.

The sound of Cora's clapping grew softer as she looked up at him again and again. Onyx calmly met her gaze, a few strands of hair falling over his deep-set eyes, giving him a sharp yet cold aura—a paradoxical mix that was hard to describe.

Cora was stunned.

It seemed... he had changed.

No, perhaps the wheelchair-bound "Arashi Researcher" had always been a disguise. The confident, composed man who could run and stand was the real Onyx.

"Handsome," Cora said dumbly.

"I don't like it when you say that." Onyx clicked his tongue lightly.

Cora pouted, angrily punching him in the chest. "Ugh—" Onyx grunted, his tall figure wavering unsteadily, and he fell forward.

Cora was startled, quickly catching him. Turning her head, she noticed Onyx's face looked terrible.

"The magic has worn off," Onyx sighed. Nearly eight hours had passed since the injection, and the side effects were showing.

"What, what should I do?" Cora asked anxiously. "I'll go get your wheelchair."

"Don't move yet. Let me rest a bit." Onyx reached out with his right hand, gently wrapping it around Cora's back, borrowing some strength. The distance between them closed.

"Cora, who do you think I've been working so hard for?"

His warm breath brushed against her neck, making Cora's toes curl. She strutted like a piece of wood. "Hmm?" The questioning tone seemed to hook her, demanding an answer.

"...Me, I guess?" Cora stammered.

"At least you have some conscience." A faint laugh echoed in her ear. The blush on Cora's cheeks spread all the way to the top of her head, making her face flush.

The cafeteria served once again as a temporary meeting room. All the high-level Aberrants from Saya Base gathered, regardless of how long they had been members. After this battle, they were all trusted comrades.

Cora pushed Onyx in, his body limp like he had no bones, lazily leaning against the wheelchair, coughing weakly now and then. Cora was careful, even whispering when they crossed the threshold as if he were made of fragile glass.

Charles glanced at Onyx, not remembering "frailty" being a side effect of the treatment.

"You said you wanted to discuss Ne Kon's matter. Have you discovered something?" Chi Zhang pointed to a distant table. "Cora, Rita saved some food for you. Go eat."

Cora responded, letting go of the wheelchair and happily running over to eat.

Losing his motivation to act, Onyx straightened up, his face no longer pale, his cough gone, and spoke seriously.

"Ne Kon is not an Aberrant."

A collective gasp filled the room. "What?"

"How is that possible?"

"If he isn't an Aberrant, why can't even an S-class kill him?"

Onyx explained calmly, "Ne Kon's mental power is very weak, definitely not originating from his own magnetic field. I suspect that a causality Aberrant placed a protective barrier between him."

"Causality Aberrant? I know someone." Mercenary leader, Samuel spoke up. "He was once a free mercenary on West Street, later joining the security team. His ability is 'Life Puppet,' which allows him to make people into puppets, sacrificing their lives to protect their master. As long as the puppet lives, the master won't die."

Such an ability sounded horrifying.

"Damn, sending others to die for you? No wonder Ne Kon is so arrogant."

"Who is his puppet?"

Onyx continued to analyze, "When Cora killed Juramani, Ne Kon showed obvious panic, exposing a vulnerable moment but quickly recovering."

Chi Zhang interjected, "You mean Juramani was Ne Kon's first puppet?"

First puppet??

Everyone felt a chill. Chi Zhang's words suggested Ne Kon had more than one puppet.

"So, how many lives does he have? Can he not be killed?"

"Does this ability have no limit?"

"Of course it does. Causality Aberrants pay with their own life force each time they use their power. And that guy was only a B-class. From what I know, he died several months ago from overuse," Samuel said gravely.

A shadow fell over Cora's heart. From Samuel's information, it was likely the causality Aberrant had overexerted himself to create the puppets for Ne Kon, ultimately dying from it.

"Three," Onyx said calmly. "Ne Kon has three puppets."

"How do you know?" The others looked at him suspiciously.

Onyx waved. "Cora, lend me your terminal." Cora, halfway through her meal, put down her bowl and ran over, passing the terminal through the crowd to him.

Onyx projected a whiteboard and began writing complex formulas in front of everyone. "Calculating the result isn't hard. By considering Ne Kon's mental power, magnetic field strength, and radiation fluctuations, we can compute...assuming his initial mental power is Y, then after Juramani's death, the first layer of causality disappears, denoted as x..."

Onyx's fingers moved rapidly, the data on the whiteboard increasing in density until he drew a final straight line. "The answer is simple. After Juramani's death, Ne Kon has two layers of protection left."

"This matches the strength of a B-class Aberrant. That guy's lifetime limit was likely three puppets."

When Onyx looked up, the cafeteria was silent. The members of Mount Yue Martial Arts School wore identical bewildered expressions, their eyes reflecting pure confusion, unaware that their chopsticks and spoons had fallen.

Clap—clap—clap — In the quiet room, only Felix's slow clapping broke the silence. "From a mathematical standpoint, it's perfectly accurate."

Onyx smiled, pinning a butterfly brooch back onto the equally bewildered Cora and brushing a grain of rice from her cheek.

"To kill Ne Kon, we must first eliminate the puppets," Onyx stated calmly.

"The question now is, who are Ne Kon's remaining two puppets?"

CHAPTER 34

The Mole

"I have a question," Charles suddenly spoke up. "Do the puppets know they are puppets?"

He had washed his face, shaved, and tidied himself up. Over the past few days, Charles had changed significantly. His unexpected reunion with Rao had broken him down completely, yet also brought him a new life. The sense of decay that once surrounded him had vanished, and he now resembled his former mature and rational self.

"They can know, or they can be unaware," Onyx answered slowly. "When a causality Aberrant plants their power, neither the puppet nor the master will feel any obvious discomfort. If done discreetly, they might not even realize it. All the suffering is borne by the Aberrant, hence why such people are often called 'spring silkworms.'"

In literature from the old civilization, spring silkworms symbolized selfless dedication. However, in this context, it was full of irony. This ability was too insidious, able to change someone's life trajectory without them knowing, making them a scapegoat for another.

Onyx paused, "As for whether Ne Kon's puppets know their identity, it's debatable."

"I think Juramani didn't know," Cora said confidently. When a warrior faces a life-and-death moment, their eyes and behavior cannot lie. When Cora fought Juramani, his strikes were fierce, his mind firm, with no hint of abnormality. If he knew he was a puppet, he would have been cautious, his moves would have had flaws, and his emotions would have fluctuated upon being killed. But Juramani showed none of these signs.

Juramani's strength was close to S-class; he was a definite powerhouse and wouldn't die easily. Ne Kon's choice to make him a puppet was extremely wise, so there was no need to inform him.

"Additionally," Onyx continued, "this life connection can't be established in one go. It requires multiple reinforcements. Also, when creating a puppet, the host body and the causality, Aberrant must be present together."

Chi Zhang further speculated, "This means the puppets are likely people familiar to Ne Kon, at least those he can see regularly."

Ne Kon held a high status, and only a few were allowed into the Unified Palace to meet him in person, which narrowed down the possibilities significantly.

The Aberrants in the cafeteria began to discuss among themselves.

"I don't understand. Couldn't Ne Kon just randomly capture someone, imprison them where no one can find them? Wouldn't that be safer?"

"I don't think so. A normal person being inexplicably imprisoned would definitely break down. If they couldn't take it and committed suicide, the puppet's potential would be wasted. Is Ne Kon that stupid?"

"He could capture several people and rotate them," the young man who first spoke said defiantly, turning to Onyx, "Hey, dude, can the puppet's identity be transferred?"

"Yes," Onyx nodded slightly.

Everyone was shocked. If the puppet's identity could be transferred, it would be like a rabbit with three burrows. How could they find it?

"But the causality Aberrant who planted the power must do personally it," Onyx added slowly.

Relieved, the crowd murmured, "Thank goodness he died early, otherwise it would have been troublesome."

"Thankfully, the remaining two puppet identities are fixed."

Samuel stood up, his voice low. "I know Ne Kon better than you all. He's called 'the Tyrant' because he dislikes anything beyond his control. I don't think he'd tell the puppets the truth."

In the New Era year 47, it was Ne Kon's twenty-seventh year as governor. Samuel had joined the Free Mercenaries at fifteen, over thirty years ago, witnessing Ne Kon's bloody rise to power.

Samuel added, "I don't know what he planned before, but after losing an important puppet in yesterday's battle, Ne Kon will probably keep the remaining two in the Unified Palace, the safest place in Deep Woods."

Chi Zhang nodded in agreement, "To summarize, the puppets are familiar or trusted people of Ne Kon, who see him regularly and are likely in the security team or the Unified Palace, and are unaware of their identity."

Who could such people be? Everyone fell into deep thought, and the cafeteria's atmosphere became quiet.

"I know someone." Charles clenched his fists gradually. "He has lived in the Unified Palace for years, is Ne Kon's closest person, firmly under his control, and can see him at any time. Most importantly, that person is still alive today."

Charles's eyes burned with a dark flame. "He is Ne Kon's only son, Ne Win."

"I used to be Ne Win's attending physician. I'm very familiar with his condition. His bone disease was congenital and would have been incurable before the apocalypse. But now, he can survive with healing Aberrants."

"Indeed, we haven't heard about Ne Win for a long time," a few local mercenaries behind Samuel whispered.

"That little psychopath used to enjoy torturing healthy children. He frequently caused trouble. The daughter of the couple at our street corner was killed by him... he's vanished recently."

"To confirm if Ne Win is a puppet, we must kill him," Onyx sighed, "but to kill him, we must enter the Unified Palace. No matter how dangerous, we must go there."

"The Unified Palace, I'll go."

Cora was the first to stand up.

Onyx and Chi Zhang glanced at her, speaking almost simultaneously.

"It's too dangerous for you alone. I'll go with you."

"I'll go with you."

For two seconds, the scene was silent. The senior brothers and sisters of Mount Yue Martial Arts School looked at the two and gasped.

Suchat and Felix quickly intervened. "I'll go too."

"Interesting. Count me in."

Samuel and Ewen Van also spoke up. "I'll join."

Almost all the high-level Aberrants on-site stood up.

Chi Zhang raised his hand to calm their excitement, "I know everyone came to Saya for survival. This assassination mission is extremely dangerous and entirely voluntary. You don't need to force yourselves."

"Chionji, I appreciate your concern, but this affects everyone's interests. I must go."

"Ne Kon is practically trampling on us. I must kill him!"

"If we don't kill Ne Kon, Saya will never have peace. Chionji, I'm willing to go with you!"

The name Chionji belonged to Saya's soul. His call was unmatched, the passionate voices rising one after another. Standing among the crowd, Chi Zhang seemed like a beacon of light in the darkness.

Onyx watched coldly for a while, then poured a bucket of cold water over them. "Shouting doesn't help. It's not a contest of who has the loudest voice."

"What do you mean?"

Onyx pointed lazily at Chi Zhang and a few others, "You, you, and you, you're all wanted or undocumented refugees. You can't even enter Deep Woods, let alone the Unified Palace."

Although Onyx's words were harsh, they were straightforward. These people couldn't approach the Unified Palace.

Was there another way to sneak in?

Cora thought of Simon Liu, whom she had encountered in Blossomville. Although only a D-class Aberrant, his unique ability allowed him to open a door on any surface. If they could find a similar Aberrant, could they infiltrate the Unified Palace?

Cora shared her idea, and Onyx nodded in agreement. "Exactly. It doesn't have to be door-opening. Other abilities could work too. With the right application, even seemingly useless abilities can be extremely effective."

"I'll have all of Saya's Aberrants re-register," Chi Zhang concluded.

Deep Woods.

Ellyn and Yuui led a group of girls, running frantically through the smoke.

"Ellyn, this is the last spot!" Yuui shouted.

"Masha, have you sensed your sister yet?" Ellyn, firing a cannon to repel the pursuing private soldiers, turned to ask.

Masha bit her lip and shook her head quickly.

Taking advantage of Ne Kon attacking Saya, Miêu Luân dispatched private soldiers to take over city defenses, allowing Ellyn and her team to raid several private camps, rescuing some girls conscripted into the "Rose Army." However, Masha's sister, Marie, was still missing.

"Could it be that your sister is still in Miêu Luân's private residence?" a girl with a wounded face said timidly. "I heard that Miêu Luân likes to keep his favorites as pets for a while before sending them to the camps when he gets bored."

Miêu Luân's private residence was easy to find, but high-level Aberrants heavily guarded it, making any rescue attempt nearly impossible.

"Let's take them back first and then check it out," Ellyn said.

Ellyn and Yuui returned the girls to the apartment and took Masha to the vicinity of Miêu Luân's private residence.

They didn't dare get too close, hiding on a street several kilometers away. Masha clasped her hands together, using her psychic ability. A few seconds later, she cried out in surprise, "My sister, I found my sister!"

Marie was indeed there. Masha had just smiled when it froze on her face. "What's wrong?" Yuui asked nervously.

Masha looked puzzled. "My sister said she is with someone named Rao and that they won't be leaving for now."

Rao?

Ellyn and Yuui exchanged surprised glances. Rao? Since the day they met at the apartment, they had lost contact with Rao, and now they heard her name again in such a context.

"What else did Marie say?" Ellyn asked.

Masha closed her eyes and focused on her sister, communicating silently.

"She told me to leave Deep Woods quickly and find reinforcements."

"What reinforcements?"

Suddenly, a commotion erupted in the city. The General and the United Army had just returned, and the news of Nguyen Van Tuan's death spread like wildfire. Soon, over a hundred fully armed mercenaries poured out from Miêu Luân's private residence.

"The situation is not good." Ellyn frowned. "With Ne Kon returning to the city, Miêu Luân has probably already heard about the Rose Army's defection. It's only a matter of time before he finds us."

Ellyn clutched her cannon tightly in her left hand. These girls had just escaped; could they really be captured again?

"Ellyn, let's go to Saya," Yuui said seriously. She had received messages from Suchat and Cora, learning about the current situation in Saya.

"I promise you, Saya differs from Deep Woods. The leader there, Chionji, is Cora's senior brother. He is fair and just. If they go there, at least they won't be abused and mistreated."

Ellyn looked down, silent. She feared her decision would push these girls into another pit of fire.

Yuui continued to persuade her earnestly, "Even Samuel has joined Saya. If Chionji were like Ne Kon, so many locals wouldn't willingly follow him."

"...Alright, we'll go to Saya," Ellyn finally agreed, nodding slowly.

The three returned to the apartment, gathered the rescued girls, and set off towards the city gate, hoping to leave Deep Woods before Miêu Luân's search began. As they approached the gate, Ellyn paused —Cơ Đan Vi and Hu Chao were guarding the checkpoint, their eagle-like eyes scrutinizing every person, especially women, who had to roll up their sleeves for inspection.

"Ellyn..." a trembling voice came from behind.

The girls, pale-faced, rolled up their sleeves. Except for Masha, who hadn't been captured yet, all of them bore a deep red rose-shaped brand in their arms.

This was Miêu Luân's victory "medal," also the "honor" of joining the Rose Army.

"..." Ellyn fell into a furious silence.

"Bastards!" Yuui turned away, cursing through her tears.

"Uh, excuse me..." a man's unfamiliar voice came from behind them. Ellyn and Yuui turned sharply, standing protectively in front of the girls, only to recognize a familiar figure—Cẩm Tú.

The man, covered in mud, smiled awkwardly. "It's me. Sorry to overhear your conversation again. I swear it wasn't intentional. I just always seem to stumble upon secrets. It's actually quite troublesome..."

Cẩm Tú kept talking nervously, realizing belatedly that he was causing more anxiety with his rambling. Finally, he got to the point. "Are you trying to leave the city? I can help you."

"You? What can you do?" Yuui asked, chin raised defiantly.

Cẩm Tú scratched his head, embarrassed, "Well, my ability is 'tunneling.' Over the years, I've secretly dug many tunnels, including a way out of the city. My friends call me 'Mole,' though I prefer 'Pangolin'..."

As Cẩm Tú started rambling again, he noticed the excited, hopeful looks on the women's faces, as if they wanted to devour him with their eyes.

CHAPTER 35

The Decision

Cẩm Tú wasn't kidding when he said he could get them out.

His awakened power was so bizarre that his friends often mocked it as useless. Cẩm Tú didn't mind; he wasn't into fighting. His only interest was studying the gold-winning works of city planning competitions, and his biggest dream was, "The world is so big, I want to see it." Deep Woods' strict entry restrictions previously indefinitely postponed this idea. Unexpectedly, after the apocalypse, his tunneling ability allowed him to come and go freely, rekindling his hope.

Cẩm Tú spent over half a year tunneling hundreds of winding secret passages beneath Deep Woods. More complex than the municipal hall of Glass Port. Without his guidance, an ordinary person would never find their way out. Cẩm Tú led Ellyn and her group to a hidden alleyway. After checking the surroundings to ensure no one noticed, he pried open a manhole cover. "The way out is rather special. You'll have to endure the sewers."

The girls, having endured many hardships, were already mentally strong and didn't complain. They lined up and climbed down one by one. Cẩm Tú went last, carefully replacing the manhole cover, muttering, "At first, I just dug randomly, but people kept coming down to explore. Guess what? They got lost! By the time I found them, their bodies were bloated like balloons..."

The girls made disgusted faces, and Cẩm Tú quickly apologized, "Sorry, sorry, I won't say anymore. I just wonder why they're so curious. Later, I had to hide all the entrances..."

The sewer was dark and damp, with occasional unidentified flying insects, water rats, and bats passing by. Eventually, they lost all sense of direction and could only follow Cẩm Tú. Ellyn's cannon was always aimed at him, never completely letting her guard down. If Cẩm Tú showed any signs of betrayal, she would immediately incapacitate him.

About an hour later, Cẩm Tú stopped at a dead end. "Step back a bit. I sealed this last time, need to dig it out again."

Yuui and the others stepped back in unison. Cẩm Tú's hands glowed with an earthy yellow light, his entire body like a high-speed drill as he bored into the soil. Soon, light shone through from outside, and a half-human-sized hole appeared out of nowhere.

Yuui scrambled out, discovering they were near the Lifeline. She looked around to confirm the direction of the Saya base. "Let's go."

Under the sunlight, Yuui's face shone brightly, even with a bit of dirt. Her beauty was undeniable. Cẩm Tú stared at her for two seconds. "Miss, you look familiar. Have we met somewhere?"

Yuui thought, "Not good," but quickly calmed herself. In such moments, she couldn't show any sign of guilt. She placed her hands on her hips and scolded, "Just because you helped us doesn't mean you can hit on me! You're not my type!"

Her yelling startled Cẩm Tú and hastily explained, "I wouldn't dare! It's just... I also want to go to Saya, but I don't have any connections. Can you take me with you?"

Cẩm Tú grinned foolishly after he finished speaking. He could have used this as a bargaining chip to make Ellyn and the others do as he asked in the city, but he didn't. Only after bringing the girls out safely did he naively make his request. This guy truly had no ulterior motives.

Just then, Yuui received a message from Cora, her lips curling slightly. "Of course."

At the Saya base, Onyx was browsing the list of Aberrants, occasionally pulling out a few files to circle and highlight on the light screen. He was contemplating various combinations in his mind, while Cora stood behind his wheelchair, idly counting his eyelashes.

Merlin peeked half his head in. "I detected them. The people you mentioned seem to have arrived."

"I'll go meet them." Cora immediately perked up, leaving Onyx and running towards the base gate.

The scars of the last war hadn't fully faded. Amidst the swirling dust, a woman with a cannon in her left hand and an empty right arm appeared. Her eyes were resolute, her steps steady, followed by dozens of disheveled girls supporting each other as they walked.

Above the base, Chi Zhang confirmed their identities and nodded, signaling, "Let them through."

Rita organized people to prepare hot water, clean towels, and coats at the end of the drawbridge, handing them to the girls. Ellyn took one, wiped her face, and looked up at the fortress-like city, feeling a mix of emotions. She had never thought that as a native of Deep Woods, she would end up displaced, relying on outsiders for shelter.

"From now on, this is your home," Rita said solemnly, hugging the youngest girl, Masha. The girls, who had been holding back their fears along the way, finally couldn't help but burst into tears.

Deep Woods, Miêu Luân's Private Residence.

"Useless trash!" A scalding teapot was overturned, and the teacup was thrown, heavily hitting the two people kneeling on the ground.

Cơ Đan Vi's forehead was hit, instantly turning red from the burn. Next to him, Hu Chao, whose head was pressed tightly against the ground, was drenched and didn't dare to move.

Miêu Luân's eyes narrowed into slits, burning with unquenchable anger. "You can't even catch a group of women. What's the use of keeping you?" Rao was kneeling at his feet. When Miêu Luân suddenly erupted in anger, the overturned teapot spilled towards her. Although she dodged quickly, her hand was still scalded red.

Marie wanted to come over, but Rao shook her head slightly, her expression calm, as if nothing had happened.

"Sir, those deserters definitely didn't leave through the city gates..." Cơ Đan Vi tried to defend himself.

Miêu Luân snorted coldly, "Are you questioning Deep Woods' city defenses? Tell me, surrounded by heavy firepower from both above and below, did those damn women grow wings to fly out, or did they turn into eels and slip through some hole?"

Cơ Đan Vi felt wronged. His inspections were flawless, but the fact remained that the women had disappeared under his watch, and he couldn't shirk the responsibility. He looked at Hu Chao, hoping he would say something.

Hu Chao remained as quiet as the dead, always cowering to a new level in such situations, accepting any beating or scolding without complaint.

Miêu Luân's nostrils flared as his chest heaved with anger. The Rose Army was his pride and joy, carefully selected and trained with immense effort. Losing most of them filled Miêu Luân with overwhelming resentment.

Was that "cunning fox" truly omnipotent? How could he find and rescue those women so precisely? Miêu Luân's sinister gaze swept over the most beautiful rose lying on the ground. Rao's fingertips trembled, yet she remained outwardly calm.

Outside the door, a servant knocked cautiously three times. "Sir, the general is here."

Everyone in the room was stunned. Why would Ne Kon come?

Ne Kon always summoned warlords to the Unified Palace. This was just a private residence, not Miêu Luân's family estate. He had just suffered a defeat at Saya Base, making his sudden visit even more unusual.

Miêu Luân coldly said, "Get up." Cơ Đan Vi and Hu Chao immediately stood, bowing their heads and standing behind him.

As the door opened, Miêu Luân's face had already returned to a smiling demeanor.

The imposing Ne Kon walked in. Though his pace was slow, his high-ranking aura inexplicably made everyone hold their breath. Ne Kon sat in the chief seat, resting his arm on his knee. He remained silent for a while, the room quiet enough to hear a pin drop.

"What advice does the general have for coming here today?" Miêu Luân asked calmly.

"Nguyen Van Tuan is dead. His Iron Eagle Team is leaderless. You and Mục Tân can split them, get some usable hands." Ne Kon said.

"Thank you, General." Miêu Luân accepted with a smile.

Ne Kon's deep eyes stared at him for a moment before continuing, "Also, promote someone from the minor warlords to replace Nguyen Van Tuan. You handle this."

He was blatantly giving Miêu Luân more power. Promoting a

high-ranking warlord came with significant benefits, allowing Miêu Luân to win over more followers. Over time, his power would only grow.

Ne Kon's second statement finally brought a hint of joy to Miêu Luân's face.

"Are your people reliable?" Ne Kon glanced at Hu Chao and Cơ Đan Vi.

Miêu Luân knew well that Juramani had died at Saya Base and thought Ne Kon might be interested in one of his personal soldiers. "If the general likes, you can take them. My subordinates are absolutely loyal."

Ne Kon waved his hand dismissively, as if it was just a casual question. "No need, you keep them."

Rao was trembling, barely controlling her emotions. It was her first time seeing Ne Kon this close, and her desire for revenge grew nearly overwhelming her. The enemy was right in front of her; she couldn't stay calm. Sweet Lily's face kept flashing before her eyes, and she wanted nothing more than to kill Ne Kon right now.

Marie noticed her trembling and moved closer. Rao's eyes welled with a tear, her knee twitching slightly.

Marie quickly grabbed her, sensing that if she didn't stop Rao, something terrible would happen.

Their movements caught Ne Kon's attention. He glanced coldly at them, his gaze sweeping over the trembling Rao and Marie.

Ne Kon knew well about Miêu Luân's sordid preferences and the true nature of the "Rose Army," a deceptively beautiful but bloodthirsty force. But Ne Kon didn't care. Miêu Luân was a clever man, difficult to control, but he exposed his weakness for women, making him easy for Ne Kon to manipulate.

To reach the top warlord position in Deep Woods as a commoner, Miêu Luân's cunning was undeniable. He knew when to advance and when to retreat, especially valuing his life.

Satisfied, Ne Kon left. His visit seemed only to say a few inconsequential words. Miêu Luân watched him leave, squinting his eyes and curling his lips slightly.

Onyx, Chi Zhang, and Cora were in a meeting when Felix wheeled in. "I have some bad news and some worse news. Which do you want to hear first?"

Onyx looked up, expressionless, while the others remained silent, not answering his question. Felix Lucas shrugged disappointedly. "Alright, seems you don't get humor."

"First, Ne Kon has issued a new law. The entire region is now on the lookout for four S-level Aberrants from Saya Base. We are now honored fugitives, and forging entry permits is no longer an option."

Felix's ice-blue eyes flickered as a series of decrypted texts were projected in front of everyone. "The worse news is, I intercepted several one-way encrypted messages. They are Ne Kon's 'request for intervention.' I have good reason to believe the Alliance has already received them."

"What is a request for intervention?" Cora asked, puzzled.

Onyx's expression grew serious. "The governor of District C has the highest authority within the district. If something uncontrollable happens, they can cede some benefits to request Alliance intervention. The Alliance would send 'special envoys' to temporarily take over local affairs and 'solve the problem' for the governor."

Cora blinked and hit the nail on the head. "Ne Kon is panicking, isn't he?"

For someone with such a strong desire for control to willingly bow down, relinquishing the supreme status of a governor and requesting Alliance intervention was unimaginable. Could Juramani's death have hit him that hard?

Onyx smiled slightly. "I think this opens up another path for us. If Ne Kon made this decision, it suggests his remaining two puppets are no match for Juramani."

"But these are just speculations. In the current situation, the special envoys from the Alliance will arrive in Deep Woods within three days, possibly more than one S-level. If we make a move then, it will be hard to deceive everyone."

Everyone felt a chill in their hearts. Their plan was assassination, not a head-on clash with S-level Aberrants!

"We're out of time. We need to get into the Unified Palace quickly." Onyx made the final decision.

CHAPTER 36

The Palace

At the heavily guarded gates of the Unified Palace, two unexpected visitors arrived. Before they could approach the restricted area, armed guards simultaneously aimed at them, warning them to stop.

"We're here to claim the bounty."

One of them slowly raised his head, revealing a hideous scar running from his eye to his jaw, giving his face a grim look. His voice was hoarse, as if fire had scorched his vocal cords, making anyone who heard him feel a chill down their spine.

Next to the scar-faced man was a silent, thin man, both carrying strange black boxes.

The captain of the guards hesitated. What bounty required them to come to the Unified Palace? But his expression changed as he quickly realized the answer. The most prominent bounty recently was issued by the general. "Kill any of the four S-level Aberrants from Saya Base and claim a substantial reward at the Unified Palace."

This bounty was high-authority and extremely difficult, almost impossible to complete. However, the reward was also astonishingly rich, including the privilege to make a personal request to the general himself. The promise of such a reward, even the chance to walk unchallenged in Deep Woods, was irresistible. Could it be that someone had actually completed the bounty?

Only an S-level could kill another S-level... The guard captain stiffened. His attitude immediately turned respectful. "Heroes, we need to verify the token."

The scar-faced man snorted coldly and, with the thin man, simultaneously pressed a switch on their boxes. A small automatic door opened from the side, revealing two bloody human heads inside!

The guard captain's heart went cold. He quickly pulled up the battle footage from Saya Base. The identities of those S-level Aberrants were unknown, and they had no biological information on them, so traditional methods were needed for verification. He glanced at the video, then paused it, comparing it to the bloody heads. After a hard look, he identified the head on the left as the disabled boy who controlled the mechanical vehicle on the city wall. The one on the right bore a striking resemblance to the refugee leader, Chionji.

The guard captain, deeply shaken, stepped forward to inspect more closely. The scar-faced man "snapped" the door shut, saying in a sinister tone, "I want to see the bounty."

"Please wait a moment. I'll report to the general immediately!" The guard captain moved aside and communicated quietly through his device. The message was relayed layer by layer, and Ne Kon's order quickly came through: let them in.

"Please, come in."

Receiving the order, the guards moved aside to clear the way.

The scar-faced man and the thin man carried their boxes through the security checkpoint. Precision instruments scanned them from head to toe, prohibiting any weapons or sharp objects. The indicator light blinked twice, remaining silent, triggering no alarms.

After entering through the main gate, they walked for nearly fifteen minutes before officially entering the Unified Palace's domain. Along the way, they encountered several patrolling Aberrants. The security level here was so high that not even a fly could get through.

The scar-faced man stared at the grand and majestic buildings before him, a peculiar smile on his face. "The general sure lives well. When we get the bounty, we'll get ourselves a house like this."

The scar-faced man and the thin man exchanged glances and burst into laughter at the thought of their future good fortune. The guard captain's mouth twitched, but he remained silent.

Suddenly, several small openings appeared at the bottom of the black box, releasing a swarm of mechanical spiders. They crawled into nearby bushes or slipped into the cracks of the buildings, unnoticed by anyone. Each spider's eight eyes glowed faintly as they swiftly collected data from the surroundings.

In the underground space, a black-haired girl retracted her listening device and leaped down from the tunnel's top, landing silently like a leopard. She took a few steps forward, and a faint light appeared. In the dark, winding tunnel, hundreds of high-level Aberrants lay in silent ambush.

Felix's fingers moved rapidly, projecting real-time footage from the mechanical spiders. First came rows of marching boots, then the view pulled back, revealing the structures of the Unified Palace more clearly as the spiders moved, mapping out the entire layout.

"Got it."

"Have you located Ne Win yet?" "It will take time."

These people were, of course, Cora Thornton and her team. The scar-faced man and the thin man were also their allies.

Onyx had discovered an aberrant with the ability to "replicate" at the base. With his quick mind, he devised the entire plan in an instant. Felix first used machinery to create fake heads, then the aberrant with replication abilities performed "plastic surgery." Finally, two unfamiliar faces were sent "openly" into the Unified Palace to scout the internal situation, while Cora Thornton and the others used Cẩm Tú's tunneling ability to infiltrate the palace through underground passages.

For the choice of heads to present as the bounty, Chi Zhang, as the leader of Saya, was an obvious choice and had no objections. Felix himself volunteered the other head.

One had to admit, the thinking of a genius was indeed hard for ordinary people to understand. The image of Felix Lucas smiling and squeezing his own head was absolutely unforgettable.

Within an unremarkable building in the Unified Palace, there was a sound of something shattering.

"Get out."

A boy, covered in brown patches and with a horrifying appearance, smashed every vase in the room, hoarsely shouting.

His sinister eyes did not resemble those of a child at all. His body was emaciated and much shorter than others his age. The Aberrants from the Guard Corps silently blocked his path, preventing him from leaving.

The boy raged. "It was bad enough that I couldn't leave the palace before, but now I can't even leave my room? Who gave you the guts to imprison me?!"

"Young master Ne Win, these are the general's orders. It's all for your safety."

"Safety? What's unsafe about me?" Ne Win showed a devilish smile. "What's the point of living like this? If I die, I die. I don't care, so why should you dog interfere?"

Ne Win reached under his bed, his expression revealing a sinister bloodlust. "I heard the head of the Saya leader has been brought in? I want to see it. I plan to make a new ball out of it."

"Young master Ne Win, you cannot leave the room..."

"Bang—"

A blazing bullet shattered the speaker's head. Ne Win wiped the blood from his face and laughed, twistedly, "Don't tell me I can't."

He used his particle gun to clear his path, forcing the Guard Corps to retreat, finally stepping out of his room.

In another tunnel several miles away from the Unified Palace, Masha sat on a bench, waiting for Cẩm Tú and the others to come back for her. She fiddled with a terminal while telepathically chatting with Marie above her.

"Sis, is the sister named Rao there?" Masha suddenly remembered something and silently asked.

"She's here. Why?" Marie glanced at Rao beside her, who was gazing at her hands, unmoving. Since Ne Kon's visit, she had become increasingly silent.

In the underground tunnel, Masha pulled out a neatly folded piece of paper from her pocket.

"Someone named Charles asked me to read this to her."

I have despised my soul seven times,

The first time when it could have soared, it was docile;

The third time when it faced hardship and ease, it chose the simple path;

Masha's innocent voice recited the beautifully rhymed poem. In the courtyard above, Marie repeated every word she heard.

The sixth time when it despised the ugly face, not knowing it was the same face;

The seventh time when it cowered in the mud, unwilling to rise.

All mistakes should end on the seventh count. From today on, I will burn my soul for you to gain a new life.

Masha read seriously, and both sisters breathed a sigh of relief in unison. That was hard to read, so convoluted. What does this poem even mean?

Rao slowly blinked, a faint smile appearing on her lips. Although she was smiling, tears of sorrow streamed down her face. "It's just like before..."

"Just like what?" Marie asked, puzzled.

"In the past, when he made a mistake and didn't dare apologize in person, he would secretly write a poem and leave it on my easel. If I opened it and read it, it meant I wasn't mad at him anymore. If I didn't, he would keep writing until I forgave him."

Charles was a renowned and respected doctor in Sycamore, but at home, in front of Rao, he was like a young man in his twenties, always clinging to her, unwilling to let go.

"Is he your husband?" Marie cautiously asked, "Did you leave him because you were angry at him?"

"No, I never..." The last few words were barely audible.

Rao wiped away her tears, her clear eyes filled with determination. "Can you ask your sister where Charles is now?"

Marie closed her eyes and sensed for a moment. "Masha says he went to the Unified Palace."

Under the layers of aberrant protection, Ne Kon received the two men who came to claim the bounty. He sat in a chair, gazing at the box in their hands. "Let me see Chionji's head."

The scar-faced man sternly refused. "Wait a moment, General. We haven't discussed the reward yet."

"You can claim the reward directly from my internal affairs officer," Ne Kon said.

"What we want, only you can give," the scar-faced man laughed wickedly.

Ne Kon frowned. "What do you want?"

"I want to live in the palace," the scar-faced man blurted out.

"Are you out of your mind? Didn't we agree on just money and crystals?" The previously silent, thin man suddenly jumped out, loudly objecting.

"What money? I changed my mind. Is that a problem?" The scar-faced man retorted.

The two started arguing fiercely over the division of the reward, their faces flushed with anger, and it seemed like a fight was imminent. Ne Kon's patience was rushing out. He raised his right hand, and many heavy weapons aimed at the two men. The arguing stopped abruptly.

"I'll ask you one last time. What do you want?" Ne Kon asked disdainfully. In the past, he wouldn't even have considered meeting such people, let alone listening to them.

The scar-faced man looked at him and suddenly grinned. "General, why don't you let me sit in your seat for two days?"

Ne Kon's pupils contracted sharply. Something was wrong. These two weren't here for the bounty! He stood up abruptly and shouted, "Kill them!"

The scar-faced man and the thin man threw the black box forward, and with a "whoosh," they disappeared before the explosion hit.

"General, they're anchor-type Aberrants!" Someone in the Guard Corps recognized.

Anchor-type Aberrants, a rare branch of spatial Aberrants, could set one or more anchor points within their mental range. No matter how far they were, they could instantly return to the anchor point when activating their ability, making them perfect for assassination, robbery, and sneaky escapes.

"Not good!" Ne Kon realized something, his face turning pale. "Where's Ne Win?"

"Beep beep—"

The black box on the ground sounded a piercing countdown alarm. The next second, a scorching heatwave shot into the sky! This wasn't the head of an S-level aberrant at all; it was a high-powered bomb!

The Guard Corps and Ne Kon were instantly engulfed.

CHAPTER 37

Blood For Blood

Suddenly, static appeared on the southwest side of the light screen projection. The real-time image flickered twice and then vanished.

"This area has an overclocked frequency band," Felix said. "The mechanical spiders' behavior patterns are disrupted, and the data can't be transmitted back."

"Hah, it seems the security here isn't as hopeless as I thought," he mocked insincerely.

"The glitch area is the core of the Unified Palace," Onyx deduced. "Ne Kon and his son should be inside."

Hearing this, Chi Zhang frowned. "But this area is vast. If we search it one by one, it'll take too long and risk exposure."

Felix cracked his knuckles and confidently said, "Need me to hack it? Five minutes, no, three minutes tops."

"What about Scar and his team?" Onyx asked instead of answering.

"They've already entered the reception hall and are stalling Ne Kon. They can hold for ten minutes at most," Chi Zhang replied steadily.

"Ten minutes..." Onyx narrowed his eyes.

"What do we do now?" Cora asked softly.

Onyx thought for a moment and turned to Felix. "You hack it. We'll come up with a way to lure Ne Win out."

"No need," Felix enlarged a section of the screen. "The kid's coming out on his own."

In the clear projection, Ne Win was holding a particle gun, forcing the guards to retreat slowly.

"Young Master, this is too dangerous. Please put the gun down."

"Please, Young Master, go back to your room."

"It's not that we don't want you to go out; it's the General's order..."

In the bright light, the brown patches on Ne Win's face became more pronounced. His uneven limbs and emaciated body made him look like a grotesque creature in human skin, step by step heading towards the reception hall.

Felix quickly locked onto Ne Win's position, and Cẩm Tú activated his power, burrowing frantically toward that spot.

"Considering the alarm response time, we have nine minutes until reinforcements arrive," Felix said.

"That's enough," Cora nodded.

Chi Zhang pulled up his hood, his face hidden in shadows, leaving only the faint outline of his prominent nose. He turned back and made a forward gesture with two fingers.

Including Ewen Van and Samuel, the Saya ability users lowered their centers of gravity, ready to strike.

Nine minutes to take down Ne Win—more than enough.

A ghostly blue light flickered as Cora conjured a military dagger, a weapon infamous for its lethality. A single strike could instantly destroy bodily tissues, causing a lethal wound and a spray of blood, ensuring the enemy's swift demise.

Just as she was about to move, she noticed an unexpected tremor in Charles's hand. This tremor wasn't from fear or terror but from the overwhelming determination that peaks when a person must do something.

Cora quietly watched him for two seconds, then walked over and handed him the military dagger. "We will succeed."

Charles looked down at her.

In Sakura, he had once been in utter despair, seeking only death. It was Cora who had pulled him back from the brink, promising with unwavering determination, "I can do it."

Perhaps it was the lingering resentment and intense hatred, or perhaps it was her dimples resembling Lily's, that made Charles choose to take a chance and trust this stranger.

At first, he watched coldly from the sidelines as the team named F777 went through many troubles to achieve their revenge. Gradually, he found himself involved, following them through the desert, into Death Hell, enduring hardships and trials, finally reaching Deep Woods.

Charles gradually realized how lucky he was to have found companions he could trust in his life.

In just a few months, they had truly overcome all obstacles to reach the last step. Ne Kon, Ne Win, today will be your last day.

Charles took a deep breath, the trembling subsiding, and took the ethereal artifact from Cora's hand. "Let's go."

The dome of the reception hall was faintly visible, and a smile of excitement appeared on Ne Win's face. Just as he was about to speak, the ground ahead suddenly split open, and a series of ability users jumped out one after another.

"Enemy attack—!!" The nearest guard immediately pressed the alarm.

"Prepare to fight—!" He didn't get to finish the word "fight" before a ghostly blue military dagger slashed through his throat. The guard's eyes widened as he fell, and only when he hit the ground did the blood from his neck gush out like a waterfall.

Cora retrieved her dagger. With a flick of her hands, a dense array of swallowtail darts appeared between her fingers and flew forward. The cold-glinting projectiles accurately struck the guards who had just reacted and were attempting to block the hole.

Chi Zhang wielded his sword in one hand while rapidly forming seals with the other. His devastating Thunder Technique cleared the way, repelling the interceptors from another direction.

Underground, Cẩm Tú burrowed like a mole, digging a new hole each time he moved. In just seven or eight seconds, he had created over a dozen openings in the ground, continuously allowing high-level ability users to emerge. In this urgent moment, he even thoughtfully dug a ramp for Onyx and Felix to move in and out with their wheelchairs.

The scene descended into chaos. Cora advanced towards Ne Win but unexpectedly collided with a flexible water shield, trapping her inside. A water-based defensive ability? But there were no ability users within five meters of Ne Win.

Cora emerged from the water shield, staring coldly at Ne Win. "Half a year ago, in Sycamore, you killed an eight-year-old girl."

Ne Win's grotesque face showed a flicker of panic when Cora was blocked by the water shield, but he quickly regained his composure. Facing her accusation, he looked indifferent and even smiled arrogantly. "Who? I've killed so many people, I don't remember."

Cora's military dagger stabbed into the water shield, but the flowing liquid neutralized it like punching into cotton. "Her name was Sweetie. Her father was a doctor. The doctor fought desperately to save you, but you killed his daughter."

"Sweetie?" Ne Win said slowly. "Can't remember."

"Sounds like a nice name." Ne Win licked his lips, his not fully developed, deformed body twitching grotesquely.

Cora's eyes showed a moment of confusion. She didn't fully understand Ne Win's words. But then she saw Charles's eyes—those eyes were blood-red, almost matching the color of fresh blood.

Cora's heart pounded, and her grip on the military dagger tightened.

How could someone as young as fourteen or fifteen be so evil?

"Boom—"

A deafening explosion came from the direction of the reception hall. The thousand-strong guard unit, alerted by the alarm, joined the battle. Cora agilely back flipped to dodge the attack and took down two more guards.

She needed to find the water-based ability user to break Ne Win's shield, but the sheer number of guards was overwhelming. She had to think of a plan... Cora quickly turned around and glanced at Onyx. Their eyes met, and in that instant, they understood each other's thoughts with no need for words.

Onyx closed his eyes, his powerful mind quickly analyzing all the abilities present. Then he abruptly opened them, locked in a direction, and raised his rapid-fire crossbow, shooting several arrows in that direction.

Cora abandoned her attack on Ne Win and followed the arrows toward the target. The water-based ability user saw her charging like a vengeful spirit and hurriedly activated his water shield.

"Zing—"

The sharp edge of the dagger pierced the water shield, creating a deep dent. The cross-shaped cut was mere inches from his forehead.

Barely escaping death, the water-based ability user sighed in relief, but then his face turned pale with fear.

Cora gripped the hilt tightly, the blue light growing increasingly blinding. Her dominant mental power reached its peak, pressing forward inch by inch. No matter how strong the shield was, it couldn't withstand her blade!

The entire water shield trembled violently. Realizing his impending doom, the water-based ability user turned pale and ran. Cora pressed forward relentlessly, breaking the shield and driving the military dagger through his spine!

A high arc of crimson blood sprayed into the air. The opponent fell slowly, his abilities dissipating.

Cora turned, her shoulder-length hair tousled by the wind. She shouted across the distance, "Charles!"

Ne Win panicked and raised his particle gun, firing wildly. "Crack —" A mechanical arm struck him viciously, knocking him over and seizing his weapon, dismantling it into pieces.

Ne Win fell pathetically at someone's feet.

Charles squatted down, looking into the eyes of this monster. "Do you remember me?"

Ne Win met his blood-red gaze. He had seen those eyes before, in a haze on the operating table, thinking he was about to die. The masked doctor had nodded at him, saying, "You will live."

Miraculously, Ne Win had survived. He remembered it well— Charles had saved him.

Ne Win sighed regretfully. "Doctor, it was just bad luck. I didn't know she was your daughter..."

He paused, his speech quickening. "If it matters that much to you, just have another one. Next time, I promise I won't..."

"Thud—" Before he could finish, Charles's military dagger plunged into his chest.

He chose his position with precision. Ne Win's face contorted in agony, but he didn't die immediately.

"You're actually afraid of dying, aren't you?" Charles twisted the military dagger, the blood grooves inside him causing severe internal bleeding and forming clots.

Charles had seen countless patients' eyes on the operating table. Ne Win might have been shouting about not fearing death, but his eyes betrayed his desperate desire to live.

"Sweetie was the best daughter in the world. She rarely cried or threw tantrums. Even when I didn't have time for her, she never blamed me, just sulked on her own. Every time she said, 'I love Daddy the most,' I felt like I could give her anything."

"That day, Sweetie finally forgave me. I bought her favorite strawberry ice cream. I bought two—first time. I told her to keep it a secret from her mom. It was our little secret."

"We had promised each other, but I never got to see her again. Because I saved you. Because I slept those extra forty minutes."

Charles methodically removed Ne Win's kidneys, spleen, stomach, lungs, intestines, liver... His hands were astonishingly steady, without a hint of tremor, while Ne Win could clearly feel his organs being emptied yet remained painfully conscious. He couldn't die.

"Someone like you will never understand what Sweetie meant to me. You don't deserve to live, let alone be human."

Charles, devoid of his former healer's compassion, now resembled a cold-blooded butcher dissecting a corpse.

Terror surged within Ne Win. As his life ebbed away rapidly, he finally sobbed like a child, "No... No! Father, Father save me!!"

Ne Win's cry for his father struck the deepest chord in Charles's heart. When Sweetie died, she must have desperately wished for him to save her too.

Charles sliced open Ne Win's ventricle and plunged the dagger into his beating heart.

Ne Win's cries abruptly ceased as he saw his own heart being removed. His body shattered, his soul fractured. Ne Win stopped breathing.

Charles's hands were soaked in blood, and hot tears streamed down his face.

In his blurred vision, he saw Sweetie with her soft braids, cuddled in his arms like a little mouse sneaking a treat. She was happily holding a strawberry ice cream, cream smeared on her dimples. "Daddy, you can't tell Mom. I love you the most~"

"Ne Win!!!" A heart-wrenching roar echoed.

A soot-covered Ne Kon appeared on the periphery. Those damned bombs had killed all the ability users in the reception hall. Only Ne Kon survived because of his causality ability. He had quickly redeployed his forces, but he was still a step too late.

Amid the fierce attacks from Chi Zhang, Felix, and Samuel, the battlefield was filled with fire and explosions. The guards were being swiftly cut down.

An opportunity!

Cora charged straight at Ne Kon, leaping high with her military dagger aimed at his head.

The ability users protecting Ne Kon acted in unison. Cora pressed forward through the barrage of attacks. Just as she was about to reach him, a misfired shell exploded mid-air, its blast sending her flying. She tumbled several times before stopping herself.

The causality on Ne Kon hadn't dissipated!

Cora punched the ground in frustration.

The piercing alarms echoed throughout the Unified Palace. More and more ability users converged on their location. They were surrounded.

Onyx's wheelchair stopped next to Cora. He extended his hand, and she used it to stand up, hearing his calm voice.

"Mental power has weakened. Ne Win was indeed his puppet."

"But I can't kill him," Cora said bitterly.

"Because Ne Kon still has one last layer of causality," Onyx replied.

The last layer of causality.

The last puppet.

Who could it be? Cora looked up, scanning the battlefield filled with heads.

CHAPTER 38

Deceived

The continuous arrival of the guard units surrounded Cora and her team. With Ne Win dead, the scene fell into a tense standoff. At this moment, Ne Kon calmed down.

The shock, anger, grief, fear, and anxiety on his face vanished, leaving only the sternness of a governor and the dignity of someone who had been in power for nearly thirty years. An aide brought him a clean uniform. In front of everyone, Ne Kon calmly unbuttoned his collar and sleeves, changed his clothes, and meticulously fastened his buttons.

"A bunch of sewer rats, trying to sneak into every hole, thinking they can steal from someone else's house," Ne Kon said with a sinister look towards Chi Zhang. "You must be Chionji. Did you cause all this to try to replace me?"

Chi Zhang stared coldly at him. "You brought this upon yourself. You are tyrannical and oppressive, mistreating the people, and allowing a twisted hierarchy to push Deep Woods into turmoil. You are not fit to be a governor."

Ne Kon arrogantly raised his chin. "Young people have some heroism, thinking they are saviors. I understand, but it's just self-deception. You speak grandly now, but if you were ever in my position, you'd probably be even more of a 'tyrant' than I am."

"Ne Kon, stop spouting nonsense!" Ewen Van shouted, recognizing Ne Kon was trying to smear Chi Zhang.

Ne Kon sneered, his gaze falling on Cora, Onyx, and Felix. These three sudden S-class individuals were completely out of his control. Their secret alliance with Chionji was the main reason he was in this situation.

"What are your goals?" Ne Kon asked coldly.

"To kill you," Cora said, her military dagger pointed straight at him.

"Ne Kon, you let your son run amok and killed my daughter. You deserve to die." Charles Franz, with blood-soaked hands, slowly stepped forward. It wasn't his blood—it was Ne Win's.

Ne Kon squinted, finally recognizing him. "Dr. Franz, I never imagined you were the mastermind. I underestimated you. If I'd known you'd cause so much trouble, I would have razed Sycamore to the ground and killed you."

Facing death, Ne Kon's arrogance infuriated the ability users on site. Cora and Chi Zhang led a hundred men to charge. The guards hurriedly responded. Explosions and abilities leveled the surrounding buildings. Countless attacks targeted Ne Kon, but he stood firm, all damage strangely diverted before reaching him.

Ne Kon's aides and secretaries, seeing the dire situation, tried to flee but were struck down by talismans from the sky. More abilities flew towards Ne Kon, but he just sneered, unmoved.

Onyx watched Ne Kon through the chaos, his brows furrowing.

If the third puppet was on site, it would be at risk of being killed amidst the chaos. How could Ne Kon be so calm?

Onyx looked at Felix, who immediately turned the light screen towards him. The surveillance was clear. Besides their core area, there were no guards in the other areas already scouted by mechanical spiders.

Onyx pondered for a moment, then raised his voice to shout at Ne Kon, "You have only one puppet left. Why do you think we can't kill you?"

Ne Kon looked directly at him. "Interesting. You even know I have puppets."

Onyx stood up with his cane and took a few steps forward. Seeing this, Ne Kon raised his hand slightly, and the guards switched to a defensive retreat. The chaotic battle paused, with casualties on both sides, but Ne Kon's losses were more severe, with only a third of his high-level ability users left.

Now it was time for a psychological battle.

Onyx smiled. "It's been five minutes since the explosion. I was wondering why none of the warlords came to save you unless... you didn't issue a support order at all."

"And there's only one reason you'd do that," Onyx said, word by word, "You're protecting your puppet and yourself. As long as it lives, you won't die."

"You remain calm because you know it's not in the Unified Palace, confident we can't find it."

Ne Kon's lips tightened. This kid's insight was terrifying.

Onyx's eyes narrowed as he rapidly processed all the relevant information.

"Your first puppet, Julamani, an ability user nearly at S-class, chosen because he's hard to kill."

"The second, your son Ne Win, imprisoned in the Unified Palace, firmly in your control, because its security was top-notch. You were confident no one would breach it before we did."

"Using these two as puppets was safe but also risky. Once someone knows you have causality abilities, they could be eliminated in one sweep. You must know not to put all your eggs in one basket. So the third puppet must be entirely different."

Onyx's calm voice echoed in the open space. "You need to ensure that even if it's not under your watchful eye, it remains safe. So it must have self-preservation abilities or be in a safer, less conspicuous environment outside."

Ne Kon's eyelid twitched slightly.

"A commoner, worker, or mercenary? Too risky. A businessman or wealthy individual? Not safe enough. Given Deep Woods' hierarchy, it must be at least second level, with significant power and status, and protected by many private soldiers. High-ranking officers and minor warlords are prone to be swallowed up or assassinated, making them unsuitable."

"So that leaves the three major warlords. Nguyen Van Tuan is dead. Is it Mục Tân or Miêu Luân?"

Onyx stared at Ne Kon's tightening hand, then smiled brightly.

"You think I'll guess Mục Tân, don't you? After all, he's an ability user, more likely to survive than Miêu Luân, an ordinary person."

"But there's something I've always wondered. The three major warlords balance and restrict each other. Mục Tân and Nguyen Van Tuan frequently clashed over overlapping interests, but Miêu Luân seems to avoid direct conflict with anyone. Why is that, General?"

At the banquet Cora attended alone, Mục Tân and Nguyen Van Tuan were at each other's throats, yet Miêu Luân remained amiable. When attacking Saya, both other warlords took part, and even Ne Kon commanded. Why was Miêu Luân excluded?

"Why favor Miêu Luân? Not out of trust, but because—Miêu Luân is your deepest hidden puppet," Onyx concluded.

Ne Kon's calm facade finally cracked.

Onyx's logical deductions and pressing rhetoric broke down Ne Kon's psychological defenses in just a few words. To kill Ne Kon, they had to kill the puppet. Miêu Luân had to die.

Chi Zhang immediately pointed to a dozen people. "Follow me."

He turned to Cora, who seemed to want to say something, and nodded. "Leave it to me."

Charles wiped his face and stood firmly before Chi Zhang. "I'll go with you. Rao is still in Miêu Luân's hands. I don't know if she's in danger. I need to go personally to be sure."

Charles turned back, bowed deeply to Cora and Onyx. "... Please."

"Stop them!!" Ne Kon shouted.

Cora conjured a stick and charged forward, sweeping away the incoming guards. Chi Zhang, Charles, and their team seized the moment to jump into the tunnels, disappearing in an instant.

Anxiety flashed in Ne Kon's eyes, but his expression remained calm. "Do you think a dozen people can kill Miêu Luân?"

"We will. And you can wait to die!" Cora retorted fiercely.

She wasn't sure how strong Miêu Luân's self-preservation abilities were, but she knew Chi Zhang. Her senior brother's character was like hers: if he made a promise, he would give everything to fulfill it.

"What if I told you that even if you kill Miêu Luân, you still can't touch me?" Ne Kon quickly regained his composure and even leisurely found a chair to sit down on.

"Not good," Felix suddenly spoke up from the back. His icy blue eyes flickered with data streams. "Detecting unknown signal interference—five starships are heading towards Deep Woods, expected to arrive in an hour."

At this critical moment, starships made the situation clear. The alliance's special envoy acted faster than they had expected.

Ne Kon also received the news. He relaxed his eyebrows and laughed out loud. "I told you, you can't touch me. I not only issued a 'request for intervention,' but also submitted an 'emergency asylum' to the alliance. By the time you find Miêu Luân, I'll be long gone from Deep Woods."

Ne Kon was planning to flee? Cora was stunned by his shamelessness.

Onyx looked at the laughing Ne Kon and smiled. "Once you submit to emergency asylum, it means you lose all your privileges as a governor. You can never return to Deep Woods. I must commend your generosity. Giving up your hard-earned power, how scared are you of us killing you?"

Onyx's sharp words cut deep. No one could rival his ability to strike where it hurt most. Ne Kon's laughter faded.

In a private military camp within Deep Woods.

A column of mercenaries was on routine patrol. As they rounded a corner and took a few steps forward, they heard a slight "crack." Before they could react, frost traps sprang up, and the icy blades sliced through their throats. The unfortunate group fell in unison.

A few meters away, bored ability users were playing cards in the camp. "Double nines! I win! Hey, what's that smell?" "Smells like rotten eggs..." "What rotten eggs, that's hydrogen sulfide... Damn it!"

Outside the camp, a giant frost-covered bomb fell from the sky, exploding on impact without a flash. Green toxic gas spread, and those who accidentally inhaled it clutched their throats, writhing in pain.

The alarm blared, and mercenaries with weapons rushed out from all directions.

"Our love seems trapped in a strange loop~ The more we love, the more confused we get, the more we love, the more bewildered~,"

A clear, enchanting voice sang. The mercenaries' eyes lost focus, afflicted by a confusion debuff. They dropped their weapons and ran like headless chickens. Silent frost bombs rained down, and soon the entire private military camp fell silent.

From a distant high-rise, hidden ability users peeked out.

Damian Blackwood, with a headband tied around his head, stood on tiptoe at the window, controlling the frost traps while helping Suchat and Ellyn the Wild Rose make "super frost poison bombs." His attacks were no longer limited to hexagonal ice prisms. They had become versatile and unpredictable. Damian's growth was clear after many trials.

"All done," Yuui glanced at the terminal and crossed off another location on the map. "Rita's operation went smoothly. The private military camps of Mục Tân and Nguyen Van Tuan have been cleared. Only Miêu Luân's remains. We need to speed up."

Their covert team's primary mission was to cut off the warlords' armed forces, preventing them from rescuing Ne Kon. To minimize noise, Ellyn used newly developed frost poison bombs instead of louder cannons.

"Something's odd," said Suchat, who had scouted ahead. "The alarm has been going off at the Unified Palace for almost three minutes, but there's no reaction from this camp."

Yuui paused. It made sense that the mercenaries didn't react immediately when they first attacked, but after the alarm had been sounding for so long, shouldn't they have been more vigilant?

"Proceed with the plan. I'll contact Onyx," Yuui decided.

"Boom—"

A deafening explosion came from the direction of the Unified Palace, followed by a piercing alarm.

Miêu Luân paused, his hand holding a cigarette, and squinted into the distance, his face partially obscured by smoke. After a while, his newly appointed secretary hurried in, reporting quietly, "Sir, the General has been attacked."

"Attacked..." Miêu Luân repeated the word. "Did the General order me to reinforce?"

"There was an order, but not for reinforcement. The General's exact words were 'stay put and do not move unless instructed.'"

"Hmph," Miêu Luân sneered suddenly. "'Do not move unless

instructed,' indeed."

He stubbed out his cigarette on the table, leaving a grim burn mark, then stood up abruptly, striding outside with Cơ Đan Vi and Hu Chao following closely behind.

"Sir, where are you going...?" the secretary called out, kneeling on the ground. Is it possible that Miêu Luân is planning to openly defy orders? Miêu Luân's voice was chilling. "Gather all private soldiers. Return to the principal residence immediately."

"Sir! Something has happened, sir!" A servant stumbled in, falling at Miêu Luân's feet. "Our private military camp was ambushed!"

"Which one?" Miêu Luân's face turned ashen.

"All of them..." The servant was heartbroken, not daring to meet his gaze.

Everyone was trembling with fear, kneeling on the ground. Miêu Luân's heavy breathing was like a guillotine ready to fall. Suddenly, he turned and headed toward the backyard.

Rao and Marie were speaking softly when Miêu Luân barged in. Without a word, he slapped Rao across the face. "You slut!"

Rao fell to the ground, her face swelling up, blood trickling from her lips. Marie's eyes widened, breaking her psychic connection with Masha, and rushed to help her, glaring at Miêu Luân. "How dare you hit her!"

Miêu Luân's expression was dark. He stepped forward, his enormous shadow engulfing Rao's frail body. Marie rushed to shield her, but was kicked away and pinned down by Hu Chao.

Miêu Luân grabbed Rao by her hair, yanking her up. "I raised you all this time, only to raise a traitor. The locations of the private military camps, you leaked them."

Rao responded coldly, "Yes."

Miêu Luân didn't need to interrogate her to confirm it was her doing. No matter what she said, it wouldn't change his wrath. Rao had used her special overlay drawing technique to send Ellyn the Wild Rose portraits, which, when the top layer was wiped off, revealed maps of the private military camps.

Enraged, Miêu Luân kicked her in the stomach, causing her to curl up in pain.

"Sir, are we still going to the principal residence?" Cơ Đan Vi asked softly.

"Yes," Miêu Luân wiped his hands, speaking coldly. "Take them all with us."

In the backyard, several girls had their eyes covered, mouths taped shut, and limbs tied tightly. They were shoved into a transport vehicle. In the dark compartment, Marie moved, trying to find Rao by scent. She lay motionless, and Marie nearly cried, nudging her with her head, trying to wake her up.

After a long while, Rao slowly awoke, gently rubbing against Marie. Sensing she had something to say, Marie quickly turned around, their hands touching. Rao's warm fingertips jotted a word on her palm.

Marie carefully deciphered it. She wrote—"sister."

Marie immediately understood and closed her eyes, desperately calling for Masha through their psychic connection.

The sun gradually set, its last rays fading on the horizon. Hundreds of fully armed ability users escorted Miêu Luân into his family's principal residence, the gates closing tightly behind them; the patrols becoming more frequent.

At the Unified Palace, time ticked by. They swiftly dealt with the remaining guards. Cora wiped the blood from her face, her eyes fixed on Ne Kon. The only layer of mental protection left around him. She was waiting for Chi Zhang's signal. Once her senior brother succeeded, she would take Ne Kon out instantly.

"The special envoy is expected to arrive in thirty-five minutes," Felix reminded.

There was still time, and Cora felt slightly relieved. Her terminal lit up with a notification, and Onyx glanced at it, his expression freezing. It was a message from Chi Zhang. "Miêu Luân has fled."

Onyx's fingers flew over the terminal. Chi Zhang concisely explained the situation: shortly after the explosion at the Unified Palace, Miêu Luân had left his residence with his men. They had come up empty-handed. This either meant Miêu Luân had spies keeping tabs on the General's every move, or he knew he was a puppet and sensed something was wrong, deciding to flee early.

Chi Zhang's next message arrived. "Heading to the principal residence. Help me locate Masha."

Fortunately, Masha was in the residence's tunnel, maintaining her psychic connection with her twin sister. After Miêu Luân fled, she and Marie moved through the tunnel, sending out updates. But the tunnel's structure made external signals weak, and Chi Zhang's terminal couldn't pinpoint her location.

Onyx tossed the terminal to Felix. "Felix!"

Felix caught it, scanned the message, and his fingers flew across the keys.

"What's wrong?" Cora asked worriedly.

Onyx squeezed her hand. Before he could speak, Ne Kon glanced at his terminal and laughed loudly. "I told you, you can't kill Miêu Luân or me."

Cora frowned, about to throw her darts to silence him, when suddenly she sensed something. She looked up alertly. Familiar spatial rifts appeared high in the sky.

"Trouble," Felix sighed while locating Masha, "the special envoy isn't here yet, but the lackeys have arrived first." One by one, tall figures emerged from the void, their powerful mental energies causing violent air fluctuations.

Three S-class ability users.

Wait, something's wrong! Cora's eyes widened.

The last person, standing over two meters tall, had a burnt, necrotic left face, muscle tissues fused together, and a ghastly white eyeball. His right face was covered with dense knife scars, making him look neither human nor ghost.

This was... the Bloody Hunter, Punk.

Deep Woods fell silent. The streets were deserted as residents realized something big was happening. Windows and doors were shut tight, and no one dared to peek. Warlords, merchants, and the wealthy watched, waiting to see how things would unfold.

Dozens of high-level ability users surrounded Miêu Luân's principal residence. Because of the urgency, Chi Zhang's group didn't use the tunnels but cut straight through Deep Woods, their killing intent clear.

In the dim night, Chi Zhang coldly issued orders. "Prepare for a direct assault. Highest priority, kill Miêu Luân."

The fierce incantations of the Heavenly Wrath spell sounded the attack. Saya's ability users unleashed their mental energies, shattering the main gates and clashing with the private soldiers.

Charles heeled Chi Zhang, holding his military dagger, fearlessly battling the private soldiers. Knocked down, he got up again; injured, he mishandled himself and continued forward.

Rao was still in Miêu Luân's hands. He had to move faster to save her.

"Boom—"

Blazing cannons leveled an entire row of buildings. Ellyn the Wild Rose and Yuui's voices rang out. "We're here to help!"

With Ellyn and Damian's area attacks, the assault on the principal residence sped up. Flames roared, and smoke billowed, with panicked figures fleeing everywhere.

"Chionji, someone's escaping from the northeast corner!" shouted Merlin, an ability user specializing in detection.

Chi Zhang and his team turned to chase northeast. Dozens of ability users protected a corpulent figure in a military uniform, fleeing desperately.

Suchat moved the fastest, his figure flashing ahead of the group. His poisoned dagger bypassed the guards, slicing the fat man's throat. Almost simultaneously, Chi Zhang's soul-destroying spell pierced his brain!

Double fatal blows—Miêu Luân was surely dead!

The fat man's body froze, stumbled, and fell slowly. His military cap fell off, revealing his full face. Just as they breathed a sigh of relief, their expressions changed. This wasn't Miêu Luân!

Miêu Luân wasn't at the principal residence. He had successfully deceived them all.

CHAPTER 39

Tomorrow's Dream

When Rao woke up again, the room was pitch black. Marie was curled up at her feet, her hands rubbing against the corner of the table, trying to fray the ropes. However, the ropes were specially made, making her efforts futile.

"Marie, where are we?" Rao asked softly. Upon hearing her voice, Marie immediately moved closer. "Rao, you're finally awake. Miêu Luân has captured us and brought us to his residence."

Rao propped herself up and looked out the window. Under the pale moonlight, her lips were as white as snow. "No, this isn't Miêu Luân's residence."

She had visited Miêu Luân's residence once before. That luxurious mansion was in the bustling area of Deep Woods, where lights never went out. However, outside was now shrouded in mist, deserted, with only Miêu Luân's private soldiers nervously patrolling. It looked more like a suburban villa.

Rao had never been here, but Miêu Luân had so many private properties that she couldn't know them all.

"Ah? But before we left, Miêu Luân clearly said we were going back to his residence..." Marie mumbled in confusion, then suddenly slapped her forehead. "Oh no, the message I sent to Masha was false. The reinforcements she found will definitely go to the wrong place!"

Marie's voice lowered as she looked at Rao worriedly. "Rao, you look terrible. Are you alright?"

"I'm fine," Rao shook her head. "Can you still contact your sister?"

"Yes, she followed us here."

"I want to know what happened in the Palace of Unity," Rao said.

"I'll ask her right now." Marie activated her powers and started communicating with Masha underground.

Ne Win was dead, Ne Kon had three puppets, and the last one was Miêu Luân. Only by killing Miêu Luân could Cora Thornton take down Ne Kon. Rao's eyes, misty and smoky, narrowed slightly. Miêu Luân had probably known he was a puppet for a long time.

When she first approached Miêu Luân, he was indulgent, but not as cautious as he was now. Gradually, Miêu Luân surrounded himself with more and more private soldiers, until he was never alone, no matter what he did. He secretly recruited various rare Aberrants, such as Hasa, who specialized in data tracking, Mulberry, who could turn into black mud, and his constant bodyguards, Hu Chao and Cơ Đan Vi...

When did Miêu Luân realize Ne Kon had tampered with him? It was unclear, but he was deeply scheming, quietly enduring, while demanding benefits from Ne Kon and seeking opportunities to free himself. Miêu Luân clearly wanted to transfer the puppet status, but the aberrant who cast the spell was dead, and other high-level causality Aberrants were extremely rare. Miêu Luân's plan had to be temporarily shelved.

Recently, Miêu Luân's gaze at her had grown increasingly strange. He clearly suspected her, had people follow her, yet didn't rush to deal with her. Miêu Luân likely kept her around not out of affection but to use her as a vessel. However, before he could implement his plan, Ne Kon was embroiled in a series of assassination attempts.

While Rao and Marie were whispering, a girl's cries suddenly came from outside. Cơ Đan Vi dragged them all out. The number of private soldiers Miêu Luân brought wasn't large, as many were sent to his residence to mislead others, but those left behind were all elite.

Soon, Cơ Đan Vi kicked open their door. "The master requests your presence. Will you walk yourselves, or shall I escort you?"

Marie bit her lip in fear, but Rao calmly replied, "We will walk ourselves."

Including Rao, six girls were taken to a spacious bedroom. As soon as they entered, they were startled by the bloody scene.

Hu Chao was holding a thin blade, slicing at a person's face. The person was covered in wounds, barely recognizable, and groaning weakly.

Miêu Luân sat with his legs spread apart, staring at him. "I'll ask you one more time. What is the old man's plan?"

The secretary sent by Ne Kon couldn't endure the torture any longer and pleaded, "General, the General submitted an emergency evacuation request. The Alliance will take him tonight. Sir, I've told you everything I know. Please, spare me!"

Miêu Luân stared at him silently.

Hu Chao spoke softly, "His seven answers are consistent, sir. Only a few more cuts left. Shall we continue?" implying that the man was not lying.

Miêu Luân lifted his finger, and Hu Chao swiftly ended the secretary's life with a last cut.

Having received the information he wanted, Miêu Luân stood up in a low mood, pacing the room. He kicked over a chair and cursed, "That damn old man!"

"Get the body out."

The servants came in silently, dragging the mutilated body away.

Miêu Luân suddenly turned around, breathing heavily, pressing down on Cơ Đan Vi's shoulder. "I don't care what it costs. Guard the door tonight. Don't let a single fly in. Understood?"

Cơ Đan Vi knelt down, lowering his head. "Cơ Đan Vi will defend you with my life, sir."

Miêu Luân nodded in satisfaction. "Go."

After Cơ Đan Vi left, Miêu Luân's expression remained dark and stormy. Like a cornered beast, he picked up a whip from the table and began lashing out in frustration, the girls in the room suffering to varying degrees. Hearing their cries of pain, he suddenly grabbed one girl's head and pressed it hard into the still-wet blood and flesh, casting a grotesque shadow over her.

The girl's screams were so horrifying that Hu Chao's eardrums twitched. Instinctively, he looked up, meeting Miêu Luân's violent gaze. He shivered, took two steps back, and retreated behind the screen, from where he could clearly see Miêu Luân's silhouette without having to witness the gruesome scene directly.

After a long while, Miêu Luân stopped. The girl, covered in blood, had fainted, barely alive. Miêu Luân then turned his icy gaze to Marie. "Come here," he ordered.

Marie backed away in fear. Miêu Luân, growing impatient, flicked the whip in the air, catching her neck and dragging her over with brute force. Marie struggled, kicking and punching, but Miêu Luân tightened the whip around her neck. Her breath grew short, her eyes rolled back, and her struggles weakened.

Rao rushed over to pry Miêu Luân's hands off Marie. Annoyed, Miêu Luân kicked her away. "Thud!" Rao's back slammed into the iron bed frame, making a thunderous sound. Her vision went white, and she lost consciousness for several seconds.

Miêu Luân stretched out, a bloody smile on his face. "Why rush? Your turn is coming soon." Good things should always be saved for last.

Hearing the commotion, Hu Chao peeked over the screen and saw Rao lying on the ground, barely alive, while Marie, her eyes closed, had deep marks around her neck and her hands twitching spasmodically under the table.

Hu Chao withdrew again. He sorely missed Mulberry, who had passed away. Given a choice, he would prefer not to be involved in this bloody business.

Time was running out.

Enduring the intense pain, Rao forced herself to stay calm. She had to do something. If Miêu Luân died, Ne Kon would lose his ultimate protection. Though she didn't have the power to kill Ne Kon herself, she could speed up his demise.

From Miêu Luân's earlier tone, Ne Kon had a backup plan. Miêu Luân's goal was also obvious: to survive the night, and both he and Ne Kon could continue living safely.

Time was running out.

Rao slowly crawled forward. Miêu Luân, frustrated with the whip, threw it on the ground and began strangling Marie with his hands.

Rao's trembling fingers reached the end of the whip. Suddenly, her frail body surged with surprising strength. She stood up quickly, expertly wrapping the whip around Miêu Luân's neck, tying it in a deadly knot, and pulling it tight.

Miêu Luân's body tensed, his eyes bulged, and he reflexively reached for the whip around his neck, trying to untie it. But Rao had practiced this move countless times, tying a complex knot that couldn't be undone easily. Miêu Luân, enraged and suffocating, let out a choking sound, trying to grab the end of the whip with one hand while using the other to slap Rao and pull her hair.

Rao resisted with all her might, holding on to the whip.

However, the strength of a strong, healthy man in a life-or-death struggle was far greater than that of a weak, injured woman. As Miêu Luân struggled violently, Rao's fingers bled, her strength fading.

Marie, waking from suffocation, saw the scene before her. Mouth agape, she silently mouthed, "Rao..."

Tears streamed down her face as she desperately clawed at Miêu Luân's arm, her nails digging deep into his flesh. She lowered her head, biting like a beast, and forced Miêu Luân's hand off Rao's hair.

Hu Chao, hearing the noise, peeked over the screen again. He saw Miêu Luân leaning back slightly, his hands on Marie, trembling. Hu Chao instantly realized what was happening and looked away again, lowering his head in silence.

Miêu Luân's face turned purple, but Rao was also at her limit, her grip slipping. Just then, a scarred hand reached out, pulling the whip tight with her. It was another girl from the room, her appearance miserable, but her eyes filled with fierce determination.

In the silent standoff, a third hand joined, followed by a fourth and a fifth...

These girls, treated as playthings by Miêu Luân, fought back with their lives. Without uttering a sound, they stumbled or crawled over, resolutely gripping the whip.

They had only one thought: Miêu Luân must die.

Miêu Luân, on the verge of breaking free, suffered another blow. His eyes turned lifeless, his brain deprived of oxygen, and his carotid arteries close to bursting. His struggles grew weaker until he knocked over a teacup.

The sudden sound of breaking porcelain alerted Hu Chao. He looked up, but his attention was drawn outside the door.

In the darkness, the sounds of fighting could be heard, the glow of aberrant powers flickering. Hu Chao frowned slightly. What was Co

Đan Vi doing? Couldn't even guard the door properly? He should switch with him, he thought, and guard Miêu Luân himself...

Wait!

Hu Chao realized with a start that he hadn't heard Miêu Luân's voice in several minutes, nor the cries of the girls. Cold sweat broke out on his forehead as he pushed over the screen to rush forward.

A sharp talisman pierced through the air, stabbing through Hu Chao's head from behind.

Chi Zhang and Ellyn rushed in with their team, and everyone was stunned by the scene before them.

The battered girls clung to the whip in various positions, the other end wrapped tightly around Miêu Luân's neck. He was stiff, barely clinging to life.

"Rao!!"

Charles dropped his military knife and ran over in a panic, helping Rao up from the ground.

Chi Zhang yanked Miêu Luân up and thrust the sword into his head with pinpoint accuracy. Miêu Luân had no strength to resist. After confirming his death, Chi Zhang sent a message to Onyx.

Miêu Luân's body was dragged away, and Marie slid off the table, falling to the floor and coughing violently. Chi Zhang hesitated, then removed his robe and turned away to cover her battered body.

Yuui and Ellyn also took out clean jackets, distributing them to the other girls.

The Aberrants present remained silent. These girls were heroes. Miêu Luân, even in death, might never have imagined that his once glorious life would end at the hands of the very "roses" he had cultivated.

Charles clumsily checked Rao's limbs, anxiously asking, "Rao, are you hurt? Let me heal you."

Rao cradled his hand. "Why are you in such a mess?"

Charles wasn't in much better shape, his face covered in blood, and his hair tangled.

Rao smiled softly. "How many times have I told you? Clothes are hard to clean."

Charles, who hadn't heard her scold him in a long time, felt both sour and sweet. "I'll clean them, I promise."

"Rao, Ne Win is dead. I killed him with my own hands. Ne Kon... Ne Kon will die soon too. None of them will escape. I finally avenged Lily." Charles choked up.

"I know," Rao smiled faintly, "You've worked hard during this time."

Charles shook his head quickly. "It wasn't hard. It was my fault before. I couldn't handle things. I always made you angry. When this is all over, can we leave Deep Woods? Go back to Sycamore, or anywhere you want to go."

"No, let's go back to Sycamore. I want to go home," Rao said softly.

The word "home" brought tears to Charles' eyes. He clumsily reached out, trying to lift Rao, but she stopped him. Charles looked up, puzzled.

"There's something I need to tell you," Rao said, placing his hand on her chest and abdomen. Charles released his spirit power, his face turning grim.

Rao's spleen was shattered.

Not only that, but her other organs were also failing rapidly because of massive blood loss and internal injuries. Though she had no visible wounds, her body was severely damaged. The kick Miêu Luân had dealt her was exceptionally vicious. Rao had held on for so long, but the successive blows were too much.

"It's okay, it's okay. I'm an A-rank healer. I can save you!" Charles rambled, his hands shaking uncontrollably as he desperately poured his spirit power into Rao.

However, Rao was just an ordinary person, her body not enhanced, absorbing the spirit power slowly. Charles's voice trembled. "Rao, don't be afraid. I'm a doctor. I'll operate on you. We'll do the surgery right away!"

Rao held Charles's hands, stopping his futile efforts. There was no time left, and she knew it. "All the things I said before were just out of anger. Charles, you are not only a good father but also a wonderful husband. I just regret that I can't be with you anymore. Don't be sad. I've regretted nothing I've done."

She cupped Charles's tear-streaked face. "This time, no giving up. Promise me you'll live well. Can you do that?"

Charles shook his head, crying, "I can't, I can't, Rao. I'm useless. I couldn't save Lily, and I can't save you."

"You are not useless. You are the best doctor in the world. Promise me." Rao stubbornly looked at him, waiting for an answer.

Charles, in immense pain, nodded with tears, "... I promise you."

"What do you promise me?"

"... To live well."

"Ne Kon is dead," Chi Zhang suddenly spoke, "Cora killed Ne Kon. Ne Kon is dead."

"Is he dead? That's good, he deserved it," Rao's voice grew softer, "Charles, I think I see Lily."

This time, the dream was a long-awaited, beautiful one. Lily was no longer crying, her dimples faintly visible as she smiled sweetly, calling out something.

Rao gobbled two steps forward and finally heard it clearly.

She was calling, "Mommy!"

CHAPTER 40

Her People

Three S-class Aberrants emerged from a spatial rift and walked towards Ne Kon. Besides Punk, the other two were dressed in identical combat uniforms. After confirming Ne Kon's identity, the leading man revealed his credentials and introduced himself, "Former Governor of Deep Woods, we are Gasta and Roy from the Alliance Special Task Force, arriving in District C33 at exactly 17:27 local time."

"Why is it just you two? Where are the envoy and the starship?" Ne Kon asked, his face showing displeasure. "I demand to leave immediately."

"The starship scheduled to escort you will arrive in thirty-three minutes," Gasta replied.

"Then I order you to kill these people now." Ne Kon's eyes were sinister as he pointed to Cora and the Saya Aberrants opposite him.

Gasta remained indifferent, showing no respect. "Former Governor of Deep Woods, our mission is to ensure your safety until the envoy arrives. You have no authority to issue commands to me."

Gasta and Roy exuded calm restraint, but Punk was different. He stared intently at Cora, the scars on his face writhing menacingly, clearly recognizing her as the one who had blinded his right eye on Manzoni Street, forcing him to replace it with a mechanical eye.

Punk took a couple of slow steps forward, then suddenly lunged.

A series of bloody explosions erupted, but Cora was prepared. She instantly conjured a shield, flicked her left hand, and threw a handful of dart tails at Punk.

Punk's face twisted as he charged like a beast. Cora transformed her shield into a blade, slashing at his legs. Punk jumped to avoid it, and Cora leaped higher, delivering a powerful kick to his jaw. "Bang!" The sound of fireworks exploding echoed, and the force of the impact caused Cora to spin mid-air before landing steadily. Punk, however, stumbled back, leaving deep marks on the ground, his jaw nearly dislocated.

The exploding sparks still injured Cora.

Her sleeve was mostly blown off. Despite her quick dodge, Punk's bloody blasts had grazed her arm, leaving a wound. Fortunately, it wasn't serious.

Samuel and the others wanted to help but were stopped by Cora. "You all fall back."

Battles between S-classes were not something ordinary Aberrants could interfere with. Punk would only slaughter Samuel and the others.

Gasta stood in front of Punk, his voice cold, "Bloodthirsty Slayer, acting on your own, first warning."

Punk sneered, "You brought me here to suppress the rebellion, right? What's wrong with me killing her?"

Gasta remained unmoved. "All actions are to follow the envoy's orders. One more violation, and I will activate the containment directive to send you back."

Punk clenched his fists.

His malicious eyes glared like a chained mad dog, but he refrained from attacking.

Gasta turned to Cora. "Are you an S-class aberrant? Which unit? What's your number? Who's your superior?"

Cora paused for a second and answered honestly, "No unit, no number, no superior... I, I'm the highest authority."

A wild S-class? Gasta frowned. S-class Aberrants were extremely valuable strategic resources, and the Alliance would go to great lengths to recruit them. It was possible that they might end up as colleagues someday, so Gasta didn't want to clash with her now. "The Alliance is on an official mission. Take your people and leave the Palace of Unity immediately."

"No, Ne Kon must die." Cora raised her sword, refusing to back down.

Seeing her obstinance, Gasta's voice grew colder. "Obstructing official duties knowingly—do you know the consequences?"

Punk gathered blood beads at his fingertips provocatively. Ne Kon, confident of his imminent escape, looked smug. Words were useless. Cora gripped her Tang sword tightly and leaped over Gasta, ready to force her way through. Punk laughed wildly, lunging forward. "She made the first move. Don't blame me!"

Gasta and Roy, feeling a headache coming on, had no choice but to join the fray. As they moved, they were blocked.

Roy faced off against Felix Lucas.

The man before him moved using six massive mechanical arms, his fingers flying over a screen, completely ignoring Roy. Felix easily intercepted him.

Roy calmly launched an attack. His ability, "Prism," manipulated the refraction rates of different colors of light, creating disorienting illusions that inflicted severe cutting damage. Roy was a master of his power, and prismatic beams shot straight at Felix, blindingly bright. Felix entered the final code and confirmed Masha's location, smiling as he sent it to Chi Zhang.

Then Felix casually looked up. The nearest prism was less than an inch from his nose. His eyes glowed with a strange and dazzling light, and binary code floated in his pupils, altering the prism's structure, disintegrating it bit by bit.

Felix's six arms swept out, and a torrent of data overwhelmed Roy's attack, dismantling the deadly prisms like small toy horses.

Only then did Roy get a clear look at his opponent: silver hair, icy eyes. He gasped, "You're... from the Lucas family?!"

Felix blinked in confusion. "Lucas family? I don't know."

Gasta was a powerful attacker. His ability, "Bioelectricity," controlled electric currents within living organisms to stun or kill targets through mental manipulation.

Facing Onyx in a wheelchair, Gasta did not underestimate him. Anyone daring to block an S-class aberrant must be formidable. Bioelectric currents attached to Onyx's organs, tissues, and cells, ready to strike. Suddenly, each current was met with strong mental resistance and eradicated instantly.

Gasta was shocked. His opponent's control over mental power was more refined than his own.

Onyx countered seamlessly, mimicking Gasta's electric paths to attack him in return. The radiation field in the air fluctuated violently. Gasta's thoughts were weighed down, forcing him to retreat and putting him at a disadvantage.

"An Initial Awakener?"

Gasta realized something and looked up sharply.

Initial Awakeners were those who had awakened their powers before the apocalypse. They absorbed more intense radiation and had more time to adapt, strengthening them. Cultivating an Initial Awakener required immense resources, including nutrient pods, laboratories, exclusive agents, and precise radiation exposure, all top-secret information that only major families in Zone B could afford. Gasta knew the Lucas family's gene optimization program aimed at creating Initial Awakeners. Who exactly was this person in front of him?

Gasta scanned the battlefield, slowly understanding. Three S-class Aberrants wanted him dead. No wonder the Governor of Deep Woods applied for asylum.

Cora, engaged in a fierce battle with Punk, maintained high vigilance and constantly watched her positioning. Although they were currently evenly matched, Punk had yet to use his other power —time reversal.

All three battlefields were locked in a stalemate, and the Alliance envoy was imminent.

Above the Palace of Unity, the outlines of five starships gradually appeared. One smaller ship suddenly fired its engine, accelerated, and jumped instantly overhead. It descended slowly, hovering at low altitude and lowering a gangway.

Ne Kon, unable to contain his impatience, stood up and strode toward the gangway. Cora unleashed a flurry of strikes to force Punk back and then rushed forward, determined not to let Ne Kon board the ship.

Gasta and Roy's primary mission was to protect Ne Kon. Seeing this, they decisively broke away and charged at Cora.

Ne Kon ascended the gangway, standing at the entrance, looking down at Cora, who was desperately chasing after him. Seeing her weapons and sword strikes deflected from his body, he sneered coldly: How does it feel to watch me leave, powerless to stop it?

Ne Kon moved his lips, about to speak, when a faint cracking sound echoed in the air. It was subtle and easy to miss, but Ne Kon felt as if lightning had struck him, his pupils contracting sharply. — Miêu Luân is dead.

Cora's spirits lifted—her brother had succeeded, and the last layer of causality protecting Ne Kon had vanished. Now, Ne Kon was completely vulnerable.

Pale-faced, Ne Kon turned and scrambled into the cabin, stumbling and tripping over himself in his panic. He barely made it inside, and the hatch closed as the starship lifted off.

Cora leapt forward, grabbing the edge of the gangway with both hands, and quickly climbed up. She hung beneath the starship like a precarious kite.

"Bang, bang—"

Blood-red fireworks exploded behind her. Prism and bioelectric attacks all targeted her, and unable to dodge, Cora endured the damage and jumped onto the top of the starship.

The starship's ascent created strong air currents, and Cora struggled to maintain her balance. She moved forward, located Ne Kon, and thrust her Tang sword downward. "Clang—" Her powerful metal ability created a deep crack in the porthole, but it didn't shatter. Ne Kon stared at her through the glass, eyes filled with terror.

"Boom—"

Blood mist rose from her abdomen as Punk's explosions grew fiercer. Cora wavered, nearly falling from the starship. At the critical moment, she gripped her Tang sword with one hand and pulled herself back up.

From afar, Onyx's eyes were chillingly cold. He pulled out his last dose of the inhibitor, ready to inject it into his leg.

"Gonna lose your leg?!" Felix's mechanical arm reached out, stopping him, his face uncharacteristically serious.

"Yeah, I'll keep you company. Happy?" Onyx smiled brightly, firmly pushing Felix away and injecting the inhibitor without flinching. Despite the excruciating pain, he stood up and ran towards Cora.

Felix fell silent. He knew his own condition well; years of illness had left his legs unable to regenerate. But Onyx, who might heal, will take such a risk. Once so proud, could he really resign himself to a life in a wheelchair?

"Madman." Felix rolled his eyes. He had to admit, this guy was becoming more and more... human.

Cora's bloodied right hand pressed against the starship's surface, her mental power surging rapidly. The starship glowed a ghostly blue, vibrating incessantly. Ne Kon's panic intensified. What kind of monster was she to tear the starship apart with her power?

Ne Kon anxiously looked at the control panel. The next jump was in five seconds.

【Five】

Cora gripped her Tang sword with her left hand, driving it inch by inch into the porthole.

【Four】

Gasta and Roy unleashed their most lethal attacks on Cora, while Punk's crimson explosions lit up her back.

【Three】

Just as Cora was about to fall again, two figures rushed forward. Powerful and cold mental energy surged, a torrent of binary data forming an inescapable defensive web, deflecting the deadly attacks of prism, bioelectricity, and bloody explosions.

Onyx and Felix were thrown back over ten meters.

Onyx, usually meticulous about his appearance, was now in tatters. Felix fared worse, with four of his six mechanical arms broken, but none of the attacks had touched Cora.

【Two】

Punk's left eye, now mechanical, flickered wildly as he activated his time reversal ability. Cora exerted all her strength, her eyes blazing with blue light. The starship's hull shattered, and her Tang sword pierced Ne Kon's heart.

【One】

"Boom—" The entire starship exploded into a dazzling display of fireworks.

Time slowed, then reversed. Before everyone's eyes, a complete starship reappeared. Punk's ability had worked!

Everyone held their breath, staring at the sky.

A lithe figure leaped down, landing silently. Covered in wounds, Cora slowly stood up.

Behind her, the starship restored by the time reversal paused for two seconds before its hull shattered again. Ne Kon's body plummeted to the ground, a Tang sword embedded in his chest.

Time reversal could only restore non-living things to their state a few seconds prior. However, the impact of Cora's aberrant power on the starship's surface remained. Even with another reversal, it would still break apart. Cora had killed Ne Kon before Punk activated his ability.

The scene fell into dead silence.

Cora's eyes flashed with blue light, her mental power pouring out, crackling like an enraged storm. She turned to Punk and his companions, demanding, "Who gave you permission to touch my people?"

CHAPTER 41

Psycho Tsunami

Behind Cora, Ne Kon's body crashed to the ground, bones breaking through his internal organs, and crimson blood spreading out. Everyone realized this once-mighty governor had met a grisly end, now dead beyond doubt. The Tang sword embedded in his chest rang like a death knell in the ears of the onlookers.

Everyone present was terrified, looking at Cora as if she were a monster. Despite being surrounded and attacked by three S-class Aberrants, she had killed the governor of District C. But what was even more horrifying was that she had single-handedly destroyed a starship. This was far beyond human limits, even for an aberrant.

The remaining four starships arrived one after another above the Palace of Unity, maintaining a high-altitude hover and not daring to descend. In the cockpit of the leading ship, a man dressed in a formal suit with meticulously groomed hair looked solemnly at Cora on the floating screen.

"Trouble, trouble," sighed Special Envoy Park Jae-woo, feeling a headache coming on. Even though he had mentally prepared himself before arriving, the complexity of the situation in District C33 was far beyond his imagination. The governor, who had applied for emergency asylum, had died, and they would undoubtedly hold him accountable upon his return. Three unidentified S-class Aberrants could erupt into a new conflict at any moment.

Park Jae-woo, a highly slick politician, was keen on climbing the political ladder and detested war and violence. From a personal standpoint, he preferred to resolve disputes peacefully, without force. Fighting would cause casualties, which would affect his performance and delay his promotion. Ne Kon's death was a fact, but perhaps there was still room for negotiation?

"Have you identified those three yet?" Park Jae-woo asked seriously.

On the starship were two more S-class operatives from the Special Task Force and a team of fully armed A-class Aberrants under Park Jae-woo's command.

An administrative assistant pulled up the files on a holographic screen and reported to Park Jae-woo, "Sir, we could only identify one, named Cora, bio ID: VUL7700523, registered in District C83, power level... A-class?"

The A-class Aberrants seated behind him gasped in surprise. "What? A-class! Look at her, does she look like an A-class?"

"District C83, that AI-governed Felalakas? This is absurd!"

"What's the registry center in Felalakas doing, missing an S-class aberrant? If reported in time, she might have been recruited already."

"Sir, her energy fluctuations are abnormal," reminded Odin, an S-class aberrant himself.

Park Jae-woo glanced at the power detection device on the control panel. The detector circling near Cora showed radiation levels spiking, with lines wildly fluctuating like a disco. The energy readings far exceeded the S-class threshold.

"We can't fight, we can't fight," Park Jae-woo thought, maintaining his expression but sighing internally. "Issue a surrender broadcast immediately."

The cannons on the four starships were all raised, and the latest heavy weapons from the Alliance were on high alert. Simultaneously, a small drone descended to low altitude, broadcasting a looped mechanical message through loudspeakers. "Attention below, lay down your weapons immediately! Any grievances can be resolved through dialogue! Step forward and face destruction, step back, and you may still have a chance. The envoy urges..."

Annoyed, Cora's eyes flashed blue, and dozens of crossbow bolts materialized, turning the drone into a porcupine.

Park Jae-woo sighed inwardly. Negotiation chances were shattered.

Because of the overexertion of their powers, Gasta and Roy collapsed on the ground, exhausted.

Punk, however, seemed unaffected. He stared at Cora with a sinister smile. "You've got guts, killing in front of me."

"I'm curious. How did you survive last time?" Blood mist rose from Punk's fingertips. "But it doesn't matter. Today, I'll watch you die."

Cora raised her right hand, and a ghostly blue halberd formed with no external aid. "The one dying is you."

"What's she trying to do?"

"Is she mad? She wants to kill Punk? Punk is a dual-ability S-class!"

The people in the starship looked surprised and started murmuring. A few months ago, when the secret of the Bloodthirsty Slayer Punk's second ability was exposed, it had stirred quite a commotion in the Alliance.

Cora charged with her halberd, and Punk met her head-on. Their exchange was so fast it was hard to follow, with equally powerful abilities and magnetic fields clashing. In terms of combat skills, Punk was no match for Cora, but his blood explosions were extremely treacherous, constantly erupting on Cora's body like fireworks.

Cora didn't retreat a step, fighting recklessly, dodging only when vital points were threatened. Her attacks grew increasingly fierce. After dodging a blood mist aimed at her chest, she lowered her center of gravity and seized the opportunity. The halberd pierced through Punk's left hand, swinging his entire body and smashing him into a building wall, which collapsed in a cloud of dust and rubble.

Punk, covered in blood, had a twisted smile. In the next moment, Cora's arm exploded in blood fireworks, shattering her joint and rendering her right arm limp. Punk's left eye flickered, activating the time reversal, allowing him to escape her grasp and return to his position a few seconds earlier.

Losing the use of her right arm didn't faze Cora. She calmly switched to her left hand, and her mental power crackled, forming another spear. She charged at Punk again.

Seeing the spear coming, Punk activated the time reversal! Cora was sent back to her previous position, but her attack continued uninterrupted. As she struck, the spear transformed into twin clubs, descending like iron plates. Surprised, Punk was struck in the chest, his internal organs damaged, and blood spurted out.

Cora's transformations were unpredictable, driven by combat instincts. Her opponents couldn't expect what weapon she'd use next. The weapons could appear at any time in any unexpected form. She could wield a sword, halberd, crossbow, or, in the blink of an eye, switch to a staff, trident, or twin blades, mixed with various concealed weapons, making defense nearly impossible.

Punk had never seen such bizarre ancient weapons and couldn't discern their characteristics, forcing him to increase the frequency of his blood explosions. Cora's wounds multiplied, but she charged through the blood fireworks as if she felt no pain.

"Sir, the radiation levels are still rising," Odin frowned.

"Is she... still human?" an A-class aberrant asked, trembling.

"Should we intervene, sir?"

Park Jae-woo's expression turned inscrutable. The Aberrants following him on this mission, except for Punk, were from his political rival, sent to monitor him under the guise of "rebellion suppression" and to catch him off guard.

After a moment of internal struggle, Park Jae-woo remained composed. "Don't rush in. Wait, longer."

Others might not have noticed, but only Punk, who was fighting Cora, was painfully aware of the increasing pressure. Gritting his teeth, Punk deliberately left an opening, lunging forward to unleash a blood mist on Cora's left arm. Cora shook it off quickly, then her right hand turned, materializing a piercer.

Impossible! Punk's pupils constricted. Didn't her right hand get incapacitated?

In that moment of vulnerability, Cora grabbed his head and smashed it into the ground, driving the piercer into his functional mechanical eye. "Ah—" Punk screamed in agony.

Through his bloodied vision, Punk saw a miraculous change in Cora's wounds. The once-deep, fatal injuries were healing rapidly, turning into superficial cuts.

Punk's eyes widened in disbelief, "You're a dual..."

Cora didn't give him a chance to speak. She flicked the piercer through his right hand, severing his tendons, rendering both his hands useless. She then materialized an axe, and with two swift strikes, severed Punk's legs.

With his mechanical eye broken and his limbs destroyed, only his left eye could still move.

"Sir, should we...?" Odin asked, unable to sit still any longer.

Jae-Woo Park watched the battle below, giving a heartfelt speech, "Go now. In such critical times, we must support each other. Punk has done his best. We can't let him bear the risk alone."

Odin and another S-class aberrant jumped down from the starship, rejoining Gasta and Roy to assist Punk. As they moved, four battered mechanical arms stretched out to block their path.

Onyx supported Felix into his wheelchair, his voice icy. "This is a personal matter. It's not appropriate for you to interfere."

Odin snorted, activating his power. Before he could strike, countless talismans descended, and a young man in a black robe appeared before them. With a thunderous roar, countless bolts of lightning struck down, creating a clear boundary between the two sides.

"Chionji!" Samuel and the others shouted excitedly. Chi Zhang had returned at the critical moment.

In the command cabin, Jae-Woo Park gasped. Another S-class? What kind of place was Deep Woods, filled with such monsters?

With Onyx's group in a fierce battle, Cora faced Punk, who was paralyzed and staring at her with hatred. He laughed maniacally, "No wonder you survived..."

"You think you can kill me? Are you ready for the consequences? I'll drag all of you to hell with me!"

Punk's dead white eye flickered violently, and his body swelled like a balloon, emitting a bright, blood-red light.

Not good, he's going to self-destruct! Cora's eyes widened slightly, and she hastily released her mental power to shield herself.

However, the energy unleashed by an S-class aberrant's self-destruction could be cataclysmic.

"Retreat!" Gasta and Odin shouted in horror. The four starships quickly turned around, and the remaining guards and Saya Aberrants fled for their lives.

Punk's dual abilities fused, planning to use himself as the catalyst for a final bloody explosion, then repeatedly revert to the moment of the explosion with time reversal. Such devastation could obliterate not just Aberrants but the entire Deep Woods.

Cora realized his intent and aimed to attack his left eye. The explosive force surrounding him repelled the source of his power. Blown back several times, she could barely keep her eyes open against the raging wind, cold sweat soaking her back. Punk's self-destruction was inevitable, but the chain explosions had to be stopped. What could she do to break it?

Think, think fast. Cora clenched her fists and bit her lip.

At that moment, a hand supported Cora.

Onyx walked against the fierce wind, coming up behind her and wrapping his arms around her. Cora's back pressed against his warm chest. Looking up, she saw the disheveled but still handsome man smiling down at her. "Unless you want to die with me, Cora, seize the moment."

Onyx squeezed her fingers gently, and his immense mental power surged towards Punk like a tsunami. His psychic blades stabbed into Punk's brain, causing his consciousness to pause for half a second.

Cora's eyes narrowed. She instantly formed a dagger, her eyes turning a deep blue, her mental power spiking to its peak. She broke through the layers of explosive force and plunged the dagger into Punk's left eye.

"Boom—"

A cataclysmic explosion erupted, leveling the Palace of Unity and shaking the entire Deep Woods. Scorching air rushed at them, and Cora turned to shield Onyx, their mental powers intertwined tightly.

The flames engulfed their figures.

CHAPTER 42

Home

Amid the choking, thick smoke, the sound of coughing echoed through the air. Bloody Hunter Punk's chain explosions were promptly stopped, but the scene remained engulfed in smoke and flames. Some surviving Water and Earth Aberrants tried to extinguish the fire, but it was futile. The fire at the Unified Palace grew stronger, and the magnificent palace was collapsing into ruins, gradually turning into scorched earth.

Chi Zhang waved away the smoke in front of him and looked in Cora's direction, vaguely seeing the silhouette of a tall man. The man wobbled and slowly fell forward, caught by a pair of slender hands.

Cora's mouth moved as she anxiously said something. Onyx, leaning on her shoulder, smiled comfortingly, lifted his fingertips, and extinguished a small clump of her burning hair. He then took out a wheelchair from his space and, with Cora's help, sat down.

Gasta, Odin, and Felix slowly stood up. After a while, four fully armed starships flew back, circling over the Unified Palace. With the successive deaths of Ne Kon and Punk, would the situation spiral into an irreversible abyss? Would the Special Envoy announce the start of a war? Everyone grew tense.

Amidst the crackling of fire sparks, Onyx's clear voice pierced through the smoke, echoing in everyone's ears. "Special Envoy, according to Article 22, Section 9 of the Alliance Wartime Emergency Ordinance, I, as the weaker party, may request a ceasefire negotiation."

Odin glared at him, shameless! You assassinated the Governor, killed an S-class Aberrant, and now you claim to be the "weaker party" and request negotiations. Do you have any sense of shame?

Unfortunately, Onyx was never one to care about shame.

In the starship, Jae-Woo Park's eyes lit up. Finally, someone who understands. Negotiating would be good.

A holographic projection slowly descended, and Jae-Woo Park's image appeared clearly before Cora and the others. As a shrewd and cautious politician, he would never risk his life by coming down in person, especially with a killer like Cora present. Now, even the starship wasn't safe.

In the holographic projection, Jae-Woo Park fell into deep thought. He then slowly raised his head, his expression stern and imposing. "I will stay in District C33 for three days to reorganize internal affairs. During these three days, I do not want to see any of you in my presence."

"Officer," Onyx responded with a loud laugh.

A secret deal was thus struck, and the imminent war dissipated into nothingness, allowing Cora and Saya's Aberrants to retreat safely.

Ewen Van and the others were dumbfounded. They had known this man was a great deceiver, but they never expected he could even fool the Special Envoy!

Gasta and Odin exchanged glances, wisely choosing to remain silent and not express any opinions.

Roy and another young S-class Aberrant showed dissatisfaction and disbelief on their faces. They couldn't understand the deeper meaning behind the confrontation between Jae-Woo Park and Onyx. Why were Ne Kon and Punk's deaths brushed aside so lightly? Why were these people allowed to leave?

To survive in the Alliance's political arena, strength was important, but it wasn't enough. One also needed a cunning mind. Every person there had countless schemes up their sleeves, and Onyx was more familiar with the rules of the gray areas than they were.

From the starship, Jae-Woo Park gazed down at the four S-class Aberrants walking away side by side, the blazing Unified Palace behind them. He exhaled, "Saya... Deep Woods... It seems the next regional level assessment of the Alliance will see significant changes."

The old C District had collapsed, and new flames were spreading. Would Saya replace Deep Woods in the future? Only time would tell.

Jae-Woo Park's gaze fell on Cora again. Her strength was unfathomable, likely surpassing S-class long ago. The Alliance couldn't use it. She would inevitably become a major threat in the future, just like Ne Kon's fate.

As soon as they stepped out of the Unified Palace, Cora's terminal lit up with a notification. "Your entry permit is valid for 0 days, 0 hours, 0 minutes. Please submit an update promptly, or you may not remain in the city."

What a coincidence. Fifteen days ago, they had entered the completely unfamiliar Deep Woods with forged identities, their future uncertain. Fifteen days later, Ne Kon was dead, their assassination target successfully eliminated, and as they were about to leave, their fake entry permit expired right on time. It was as if fate had written the perfect ending.

The next day, at Saya Base.

Charles examined Onyx's legs, his expression grave. "It doesn't look good. The excessive injections have affected the nerves in your left leg, and the muscle atrophy will only get worse. Now it's your legs, but if this drags on, it will soon spread throughout your body."

Since the morning, because of the aftereffects of the closure, Onyx's legs had lost all sensation, and he couldn't stand even with crutches.

"What do we do?" Cora asked nervously.

"Go back to Sycamore. I'll contact colleagues at Nine and arrange for surgery as soon as possible." Charles didn't hesitate to mention the hospital.

Yuui Hayashi was about to say something but stopped, worriedly looking at Charles. "Are you... okay?"

Despite the bloodshot eyes and dark circles that revealed a sleepless night, his expression was eerily calm. When Rao died in his arms, Charles's collapse and pain were beyond words, and Yuui Hayashi was worried about his mental state.

"I know what you're worried about, but I... I promised her."

Charles clutched a small bottle around his neck, his eyes tender and reminiscent. Rao left peacefully; she was just accompanying him differently now. What he had to do was take her home and then live well as she had wished.

"Knock, knock."

There was a rhythmic knock on the door.

As soon as Cora said "Come in," a group of people jostled in, all martial art fellows from the dojo, led by none other than the heavily bandaged Morgan. He grimaced in pain but still hooked an arm around Cora's shoulders. "Little Junior Sister, I heard you were unstoppable at the Unified Palace yesterday! Damn, I missed it. I don't care. I want a rematch with you!"

"You're just trying to save face. A match with Little Junior Sister is just a beating for you, but you want to call it a sparring session," Rita dismantled him mercilessly.

Chi Zhang leaned casually against the doorframe, watching the noisy room with a relaxed posture. He wasn't wearing his usual robe, but a casual outfit he used to wear during their training days on Mount Yue. With the martial art fellows around, he was not Chionji, just the senior martial art brother.

Cora's hair was a mess from Morgan's rubbing, but he was so bandaged up that she couldn't even hit back.

"Ah!" Morgan suddenly yelped.

"What's wrong?" The others looked over nervously, afraid he had accidentally hurt himself, impacting his recovery.

Morgan. "I just remembered something."

Ewen Van glared at him irritably. "Just say it. Why the dramatics?"

Morgan grinned cheekily. "Now that Ne Kon is dead, the base can develop in peace. Chi Zhang, aren't you and Little Junior Sister getting married? Hurry, before some pretty boy outside steals her away!"

Ewen Van instinctively glanced at Onyx's expression. Morgan hadn't been in the action yesterday and didn't know the details, but they had seen it clearly. It was too late. Right in front of Chi Zhang, Little Junior Sister and that "pretty boy" had embraced.

Ewen Van coughed theatrically and gave Morgan a look, but Morgan, oblivious, continued muttering, "Speaking of which, what do you need to prepare for a wedding? Should I get some new holoscreens as a gift? Hey, Chi Zhang, say something."

Morgan's interruption jolted Chi Zhang, lost in thought, back. He stood up slightly straighter and looked at Cora. The others realized he was about to speak and fell silent.

Chi Zhang spoke slowly, "Cora, have you considered staying in Saya?"

CHAPTER 43

Family

Chi Zhang was naturally calm and composed, making it difficult to discern his true thoughts from his outward appearance. It seemed like he mentioned it casually, but it might have been deeply thought out. No one knew what he was thinking when he said it.

Cora blinked, momentarily confused. "Huh?"

Before she could answer, the members of F777 exploded with outrage. Chi Zhang was stealing their leader right in front of them. No, it was more like he was tearing down the entire wall! Cora wasn't just the captain of F777, she was the linchpin holding everyone together. If she left, the team would fall apart instantly!

"No way!" The first to jump out was Damian, his curly hair standing on end. "Sister is ours!"

"What do you mean, ours? We watched Little Junior Sister grow up!" Morgan retorted, unwilling to back down.

"But Sister enjoys playing with us now!" Little Diamond was so angry his voice cracked.

"You said it yourself. It's just playing," Morgan, wrapped tightly in bandages, seized on the flaw in his argument, a cunning light in his eyes. "When you're tired of playing, you come home. The dojo is gone. Saya is our home now."

Morgan used "home" as his trump card, and Damian was at a loss for words. He quickly turned for help, but Felix raised an eyebrow with an amused expression, Suchat's icy face showed no emotion,

Yuui covered her mouth with a smile, clearly not planning to intervene, and Dr. Franz... his mood was bad, so it was better not to trouble him.

Damian looked pleadingly at Onyx in the wheelchair. Why wasn't he saying anything? Whenever he tried to get close to Sister, this man would hang him up and threaten him. Now someone was about to steal her, and he was just sitting there?

Even those who knew the details, like Ewen Van, sensed something was off. Although Onyx was now in a wheelchair, they shouldn't forget he was a master manipulator who never suffered losses.

Onyx didn't rush to express his opinion. He absentmindedly squeezed Cora's fingers and blurted, "Cora, my leg hurts."

Cora immediately grew concerned. "Where?"

Everyone could see the concern in her eyes. The once stuttering, shy, and inarticulate Little Junior Sister had become more cheerful and confident, thanks to this man.

"Cora, please don't mind their jokes about the 'marriage agreement'," Chi Zhang said in a calm tone, but then dropped a bombshell. "But your affairs, I will take responsibility for them."

When Cora first arrived at Mount Yue, she was like a skinny little monkey. Master Zhang felt sorry for her and let her share a birthday celebration with Chi Zhang. They sat side by side in front of the cake, blowing out the candles awkwardly. Year after year, they celebrated their birthdays together, and everyone joked that Chi Zhang would marry Cora—since neither of them denied it, the joke became a tacit truth among them.

Chi Zhang had no special feelings for Cora; he just felt responsible for her, treating the adopted girl like a real sister. In fact, he felt responsible for everyone at the dojo, but with Master Zhang gone... his responsibility for Cora might have been more because of familial affection.

"It's too dangerous for her to stay with you," Chi Zhang said.

Assassinating Ne Kon, resisting Punk's explosions, everything Cora did now was like walking a tightrope.

"Is she safer with you? That's overly confident," Onyx retorted, not backing down.

"Cora is from Mount Yue, and we will all take care of her," Chi Zhang calmly countered.

"Please, Brother Chi, understand that Cora doesn't belong to anyone. She is free. What right do you have to control her?" Onyx sneered.

"I'm her brother. If she wishes, I can be more than that. But whatever my role, it's more qualified than you," Chi Zhang's dark eyes were firm, his sharpness unmistakable. "You ask about my role, but what about you? Who are you to her?"

Onyx was stunned.

What role did he have? Who was he to Cora? The man, usually unbeatable in arguments, was uncharacteristically silent. In the end, Cora was the firm ally he chose, while he was just someone she picked up... an outsider. He indeed had no right to control her.

Seeing the tension, Cora stepped forward and earnestly told Chi Zhang, "Brother, I won't stay for now. Besides, I have things to do."

She had to cure Onyx's leg, go to Felalakas for the T.T.T. finals, fulfill Yuui's wishes, and maybe someday visit District B. Once everything was settled, she might return to Saya.

Chi Zhang listened in silence for a long time, not forcing her. "Alright, whenever you come back, Saya will always be your home."

"Yes, Little Junior Sister, Saya will always be your home!" her martial brothers and sisters echoed loudly.

"Mm!" Cora nodded happily. She knew they were her most solid support.

Before leaving Saya, Cora specifically sought Chi Zhang. "Brother, Master left something for you."

Before her eighteenth birthday, Master Zhang had given two gifts, one of which was entrusted to Cora to pass on to Chi Zhang. Unexpectedly, after descending the mountain that day, a solar storm hit, and the apocalypse began. They temporarily put the matter aside. After more than half a year, she and Chi Zhang finally met again under such complicated circumstances.

Cora had already opened her gift: an ancient-looking calming charm, cool to the touch, made of a unique material that neither water nor fire could destroy. She didn't understand why Master gave her this, but she kept it carefully.

Chi Zhang opened the plastic bag. Inside was a transfer agreement, wherein Master Zhang had given all his movable and immovable property, as well as ownership of the Mount Yue dojo, to Chi Zhang. He was a strict master, but not a competent father. Their relationship had been worn down by repeated conflicts, yet thankfully, it had never disappeared entirely.

Chi Zhang rubbed the thin pages silently for a long time. Now, with Saya in dire need of reconstruction, this money was like timely help, enough to sustain him for a long while.

Chi Zhang said, "By the way, Ruby wants to ask you for help."

Chi Zhang had always had doubts about Master Zhang's death. According to the memories Ruby had extracted from Eamon's mind, a group of uniformed men had killed Master Zhang. Recently, Ruby had been inquiring about these people among the base's personnel, trying to uncover their origins. Given the complex backgrounds of Cora's team members, she wanted to see if they had any clues.

After listening to Ruby's description, Cora shook her head. "I don't know."

Ruby shrugged in disappointment.

Cora added quietly, "But Onyx definitely knows."

In her mind, Onyx was the all-knowing one about Alliance affairs.

The three of them found Onyx and met with Chi Zhang again. The two acted as if nothing had happened. Onyx, using the information Ruby provided, casually sketched a few strokes on the holo-screen, drawing a fierce vulture. "Is this the symbol?"

Ruby nodded excitedly. "Yes! Exactly the same."

Onyx frowned. "Are you sure?"

"Positive. I extracted it directly from Eamon's memory. The vulture symbol was something he saw with his own eyes," Ruby confirmed.

"You know these people," Chi Zhang keenly observed.

"Not really know, just heard of them," Onyx said. "They are from Vulture, the Alliance's top intelligence agency. Your master's death was no simple matter."

The Vulture Unit, also known as Vulture, was the highest intelligence agency of the Alliance. Their primary tasks included collecting various types of information, both openly and secretly, as well as investigating subversion, assassination, and bombings.

Why did the Alliance's intelligence agency target Master Zhang and kill him? What secrets did Master Zhang hold? This matter seemed to plunge into deeper mysteries, becoming more and more complex. Cora worriedly looked at Chi Zhang.

Chi Zhang clenched his palm, speaking calmly, "Thank you. I will sort this out."

Cora stood at the lookout, gazing down.

In the distance, a dark crowd crossed the lifeline, advancing slowly towards Saya amid the roars of zombies outside the iron net. This was not an army attacking Saya, but people bringing their families to seek a new life. The entrance to the base was bustling, and nearby Da Nang and Emerald City had also been incorporated into Saya, becoming one entity.

The situation in Deep Woods was transforming. Of the three major warlords, only one remained. Mu Qin was now too busy to care. Jae-Woo Park's swift and decisive actions not only limited the warlords' powers, but also abolished the distorted class system. Soon, a new governor would take office. But with the chaotic and declining Deep Woods and the rapidly developing Saya, no one could predict the future.

Inside the base, the liberated girls of the Rose Army spontaneously gathered, offering flowers to a pure white statue and singing local ballads. The statue, beautiful and holy, bore a nameplate reading. "In memory of the strongest Rose, Rao, who led us to fight against an unjust fate."

Ellyn the Wild Rose stood quietly at the back, holding a cannon barrel with one hand. Yuui patted her shoulder. "Hi Ellyn, we're about to leave. We're here to say goodbye. What are your plans?"

"I'm going back to Felalakas to continue the finals," Ellyn initially looked serious but gradually smiled. "But I won't fight desperately anymore because my wish has been fulfilled. See you at the finals. Even if we're friends, I won't go easy. That's the pride of a free mercenary."

"Neither will we. See you at the finals," Yuui smiled brightly.

Samuel patrolled the base, his upper body bare, a giant snake tattoo vividly moving. But no one feared him; children gathered around, wanting to touch him in awe.

Merlin and Cho Lu, one learning mechanical skills from Felix, the other eagerly listening to Charles Franz's lectures, were the ones most reluctant to see F777 leave.

Chatterbox Cẩm Tú sneaked glances at Marie, stammering. "You and your sister don't look alike. Of course, your sister is cute too, but I think... I think you're prettier...."

"What do you want?" Marie glared at him warily.

"I mean, you, you're very brave. I admire you!" Cẩm Tú stuttered.

Cẩm Tú's face turned red as he spoke, scratching his head awkwardly.

Marie still had injuries on her face, her mouth swollen, but her eyes were bright.

Cora stood in the wind, observing the scene below.

Onyx's wheelchair stopped beside her. "Are you reluctant to leave?"

Cora shook her head. "We will come back."

"Cora," Onyx called her name and smiled gently, "After my surgery, let's talk. There's something I want to tell you."

To Be Continued...

About Me

This is Jennifer. I have a deep passion for young adult romance and science fiction, with a penchant for weaving in the extraordinary, like zombies, into the ordinary.

About the Series

"Ethereal Artifacts" was originally serialized via a web novel platform. It's my first long series with all elements I like in my life: post-apocalypse, zombies, dystopian, cyberpunk, and of course, strong female leads.

Please Review

Your opinions matters! It is important for authors to improve themselves.